P9-DVV-997

TOO BAD TO DIE

TOO BAD
TO DIE

FRANCINE MATHEWS

RIVERHEAD BOOKS

A MEMBER OF PENGUIN GROUP (USA) | NEW YORK | 2015

RIVERHEAD BOOKS
Published by the Penguin Group
Penguin Group (USA) LLC
375 Hudson Street
New York, New York 10014

USA · Canada · UK · Ireland · Australia
New Zealand · India · South Africa · China

penguin.com
A Penguin Random House Company

Library of Congress Cataloging-in-Publication Data

Mathews, Francine.
Too bad to die : a novel / Francine Mathews.
p.   cm
ISBN 978-1-59463-179-5
I. Title.
PS3563.A8357T66 2015   2014017323
813'.54—dc23

Printed in the United States of America
10 9 8 7 6 5 4 3 2 1

BOOK DESIGN BY MEIGHAN CAVANAUGH

For Stephen, my commando

PROLOGUE

MAY 22, 1917

THE TOO BAD CLUB

He learned about Mokie the day the new boy arrived.

May was utterly the wrong time of year for new boys, of course. There were only a few weeks left before the Long Vac. Which meant there was probably something very wrong with this one, some reason he'd been shifted to Durnford so late in the term, an infraction so unspeakable he'd been booted out on his nine-year-old arse from the last obscure refuge that had agreed to raise him.

The new boy was bony and slight, a pale-faced number with springy tufts of brown hair all over his knobby skull. He had a sharp chin and wide cheekbones, and this, combined with the tuftiness of his head, suggested a young hawk fresh from its shell. The boy's eyes were hawkish as well, winkingly bright, the color of cold pond water. They studied Ian as he stood, ramrod straight and miserable, before the Head's closed study door.

"Hiya, kid."

Crikey, Ian thought. *A Yank.*

"Are you up for a beating, too?" The boy slouched over, hands shoved in his pockets. "What does he use? Cane or slipper?"

"Depends."

"On how bad you are?"

Ian nodded warily. He had no time for Yanks who appeared without explanation in late May. His heart was racing as it always did when he faced Tom Pellat's door, awaiting his turn, the methodical swack of a plimsoll on a padded bottom filtering thickly to his ears. TP usually slippered his boys, but he'd been very angry this morning when Ian's Latin grammar was pulled foul and dripping from the privy. Ian hadn't tossed it there, but he knew that if he told who *had,* his head would be stuffed in the privy next. He was afraid TP would cane him. Canings drew blood. His face would crumple and he would disgrace himself.

The Yank thrust his shoulders against the wall. "I try to get a beating the first day at every school. It helps me size up the Enemy. Figure out what he's made of."

"TP's a good sort, really," Ian said. "He doesn't beat us for *fun.* It's for the Greater Good of England."

The Yank snorted. "I don't give a darn about *that.* How often does he do it?"

"Well . . ." Ian shifted uncomfortably. "Three or four times a week. But then, I'm *very* bad. How many schools have you been to?"

The Yank jingled a few coins in his pocket. "One at home, when I was little. Then two in Switzerland—I had to leave both of those. And then, in Vienna? Gosh—I lost count."

"Vienna? You mean—*Austria*?"

He grinned. "Good ol' Hapsburg Empire."

"You've moved rather a lot," Ian observed curiously.

"My dad's with the embassy."

"My father's at the Front," Ian said. "He's a major of Hussars."

"What's uhzars?"

Ian scowled. "A cavalry officer. Don't you know *anything*?"

"Not about England." The Yank stuck out his hand. "I'm Hudson, by the way. What's your name?"

"Fleming." Although mostly he was called Phlegm. With a particularly disgusting gob of spittle attached, when most people said it. He shook Hudson's hand and hoped his own was not too damp.

"Wait a sec—" Hudson stared at him. "You're not the *grind*? The Fancy-Pants everybody's in love with?"

"That's my brother. Peter. Only he's been sent home. *Tonsils.* He's eleven."

The Yank whistled through his front teeth. "I don't know how you stand it. I just got here, and all I've heard is 'Fleming says . . .' and 'Fleming thinks . . .' If I had a brother like yours, I'd slug him. Or change my name."

Ian bit his lip. His name was Mokie's name and he wouldn't change it for worlds. "Peter's not so very grand, really. Mamma says he's delicate. He has to have flannels on his chest and drink nasty tonics. He shall probably be Taken, Mamma says, because he's too good to live."

"Grinds always are."

"I shall live forever," Ian said gloomily.

The plimsoll sounds had died away in TP's office. He fancied he heard sniffling, a wet admission of inferiority. It would be his turn next. He closed his eyes and saw a length of rattan hissing through the tobacco fug of TP's rooms.

Nobody would dare to stuff Peter's Latin in the privy. Peter would never be caned in his life.

"My mother was too good to live," Hudson said suddenly. "There was a baby, too, but it didn't live, either."

"I expect it was a girl, then," Ian offered.

"Dad didn't say. He just packed us up and made tracks for England."

Ian listened for TP's footsteps across the worn wooden floor. The brass knob would turn with a metallic screech and there would be TP's face, purple with the outrage of Ian's grammar.

"We buried my mom there. In Vienna." Hudson's voice was a bit shaky and his knees were buckling. He slid slowly to the ground. "Dad said we had to. Her family's Austrian."

Ian whistled. "You mean you're related to *Huns?*"

"Not after this war."

Ian rocked uneasily on his heels, too well trained to sit on the floor. It must be terrible to be a Yank with a father who didn't fight and a mother who was too good to live but was still the wrong sort, after all. Hudson was taking a chance, telling Ian about himself. He clearly lived in an appalling state of innocence that would get him killed at Durnford School within the week. Ian thought, suddenly, that he would have to be Hudson's friend now, whether he liked it or not. He would call him Hudders and show him the best places for tiffin in the village, and the best spots for plover's eggs anywhere on the Isle of Purbeck.

The door behind him opened. A small boy sidled out, his hands to his backside. His nose was streaming.

"Ah. Fleming." To Ian's surprise, TP was not grim and furious. He wore a tender expression Ian had never seen before, and the strangeness of it was terrifying.

Peter, he thought. *Taken.* His stomach twisted and he was afraid he might be sick.

"Come inside; there's a stout lad." TP scowled at the pile of loose limbs that was Hudson. "Get off the floor, boy. I won't be wanting *you* today."

THE HEADMASTER moved a pile of letters from an aged club chair and suggested Ian sit on it. He pulled up a hard-backed one himself, his large hands dangling between his knees. TP was beloved for the way he bellowed *"Nell!"* whenever he misplaced his wife, for his magnificent mustache and spectacles, for his ancient tweeds and his willingness to dive with the boys off Dancing Ledge into the frigid English Channel. He had Tennyson by heart. He was less well versed in tragedy.

"There's been a telegram," he said.

"From home?"

"Afraid so, old man." TP cleared his throat with a noise like gargling. "You must be proud, Fleming. Very proud. He died for King and Country."

Peter. With his throat bound up and his special treats. Ian hadn't known it was for England. A buzzing began in his ears and TP's face blurred at the edges. The buzzing grew louder, and behind it the thud of his heart, as he glimpsed the thought at the edge of his brain, the words he must never say. *Not Peter. Somebody else.* TP was still talking, the same tender look on his face. Ian was going to scream.

". . . a hero, Fleming. We must all wish for such a glorious end. *Dulce et decorum est pro patria mori.*"

Ian sat rigidly in his chair while the Latin washed over him. He would not think of Mokie. Who, if he once walked into Ian's brain, would be killed absolutely and forever.

". . . mortar attack," TP was saying. "Near St. Quentin. Your father meant to take the trench. He'll be mentioned in dispatches, I expect. Perhaps even in the *Times*. You must do your best to be worthy of him, Fleming."

Ian felt his throat constrict, his air cut off. He tried to swallow.

The Headmaster grunted. "Good man. Now stand up and take your punishment."

Ian got to his feet. He bent over.

Six of the best, from his own plimsoll. He didn't care, this time, how hard he cried.

"I GUESS HE WAS TOO GOOD TO LIVE," Hudders whispered from his cot after Lights Out that evening.

Ian did not reply. He'd cadged a candle from Commons and wedged it in a crack in the floorboards. His head dangled from the side of his bunk; the copybook was on the floor and his fingers gripped a bit of pencil painfully.

. . . the wistling sound of shells acrost the muddy grownd.

Forard! cried the stern Majer. He razed his arm and advanst there was a birst of light and . . .

"What are you doing?" Hudders asked.

Ian kicked out with his legs.

"You're *writing*? What is it? Let me see."

"Shhhhhh," Ian hissed. Writing was his secret, his way of flying through the unheated rooms and grimy windows of Durnford School and back to London, or maybe Arnisdale, where the dogs were, and Cook let you sit on a stool by the kitchen stove on wet days, eating lamb pies with drippings. He kept the copybook under his mattress, along with his Bear, and he never took either of them out until the deep sound of breathing throughout the dormitory assured him that he was safe.

"I play the violin," Hudders whispered.

"Crikey." Ian looked at him. "Don't tell *anyone*, understand? They'll think you're wet."

There was a silence. Ian closed his copybook and blew out his candle stub. He shoved it and the copybook under the far side of the mattress, where Hudders wouldn't think to look.

"Did they *make* you learn to play?" he asked. "Your parents, I mean?"

"Didn't have to. I like music. Everyone does in Vienna."

"Well, you're not there anymore." Ian pulled up his blanket. He felt queer inside. Hudders had done it again—he'd *told* him something he should never have said out loud.

"I play the piano, too," Hudders said.

"*Shut up,*" Ian whispered fiercely. And then, in a silent voice inside his head, the words he would utter before bed until the day he died—

Please, dear God, help me to grow up to be more like Mokie.

He lay there in the dark feeling awful. He had wanted to write about Mokie as a Hero—the sort of father who would die for King and Country. But the words had come out like a Rider Haggard story. Nell, TP's wife, read *King Solomon's Mines* to the boys at night. It was a cracking good adventure, but it wasn't real. Mokie, dead, was horribly real.

He tried to remember what his father looked like. The sound of his voice. He wondered if it hurt terribly to die, and whether Mokie was watching him, now, from somewhere. Ian closed his eyes so as not to see his father's face among the cobwebs in the dormitory ceiling.

Mokie had come home from the Front for Christmas, and they had all gone up to the lodge at Arnisdale for a few days. Mokie was very tired and Mamma had talked nonsense more than usual, because his father spent all his time out on the Scottish moors with his pack of bassets, stalking things instead of going to parties. Ian had followed the scent of pipe tobacco to the stables. Mokie's face was pressed into his polo pony's neck. His fingers were knotted in its mane. The smell of horse and tobacco mingled with the sound of his father's sobbing. Ian had felt sick. Just like today, when he'd thought it was Peter who'd died.

"I'm to be worthy of him," he muttered to Hudders. "Only I don't know how."

"Your dad wouldn't care, I bet. You were his pal, weren't you?"

Ian shrugged in the dark. "There are four of us boys. Everyone likes Peter best."

"Did your dad give you a pet name? You know—one that only he used?"

"He called me Johnnie. That means Ian in English."

There was a pause as Hudders worked this out. "I thought Ian *was* English," he said cautiously.

Crikey. He didn't know *anything*.

"Still." Hudders's whisper was triumphant. "That means you were his *pal*. Even though you're beaten three times a week. I bet your dad liked you much more than your old grind of a brother, with his tonsils cut out."

Ian curled in a ball and thought about it. He thought about Peter, who could cry in Mamma's bed with Michael and Richard because Mokie was killed. They would feel special because they were sad—not like him, blubbing because he'd been slippered. He would never be a Hero. He was glad that Hudders at least was lying there, between him and death.

"Let's have a club," Ian whispered. "Just you and me."

"What kind of club?"

"For people who are too bad to die. And if any of the others are bad enough, we shall allow them to join."

Hudders sat up. "But if they're good, we won't tell them a thing. Even if they pull out our toenails."

"Agreed. And violins, or writing, shall *always* be allowed. It doesn't matter whether they're wet."

Ian offered his hand. Hudders shook it.

"The Too Bad Club," he said. "For guys like us, who are forced to live."

DAY ONE

CAIRO

Thanksgiving Day,
November 25, 1943

For nearly four thousand years the Great Pyramid of Giza had flung its shadow like a massive shroud across the desert and silenced those who gazed upon it. Before the forging of steel, it was the tallest man-made structure on earth; and even after steel dwarfed it, the stones remained terrifying in their bulk. Their blind faces. Their inspiration of dread.

The pyramid was a Wonder in an age that had outgrown them, or thought it had, and people were more desperate to see it when its size was no longer the point. They liked to believe that in surpassing the Great Pyramid, the Modern World had conquered what it represented.

Which was Death.

The founders of Giza's Mena House Hotel knew good value when they saw it. They were English, and understood that travelers paid more for a view. They bought Khedive Ismael's old hunting lodge in Giza and added balconies to every room, expecting their guests to sit on them and gaze at the pyramid in the fading desert light. For decades, most of the guests did. They were grateful and blessed as they drank their gin. They talked of hiring camels and crawling through tunnels to the burial chamber of Khufu.

Not Pamela.

The Great Pyramid filled the windows of her father-in-law's rented villa, a stone's throw from Mena House. Pamela might have hurled a book at it, or perhaps an empty champagne bottle. One of her strappy dancing shoes. But she drew her curtains instead, and blocked out the sight.

The pyramids—Great and Small—sickened her with their stillness. The flat, impenetrable stones devoured light and exhaled darkness. They sat like God at her elbow, assuring her that she was tiny and mortal, and she hated them for it. In the rare moments when she was alone like this, Pamela could feel a grave beneath her toes, and it frightened her. She was waltzing on the edge.

She turned her back to the window—her gorgeous, supple, peach-flushed back—and stared at herself in the mirror. Like everything Pamela possessed, her evening gown was far too expensive for war. It informed the world that she had powerful friends. And that they gave her things.

Her hair glowed like warm brass. Her dark blue eyes were restless. She wanted a good time tonight, because in two days they would all fly to Tehran, and Averell would be there. She would drink deep and seduce every man within reach. She had a talent for it.

Pamela leaned toward the mirror. Smoothed her lipstick with the tip of a finger. It was a deep red Guerlain shade from New York; Ave had brought her several of the special green-topped lipsticks the last time he visited his wife. Which of the men, she wondered, would want to kiss her tonight? And give her power over him—for as long as she liked?

Moody, dangerous Ian—or his piano-playing friend?

She smiled at her reflection. Pamela Digby Churchill was very like a mirror. A hard and beautiful surface few things could crack.

THE MAN IN THE WHEELCHAIR found the bulk of the Great Pyramid a comforting presence in his sitting-room window. He was smoking a cheroot near the open casement, unconcerned by the desert's dropping temperature at dusk. It had taken him nearly two weeks to reach Egypt, first by naval vessel and then by air, and he felt drained. The constant effort to pretend otherwise—to appear strong and sharp and to stand upright for the cameras, even if it meant supporting his useless lower frame with his whitened knuckles pressed hard against a desk's surface—was growing tedious. He wanted time and space to think. These brief moments in the shadow of vast stones were precious, like a deep breath drawn at high altitude.

"Sam," he said, removing the cheroot from his mouth, "is there some kind of threat I should know about?"

"You mean besides the Germans, Mr. President?"

"Rommel turned tail a year ago. You know that."

Sam Schwartz, Franklin Delano Roosevelt's Secret Service chief, peered out the window. The villa placed at their disposal belonged to Alexander Kirk, the U.S. ambassador to Cairo. It sat within spitting distance of the Mena House Hotel, where this conference was taking place. Roosevelt found the villa comfortable and airy; Kirk was a flamboyant man who spent his cash well. The food was better than the White House's. His son Elliott and his daughter Anna's husband, John, were both traveling with him, and they seemed to be having a high old time. Nobody'd mentioned security. But Schwartz would be acutely aware of it: he'd prepped Kirk's villa for this visit, installing wheelchair ramps and making sure the Signals equipment was specially wired. Roosevelt had glimpsed Schwartz's men at strategic spots, indoors and out, with a startling number of Thompson submachine guns. One of the smaller hotel dining rooms had even been doctored with a false ceiling and soundproof walls, so that no hint of high-level discussions could reach Cairo—where any number of spies would love to pay for it. When he and Churchill sat down to talk, Roosevelt thought, the whole world tried to listen. Their chats determined who would live and die.

"The State cables are clear, sir. Nobody outside of Egypt even knows we're here," Schwartz said. As though Franklin were a small child who needed soothing. Or a cripple, trapped in a rolling chair.

After twenty years, Roosevelt was used to the numbness in his legs—but he'd never learned to accept his vulnerability. If an attack came, he'd be unable to run from the whistling bombs or the sudden hailstorm of machine-gun fire. What galled him most was the idea that somebody else might die in a crisis because they'd turned back to save *him*. But from the moment of landing on the dirt airstrip at Giza a few days before, he'd known there was no safer place in North Africa. Mena House was an armed camp. Acres of gardens, stables and chicken coops, a languid pool terrace, and a golf course were cordoned off with barbed wire and a brigade of British infantry. Five hundred anti-aircraft guns were pointed at the sky. The hotel's guests had been dismissed the previous week, and the entire staff was offered a vacation with pay. Enlisted men now worked as Mena House waiters. A tent city filled with soldiers from all over the U.S. and the British Empire stretched behind the hotel. They had overrun Alex Kirk's villa, too. The transformation blared to the world: *Stand back or die.*

"Why do you ask?" Schwartz persisted.

Roosevelt drew a lungful of smoke. "There's an RAF observation post on the summit of the Great Pyramid. Wasn't there yesterday."

The Secret Service chief smiled faintly. "That must've ticked off a few pit diggers."

"And see the snipers? Positioned at intervals on the rest of the pyramids? Winston's got wind of something."

Schwartz's smile faded. His eyes strayed from the snipers to a single telephone, connecting Churchill's villa with their own.

"Fleming," Roosevelt said thoughtfully. "Young Hudson's friend. He'll know."

———————

MAY-LING WAS drinking tea in the drawing room of the Royal Suite, shoes kicked off and her slim legs tucked beneath her. Unlike the Western potentates, she and her husband were lodged in Mena House itself. They commanded a drawing room, several bedchambers and baths, quarters for their personal servants, a private dining room, and a kitchen, where she could prepare her husband's opium pipe at night. No one but the two of them knew she did this. There was a dressing room filled with Western and Chinese clothes where her personal maid presided over several Louis Vuitton trunks—one just for hats, another for shoes. She had brought twelve handbags and thirty pairs of gloves to Cairo. The dust, she'd heard, was terrible.

During the past year, May-ling had toured the length and breadth of the United States, which was like her second home. Correction. Her only *real* home. And she had shopped well. Only the most elegant and exquisite clothing adorned her body, because she was the face of a civilization.

Madame Chiang. The uncrowned empress of China.

While the Generalissimo fought his own people and the Japanese—months of losses, of vicious and brutal death—she had addressed both Houses of Congress. She had raised her glass to well-meaning patrons in Poughkeepsie and Detroit and Sioux Falls and Menlo Park. Americans hated the Japanese after Pearl Harbor and were desperate to find an Asian they could trust. May-ling spoke English with a southern accent. Her brief childhood was misspent among the mosquitos and missionaries of Georgia. Unlike her Buddhist husband, she was a Methodist, and a graduate of Wellesley College. Americans were fascinated by her exotic beauty and her obvious smarts. She'd collected millions of dollars for the Kuomintang cause.

"And what have you spent it on?" she demanded, as her husband fitted a cigarette to his lighter and crossed one perfectly creased trouser leg over another. "Payoffs to your cronies. Rivals whose loyalty you have to buy. And women, of course. There are always women."

"Just as, I understand, there have been men."

She did not answer him; he had the best possible sources and he was uninterested in protest or denial. She merely held his gaze and refused to think of what might incriminate her.

"You will sit next to Churchill tonight," he instructed. "Distract him. Bring his daughter into the conversation. She watches me too closely for my taste."

"If you knew anything about women, you'd realize Sarah is unimportant," May-ling flung back at him. "When the old man wants something, he trots out the other one. *Pamela*." She uttered the English name with distaste. Her husband had danced with the girl last night and enjoyed it. He was a connoisseur of women, but Round Eyes with red hair and pillowy breasts were rare in his experience.

"The Golden Devil is a fool," Chiang Kai-shek said mildly. "And you are jealous."

"*You* are a fool." She took a delicate sip of tea. They had found green leaves for the celebrated guests and her maid had brewed the pot herself; still, the result was disappointing. "Wasting the Americans' money. What will you say when they ask what you've done with it?"

"Tell them I need more." He gazed at her through his cigarette smoke, amused. "That's how these things work. That's why we're here, to demand that Roosevelt bomb the Japanese from bases in China he'll pay us to build. With materials *he* will provide. And American engineers. The bombs will be American, too, and so will the planes and pilots. We'll let the Round Eyes defeat our enemies—and pay us for the privilege."

"And if Roosevelt refuses?"

He rose and crossed the room to her. Sank down on the sofa where she was perched. Gripped her chin with the strength of a vise. The other hand held his burning cigarette close to her perfect cheek. He had ordered the death of millions with those hands during the White Terror. He called the victims *Communists,* but some of them, she knew, he'd once called friends.

"Never question my methods. American money keeps you alive, *darling.*"

She'd taught him the English word, the only one he knew, when he'd divorced his chief wife and three concubines. She'd thought then it was because he loved her. Wanted her. She knew now that the only thing he wanted was power. Her sister was Sun Yat-sen's widow; Chiang was Sun's political heir. He'd married May-ling for her family.

The glowing end of his cigarette wavered near her eye.

"It's too bad you're not invited to Tehran," she said, defying her danger. "That's where the real decisions will be made. This conference means nothing. These lords give you money to keep you quiet—like scraps of meat thrown to a dog. But they expect you to bite Japan's neck. And then what use is the vicious beast to them? You're a cur they can't trust. A cur they will put down. You're the one being used, Kai."

"You will sit next to Churchill," Chiang said softly. "You will find out why he's afraid. I can smell the fear coming off his skin like rancid fat. Find out what he wants from this conference in Tehran, *darling.* For China."

"For you, you mean."

"I *am* China." He released her. "England's enemies pay highly. And China wants something to sell."

"GOD, SHE MAKES ME FEEL FILTHY," Sarah Churchill Oliver muttered as she wrapped her kimono around her slim body and quietly closed the bedroom door. "Just the look in her eyes. *Smug.* And *knowing.* She guessed you were in here."

"Probably knocked on my door first." Gil Winant's mouth lifted in a smile. "What'd she want?"

"Said there was a wire for Commander Fleming, and did I know where he was? I suppose she's after poor Ian now. One more tame tiger on Pamela's leash. I told her to go up to the hotel. Somebody'll buy her a drink."

"I was surprised to see her on the plane, frankly. Diplomatic missions aren't her style."

"Father wanted her to come." Sarah sounded forlorn. "She plays bezique with him when he can't sleep. His nights are getting worse and worse, Gil, and this flu isn't helping."

"Well, if a game of cards with a doting daughter-in-law can win the war for Britain . . ." Winant rolled off the bed and reached for his jacket. "I'm sorry you have to put up with her, Sal. I thought we'd seen the last of her once she got her own place in Grosvenor Square."

"Not a chance, Mr. Ambassador. Our Pammie has her claws in the Prime Minister of Great Britain. She's borne his grandson, for God's sake. And named him Winston. She'll never let us go. She can call herself a Churchill until she dies—even if she *does* divorce my brother, Randolph, one of these days." Sarah leaned against the bedroom door and studied Gil coolly. "Did you know she sleeps in the War Rooms sometimes? In the top bunk, right over Father? He won't hear a word against her. No matter how many men she bags."

The list was growing, as they both knew. Averell Harriman, possibly the wealthiest American in the world and Roosevelt's ambassador to the Soviet Union, was quietly paying for Pamela's new apartment and most of her expenses by a circuitous banking route from Moscow; but now that he'd left England, she was frequently seen around London with everyone from Jock Whitney to Bill Paley and his famous reporter, Edward R. Murrow. Pamela liked acquiring Americans, but she wasn't exclusive; Lord Beaverbrook, the British press baron, supported her infant son and his nanny at Cherkley Court, the Beaverbrook estate in Surrey. A complement of variously starred generals supplied Pamela with the necessities of life. Fresh beef. Silk stockings. Trifles studded with diamonds and emeralds. Emeralds were particularly striking with her titian hair.

"She probably gets a lot out of her men," Winant said thoughtfully. "And I don't mean money. She learns things, Sal. And passes them on. I bet your dad finds that damned useful. Love Pam or hate her, she's got the makings of a great political courtesan."

He was right, of course. They both knew Pamela Digby had won Churchill's heart from the moment she sailed into the family and took Randolph off their hands. As a child, Sarah's brother had been difficult; as an adult, he was a hard drinker, a hopeless gambler, and a bruiser with an uncontrolled temper. For a few months, Pamela had seemed like a God-given answer. A steadying influence. A good woman whose love could save even Randolph. The fact that Pamela was neither steady nor good was apparently beside the point. Randolph's abandonment—and Pam's determination to ignore it—had only ranged his parents more firmly on his wife's side.

It occurred to Sarah that Gil was right. Her father appreciated the courtesan in Pamela. Used it, even, in a way he would never appreciate or use any of his own daughters. Sarah felt suddenly like weeping. She had spent much of her youth trying to escape the Churchill name, the Churchill madness—running away to the stage and an unhappy marriage with a showman who was too cheap and too old for her—and now, in the midst of this bloody war and her father's visible decline, she wanted nothing so much as to *belong* to him. One of the most brilliant and demanding personalities on earth.

Gil didn't have to be told any of this. He seemed to understand everything important about Sarah and her troublesome family. Not because he was one of Roosevelt's trusted men or had twice been governor of New Hampshire or because he had raised two sons himself. Gil was a philosopher and a lover of poetry, a quiet and inward-looking man whose simplest pronouncements rang with existential truth. He hated to speak in public, but he'd won British hearts by risking his life in bombing raids and promising far more help than America would ever give. Sarah suspected he'd gladly die if it would save her country from annihilation—and he'd do it in a heartbeat to save her. Which meant that she'd already destroyed something precious in Gil Winant. Because the man with more integrity than anybody in England had left a wife behind in the United States.

She was no better than Pamela after all, Sarah thought. An adulteress who took her happiness in both hands. But unlike Pamela, she was strangling it with guilt.

"Ever had turkey?" Gil asked her now.

She shook her head.

"It's dry. Go for the stuffing instead." He kissed her cheek. "See you at dinner."

He glanced down the villa's empty hall, then slipped noiselessly from her room on stocking feet. Sweet of him, but Sarah wondered why he bothered to tiptoe. If Pamela knew they were lovers, so did the entire British delegation.

"I LOATHE and abominate that sly dog of a Chiang," the Minister for War Transport, Lord Leathers, was saying petulantly as he sipped his whiskey. His short legs were stuck straight out on the wool carpet, as though discarded by his round body. "He wants to bugger our understanding with President Roosevelt. Nattering on, in his slit-eyed way, about *Colonials*. Playing up the democratic bit. Deploring our nasty British *ambitions*. Our postwar plans to buy and sell them all, from Shanghai to . . . to . . ."

Leathers's knowledge of the world momentarily failed him; he had left school at fifteen. A shipping magnate with a shrewd and canny sense of sea lanes, certainly, but no Public School education. That was what Ian was for.

"Guangzhou?" Ian suggested delicately.

"Indeed!" Leathers grunted, and raised his glass.

Ian topped it off. "I'd like the name of his tailor. Fellow's extraordinarily well dressed."

"*Blasted* Orientals," Leathers continued, swallowing. "You'd think enough of our sort had died in that Boxer business to satisfy the bloodlust of 'em all. But *no*. Our yellow friends would rather the Japanese raped their women from here to there and sideways than we turned an honest pound selling *tea*. I *ask* you, Ian—"

"Don't," he interrupted, pouring out three fingers of Scotch and handing it to Michael Hudson. "Ask Hudders. He's the one who's got the President's ear. Does Roosevelt give a damn what Chiang Kai-shek wants, Michael? Or is he just throwing the Chinese a bone?"

The three men had met in one of the hotel's side lounges to brace themselves before dinner, which would be a protracted and formal affair—Roosevelt was hosting the American celebration of Thanksgiving tonight. He'd brought twenty-two turkeys to Egypt, along with his aide Harry Hopkins, a few generals, and assorted hangers-on like Michael Hudson.

Hudson had flown uncomfortably into Egypt in the cargo plane carrying Roosevelt's car. His job was something vaguely to do with Lend-Lease, the American program that allowed Britain to borrow everything from old ships to new hospital beds. Hence his chumminess with Lord Leathers—who had negotiated the British end of that deal. His chumminess with Ian Fleming had long since been explained. It was their chiefs' sixth bilateral meeting in two years, and the sight of Hudders and Flem clinking glasses in various conference rooms was old hat by now.

Ian knew that Hudson's title was simply cover for far more interesting work: he was one of Wild Bill Donovan's handpicked aides—a spymaster in the Office of Strategic Services. Ian had helped draft the blueprint for the OSS a few years back, during an official visit to New York. He'd probably gotten Hudders his job.

"A Yale man," he'd suggested, "by way of Eton and Durnford. You can't possibly find a better liaison, Bill. He already knows how the English think."

Ian was personal assistant to the Director of Naval Intelligence, a deeply conventional and unimaginative sailor by the name of Rushbrooke. He did not like Rushbrooke much; he thought his mind small and his courage stillborn. As a consequence, Ian spent a lot of the war ignoring Rushbrooke's instructions and issuing his own. Liaising, when possible, with his American friends.

He was still whispering to Hudders in the companionable dark, plotting the ruin of their enemies. The Too Bad Club was alive and well.

"Of course FDR cares," Hudson said now. "Our boys are dying every day in the Pacific. Chiang's fighting the Japs. We need *him* just as much as you Brits need *us*."

"But does America need England anymore?" Ian threw himself into a chair by the carved sandstone fireplace; coal was burning feebly in its depths. "The PM's beginning to wonder. A few months ago it felt like a marriage made in heaven, Churchill and FDR. But the starch is off the bedsheets, the bloom is off the rose. Admit it, Hudders—we Brits bore you. We talk too much and haven't a fiver between us."

"Hear, hear," Leathers intoned.

There was an uncomfortable silence. The truth usually shut people up, Ian thought. He'd planned the Cairo meeting as he'd planned all the others between Churchill and Roosevelt, and he knew the Chinese were only a sideshow. Cairo was just the first stop on a far trickier journey ending in Tehran—where Roosevelt would meet Joseph Stalin for the first time.

Uncle Joe, as the American press admiringly called him.

Stalin had been keeping Hitler busy for years now, tossing cannon fodder at his guns on the Eastern Front. He'd tried to use the Nazi war machine to his own ends, but he'd been stabbed in the back and lost millions of people to starvation and siege. The Soviet strongman wanted only one thing from his allies in Tehran: Overlord. Their promise to invade Europe. As soon as possible. So that Hitler would turn around. So that Hitler would go home.

Talk of invasion made Churchill nervous. He didn't think his army was ready to attack Hitler in France, and he wanted Roosevelt's support for a simpler approach. A series of lightning raids, maybe, from various parts of the Mediterranean. More time, perhaps, to train for a brutal amphibious landing across the unpredictable Channel. Stalin would pressure them in Tehran for a date and a detailed plan, anything that would guarantee him a pitched battle on Hitler's Western Front within six months. But Churchill was stalling. A commitment to Overlord meant concentrating all his military effort on one terrible stroke; and if Overlord failed, it would take England down with it.

Churchill was deathly afraid of putting his head into a noose of Stalin's making. It was vitally important that he explain his position to Roosevelt, here in Cairo, before their joint delegation arrived in Tehran. He and Roosevelt had to stand together—present a unified front against Stalin's demands.

But Roosevelt was playing hard to get.

THE PRESIDENT had been polite but distant to his British friends since his plane had touched down three days before. He'd seized every opportunity to draw Chiang Kai-shek aside, instead, and to talk Broadway shows with his stunning wife. So far, Churchill hadn't been able to get a word in edgewise. And they were flying to Tehran in thirty-six hours.

Hudson lifted his glass in salute. "Hey. No England, no Scotch. How in the hell did you find this bottle in Cairo, Johnnie?"

"Brought it with me on Leathers's plane." The Scotch was Ian's personal poison, a single-malt bottled in secrecy on the remote Scottish island of Islay. The Laphroaig distillery had been converted to a military depot since the start of the war, but precious bottles could still be found. Ian's family was Scots. One of his bottles had smashed during a rough patch of turbulence over Rabat. Leathers's plane cabin smelled like caramel and peat.

The Minister for War Transport snorted. "Needn't have bothered," he said. "The PM has flown in enough drink to flood the Nile."

"Let's hope he can swim, then."

"That's why he brought me," said a voice from the doorway. "Keep his head above water and floating in the right direction."

She was a mirage of gold and turquoise, a perfect hourglass in shimmering silk. Her smile was aloof and enigmatic. Ian had seen that feline look before, lit by flaring torches, on the wall of a pharaoh's tomb.

But Pamela was the sort of woman who bored him silly. The kind who might as well be a pet, something fed and cosseted and groomed. Played with when she demanded it. Never an equal. Never anything but *owned*.

"Mrs. Randolph." Leathers harrumphed and struggled to his feet.

"Pamela," Ian murmured.

Michael merely saluted with his drink. She had the ability to strike him dumb.

She fixed her glowing gaze on Ian. "I've got something for you, Commander. A telegram. Passion by post, direct from the PM's *private* wireless. A penny says it's Ann!"

A faint line furrowed Ian's brow. He set down his Scotch and held out his hand. "Give," he said quietly.

"You might offer a girl a drink."

"Hudders, the girl wants a drink."

Michael rose hurriedly to his feet. "We've got whiskey here, but I'm sure you'd prefer—"

"Champagne," she murmured. On Pamela's lips, the word was a

bauble. Something to toss in the air and catch in the teeth. Michael was mesmerized. He held out his arm. She took it.

"Pamela," Ian said wearily. "The telegram?"

She drew it from her bodice like a harem girl of old. Still warm from her skin when she handed it to him. He noticed Leathers *almost* try to touch it.

"If you'll excuse me," he said.

And left the Minister for War Transport in possession of the Laphroaig.

THE TELEGRAM was not from Ann O'Neill, of course. Ian's latest flirt could hardly gain access to Churchill's private commo network.

It was from Alan Turing, an eccentric and solitary man who lived out his days in Hut 8 at a place called Bletchley Park, working for something known affectionately as the Golf, Cheese, and Chess Society— the Government Code and Cypher School. Turing was an odd fish in most people's estimation, but Ian had learned long ago to ignore most people.

He strolled out onto the Mena House terrace. The Great Pyramid's hulking silhouette blotted out a few stars. A November chill was rising from the desert; he was completely alone for the first time in days. He tore open the telegram.

The Fencer's in town. He's brought a girlfriend with him.

Ian's fingers tightened, briefly, on the paper. Then he reached into his jacket for his gold cigarette lighter and burned Turing's words to ash.

CHAPTER 2

The Prof, as Alan Turing's friends called him, was an indisputable mathematics genius, with degrees from Cambridge and Princeton and a mind that shook up the world like a kaleidoscope, rearranging it in unexpected and intricately beautiful ways. He saw the war as waged not by Fascists or heroes, tanks or bombers, but by bits of information reeled out into the ether in a code so complex and constantly mutating it was virtually impossible to break: the German Enigma encryption.

Ian didn't understand Turing's mathematical world in the slightest. Codes, and breaking them, were games he'd played with Hudders in their public school days. But the Enigma problem was urgent—the German naval cyphers, in particular, were the most complex encrypted communications known to man, and they told submarines where to sink Allied shipping in the Atlantic. Thousands of tons of cargo Britain desperately needed were torpedoed daily. Countless lives were lost. Breaking the codes was critical to survival—not just for the men drowning in the frigid Atlantic seas, but for all of Europe going under.

Turing had set up a series of "bombes," as he called them, at Bletchley. These were electromechanical machines that mimicked the rotor and plugboard settings of an actual Enigma encoder, sifting through millions of variations in those settings for the one correct combination that could translate gobbledygook into plain German text. Ian had no idea how the bombes worked. Turing had tried to explain it to his layman's mind in terms he would understand. But the Prof spoke in stuttering, truncated words that seemed to reel off his own rotors. Snatches of code, opaque in meaning.

"Expect the world to make sense. Certain co-co-co-*here*nce. Isn't the key. Not to codes. Not to life. Co-co-herence *hides* meaning. Seas hide a shark. Ha! Contradic-ic-ic-tion's what matters. Fin on the sea's surface. Tells you the shark's *there*. Contra*dic*tion gives up the gh-gh-ghost."

From a single contradiction, Ian translated, *you can deduce everything.*

The Enigma's contradiction was that no letter could ever be encyphered as itself. If the bombe's trial settings produced that result for an intercepted German message, the combination was instantly discarded. Which meant one less set of variables in the cipher universe. And so on, and so on, for days and hours, disproving every incorrect combination of settings until only the right one remained. The combination that broke the code.

Ian had met Turing two years ago, in the old loft of the converted stable that was Bletchley Park's Hut 8, where the Enigma naval ciphers were parsed by Turing and his team. The mathematician never met another person's eyes and avoided physical contact; he winched lunch baskets up into the loft with a block and tackle and sent requests back down on slips of paper with his dirty plates.

"C-c-could learn *heaps* from a single Enigma r-r-rotor," he'd said when Ian climbed up the treacherous ladder and introduced himself. "Or a c-c-codeb-b-book. German bits left b-b-b-behind when there's a raid."

What he was saying, Ian figured out, was that they needed the right sort of men on the ground after an enemy rout. The sort who knew how to spot treasure among the wreckage of German Signals equipment or torpedoed ships, and pocket it for analysis at Bletchley. It would save Turing time. But nobody was actually looking for such things in the heat of battle; anything haphazardly salvaged appeared in Hut 8 like a bit of the True Cross.

The Prof's words had lingered in Ian's mind. Like everybody in Naval Intelligence, he tried to do whatever Alan Turing asked. On the train back to London, Ian scribbled down a few words: *Special unit. Targeted collection. Intelligence support.* Rushbrooke's predecessor at Naval Intelligence, Sir John Godfrey, was enthusiastic about the idea.

"It must be a small group of fellows," he warned. "Thoroughly trained in survival techniques. Nontraditional warfare. *Commandos,* we'll call them. Churchill will like that name."

Co-Co-Co-Commandos.

"I want to volunteer, sir," Ian had said, with the first real pulse of excitement he'd felt since the beginning of his war.

But no, Godfrey replied with a regretful shake of the head. Ian was too valuable. Too creative in the deception operations he'd unleashed against the Germans over the years. He knew far too much about the inner workings of Naval Intelligence. They could not risk his capture in the field.

A year later, Rushbrooke said the same.

And so it was *Peter* Fleming who'd volunteered for Commando training in the wilds of Scotland instead . . .

The closest Ian came to action was the deck of a landing boat off Dieppe, when his Red Indians, as the intelligence commandos were called, had gone in on a raid. Ian's heroics that night were limited to comforting an eighteen-year-old kid under fire for the first time. He might look like a hero—tall, broad-shouldered, Byronically handsome, with a broken nose women swooned over—but he was denied all opportunity to prove himself. Ian was a *planner.* The brains of every operation.

And his desk job was driving him mad.

He'd taken to writing down the wild ideas in his head, lately—improbable contests with a sinister enemy—just to vent his frustration. It was *King Solomon's Mines* all over again. Cracking good stories, none of them real.

What would Mokie think of him now?

He pocketed the lighter and dusted ash from his fingertips. *The Fencer's in town . . .*

He needed more information than Turing would give in a one-line telegram. And, unfortunately, that meant grappling with Grace. She'd assume he'd invented a reason to see her, when in fact he wanted nothing less. But it couldn't be helped.

He stepped off the terrace and made for one of the sanded paths that led directly from the hotel to the Prime Minister's villa.

"No evening gown for Gracie?"

"Ian!" She glanced over her shoulder, a distracted look in her gray eyes, and snatched irritably at the earphones she was wearing. They'd muffled the sound of his approach to the Signals Room, and Grace would resent the fact. *A security breach,* she'd say. In the future he should expect a cordon of alarms to herald his approach, if not a locked door.

It could be a metaphor, Ian thought, for his entire history with Grace Cowles.

She was an expert Signals operator, a composed and efficient twenty-six-year-old from Lambeth who was cannier than her education and more vital to the British war effort than most people knew. Grace served as General Lord Ismay's right arm—and Ismay was chief of Churchill's military staff. Since Ian coordinated intelligence and Grace disseminated it all over the British field, they'd been thrown together for years. Ismay could not function without her.

Only last week, Grace had flown to Moscow; a few months before, she'd worked the Quebec conference; and before that, she'd shared a silent cab with Ian down Pennsylvania Avenue. There'd been a time in London last summer when they'd shared dinners and films, too—*The Thin Man,* he remembered. Grace probably didn't. She'd embarked on a ruthless campaign to forget his existence. And she was the kind of woman who took no prisoners.

He ran his eyes over her elegant figure, the way her dark hair coiled sleekly behind her ears. He'd known the hollow at the base of her neck and the scent of her skin. He'd taken her to bed on nights when the blitz shuddered and screamed in the air around them and hadn't cared, then, if they'd died in the act. But her eyes were hard and flat tonight; the windows to her soul, a brick wall. Her fingers twisted impatiently on her earphones. In a few seconds she'd throw him out.

"You're on duty," he said.

"Obviously. And you should be with the Americans."

"They might have let you try the President's turkey."

"Choke on it, more like," she retorted, "watching poor old Pug swallow the bloody insult Roosevelt's offered him. The President's demanding we agree on a chief to coordinate American and British bombing—a Yank, no doubt. With about as much experience of real war as Eisenhower. Pug's *furious.* Could barely knot his tie, poor lamb. I expect he'll have a stroke before dinner's out."

Ismay was Pug to his friends, although Ian doubted Gracie called him that to his face.

"You took down the cable from Bletchley?" he asked.

"Yes." Her mouth pursed. "Don't fret, Ian. I won't talk about your Fencer and his girlfriend. I'm not that interested in your social life."

"I didn't think you were. But I need to reach Turing. As soon as possible."

She picked up a pad and pencil. "Fire away."

Ian shook his head. "It's urgent. I'd like to place a trunk call to Bletchley on the Secraphone."

Her eyes strayed to a black Bakelite telephone with a bright green handle. The nondescript box beside it was filled with something that scrambled voice frequencies. A similar box on Turing's end would unscramble them.

"You're not supposed to know it exists."

"But I do." He stepped toward her desk, that safe barrier, willing all his charm into his voice, caressing rather than challenging her. "It's absolutely vital that I use it. You're my only hope, Grace."

"I've heard that lie before." Her eyes narrowed. "Is this to do with the stray Dornier?"

"What stray Dornier?"

She brushed a strand of hair from her forehead. "Spotted over Tunis. Possibly zeroing in on us. Pug ordered snipers in the heights and an RAF post on the top of the pyramid on the strength of it. He doesn't want this conference to end in a blaze of German glory."

Ian's hands were propped on Grace's desk and his body yearned toward her. It was she who'd ended things between them, and he'd never quite gotten her out of his system. He suspected she knew that and enjoyed having the upper hand. Enjoyed denying him. He was intoxicated by her closeness, the fold of her mouth when she smiled, and his mind was only dimly processing the fact of the Dornier, which would be the 217 model, not the lighter and older 17, a reconnaissance plane and bomber that could outrun most defending fighter craft. Certainly most fighter planes the RAF could throw at it. Particularly in North Africa. The gun site on the Great Pyramid suddenly made sense.

"Do you know," he murmured, "that your left eye has a green cast in the iris?"

She swatted his head, hard, with her steno pad.

"For the love of God. Romancing the bloody secretaries again?"

Gracie came to attention, her eyes fixed on the door; Ian spun around. "Prime Minister."

———

WINSTON SPENCER CHURCHILL was nursing a foul bout of bronchitis with cigar smoke, whiskey, and petulance. He was frowning now, a portrait in annoyance and white tie.

"Val Fleming's boy," he muttered. "Peter, is it?"

"Ian, Prime Minister. Peter's my brother."

"Ah, yes. Splendid chap. *Commando*. Read his book on Brazil."

Everyone had. Ian said only: "That will give him the greatest pleasure, sir."

"I didn't say I enjoyed it," Churchill barked. "Knew your father once upon a time. Excellent fellow. We shall not see his like again."

It was true Mokie and Churchill had been friends. Members of Parliament together. Churchill's younger brother, Jack, had served with Val Fleming, and Ian remembered hating him as a boy—hating anyone who'd failed to die in the stinking mud trenches. It was infuriating to know that even one man had escaped to take his morning tea in the comfort of London, to snap open the newspaper his valet handed him and carelessly ruffle the head of a hunting dog or a ten-year-old son, while thinking idly of his breakfast. Survived, when Val Fleming hadn't. They never saw Mokie's body. It was buried with all the other waste among the poppies and the sagging trenches.

Ian drew his wallet from his jacket. There was a newspaper clipping tucked in one of the folds, much creased and yellowed with age.

"I wonder if you might sign this, Prime Minister," he said.

Churchill's paw reached for it. "Lord! My tribute to Val from the *Times*. How do you still come to have it?"

"*He could not share the extravagant passions with which the rival parties confronted each other*," Ian recited. "*He felt that neither was wholly right in policy and that both were wrong in mood.* You cannot know how those words marked my childhood, sir."

"For good, I hope," Churchill growled. "From what your mother says, you're a bit of a scoundrel. Left Sandhurst under a cloud, didn't you?"

"Yes, sir."

The PM swept Ian's length with frowning eyes. "Have you a pen, Cowles?"

Grace offered him one.

He scrawled his signature in the faded margin of the piece. As he handed it to Ian, he was swept by a fit of coughing. They watched as Churchill doubled over, his jowls heaving. A man of his corpulence did not double easily. Ian wondered whether Gracie worried, as he did, that Churchill might drop dead, worn out by this war. And abandon them to their various fates.

"What's all this?" the PM demanded, his eyes streaming as he surfaced. With a gesture of his cigar he encompassed Ian, Grace, and the Signals equipment. A clump of silver ash fluttered to the Turkish carpet.

"Commander Fleming received an urgent cable from Bletchley, sir," Grace said. "He's requested the use of the Secraphone to answer it."

"Ah." Churchill drew a fraught breath and paused to bury his nose in his handkerchief. "You'll tell me what it's about? After dinner?"

"Certainly, sir," Ian said.

"Good man. Carry on, Cowles."

"Yes, sir. Enjoy your dinner, sir."

Churchill grunted.

His valet materialized with coat and hat. The Prime Minister allowed himself to be babied into them, his jaw contorting with the threat of another cough. He lifted his hand vaguely in Ian's direction and moved heavily toward the villa's front door.

"You still love him," Grace said.

"Churchill?"

"Your father. When was that piece written?"

"May 1917."

He recalled a plimsoll. A straight-backed chair. The summer that followed.

His impossible mother, painting every room of the hunting lodge black.

"And you've kept that bit of paper, all these years."

Annoying, to be analyzed by Grace Cowles.

"Now it's signed, I'll have to insure it." Ian pocketed his wallet. "I'll wait for that call, if you don't mind."

"Provided you sit in the lounge," she said briskly. "This could take upwards of an hour. Why do you always pretend, Ian? That you don't feel things?"

He looked at her.

"I feel things," he said. "Hunger, for instance. Lust."

"Loneliness. Pain. Fear?"

"Hunger," he repeated. "Is there food?"

"There's a cook. I'll have something sent out to you. Omelet do?"

"Of course."

"Drink anything you can find. He'll never miss it."

She reached for the bright green receiver and began speaking in coordinates, one exchange to another, the long relay of scrambled frequencies reaching across continents, Ian already dismissed.

Pamela, he thought, would have teased him relentlessly for information, like a poodle worrying at a ball. But Grace was too well trained in the white lies of war.

What if he said to her: *Not the Dornier. An enemy agent.*

They were surrounded by guns and concertina wire. But facts—the date and location of the greatest land invasion in Europe's history—could slip through both.

What would Grace say if he admitted he was afraid?

IN THE CHARMING salon of the PM's rented villa he chose a club chair by the coal fire and warned himself he must not fall asleep. He was exhausted to his bones—the reaction of an introvert to constant, enforced interaction with other people. In London he might have disappeared into White's club or gone to ground in his own flat, which had miraculously escaped being leveled by German bombs. It was filled with his carefully chosen collection of books in their special bindings, the walls lined in pinstripe-gray fabric. He invited very few people there. Ian, by nature, was a loner.

He was especially distant around women, who often seemed like an alien race. How could they be anything else, when from the age of eight he'd been raised by and with men? First Durnford, then Eton; and after his prepping and athletics were done, the martial heartiness of Sandhurst. At home there were three brothers. He craved the company of women as a cave dweller craves sunlight. But he was afraid of that light as well, because his mother had always blinded him.

Eve Fleming was a Force. She had been a good political wife while Mokie was alive, but at his death she turned Bohemian, selling the house they'd loved in Hampstead (once owned by William Pitt), and buying a cavernous space in Cheyne Walk surrounded by painters' studios. She was a beautiful and beguiling woman whose looks endured over the years. She favored trailing silk gowns with diaphanous veils. Mokie's money went to the boys if she married again, so she stayed single and had passionate affairs.

Of the four Fleming sons, she managed not to damage three of them.

Ian worshipped his mother for years. Eve, on the other hand, worshipped Peter. Ian looked rather like his elder brother but was utterly different—an athlete, where Peter was a scholar; a man of passions and moods, where Peter was cool and steady. A failure, where Peter was a flaming success. The fact that he actually *liked* his brother made it worse. Hating Peter would have been far more satisfying than depending on him; instead, Ian was forced to admit his inferiority in everything but sports. At fifteen, he won the Slater house colors for his play in the Field Game, Eton's odd mix of soccer and rugby; and his height made him a natural cricket bowler. But in general he disliked teams. Steeplechase and hurdles and long jump were Ian's real meat. With Hudders stumbling behind him, one rain-sodden mucky February, he pounded round the mile at Eton in just under five minutes; Hudders came in twenty-third, and vomited while Ian was lifted on the shoulders of his Slater housemates. It was not enough, however. He might be named Victor Ludorum—Champion Athlete of Eton—two years running, but his grades were shite. Eve made sure Ian knew how profound a Disappointment he was to both parents, living and dead.

She was certain that Sandhurst would be the making of him. What use was an athlete, if not as cannon fodder? And Mokie had liked the cavalry. But Ian slept with a tart in his final year and contracted VD. Furious, Eve pulled him from the academy a few months before graduation.

Obviously, she'd talked about it, too. Even Churchill had known he'd left Sandhurst "under a cloud."

Please, dear God, help me to grow up to be more like Mokie, he thought. Not without irony.

His response to his mother's disapproval was to lead a careless and rakish life. There were women. Sudden forays into strange countries with dangerous friends. A maudlin collection of poems he published himself.

Peter married a famous actress from the London stage and settled on the old Fleming estate in Oxfordshire. He went on far-flung adventures and wrote about them for a living.

Ian prepped for the Foreign Office, but didn't score high enough for a post. He wrote long letters full of disillusionment back to Hudders, who replied with a bitterness of his own. They were both going through difficult patches—Hudders with finances, Ian with women; he'd broken an engagement and was almost sued by the girl's father. He cast about aimlessly for a passion he could not feel. He dabbled in journalism for Reuters, tried stockbroking in the family firm. When the boredom was too much, he devoured thrillers and spy novels, the one lasting effect of his Durnford education. The outbreak of war in 1939 came as a relief.

Ian discovered, at last, something he was exceptionally good at. Something nobody else could do with quite his brilliance or flair.

Lie to the Enemy.

In the Office of Naval Intelligence, where he was hired as the chief's assistant, Ian spent his days writing fiction: elaborate deception operations intended for the Nazis to swallow—hook, line, and sinker. It was Ian who suggested dumping a corpse padded with fake Top Secret documents on a beach in Spain, where German agents were sure to find it; Ian who came up with the idea of luring a German ship to rescue British pilots falsely downed in the Channel. The object that time was to overpower the crew and steal their Enigma encoding machine—for Alan Turing's use, of course.

Ian was good at planning conferences as well—he'd been behind all of the meetings between Churchill and Roosevelt over the past four years—but his true gift was for conspiracy. He was a natural deceiver. He delighted in the confusion of his enemies.

It was the kind of success, of course, that he could never tell his mother about.

THE OMELET ARRIVED. Oranges came with it, and dates; bitter black coffee and *eesh baladi,* the flatbread the Egyptians made so well.

Ian ate and smoked and pursued his thoughts.

Consider the Fencer, now. Ian had been obsessed with the German agent for months, to little purpose. He did not know his name. He had never seen his face.

He was not even sure that the Fencer was male.

Alan Turing had stumbled across the code name in the course of parsing intercepts at Bletchley: *der Fechter*—the Fencer—recurred in the private correspondence between Adolf Hitler and Walter Schellenberg. Schellenberg was an SS brigadeführer in the foreign intelligence branch of the Sicherheitsdienst, the Nazi Party's security service. The Fencer reported to Schellenberg, it seemed, but he was Hitler's weapon of choice: the agent consulted in the direst circumstance, the eleventh hour, the last stand. Not simply an assassin, Fleming knew, but a singular intellect who commanded entire teams of operatives and killers.

It was the Fencer who planned the Venlo Incident in 1939, when the Duke and Duchess of Windsor were pressured to "defect" to the German Reich; but the royal failure to jump was blamed on Schellenberg, who'd served as Hitler's courier. The Fencer survived to manipulate the Duquesne spy ring in New York two years later, which the FBI said they'd penetrated from the start. Thirty-three German agents were rounded up and convicted of treason a few days after the United States entered the war. But Ian knew what the FBI wasn't telling: the Fencer had deliberately blown Duquesne and his spies. They were a necessary diversion from a far deadlier ring the Bureau had yet to pinpoint.

When German Deputy Führer Rudolf Hess parachuted wildly into Scotland, babbling about peace talks, it was the Fencer who shut him up: Hess refused to cooperate with MI5 because he was terrified the Fencer would kill his wife, Ilse, if he did. Ian figured Hess was right to worry. The Fencer was good at revenge. Take Prague, where Reinhard Heydrich had been assassinated a year and a half before. By the time Adolf Opálka and his Czech Resistance team threw a grenade in Heydrich's car, the Fencer had already penetrated Opálka's network. After he and his men shot themselves in a Prague church crypt and Opálka's family were sent to their deaths at Mauthausen, it was the Fencer who suggested a broader example for the Czech Resistance. British intelligence estimated nearly five thousand Czechs were murdered as a result.

And just two months ago, he—or she, Fleming mentally conceded—had planned the daring rescue of Benito Mussolini from an Italian mountaintop. The Fencer had tracked the imprisoned dictator for two months as his captors moved him from hiding place to hiding place. Then a Nazi team snatched Mussolini without a shot being fired.

From an inaccessible peak. Reached only by cable car.

The Allies were still chattering about it.

The Fencer could plan. The Fencer could execute. And none of his enemies lived to breathe his name. *That* was power, and that was why Hitler used him. It wasn't for his loyalty to the Reich—because nobody knew if the Fencer was even German.

Ian let a sip of coffee burn its way down his throat. *The Fencer's in town, and he's brought a girlfriend with him.* Hitler's agent, man or woman, certainly got around. That suggested to Ian that the Fencer was no soldier. A soldier went where he was told. This agent was a law unto himself.

Among the few Allies who knew of the Fencer's existence, rumor and speculation were rife. Some said he was not one man but several, with a fancy code name deliberately dangled before Western eyes as a red herring. Some said he was a German aristocrat descended from a military family, named for a fencing scar on his face. From stray references in the Enigma traffic, Turing suspected the Fencer was the same man who'd taken over the murdered Heydrich's job: Ernst Kaltenbrunner, Hitler's new Gestapo chief. Kaltenbrunner's name turned up in the Fencer traffic—he did much of Walter Schellenberg's dirty work for him. And, most significantly, a saber scar bisected his left cheek.

"Won't wash," Ian said impatiently. "They'd have no need for a code name if the agent's Kaltenbrunner. Besides—you know the fellow's too obvious, Prof. You don't make your Gestapo chief your prize secret agent. How could he possibly run the shop in Albrechtstrasse if he's pirouetting in a cable car with Mussolini?"

"Maybe it's a kind of Nazi club," Hudson suggested. He'd learned of the Fencer's existence when the FBI rounded up the Duquesne spy ring. "You know, like the Death Head guys. Only this time it's scars. Although I suppose it's ridiculous to think that more than one guy is running around with a saber cut on his face."

"I thought you knew Austrians!" Ian retorted.

Hudders had left Vienna too early. But for several summers during his Eton days, Ian's mother had packed him off to Kitzbühel to prep with an old Oxonian who understood how to motivate boys. Eve had no idea that Ernan Forbes Dennis had once worked for MI6, in the dark days following the First World War; but he remained a canny intelligence talent spotter for life, his nearsighted gaze roaming shrewdly over the raw youths under his care. Forbes Dennis advocated bracing climbs to the top of the Kitzbühler Horn, icy plunges into the Schwarzsee, and tedious efforts at German translation. Unbeknownst to Eve, Ian had spent nearly as much time in Austria seducing the local Viennese girls who summered by the lake.

And he learned that fencing duels were primal rites of passage among Austrian college boys. They were waged with sabers, the old cavalry sword, and were strict affairs of honor. The duelists wore no masks. The point, indeed, was to cut each other—and bear the mark of combat for the rest of one's life. Hudders and Turing might speculate about the Fencer all they wished. Ian found their guesses vaguely amusing, but he dismissed them entirely. He didn't care where the Fencer came from or if he'd ever held a sword. The agent might be scarred, but Ian doubted the wounds were visible. It was the Fencer's mental game—his perfect calculation behind an impenetrable mask—that intrigued Ian.

To operate as seamlessly as the Fencer did, he had to live completely *outside* the Nazi hierarchy. That was the only way that nobody—neither Axis nor Ally—could identify him. The Fencer accepted Hitler's missions because Hitler expected the impossible—and the Fencer liked to deliver. Ian sensed a familiar arrogance in the cool cunning of the Fencer's operations; it was similar to his own. The Fencer believed he was nobody's lackey. He might do as Hitler asked, but the Führer existed for *his* purposes—not the other way around.

Ian knew the two communicated by way of Enigma signals—Turing's intercepts proved that much—but Hitler had probably never met his top agent. Ian suspected that the bulk of those the Fencer employed—his crack teams—had never seen him, either. Otherwise, the agent would long since have been blown. *No.* The Fencer must assemble his people from a long chain of go-betweens, each of them strangers to the other, and abandon them once a job was done.

A Nazi outsider. Well and good. But a world war was on; nobody—*nobody*—could survive without choosing sides. A spy needed something to sell. Needed doors he could open. Facts he could use. A spy needed trust from the people he betrayed.

He needed Allied leaders and Allied secrets.

He needed to look like the Allies' friend.

Completely trustworthy and completely above suspicion. Perfectly hidden in plain sight.

A spy like that, Ian thought, could do a world of damage.

He set down his coffee cup and reached again for his cigarettes. God, it'd make a great story—

When this war was over, he was going to write the thriller to end all thrillers. And make a bloody fortune doing it.

He glanced around for paper. He found some engraved with the villa's address in the drawer of a table.

The British spy known only as 007 trained his gun on the menace in the shadows. "You cannot escape," he said. "I've blocked the passage. Now let's see who's really behind the Fencer's mask—"

He was still scribbling when Grace called him to the phone thirty-seven minutes later.

"C-C-CABLE traffic c-c-calls it Unternehmen Weitsprung," Turing said. He took his time with the German and it came out clearly. "That's—"

"Operation Long Jump," Ian supplied. He was fluent in German, thanks to those adolescent months in Austria and Switzerland. "What's it about, Prof?"

He waited for the scrambler to deliver his words and for Turing's to return: an eerie sound, like the howling trapped in a seashell.

"No idea. Got Hitler's approval. I g-g-gather he knows about your p-p-party in Tehran. Some Amer-mer-mer-ican traffic went m-m-missing. Turned up in B-B-Berlin."

So the Germans knew the Allies were gathering in Persia in thirty-six hours. Most of the world was in the dark; security was so tight even Pug Ismay had pretended to come down with the flu, rather than reveal he was leaving England.

"You've definitely placed the Fencer in Cairo?"

"With an operative. F-F-First time I've known him to g-g-go halves on anything. Cable c-c-calls her das Kätzchen."

"The Kitten?" Ian said blankly. "Run across that code name before?"

"Never. She c-c-c-could be merely c-c-cover, of c-c-course."

"Must be. He'd never risk revealing who he is."

"Unless she's m-m-meant to die."

Yes, Ian thought. The operative was probably dead from the moment she earned her pet name.

"In any c-c-case, Ian, your f-f-f-friends are in the Fencer's sights. And he knows too d-d-damn much. Traffic's full of the PM's c-c-cold and a bad j-j-joke FDR told the Chinawoman. Ismay foaming b-b-b-because Roosevelt wants B-B-British b-b-bombers under American c-c-command."

"Good guesses," Ian attempted. "Not reporting."

"Then why does H-H-Hitler know your American ch-ch-chum is hot for Harriman's m-m-mistress? Or that our own S-S-Sarah is having it off with the A-mer-mer-ican ambassador?"

Ian's fingers gripped the receiver. "What the hell are you trying to say, Alan?"

"He's *there,* old thing," Turing said distinctly. "Right in the m-m-middle of Mena House. B-B-B-Buggering all of you. The Fencer's *one of us.* And he's wormed his way r-r-right up your arse."

The thriller to end all thrillers. He'd never meant it to be true.

Static howled along the continents between them.

CHAPTER 3

That final month at Durnford before they broke for the summer was a strange one for nine-year-old Ian. He woke up each day with the knowledge that something horrible had occurred, something terrifying he must fight. He would lie on his cot with the sweat-damp sheet twined around him, face buried in the pillow, and will the fear to stay at arm's length. While his half-conscious mind directed all its fury on this single task, the rest of him was waking. Hearing the other boys as they trudged to the cold washbasins and privies. The slap of towels on naked bottoms. Hudders, sitting patiently with his knees under his chin, trying not to breathe too loudly as he stared at Ian's rigid back.

And then he would remember.

Mokie. Blown to bits by a mortar. Pieces of him on the ground.

"It gets easier, you know," Hudders whispered the first day after Ian heard. "You start to forget what they look like. At first that makes you feel lousy. Because if you can't see them—in your head, I mean—then they're *really dead*. But after a while it's okay, Johnnie. You *have* to forget."

Michael Hudson had no idea what the Cult of Heroes was like in the Fleming household. None of Val's four sons would ever be allowed to forget him. Eve intended them to be martyrs. To yearn for the approval of a phantom. It was, she said, the Fleming Way.

Ian sleepwalked through the end of term. He stopped even trying in the subjects his headmaster, Tom Pellat, loved—Latin and Greek and English poetry. He could not declaim his passages of Tennyson. He was slippered with astonishing frequency, until the bruises refused to wane and he was seen, when stripped down for swims on Dancing Ledge, to sport an arse as violent as a thunderhead.

These swims were his sole relief. There was something about plunging from the heat of the afternoon into the chilly wash of the Channel that cut dead every sensation of self-pity and horror that dragged at Ian's mind. He would dive downward, skimming his fingertips along the edges of the granite shelves that made up Dancing Ledge, and stare until his eyeballs ached at the diffuse cloud of bubbles that carried his life back to the surface. Usually he flipped and caromed to the sun, breaking through the aquamarine in a shower of benediction. A huge breath. A float on his back. Water filled his ears and he was free of the Durnford oppression, the ceaseless caterwauling of prepubescent boys. No sound but the unplumbed soundings of the sea.

On this day, however, he stayed down with the stones.

His fingers trailed along the shelving. He forced his eyes open, forced himself deeper. His legs pumped into blackness. What lurked in the granite shadows? What monster might he find, if only his breath held out?

Death, said the voice in his head. It had been talking to him for days now.

Gooseflesh rose on his ribs. His lungs were taut as a hot-air balloon. It was important, Ian thought, as his legs rippled through green, to reach the bottom. The *true* bottom. And see if Death was there. With Mokie. If he could see Mokie just once, and apologize—for not being *worthy* of him . . .

It would be good to stay below. Safe in the stones and darkness.

He had dived beyond light. The water was very cold, and his aching eyes saw nothing. His lungs were going to burst and then he would be in pieces on the bottom, just like his father.

A claw drove through his scalp, tearing back his hair and snapping his chin up. He shook his head in a frenzy, trying to free himself, and then another claw was on his arm and he was being pulled upward, helpless, away from the freeing dark. The claw in his hair and the one on his arm were pitifully small, and as they rose toward the light Ian could see the grubbiness under the bitten fingernails, the scabs on the knuckles where Hudders had punched a wall. You're too weak, Ian thought desperately, too weak to save me—and he expelled all the air in his lungs in a single burst, waiting for the sea to fill them instead.

They were almost there—almost to the surface—when Hudders let go.

It was his feet, pumping like a dynamo, that wavered first. Then the claws released one by one—first the hair, then the arm—and Ian was rising while Hudders fell back, a staring stone dropping soundlessly into the depths. Ian kicked upward, his chest viciously compressed, and broke through to air, gasping. *Gasping.* He was going to be sick, but he did not have time for it, and so he hurled himself back down on the gift of clean air, everything pins and needles, his whole body aching. He kept his eyes open. There was a trail of bubbles. Hudders's breath. He reached for it and won.

LATER, TP—TOM PELLAT—said that Ian was a hero. That he had saved the life of the New Boy who did not really know how to swim, being a Yank and one raised by Huns, at that. It was too complicated to explain to TP, and besides, Ian thought, it was Hudders who ended up in the infirmary for two days, being fussed over by Nell. They were both special in their own way—Ian the Hero, Hudders who'd Cheated Death.

They never talked about it until the final afternoon, when Eve's chauffeur came for Ian. Hudders's father—a thin, desolate-looking man who worried the brim of his homburg between his fingers—waited by a car Ian thought was hired.

"Remember," Hudders said fiercely as he gripped Ian's hand. "We're both of us too bad. See you after the Long Vac."

"GRACIE."

She'd given him privacy during the Secraphone call, closing the Signals Room door while she smoked in the sitting room beyond. Now she stubbed out her cigarette and uncrossed her legs; she looked tired, Ian thought, and he wondered if she, too, was prey to faceless terrors. But when she got to her feet she was Grace again.

"What's the PM's night look like?"

Her brow creased. "Brandy with FDR, then bed. Must you brief him?"

Ian hesitated. Every nerve in his body screamed at him to run—straight to the President's villa, where even now dessert plates were being cleared and wineglasses topped off with Roosevelt's Bordeaux and Michael Hudson was leaning close to catch what Pamela Churchill had to say in her breathy nursery voice. Music in the distance and Sarah's dance pump trailing along Gil Winant's leg beneath the gleaming table . . . until the flash of light and the sound of earth rending and the dense smoke mingling with cries of agony . . .

But no. The Fencer must be sitting at that table. He wasn't likely to blow himself up.

And what would Ian say if he burst breathlessly into that room?

He had a warning without proof. He had Alan Turing's word about a decoded message. There were people in Churchill's government who thought Turing was mad. If Ian cried *Wolf!*—with no name for the wolf and no idea whose throat it was savaging—he'd be sent home on the next plane and dismissed from the service.

"He asked me to let him know what it was all about," he temporized. "But, frankly, the PM looks all in. I'd rather put it off, and let the Old Man get some shut-eye."

Her lip curled scornfully. "So there was nothing *Urgent* about that call. Just another of Turing's queer starts."

"If you like. Thanks for letting me use the Secraphone, all the same."

She shrugged off Ian's gratitude. "Don't tell anybody it exists. It's meant to be frightfully hush-hush."

"Gracie! Did you risk your job for me?"

"Don't flatter yourself, Ian. I had the PM's blessing," she said curtly. And closed the Signals Room door in his face.

HE FOUND Michael Hudson seated at Alex Kirk's excellent baby grand in the President's borrowed villa, his fingers flickering through a Cole Porter tune. *I've got you under my skin . . .*

Michael had a good voice. Not that Ian knew much about singing—the cinema was more in his line—but he could listen to Hudders without wanting to plug his ears or strangle his friend. And Michael's piano held the room. Everybody except Roosevelt was swaying around the baby grand, drinks in hand, as though Rommel had never shelled his way through Egypt a year ago. That was Hudders's gift: he could transport people. He was a ray of sun, a counterpoint to Ian's darkness.

Ian closed his eyes and let the music take him back. To other rooms, filled with people who suddenly found Michael Hudson attractive. Who yearned to be his friend. With his hawkish nose and thin, vivid face, he was no beauty. But strangers immediately trusted him. They never trusted Ian.

He remembered a girl both of them had known about ten years ago. Her stage name was Storm. A "bubble girl," as they were called, music hall dancers who bounced about with very little on. Ian had pursued her for months, awed by the careless glamour she trailed behind her like a feather boa. *Not tonight, dear,* she would tell him mournfully. *I'm too tired. There's a special performance tomorrow for some City toffs.* It was only after Michael asked to borrow Eve Fleming's Daimler that Ian realized he'd been ruthlessly cut out by his best friend. The Daimler's backseat was littered with black boa feathers.

How did Michael do it, exactly?

It was the introvert's eternal question, Ian thought. He loved Michael Hudson more, perhaps, than he loved any of his brothers, even Peter—and yet he was no closer to understanding his friend than he had been when they were nine. Michael's charm was effortless; he won hearts without even realizing they were in play. He looked so boyish, genuine, open, guileless—the entire world took him on faith. Except, perhaps, *Ian.* Ian knew the subtleties of Michael's mind, the way his restless intelligence constantly sifted facts for deeper truths, stranger warnings. Michael loved to pick apart arguments. He questioned Ian's assumptions and turned principles on their heads. Following his logic was like tracking the path of a Ping-Pong ball.

Ian was bemused, this evening, by his friend's apparent enslavement to Pamela Churchill. Hudders liked to seduce women for the same reason Ian did—purely to prove to himself that he could. He was convinced that his wit would always be more devastating than Ian's looks. He was right, but Ian didn't mind. The game mattered more to Hudders than it did to him.

Ian glanced away from the piano and noticed Pug Ismay in conversation with Harry Hopkins. Hopkins was gaunt and unpolished, and inclined to be querulous when he'd had a drink; he seemed determined to kill his stomach cancer with alcohol. Gil Winant, an arrested expression on his face, was listening closely to John Boettiger, Roosevelt's son-in-law. Boettiger published one of Hearst's newspapers, Hudders had said, but he was wearing a uniform now. Like all of them.

Hudders's voice rose over the babble of conversation, pulling Ian's gaze back.

Don't you know little fool, you never can win?
Use your mentality, wake up to reality,
But each time that I do, just the thought of you,
Makes me stop before I begin,
'Cause I've got you under my skin . . .

Christ. For Michael, Pam Churchill was the only person in the room. Ian couldn't entirely blame him—if you didn't *know* Pam, she was a potent cocktail of sex and class. When she zeroed in on a man, even one like Hudders who really didn't interest her in the slightest, she could make him feel like the most desirable animal on earth. She was gazing at Michael now, as though he was all she'd ever wanted. A fiction she'd adopted to suit the setting and her mood. Having Little Winston two years ago had improved her public poses, Ian thought; she'd learned this one from photographer Cecil Beaton. Her arms were loosely folded around her drink, cradling her sumptuous breasts; her head was slightly bent, like a Madonna's. Pam's secret was that she never looked like a tart. It was only later, Ian reflected, when she'd taken everything you had, that you found out what she was.

He was conscious of eyes on his back, and glanced over his shoulder. Roosevelt was leaning heavily in his wheelchair, a cheroot between his fingers, a wide and fixed smile on his face as he watched Hudders perform. At that moment, his son Elliott—a man roughly Ian's own age and already twice married—reached impulsively for Madame Chiang and swung her into a makeshift tango. Too intimate a dance for the company and their level of acquaintance, but the music demanded it.

May-ling looked both startled and oddly pleased. Elliott was grinning broadly.

The President's pince-nez reflected the light in such a way that Ian could not read his gaze. But Roosevelt was plainly staring at him.

"Sir," he said.

"You're Fleming. Hudson's friend from boarding school."

"I am, indeed." Ian inclined his head, hands grasped behind his back—the traditional British act of condescension, masked as deference.

"Perhaps you can explain something to me."

"I'm at your service, Mr. President."

"Why is there suddenly an RAF gun sight on top of the Great Pyramid?"

"Because the best hope of civilization is collected here in one small-ish villa."

Roosevelt cocked his head. For the first time the light shifted and Ian caught the shrewdness in his eyes. "The best hope collected days ago. The gun sight showed up this morning. Sure nothing in particular inspired you?"

"A stray Dornier, sir. Reported over Tunis. Not seen, to my knowledge, since."

"That's the second-generation Nazi bomber, correct?"

"It is. We knocked a few out of the sky in Rommel's retreat last winter, and have been chasing them ever since."

Roosevelt inhaled some smoke and released it, lips pursed. "If anything that interesting comes up between here and Tehran, you'll talk to Sam, won't you?"

"Sam?"

"Schwartz. Head of my Secret Service detail. He's a fellow you should know."

"Then I'll remember his name," Ian said.

He was aware of the piano keys drifting into silence. Hudders rising from the bench, laughing in a self-deprecating way. Madame Chiang was bowing politely as though she'd enjoyed her tango crucifixion. Her husband looked dangerous—like he might slap his glove across Elliott Roosevelt's face—but Pamela Churchill drifted by, murmuring to Chiang with a smile, and the moment passed.

Hudders's eyes flicked up and met Ian's. His expression of good humor faded. Without the slightest appearance of haste or alarm, he slipped out of his charmed circle and made his way to Ian's side. Leaned toward him and offered a light.

"What is it?" he asked quietly.

"High Drama. Conflagration." Ian expelled a lungful of smoke. "The Too Bad Club meets in my room in a quarter of an hour."

CHAPTER 4

A collar stiff with starch. A waistcoat, tails, and top hat. Pin-striped morning trousers. Eve made him wear the new school uniform for a fortnight before he arrived at Eton during the Michaelmas half term in 1921. Peter had already been there for two years, and they were both stuck in the Timbralls, a redbrick house that sat on the Slough road, because it had been Mokie's house when he was at Eton. Everybody referred to it as Slater's. Sam Slater, the master, was feared by his boys. They might not know the word *sadist,* but they could have defined it for anybody who asked.

Michael Hudson's house was College, which meant he was a King's Scholar and his fees were mostly paid by the school. This was embarrassing to both of them for several reasons. Ian didn't want to ask if Hudders was at Eton on charity, and Michael didn't want to say. The alternative—that Hudders was so brilliant he'd been awarded a scholarship for his wits alone—was too awful to contemplate. It meant that Hudders was a *grind.* Worse, he was a grind who never acted like one. Ian could not recall Michael burying himself in books at Durnford. He was more likely to pinch an older boy's bicycle and cut class entirely. The idea that Hudders was capable of pretending to be a rotter when in fact he was a grind was mind-boggling to Ian. It threatened the entire foundation of the Too Bad Club. He preferred to believe that Hudson's father was simply impoverished, no matter how many embassies he toiled in.

Then there was the black gown Hudders was required to wear over his morning dress. It went with being a King's Scholar and set the College boys apart. They were meant to be prepping for King's College at Oxford, and the gowns were a constant reminder. The rest of the school called King's Scholars *tugs*. Ian thought this was because it was so tempting to tug on the fluttering edge of the gown and pull it off, but Peter explained it was from Latin—*togati*, meaning *wearers of gowns*. Ian had never liked Latin, and Hudders made a habit of balling up his gown and tossing it in the corner as soon as classes were done for the day. But it was another difference that hadn't been there at Durnford, and it made them both self-conscious.

Ian fagged that first year for one of Peter's friends in Slater's. Peter was the kind who never allowed anybody to hurt his brothers, and, if forced to choose between his friends and Ian, stood shoulder to shoulder with Ian every time.

Michael Hudson had no brother. Ian tried to be one when he found Michael waiting in front of Slater's one January night. He'd been birched by Pop—the Sixth Form boys who made up the exclusive Eton Society—for pinching someone else's tiffin box from home. Michael never got tiffin boxes. When you were caned by Pop, you knew to go in your oldest trousers because the birch cut through the fabric and left your buttocks bleeding. Michael had made the mistake of wearing his uniform pinstripes.

"Don't you have a second pair?" Peter asked incredulously when Ian brought Hudders into his brother's room and lifted the tails of his suit jacket. The tails hid a sorry mess of torn trouser fabric and dried blood. The birch had cut right through Michael's undershorts. Ian felt a sickening urge to giggle.

"They give King's Scholars the uniform," Michael said indifferently. He was trying to act as though it didn't matter if his morning dress was in rags. "I didn't want to ask for more. I didn't know if it was allowed."

Peter looked at Ian, his brows lifted. The Fleming boys got their clothes on tick at Tom Brown's in Windsor, where the Eton uniform had been tailored for over a hundred years. They were used to walking down to the High to be measured, and the bills were sent to Eve. Peter pulled at Hudders's jacket, searching for a label. "It's Brown's, all right," he said slowly. "But it's too late to go to the shop now. You'll have to borrow a pair of ours. Maybe you can get leave for Windsor tomorrow."

Michael was closer to Peter's height than Ian's. Peter rummaged in his trunk for a pair of pinstripes that might fit.

"No," Hudders said quietly. "It's good of you, old man"—he'd been in England four years now, and barely had a Yank accent anymore— "but I think I'll just wear these."

There was a silence. Ian could not look at his brother. Hudders would be caned again if he wore a rubbishy pair of pants to class. It wasn't allowed.

"If I get new trousers, it's as though they've won," Hudders explained.

"Of course they've won," Peter retorted. "This is *Pop* we're talking of. Pop runs the school."

Peter would be admitted to the Eton Society when he reached the Sixth Form. He was that sort of boy.

"It's okay." Hudders shrugged. "My tails and gown will hide most of it."

He twitched his suit jacket over the horizontal lashings in his seat bottom. He was right, Ian thought—with the black gown thrown over the top, the state of his trousers was invisible. But it was risky, all the same. There were places the gown wasn't worn. Or the suit jacket. Hudders was bound to be seen and punished.

Michael's face was rather pale and he made a point of not sitting down as he lingered in Peter's doorway. He hadn't come to Slater's for trousers, Ian thought, so what was it he'd wanted? Comfort? Salve for his bleeding buttocks?

No. He'd just wanted someone to tell.

Slowly, Ian undid his fly and slipped out of his pants. He reached for a pair of scissors on Peter's desk and before either of the boys could stop him, he drove the points through the seat. The bespoke wool fabric ripped cleanly. He did it again. And again. Then he put the trousers back on.

"You twit," Peter said. "Mummy will be *furious*."

"They shan't win." Ian's voice was overloud; he was terrified by the enormity of what he'd done. "Not while we stand together, Hudders."

It was a hallowed British hope. One Mokie would have recognized, from his wretched Belgian trenches. Ian had no black gown to hide his sins.

He was birched the next day. Peter put an unguent on his weals without comment. He ordered new trousers the next time he visited the High.

Years later, when it was time for their form to be chosen for Pop, it was Michael who made it. Not Ian.

"I DON'T BELIEVE IT," Hudson said now, as he sat in Ian's room at Mena House. "Turing's off his nut. The Fencer cannot possibly be one of us."

They'd managed to break away from the Thanksgiving party without appearing as though they had somewhere better to go, staggering their farewells with a ten-minute interval. Ian had left first. He had the Laphroaig waiting when Hudders arrived.

"The Prof was absolutely clear. Somebody's reporting to Berlin in real time."

Hudson snorted. "Probably got his intelligence from the Society column in *The Egyptian Gazette*."

"Have they printed the fact that Gil Winant is sleeping with Churchill's daughter?" Ian took a sip of whiskey. "Or that you're doing your damnedest to get Pam Churchill to sleep with you?"

"I doubt even the *Gazette* would be so fatuous," Hudson retorted coldly. "Why do you despise her so much, Ian?"

"Because she wastes people's time."

"I notice she hasn't wasted much of yours."

Ian laughed harshly. "You think I'm jealous? Michael, I've known Pamela Digby since her first Come Out, when she was a pudgy wallflower with bad clothes and a spotty face. The years have gilded but not improved her."

"She's an angel."

"*Fallen* angel."

Hudson's mouth twisted, and for an instant Ian thought he might toss his Scotch in his face. His fingers compressed whitely on the glass. He set it down carefully and turned toward the door. "You're drunk. We'll talk in the morning."

"Hudders."

He stopped.

"Look—I apologize. I'm a vicious brute. But this is serious. The Fencer is deadly serious."

"Agreed," Hudson said tautly. "But Turing's talking bullshit. Come on, Ian—look at the candidates! Who's around that dinner table? *FDR and Churchill.* A couple of their kids—but I don't see Sarah or Elliott in the role of Nazi spy, do you?"

"Elliott's a colonel in the Army Air Corps, and he commands a reconnaissance wing over Tunisia," Ian pointed out. "He led his boys in Operation Torch last year and he's rumored to have developed some interesting night recon techniques. You know he's popped up as air attaché at nearly every conference we've organized, Hudders. He's up to his ears in secrets."

"Because he's the President's son," Hudson retorted dismissively.

"And a horse's ass, in my humble opinion. Who else have we got here at Mena House, Flem? The Generalissimo of China, who's at war with Hitler's ally. His wife. *Scratch.* George C. Marshall and General Lord Ismay. Poor old Harry Hopkins, who's going to die right in front of us. You and me."

"And Pamela," Ian said quietly. "A kitten if ever I knew one."

Hudson stared at him in disbelief. "Jesus Christ. You can't be serious. The PM's daughter-in-law? Not even remotely possible."

"What if you're wrong, Michael? What if Turing's dead-on, and we've got a German spy in our midst? How much time do we have to stop him in his tracks? The Fencer isn't interested in Sarah's affair or Pammie's latest conquest. He's not even interested in Pug Ismay or Bomber Command. He's here for bigger game. Much bigger game."

"Like?"

"Overlord." Ian drained his glass. "The Allied invasion of Europe. Two hundred thousand men and six thousand vessels thrown at Hitler's best. The Nazis will want to know where and when to show up."

"Nobody can tell them that."

"In a few days, we'll all know. That's what Tehran is meant to decide."

Hudson frowned at him. "Are you sure, Ian?"

"It's an amphibious landing, Michael," he said patiently. "I handle the intelligence for amphibious landings. *Of course I'm sure.* I planned the bloody conference."

"And if Hitler can find out six months in advance where the blow will fall—"

"Two hundred thousand men will never get off the beach."

Hudson ran his fingers through his short hair, ruffling it absurdly. He looked birdlike, reminding Ian of the kid he'd once been. Craggy thin. The eyes hawkish. "Nobody's going to believe this. Neither your chief nor mine. You haven't even got Turing's intercept."

"I know. Which is why we're not going to tell them."

"What?"

He'd startled Hudders. "Not until we know who it is. And how he's operating. Not until we have *proof.*"

"Where do you propose to get it?"

"In Tehran."

The ghost of a smile played over Michael Hudson's mobile mouth. "You're tackling this alone. Without Rushbrooke's approval. And the entire Allied victory hangs on it?"

"Well—I had hoped you'd help me, Hudders."

"Holy shit," Hudson said. "Ian Fleming goes commando."

CHAPTER 5

The man in the wheelchair was close to exhaustion that night— the result of his self-appointed role as Thanksgiving host, the necessity of grinning broadly at all and sundry, the difficulty of fending off Winston, admittedly his good friend but increasingly an encumbrance. Winston's approach to alliance was defensive—he hoped to use the Soviet machine to win the war without giving an inch in return— and he wanted Roosevelt's word that he would do the same. But Roosevelt saw geopolitics in a cannier way. A more brutal way. It was not about friends. Still less was it about the Old World draining the strength of the New. He'd helped the British as much as possible with his Lend-Lease Agreement—even though he'd had to bludgeon Congress to release a bunch of mothballed American destroyers not worth the dry docks they were rotting in—because England was the last wall standing between New York and Hitler. Once Hitler was dead or defeated, England would be irrelevant. Roosevelt knew the country was nearly bankrupt; the pound was tied to gold reserves that were almost exhausted. It would be a decade, at least, before the British economy recovered—if it ever did.

He could understand Winston's obsessive focus on the European theater. Europe was Winston's world. He was a self-appointed guardian of a way of life that had committed collective suicide in Belgium thirty years ago. But Roosevelt's theater was the entire globe. His ships and men were drowning in the Pacific, fighting a hydra that formed and re-formed in successive island jungles, with the specter of an eventual land invasion of Japan he could not begin to contemplate. Roosevelt wanted the European war finished, soon, before his men and arms were exhausted, so that he could annihilate the threat in the East.

That meant a massive Channel crossing and landing in France in the next six months. Stalin needed it, and so did he. A steel hammer blow on Hitler's western flank, so that the man was surrounded. The landing might fail, of course—it might be a hideous mess of men and machines blown to pieces on the beaches. But if the Allies did it right—with enough force, enough will, and Americans running the show—they'd drive Hitler back into his last Berlin bunker.

Roosevelt could see the hesitation in Winston's eyes. The bulldog thrust of his lower lip. The almost childish stubbornness to have his way. He'd watched English soldiers go down in death countless times before, on his orders, and he did not want the most daring attack of the war to end in disaster. Winston's stakes were high—if Overlord failed, England would be mortally vulnerable. He was pushing an alternative plan: pepper the Nazis with smaller skirmishes all over Europe. Eat away at their edges. Roosevelt knew Winston's approach would prolong the German war machine for another year at least. He didn't have time to let Hitler die a slow death. Neither did Stalin. The fate of his Pacific war could not be decided by Winston's dithering.

We're not pulling his chestnuts out of the fire, Roosevelt thought mutinously. It was a pet phrase of his. Because the British Empire is finished.

The postwar world would fall between two poles—Russia and the United States. Communism and Democracy. East and West. Stalin and whoever replaced Franklin Delano Roosevelt. He could not go on being president forever. He was sixty-one years old, and the job was wearing him out. It was an open question whether he'd run for a fourth term in the spring, but he hated leaving the war unfinished. One more reason Overlord mattered. He might be able to leave office if Hitler was defeated.

His valet helped Franklin stand and lifted his right leg gently to the level of his waist. Then he slipped a pajama leg over the foot. Elliott could have done this sort of thing for his father, but Elliott was drinking in the salon downstairs with Alex Kirk and John Boettiger. Winston and his girls had gone home for the night. The PM's bronchitis was worse every day. Even Pug Ismay had caught it now. Roosevelt smiled mirthlessly. He could probably track all kinds of liaisons just by recording who came down with a cough. Espionage was too easy.

Espionage.

The valet lifted his left leg into the trousers. Offered Franklin his pajama shirt. He was twitching it over his shoulders, safely back in his chair, when there was a knock at the door.

"Come in."

Sam Schwartz's head slid around Roosevelt's bedroom door. "Just checking, sir, whether you need anything before I head up to the hotel."

"I'd like you to read something, Sam."

The letter from Stalin was lying in its official envelope on his bedside table. It was typewritten in Russian, but Chip Bohlen, a young Russian expert Roosevelt had brought with him, had translated it. Franklin rolled his chair over to the table, Schwartz carefully following behind. "I want your opinion."

Schwartz's gaze traveled swiftly across the lines of translated text. "Uncle Joe wants you to stay at the Soviet Embassy?"

"Says the drive between our legation and theirs exposes me to risk in Tehran. From some sort of 'demonstration.' He seems to think a Nazi with a gun could wreak all kinds of havoc. Says I'd be more comfortable at his place, too."

"Sounds like a lot of hooey to me," Schwartz said dubiously. "Why's he want you inside his embassy so bad?"

"I'm guessing Stalin doesn't want to make that dangerous drive. The Soviets aren't too popular in Persia these days."

The Secret Service chief returned the pages to their envelope and set it back on Roosevelt's table. "The British and Soviet embassies are right next to one another in the same walled compound, sir. Ours is only a mile away. I think my fellas can guarantee your safety for a mile."

"I believe you, Sam. You've never let me down yet. And what's a German agent or two in Tehran? I bet there's more than that in Washington and New York."

"I doubt the Nazis even know you're headed to Tehran," Schwartz said. "I talked to Dreyfus only this morning, and he never mentioned trouble." Dreyfus was the American envoy to Persia. "But the Sovs and the Brits have been holding down the city between them. Stands to reason their information's better than ours. Has Mr. Churchill said anything, sir? About that gun placement on the Great Pyramid?"

"Commander Fleming assures me it's nothing," Roosevelt mused. "He spun me a tale about a German fighter plane out of Tunis. I pretended to believe him."

Uncharacteristically, Schwartz began to pace. "I don't like dropping you in Stalin's lap, sir. Even if he *is* an ally. If you need to be closer to the conference, stay with Mr. Churchill."

"Winston would love that. But it would alienate Uncle Joe. Both of us landing in Tehran and pitching camp together! He'll be suspicious as hell before the three of us even sit down at the table."

Schwartz simply looked at him.

"Ever been to Tehran, Sam?"

"No, sir."

"Why don't you leave tomorrow—and check the place out? Go over Stalin's guest room. Take a gander at ours. Look at Churchill's if you like. I want us to have every option available."

CHAPTER 6

As darkness swept over Giza, the first flakes of snow began to fall fifteen hundred miles to the east, in the foothills of the Alborz mountains north of Tehran.

A thousand feet higher, snow already lay deep in the twining branches of the ironwood trees; it had been falling since September. The principal peak, Mount Tochal, rose to thirteen thousand feet, and its height would not be free of ice until June. But here, in the forest at the head of the Jajrood River, they'd been lucky, Skorzeny thought—it was not yet winter when they'd set up camp and begun to fight the Persian leopards for their prey. Those clement days were dwindling as November came to a close.

He was tending a small fire in the lee of a rock outcropping, standing watch while his five men slept. The remains of a roasted ibex lay on a canvas tarp; they'd eaten as much meat as they could hold, aware that it might be days before they hunted again. He would toss the bones off a cliff to draw the leopards and wolves away. The fire helped protect the encampment, but the snow might douse the fire soon. Until it did, he would warm his hands, gazing toward the outskirts of Tehran, some fifteen miles distant.

Lights still burned in the city; unlike Berlin, there was no curfew.

No blackout. No bombers screaming out of the west. It must be nice to be an occupied country, he thought acidly. Relieved of the duty to fight. Like all those French he'd seen in Paris a few months ago, dawdling in their cafés. That was why the Reich would win the war: they did not know what it was to relax.

Skorzeny, at least, never had.

He'd been ten when the Austro-Hungarian Empire fell and the Kaiser had surrendered to the Allies in defeat. The years that followed—his schoolboy years—were shameful in their privation, or would have been, if his father had not showed him the higher purpose of suffering. The Skorzenys were a respectable, middle-class family whose landholdings in the last century had been in what was now called Poland. Versailles had redrawn the map of Europe, taking from the losers and labeling them criminals. Versailles had made the Skorzeny family poor.

It's a good thing you've never tasted butter, his father said when Otto complained. *Be glad you've got bread.*

He rose and threw a piece of wood on the fire. The flakes were falling faster now, but the rock offered some protection from the wind, and the flames leapt briefly as the coals shifted, licking at the new fuel. The old man had known what he was talking about. Otto was thirty-five years old and he'd come to crave the tests of discipline and pain that filled his days as a colonel in the Waffen-SS. He could not live without physical combat, or constant danger, or the adrenaline rush that filled his blood as he crouched on the edge of an open fuselage, ready to step out into the night sky.

He'd learned to channel pain as a young man in Vienna, where he'd dueled his way into college legend—thirteen affairs of honor, a record for his year. It was the tenth duel that had scarred him for life. But the lessons of fencing—of combat with a sword—he still carried with him.

You cannot waste time on feinting and sidestepping, he thought. *Decide on your target. Go in.*

Otto stood for a moment, rubbing his back, which was almost impossible to find beneath the layers of his clothes. He burrowed among the cuffs of his sleeves for his wristwatch: nearly three o'clock in the morning. He glanced at the night sky. The storm had clouded the lights of Tehran and blotted out the rifts and crags of the landscape. If it kept up, they would have difficulty breaking camp in a few hours. To move in darkness and snow, however, would be deadly.

There was a noise behind him.

He turned with instinctual speed, his right hand already on his gun. He was a giant of a man at six-foot-four, broad-chested and powerful, with a head as square and heavy as a St. Bernard's. His size was one reason the Führer had chosen him as a bodyguard; his kill rate was another. But then he relaxed. It was only Fuchs. Up early, like Otto.

Fuchs was compact and lean, barely five-foot-eight, the last man anyone would expect to carry the heavy radio on his back when they'd parachuted into the Caucasus. He'd turned nineteen last week, far from his hometown of Hamburg. Skorzeny had chosen the boy for this duty himself. Knowing Fuchs probably wouldn't get out alive. But Fuchs had made it this far. Thirty of Skorzeny's men hadn't.

The Russians were waiting on the edge of the drop zone when the Nazis' parachutes slipped amoeba-like from the night sky. He still didn't know whether they'd been betrayed in Tehran or Berlin. He'd been the last to jump—as commander he'd wanted to make sure everyone got out of the plane—and by the time his legs buckled beneath him he was surrounded by the sounds of hand-to-hand fighting. The plane and the wind had carried him to the far edge of the drop zone, and as soon as he was free of his chute, he'd strangled the man who tried to take him and ran for the woods as fast as he could go. Fighting the Russians further was dangerous. If he were captured, he had a capsule of cyanide. Each of them did. No Russian would make Otto Skorzeny talk.

By daylight, the ones who'd survived had found one another. Richter, a raw recruit. Hoffman, the lanky kid from the north. Lange, who could fire a rifle on skis. Braun, a veteran like Otto. And Fuchs—

who'd managed to save both his skin and the radio. Skorzeny was beginning to think Fuchs was a fucking good-luck charm.

Fuchs saluted.

Skorzeny holstered his gun. "Come to the fire," he said. "Can't you sleep?"

The boy shook his head. "I've had contact."

"Berlin? Or Tehran?"

He couldn't trust either of them, Skorzeny thought. Berlin insisted their Tehran people were clean. But those Russian pigs had come from somewhere. And rounded up most of his men. A British informant? American?

"This was from Cairo," Fuchs said.

DAY TWO

CAIRO

FRIDAY,
NOVEMBER 26, 1943

CHAPTER 7

I can't really say I've been here until I've had a Suffering Bastard at Shepheard's Long Bar." Pamela Churchill gazed out over Old Cairo and pouted.

She was a trifle hot, having insisted on wearing her furs to the Citadel of Mahomed Ali. The temperature was close to sixty-five degrees, as it generally was in November. The furs—a sable stole, in this instance, sent by Ave from Moscow—dangled limply across her elbows. Her smart hat was cocked over one eye, and her strawberry-blond curls lay crisply on the lapel of her smart suit jacket. One glance at so much smartness, so much effortless luxury in the midst of desperate rationing, and every Tommy gazing up at them from below would be convinced the war was over.

The British garrison—complete with living quarters, stables, and tennis courts—was housed in the medieval citadel, in the heart of Old Cairo, between the gates of Bab el-Zuwayla to the south and Bab el-Futuh in the north. The Islamic University also lay in this quarter, which was filled with ruins and people, tourists and Egyptians clothed in white *galabeyas*; near it was the Khan el-Khalili Bazaar, where alabaster vases translucent as a young girl's skin could be bought for a bit of haggling. Also silver and rugs. Perfumes and beads. On this final day of the Sextant Conference the women of the Allied delegation had lobbied for a visit to *real* Egypt, as they called it—turning their backs on the Great Pyramid and the endless sand running to the horizon.

Commander Fleming had martyred himself and volunteered to escort them. So, too, had Elliott Roosevelt—who made sure that Madame Chiang was in the American car, not the British. Gil Winant had tucked himself into the jump seat next to Sarah Oliver, leaving Pam to sit opposite with Ian. But Michael Hudson had stayed behind at Mena House. And Pamela was bored.

She was trying to charm Ian so that he'd talk to her about Michael, but her patience was wearing thin. She found the hereditary coldness of Englishmen defeating, and Ian was the coldest of the cold. Possibly because he was actually Scots. She had no idea what Ann O'Neill saw in him. Pamela's friend had married a peer and taken a wealthy lover when her husband went to war—and now she was infatuated with *Ian*. A mere *commander*. Not even in the real Navy. True, he was broad-shouldered and dark, with heavy-lidded blue eyes that promised all sorts of mischief. He came from a banking family and had been to Eton. But Pam guessed his fortune didn't run to much. Second son. She would have to invite Ann to a sherry party in Grosvenor Square when she got home. Talk some sense into her. Introduce her to a few Americans.

"Ladies aren't allowed in the Long Bar," Ian said. "Joe won't have it."

Joe was the Swiss barman who ruled all drink at Shepheard's, Cairo's most fashionable British hotel. Pam knew when she was outgunned.

"Your ducky friend Michael would bring me a drink in the Ladies' Lounge. Don't we have time to run over to Shepheard's in a taxi? I simply *must* have a Suffering Bastard."

"Isn't Randolph enough? Or is he merely a stupid one?"

She drew a sharp breath, eyes dilating. "You cad."

Ian grasped her arm, propelling her unwillingly along the ramparts. "Guilty as charged. But I've been meaning to have a word with you, darling, about my ducky friend. He's a good man and you're not to play with him. You've broken enough hearts."

She stared straight ahead, all her effort focused on setting her high heels correctly on the uneven stone paving. The citadel was a ghastly place. Sarah and Winant had moved out of sight. Madame Chiang despised her, and besides, she'd disappeared with Elliott Roosevelt. Pam was restless and jumpy, and she desperately wanted someone to be *kind* to her. She'd chosen badly in Ian.

To her horror, tears were welling under her lashes, and that meant they would smear. She would visit the Cairo Bazaar with charcoal smudges all over her flawless skin. She hated Ian for it.

"Pammie!" He stopped short. "What's this? Has no one ever said *no* to you?"

"Why should they? I don't ask for much," she gasped. "You haven't an earthly idea what it's like, do you? All you've heard is the *lies*. How I took Randolph for his name and dropped him as soon as I was pregnant. How if the baby *hadn't* been a boy I'd have been *much* more faithful until I'd produced an heir. How I'm a social climber who'll use *anybody*. Did you know, Ian, that Randolph beats his women when he's drunk? Or that he's drunk all the time? Did you know he's never met a wager he wouldn't take—and has wretched luck? He lost two years' income in a single night at cards a few weeks after we were married— and reported for duty the next day, without so much as a line to me! I was nineteen years old and abandoned, Commander Fleming, without a shilling to my name—"

"Pregnant, friendless, and forced to throw yourself on the mercy of the Prime Minister of England," Ian intoned. "Not to mention a billionaire old enough to be your father."

She slapped him.

He enfolded her gloved hands in both of his and held them, smiling. "How conventional. The decent girl outraged. Don't disappoint me, Pammie—I was sure you were the best at what you do."

"And what is that?"

"Anything for money."

She stared at him, her color mounting and her throat constricting.

"Have you been talking out of school?" he went on. "Sharing secrets you oughtn't to know? For a nominal fee—say, a couple of gold bracelets and enough silk stockings to see you through the war?"

"I can't help it if men like to give me things."

"But what do you give them in return? Besides the odd orgasm."

She might have raged. Or struggled against him. But instead she went suddenly limp. Pamela *sagged*. And Ian was forced to free her hands and catch her before she fell to the ground. She could feel his astonishment through his coat sleeves, and it amused her. He *didn't* know everything there was to know about Pamela Churchill, after all.

He helped her to a stone seat carved into the wall of the Citadel and offered her his handkerchief.

"Ave's not a billionaire," she said sulkily. "He's only worth a hundred million. Most of it tied up in rolling stock. It's a railroad fortune, you idiot." And then she burst into tears.

THE STORY, as Ian understood it, was simple.

Pamela was in love.

And it was going to cost her everything she had.

"He's such an extraordinary man," she murmured. "So *honest*. Such *integrity*. He was born in a log cabin, Ian, without running water or electricity! This war is absolutely killing him, you know, because he won't spare himself—he's up all night, reporting on the bombs and the hideous destruction, even though he might be blown to pieces himself. And when he speaks!" She grasped his lapel, spurred upright by the purity of her love. "He commands a nation!"

He was Edward R. Murrow. An American radio reporter the BBC had given a microphone and a booth in the hope he'd galvanize his

U.S. audience with dramatic broadcasts from burning London. Pam had met Ed ages ago but had only realized he cared in the past few months. They'd been meeting secretly, because of his wife. Max Aitken had been very kind. He'd had them down to Cherkley for weekends. Perfectly natural for Pamela to visit, of course, because her small son, Little Winston, was living there, safely out of the dangers of London bombing—but Ed was a delightful addition.

Max Aitken was Lord Beaverbrook. Ian knew him slightly—he was a friend of Ann O'Neill's, too. Ann ran in newspaper circles; she doted on press barons. Max liked to foster love affairs among his hangers-on, but Ian was surprised he'd sponsored Pamela's latest mess. Ed Murrow seemed like a good man. Ian had run into him in London; they were the same age, thirty-five, and they knew the same people. And Ed Murrow had seemed to love his wife.

Everyone was familiar with the sight of Janet and Ed, arm in arm, walking from the BBC headquarters after midnight for a drink at the neighboring pub. Until it had been leveled by a German bomb, of course, along with a score of reporters. Janet hadn't been around as much after that.

"Must you be a home wrecker?" Ian chided Pamela. "First Harriman, now Murrow. You'll end the poor sod's marriage and then you'll end him. Stick with your railroad tycoon, my child. He won't divorce his wife, either, but he'll make it worth your while to wait."

"You don't understand," she breathed. She could look infinitely beguiling with tears on her face; other women got red and ugly, but Pamela glistened. "I can't bear to think of meeting Ave in Tehran tomorrow. It's absolute torture! Being claimed as his . . . *chattel* . . . when I love Ed. Only think, Ian—he's penniless! Or as good as. A log cabin! And yet I'd follow him anywhere. That's how profoundly he's changed me. I've never felt this way before."

"I suppose it's easier to be noble," Ian observed, "when Ave is paying your rent."

"He *is* a lamb," she conceded. "But as you said, Ian, old enough to be my father. So I ask you—what am I to *do*?"

"Move out of Grosvenor Square."

"Oh, probably. But not—not *immediately*. I'm sure something will be arranged. Once Ed breaks the news to Janet. And we're able to live for ourselves. He'll have nowhere to go for a while, of course, so he *may* have to doss with me. But that would only be temporary—"

Ian contemplated the picture of Pamela welcoming one American in a flat financed by another, and said gently: "But where will your Suffering Bastard go?"

Her face hardened. "If you mean Randolph—to hell, I hope. By the fastest road possible."

"Why did you marry him, anyway?"

"He asked. The first night we met. Nobody had ever asked before."

It was, Ian thought, the most pathetic admission he'd ever heard. Girls of Pamela's class—genteel, poorly educated, with generations of forebears but no money behind them—had only one respectable course in life. Marriage, as soon as possible. She had been, what—nineteen? Twenty?

"He'd asked at least eight other women before you, to my knowledge," Ian said drily. "His record was three in one night."

"So tell me," she retorted. "Which of us is really the Suffering Bastard?"

She turned on her heel and went in search of the others.

IAN SMOKED a cigarette alone and gazed out from the Citadel's heights. It was nearly two o'clock in the afternoon, and the shadow of the mosque's great dome was moving slowly across the outer courtyard. The vast complex had been built on a promontory below the Muqattam Hills by God knows whom, long ago, but it was Saladin, that hater of Crusaders, who made it a fortress to be feared. Ironic, Ian thought, that the sons of Crusaders now owned the place.

While he smoked and considered the twelfth century, deeper in his brain he was thinking about Pam Churchill's story. He had behaved badly to her. Hudders would be shocked. He had definitely been a cad. He felt no remorse, however. He was convinced that Pam Churchill was what his mother called a "thorough wrong-un," and Eve should know. If Pamela wasn't selling information to the Enemy, she was certainly profiting from the war—by offering the only commodity she had. Sex. For the exchange of valuable goods. It was a form of profiteering Ian found as distasteful as the gouging of industrialists, in the markets for guns and steel.

The intriguing piece of her tale, from his point of view, was not how she felt about Murrow or Harriman but the meddling of Beaverbrook, who was not only a publisher of immense power and some wealth, but a minister in Churchill's government. Beaverbrook was a friend of Harriman's—so why had he helped Pamela two-time him? Because Beaverbrook liked being in Pam's pocket? Liked the tidbits of gossip—or intelligence—she gave him? Pamela must drop a lot of it—from Churchill, Harriman, and now Murrow. In return, Beaverbrook encouraged her to follow her instincts—into whatever powerful bed they led her . . .

If she was the Kitten, who was her Fencer?—Beaverbrook?

Not likely. Too divorced from Cairo and Tehran.

Ian drank in his cigarette smoke.

What of the obvious? What of Averell Harriman?

He was one of the wealthiest men in the United States, and he moved freely all over the world. He had the President's ear: Harriman had spent the past two years in England as FDR's point man on Lend-Lease. His charm and generosity were legendary—and they opened every door. Even Churchill invited him to Chequers most weekends, despite the fact that he'd made a cuckold of Churchill's son. Hitler couldn't ask for a better agent.

Only a few months ago Roosevelt had sent Harriman as his ambassador to Moscow and upended his cozy London life; Ave hadn't loved the change, but he'd gone. From the heart of Russia and the heart of the American government, he could supply Hitler with any amount of intelligence. Even if it meant losing his mistress . . .

Which brought Ian to Ed Murrow. The hero of a million American households for his tense nightly broadcasts from London. The man who dispatched a team of cub reporters all over England and Europe to ferret out information. The trusted authority on world war. That, too, wasn't a bad cover job for a Nazi spy.

But Ian balked at the idea that either Harriman or Murrow could be a traitor; and he knew if he voiced his suspicions to Churchill or Roosevelt, they'd have him committed. If Alan Turing was right, the Fencer was a friend at the Mena House table. On that ground alone, Murrow and Beaverbrook ought to be struck from the list; but Harriman was joining them all in Tehran. And if Pamela was indeed the Kitten, why couldn't *she* be sending the messages Turing had intercepted? Did she have a radio transmitter hidden in her room at Churchill's villa—and could she speak German?

There are other women here besides Pamela, you know, Hudders had said wearily last night. *You've got to take a hard look at all of them. Any could be the Kitten.*

Or the Fencer herself. Ian hadn't ruled out the idea that Hitler's agent might be a woman. Very well. That was why he'd come on this shopping expedition—to clear his mind and *think*. Ian tossed his ash over the rampart and inhaled some more smoke. There were only a few women among the Allied delegations, but each of them was a corker. And each had a partner she could play.

There was Sarah Churchill Oliver, for instance, and her lover, Ambassador Gil Winant. Sarah had unquestioned access to Churchill and most of his political allies. Winant was beloved in England—unlike his predecessor, Joseph Kennedy, he'd made a broad show of support for England even before Pearl Harbor brought America into the war, but—

But if Winant is secretly working for Hitler, Hudders had argued, *wouldn't that be his best possible cover?—Along with Sarah?*

Ian considered Winston Churchill's middle daughter. He wouldn't exactly call Sarah Oliver a kitten—although she was damned attractive and rumored to be fairly wild when she was tight. Sarah was too bright to be simply somebody's pet. She was a highly regarded member of the Women's Auxiliary Air Force, something in Photographic Intelligence. Studying aerial reconnaissance pictures of Nazi sites, Ian thought. Which in itself could be damning.

He knew Sarah was separated from her husband, Vic Oliver, an aging bandleader and funny man whose peccadilloes were wearing thin. The Olivers had never been terribly successful and the Churchills were notoriously short of cash, so if Sarah meant to change her life— divorce Oliver and claim Winant after the war was over—she might be looking for a few payments under the table. And she was a trained actress. Able to pull off any role. A smashing candidate for Nazi spy.

But would even a willful girl who'd once run away to the stage betray her father so completely? Particularly when that father was Prime Minister Winston Churchill?

It was hard to imagine. Hard to swallow. Ian ground the butt of his cigarette under his heel and squinted down the ramparts, shading his eyes with one hand. Surely that was Madame Chiang? He remembered her scarlet silk cheongsam and matching coat, beautifully cut in a way that bridged Asia with Paris, perfect for the climate of Egypt as Pammie's sables never could be. That blot of bloodred color under a black Robin's Hood hat was unmistakable. She was grasping Elliott Roosevelt by the hand, pulling him with a secret smile in the direction of the Citadel's heights.

What's her game? Ian wondered. Play with the President's rake of a son while the Generalissimo is tied up with business? Or pry what she can out of Elliott, under her husband's orders? She was no spring chicken. Probably ten years older than Elliott—who was thirty-three. But there was no denying that Soong May-ling was a strikingly beautiful woman. Her perfect oval face was fine-boned and full-lipped, her chic knot of black hair drawn back like a ballerina's. She was slender as a blade of grass, and moved with a dancer's grace. Ian could perfectly understand Elliott's interest. With two broken marriages and a string of affairs behind him, he'd be an easy mark for a Nazi agent.

You know she slept with Wendell Willkie, Michael Hudson had told him last night. *When he showed up in China last year. The few people who know think that's why she toured the U.S.—because she's in love with Willkie and leaving her husband.*

Ian hadn't known. And if this was news to him, it would be news to most of the world if it got out. He'd never met Wendell Willkie, who'd famously lost the 1940 presidential election to Roosevelt. Willkie had made the best of his disappointment by joining Roosevelt's administration as an ambassador-at-large. He'd spent the past several years flying all over the world in an old Army bomber named *The Gulliver*. Besides China, he'd visited Stalin in Moscow.

And the new Shah in Tehran.

Ian stopped short. Could *Wendell Willkie* possibly be the Fencer? It would make a perfect revenge for losing the last presidential election. Pose as Roosevelt's loyal man, and sell out the United States in the middle of Roosevelt's war.

But Willkie wasn't in Cairo. Chiang Kai-shek was. If he'd been flying on to Tehran, Ian thought, the Chinese strongman would require watching. Tonight, however, was the last evening the Chinese would spend with their Allies. Ian would have to keep them under his eye.

There was one more woman Michael Hudson had forced him to assess: Grace Cowles. The very last woman he wanted to suspect. But Hudders was right. Gracie was already up to her neck in spycraft.

She had pled work this morning and turned him down when he'd invited her on the Cairo jaunt; no surprise there. She avoided him like typhoid now. There'd been a time when that wasn't true, he remembered, as he lit another cigarette and began to stroll toward the rampart's steps. A time when she'd seemed to feel as much hunger for him as he'd felt for her. But what if her passion had been a sham? What if she'd surrendered to him not because he was devastating in bed but because he was Assistant to the Director of Naval Intelligence?

It was a damnable thought. But possible. Whether from a deep insecurity, trained cynicism, or his abundant respect for Grace's inscrutability, Ian could easily cast himself in the role of her fool. He was a source to be exploited. An easy mark, rolled and left.

Why break it off, then, before the conference was done? his gullible self pleaded. *Why give me the toss when Overlord is in the works?*

Because Grace didn't need Ian for that. He might have been useful when he was planning Deception Ops against the Enemy, but Grace could get the details of Overlord from Pug. As Ismay's disseminator of secrets to his commanders in the field, she was brilliantly positioned to betray all their trust, flying around the world with Churchill's Chief of Military Staff. She had her ear in the PM's War Rooms and her fingers in every Signals pie; she was running communications in Cairo and Tehran! She might have an Enigma encoder in her luggage right now, and nobody would even notice. She could send a message to Berlin without thinking twice. Gracie was the obvious choice for traitor. Except Ian for the life of him couldn't see General Lord Ismay—of Charterhouse and Sandhurst and the 21st Prince Albert Victor's Own Cavalry—as having the slightest interest in selling Britannia to the Nazis. Grace's Fencer—or Kitten—must be somebody else.

He'd have to keep her very much in his sights for the rest of the conference. And neither of them, Ian thought uneasily, would like that.

HE TURNED AWAY from the broken rooftops of Old Cairo, its desert colors and plumes of smoke, and saw her.

A sloe-eyed woman with fragile skin and a petal-like mouth. Her blond head was inadequately veiled with a silk scarf, the color of saffron. When his eyes met hers, she smiled slightly. The rose-petal mouth unfurled.

Despite her dress, she was not even remotely Egyptian.

"Light?" she suggested, lifting a cigarette in her delicate fingers.

She could not be more than twenty.

As he offered her the flame, her hand briefly cupped his and she leaned toward him. Then she smiled again and turned away.

She'd left a slip of paper in his palm.

He moved casually back toward the ramparts and rested his elbows on them, as if intent on the Cairo traffic below. Then he opened the girl's note.

The enemy of my enemy is my friend.

He glanced up and searched the crowd of tourists. In the distance, a saffron-colored wing of silk was flying. Ian decided to follow it.

CHAPTER 8

The girl led him swiftly down the Citadel's ramparts and out into Mahomed Ali Square. He thought she might cross it and make for the Old Helwan train station directly opposite, but instead she turned north and hesitated in the chaotic circle of traffic that was Rumeleh Square. While she did, he crossed to the official cars waiting for their party—Alex Kirk's with an American flag fluttering on the hood—and leaned through the window of the British one. A Canadian sergeant was behind the wheel. He saluted Ian.

"When the ladies return with Mr. Winant and Colonel Roosevelt," he told the driver, "go on directly to the bazaar. I'll join you there."

He glanced over at the corner where the girl still stood. A donkey trap slowed as it approached, but she shook her head. A few seconds later Ian saw her point her finger at the road—universal Cairene for "taxi."

One stopped. She got in the back.

He made a business of lighting a cigarette and moving slowly away from the official cars to a newsstand, but he was fairly obvious with his height and his British uniform and there was no point in trying too hard to fade into the background. She'd contacted him with her bit of paper. She expected him to follow. Any subterfuge was for the benefit of those enemies she'd mentioned. Rommel might be long gone, but Cairo was riddled with German spies.

As soon as her taxi moved into traffic he strolled forward and hailed another. This was complicated by the fact that every driver in Cairo negotiated his price before agreeing to take a fare—but Ian handed the Nubian a fistful of Egyptian lire and told him it was "war business." The girl's taxi was headed around the circle and into the broad arrow that was Sharia Mahomed Ali. Ian's followed it.

Sharia was the Arabic word for *way* or *street*—and this one was a boulevard that ran for several miles straight from Old Cairo to the fashionable district of Ezbekiyeh Gardens, past various mosques and government buildings, the King's palace and the Arabian museum. It ended in front of the Opera House, and, with a bit of jogging left, Ian found himself in Ibrahim Pasha Street.

Up ahead, past the Tipperary Club, was Shepheard's Hotel.

It seemed the girl in the saffron scarf wanted a Suffering Bastard, too.

Ian ignored the shaded terrace where Khawāga, or European Cairo, surveyed the life of Ibrahim Pasha Street from the comfort of wicker chairs. He plunged straight into the dim coolness of the Moorish Hall.

The saffron scarf was not to be found among the plump club chairs drawn up to the octagonal tables; and so he nodded to a bellman idling by Reception, and made for the grand staircase flanked by bare-breasted ebony caryatids. One of Ian's friends once described Shepheard's— which had dominated expatriate life in Cairo for a hundred years—as Queen Victoria's Egyptian Tomb; and the description was apt. The ballroom groaned under red damask and fake pillars of Karnak; the smoking room might have been a pyramid's central vault, upholstered in club leather. Even the loo was ponderously inhibiting; men preferred to relieve themselves in the alleyway *behind* Shepheard's rather than inside it. "Too British Museum," Ian liked to explain. "One expects a docent to wipe one's arse."

The Long Bar just off the main staircase was only dotted with drinkers this November afternoon. It was early yet for officers and government people. No girl in a saffron scarf, of course; just a smattering of civilians of uncertain origin. North Africa was awash these days with refugees of every stripe and class—but only the most affluent and presentable were admitted to Shepheard's.

He strolled over to the bar and nodded at Joe. "Gin and tonic," he said.

While the grizzled Swiss reached for a bottle, Ian casually surveyed the room. In the far corner, almost lost in the draperies of the last window, sat a gray-haired man with a magnificent mustache. He was turning over the pages of the weekly *Étoile Égyptienne*. There was a saffron scarf neatly folded in the breast pocket of his dark gray suit.

Ian paid for his drink and made his way to the newspaper rack. In the Long Bar, the top papers in the world were available—some only a few days old—and all were ironed and hung over separate wooden dowels. He fingered Beaverbrook's flagship rag, the *London Evening Standard*. He'd read this edition at White's club before flying out of England.

The gray-haired man rose from his table with an audible sigh and joined Ian at the rack. He replaced the *Étoile Égyptienne* on its dowel. "So much betrayal in the news," he said mournfully, his voice part gravel, part honey. "One no longer knows whom to trust."

"Well—as they say, 'The enemy of my enemy is my friend,'" Ian replied.

The man smiled. "An old Arabic proverb. You've learned from your wandering in the desert, Commander."

Ian set down the *Standard*. "May I buy you a drink?"

"Vodka martini. Shaken, not stirred."

———

CALL ME NAZIR, he said. *Everyone does—and I've long since forgotten my real name.*

It was clear he was no more Egyptian than his granddaughter, Fatima, whom he explained was the girl who'd led Ian to Shepheard's. She was now back behind the counter of the small shop in the heart of Old Cairo where Nazir sold scavenged antiquities. A Russian family, Ian assumed—although it was possible Nazir was Georgian, like Stalin himself. Uncle Joe liked to keep his countrymen in positions of power, and Nazir's position was very powerful indeed. Ian gathered from hints and boasts and things left unsaid that Nazir was the Soviet NKVD chief in Cairo.

The NKVD, or People's Commissariat for Internal Affairs, was responsible for many things in the Soviet Union. They ran the traffic police, the firefighters and the border guards; they secured the national archives. But what the NKVD was best known for, in Ian's world, was knocking on doors in the dead of night and spiriting people away to the gulag. Within the Soviet Union, they served Lavrentiy Beria, Stalin's chief of secret police. Outside it, they were his assassins and spies.

In Cairo, Nazir explained, they sold antiquities—because he had been a passionate Egyptologist since his youth, and could not imagine doing anything else. Besides, his network of Cairene pit diggers knew everything that happened in Egypt half a day before it occurred. They were a natural intelligence force. And they didn't ask to be paid. A fair price for pilfered artifacts was enough; information was free.

"Good Communists, then, too," Ian observed generously.

"Aren't we all?" Nazir inclined his head. "We hate the Germans equally. Nazir's pit diggers and Fleming's Navy."

Ian did not bother to ask the Russian how he knew his name, or how he had traced him to the Citadel. Nazir would not have said; and besides, he was enjoying his role as all-seeing intelligence chief far too much. Ian preferred the *why* of things to the *how.*

"You remember our countries' joint invasion of Iran, two years ago?" Nazir persisted.

"Vividly."

"Together we ran the Germans out of Tehran and toppled the King."

"And replaced him with his son."

"Mohammad Rezā *Shāh* Pahlavī. He is not entirely easy on his throne." Nazir shrugged. "And what boy would be? With English and Russian soldiers running the town, and Nazi spies all over the place, pretending to be Swiss or American—even *Russian,* the fools—who would sleep much at night? Especially in the face of this conference tomorrow. All three of them in Tehran! Churchill! Roosevelt! And my God—*Stalin!* I'm surprised young Rezā hasn't drunk himself to death in a bathtub by this time."

"You're well informed," Ian said.

"It's a living." Nazir shrugged. "When my colleagues in Iran stumbled across some German paratroopers in the hills outside Tehran— and tortured a few of them—they thought I should know. Does the phrase *Long Jump* mean anything to you, Commander?"

"I was better at the steeplechase myself." Ian studied Nazir. "But I suppose anytime you step out of a plane in midair, the jump must feel like a long one."

The Russian smiled, his mustache lifting like a walrus's. "These paratroopers are Nazi commandos. Who take their orders from an agent known as the Fencer. And my friends in Iran only captured some of them. The rest are still training in those hills. This is news to you?"

Ian set aside his glass. "I'm aware that Hitler wants to know why the Allies are gathering tomorrow. It's the Fencer's job to tell him. But why the Fencer needs commandos is beyond me."

"Oh, my dear sir," Nazir said softly, his mustache lifting further in amusement. "You thought the Fencer wanted *intelligence* from the Big Three? If only it were that simple. His orders, in fact, are to kill them."

IT WAS A GLORIOUS DAY, and she was stuck inside yet again, monitoring dreary Signals traffic. Her lot had seemed bitterly hard to Grace that morning as she watched the other women laughingly arrange themselves in a cavalcade of cars, dressed to the nines, with three attractive men as their guides. She had turned resolutely away and seated herself at her desk, headphones in hand. She was a serious girl—she understood the stakes in this war and was thankful that Pug Ismay trusted her with so much—but once in a while she felt desperate for *fun.* An uncomplicated dance with a dashing stranger and a great swing band at Café de Paris. A coupe of champagne, then perhaps another. A pretty dress that wasn't borrowed or four years old. A real pair of stockings, instead of black greasepaint seams drawn on her bare legs.

The things Grace envied were the sort Pam Churchill took for granted.

What was it like, she wondered, to think only of yourself, instead of your duty?

"Are you ever far from that desk, Miss Cowles?"

Grace glanced up and smiled at the boyish figure leaning in the doorway, her heart accelerating. He wasn't devastatingly handsome, like Ian, but Michael Hudson had only to enter a room for her self-possession to vanish.

"I'll relax on the plane tomorrow," she said, "but until then, Pug owns me."

"Pug's celebrating." Michael strolled toward her, and Grace felt a flutter of nerves along her spine. "He got what he wanted. Bomber Harris stays in command of his flyboys—with a promotion to Air Marshal, too. I guess we Yanks'll just have to learn to work with the guy."

"Or work around him," she suggested.

He grinned crookedly. "Always a possibility. You know your RAF calls Harris 'Butcher' behind his back? Not because of the way he bombs the Germans. Because he doesn't give a damn how many British pilots he kills doing it."

"That can't be true," she said swiftly. "We all know the debt we owe them—our poor boys . . ."

"I'm sorry." His voice was suddenly gentle. "You lost someone."

She hesitated, then dipped her head. "My brother."

"Bomber or fighter?"

"His Spit went down over the Channel," she said.

"Battle of Britain?"

She gave a brief nod. The glow Michael had given her had vanished. She was remembering her mother's guttural sobbing in the middle of the night, and the way she had lain awake herself, imaging the spiral of smoke careening toward the flat gray sea. Will was nineteen. He'd been a pilot only three weeks.

"Are the photographers done at last?" She was good at steering conversations away from herself and back to neutral territory. It kept her from saying too much—and in her job, a tendency to talk was fatal.

"Just about," Michael replied. He got up and strolled to the villa's window, peering out toward the distant hotel. "The PM wants a shot with Madame Chiang—but she's not back from the shopping trip yet. So the guys with the cameras are cooling their heels."

It was after four o'clock, Grace noticed, and the dignitaries would be thinking of their drinks and dinner. "Poor Ian. Surrounded by so many women. He won't know whom to seduce first."

"He's working, not playing, Grace." Michael turned resolutely and studied her. It was the first time he'd called her by her name, and she registered the fact in one part of her mind while listening to him with another. "He drove off with the girls this morning because he wanted them out of Giza—and this villa empty. Nobody wandering in. Not the

PM or his daughter or Mrs. Randolph. He asked me to search the two ladies' rooms."

"Whatever for?" She got to her feet, her back against the door to the hall, so that Michael could not act on his words. Not yet.

He shook his head. "I wish I could tell you. I really do. But Ian's afraid to put you in danger. The less you know, he said . . ."

"Bloody fool." Her voice was savage. "This is about his trunk call, isn't it? To Bletchley?"

Michael nodded. "It's vitally important. Life-or-death stuff. We're on the trail of someone dangerous."

"And you expect to find him in Sarah or Pam's rooms? You do *realize* what you're suggesting?"

"Unfortunately, yes."

"You aren't searching the men?"

"Not yet."

Grace expelled an angry sigh. "What is it about Ian Bloody Fleming, anyway? He always assumes the worst. Particularly of women. Of *course* we're the Enemy. Traitors, one and all."

"I wouldn't go that far," Michael objected. "He's crazy about you, Grace."

She laughed out loud. "Tell me another, Mr. Hudson. The only person Ian cares about is himself."

"That's not what I hear."

"Good God—has he been crying in his Scotch?"

"No," Michael retorted. "But I can tell when a guy's been punched in the gut. Why'd you do it, Grace?"

She hesitated. It was tempting to pour out her heart to Michael— his open, American face was as guileless as Jimmy Stewart's. But anything she said would go right back to Ian. She refused to let him know he'd hurt her.

"He's not to be trusted," she said flatly, "with anything of value. I imagine that, as his friend, you're not to be trusted, either. I won't allow you into the ladies' rooms."

He sighed. "I promise I won't finger their underwear."

"That's not the point," she said. "It's the principle of the thing. You're not *cleared* for their underwear, Mr. Hudson."

"Michael," he said.

"You're not a British subject," she persisted. "I'd be committing a breach of security if I allowed you anywhere inside the private rooms of this villa."

He moved closer to her. Reached tentatively for her arms, as though they were glass and might break. Grace felt his touch slide down her shoulders, warm and insistent, and knew an impulse to fold into him. She had carried so much for so long—

"Every room in the villa?" he asked softly. "You won't let me into *any* of them, Grace?"

Pam Churchill never had to make these kinds of choices.

Grace stepped backward, away from his hands. "Not a single one, Mr. Hudson. Will you let me get back to my work, now—or must I summon a guard?"

CHAPTER 9

*E*ve was pregnant by her lover, the painter Augustus John, in the summer of 1925. She closed up her house and departed for the Continent to have the baby, whom she named Amaryllis. Both were back in London by December. Eve insisted the child was "adopted," and that was the story eighteen-year-old Ian told Hudders, but there were sniggers behind cupped hands and derisive looks in Slater's. Nobody would have dared to gossip in front of Peter, but Peter was gone to Oxford. Ian pretended he didn't care, but his anger was savage. His grades plummeted. And then, abruptly, in April of his final year, Eve pulled him from Eton.

She had decided he wasn't Oxford material. Ian was sent off to a Sandhurst crammer, a Colonel Trevor who lived in Bedfordshire. The general stupidity of his fellows at Trevor's was staggering, but Eve was unmoved.

"If you can't be bothered to learn," she said, "you shall have to fight."

Michael Hudson graduated from Eton and left for the foreign world of Yale. He arrived in New Haven with British affectations and an accent he quickly learned to lose. He was adept at rugby and cricket instead of baseball and football. He had no family in the United States—his father being posted at this point to Ankara. Michael wrote pathetically cheerful letters to Ian, who urged him to spend his Long Vac with Eve and Amaryllis and his brothers in Cheyne Walk. But Michael did not come.

He did not come the following year, or the year after that; and then the worldwide slump took hold, and there was no money in America for Atlantic passages.

Ian moved in and out of Sandhurst, under his proverbial cloud.

It was 1933 before he saw Hudders again.

IT WAS THE SOUND of a piano, oddly, that stopped him as he strolled through the lobby of the National Hotel. Confident and careless, like the Cole Porter tune being played. *What is this thing called love? This funny thing called love . . .*

He'd been thinking about a drink and the dubious food he'd had over the past six days. He'd flown from Croydon to Tempelhof, then caught the six o'clock Nord Express from Berlin to Moscow. Russian trains still operated on prewar rail fittings—a wider-gauge track than the rest of Europe—so at the border he detrained and took a seat in a different carriage, much colder than the last. In Moscow that night his Reuters contact drove him to the National because, he explained, the entire Western press corps stayed there. It had one of only two bars in Moscow that served gin.

Ian had been sent to Russia in a tearing hurry because six British engineers were about to be tried for espionage. Their firm, Metro-Vick, installed generators and turbines that provided electrical power to the country. Metro-Vick had operated in Soviet Russia for decades, but at the moment, the Soviet-British trade agreement was under renegotiation. Stalin didn't like the terms he was getting. He felt himself and his country to be at a disadvantage before ruthless capitalist negotiators. So he accused a few Englishmen close at hand—the employees of Metro-Vick—of spying, and arrested them.

It was possible the engineers would be executed.

This was the hottest story Ian had followed at any time during his sketchy Reuters career. But after only a single day in a Soviet court, he suffered a quelling sense of boredom. It was purely a show trial, with a gravel-voiced judge and a handpicked if raucous crowd of spectators. Even Stalin wasn't stupid enough to risk a trade embargo with England merely to pop a few guns at the British. Ian laid a bet with his cronies—chaps from the International News Service and the Associated Press—that Metro-Vick would get off with a wrist-slapping. Their Russian conspirators, of course, would get the gulag.

. . . just who can solve its mystery? Why should it make a fool of me?

The song tugged at his brain. Ian pushed through the glass doors into the bar, his eyes straining through clouds of cigarette smoke. Most of the tables were filled with Westerners in good suits; a few were held down by the local secret police, obvious in their ill-fitting clothes. Three women, all professional. One of them was leaning over the piano with a glass of gift Scotch in her hand.

The back of Hudders's head was as instantly recognizable to Ian as Peter's or Eve's. The cords of the neck and the fragility of the skin where it met the brutal hairline. The imbecility of the ears, which resembled a monkey's. He noticed, too, the thinness of the shoulder blades and the way they knifed backward as Michael Hudson played. He had not been eating well for some time.

"What are you doing in Moscow?"

The bottled blonde with the Scotch glanced up. Hudders swung around, his fingers trailing off the keys.

"Looking for you, Johnnie," he said.

THEY WERE thrown out of the bar at two o'clock when the Communist Watchers decided it was time to go home. Hudders wasn't staying at the National—incredibly, he had an apartment in Gorky Street. He *lived* in Moscow.

"You left America. And never told me."

Michael studied the vodka in his glass. He'd introduced Ian to the Russian poison even though they were sitting in a Westerners' bar. *You can't drink in Moscow,* he'd said, *without drinking vodka.*

"My father died," he said simply. "While he was posted in Ankara. Typhoid. I never told you that, either. It seemed so . . . *tired* a way out, after Mokie."

The State Department would have sent his father's body home in the hold of a cargo ship for Michael to pick up on the docks of New York, but he had no idea where to bury it. Hudson Senior had not set foot in his native country, really, for over thirty years. So Michael boarded a ship instead, and after several weeks of travel, reached the high and empty steppes of Asiatic Turkey. The new capital of Ankara had been peopled since the Bronze Age. Hittites built its streets, Phrygians dug its fountains. Lydians and Persians, Macedonians and Galatians, Byzantines, Seljuks and Ottomans succeeded one another down the millennia. Michael thought his father—that quiet and dusty bureaucrat of the world—should lay down his bones with the rest of them.

"And once that was done," Michael shrugged, "I saw no reason to go back. The U.S. was never really my country, anyway."

You should have come home, Ian thought.

He kept traveling east, by train and hired car, to Mount Ararat and the Transcaucasus. He reached the edge of the Caspian Sea and worked north through Astrakhan and Krgyzstan and the Urals. And then, as the winter of 1932 was coming on, he turned back toward Moscow.

"Siemens was looking for a fixer," he said simply. "Somebody who could talk to both their engineers and the Sovs. Think about it, Johnnie! *How many Fascists and Commies in a room does it take to change a lightbulb?* But I can talk to anybody. It's in my blood."

The bitterness, Ian thought, was new. The collateral damage of age.

"So you do pretty much what the Metro-Vick people were arrested for," he suggested.

Michael grinned. "I just do it better."

"But doesn't it grow tiresome?" Ian asked tentatively. "Never hearing a word of English?"

"That's why I spend my nights in hotel bars," Michael said. "For the conversation. But there's nothing really for me in the U.S. No family. No jobs to speak of, with this damned Depression."

"The Russians can't possibly pay."

"Well—" Michael tapped his glass on the counter and said a few words to the barkeep Ian didn't understand. More vodka was poured. "You've heard about the famine?"

Ian nodded. Another reason Stalin was angry at the West—newspapers had blared the news that his people were starving. Communism didn't work. Nothing grew in the vast wasted plains and there was nothing for sale in the shops. Stalin blamed *saboteurs* for the bad press and restricted the travel of Western journalists. If it wasn't reported, it wasn't happening.

"At least they've got light," Michael said, "thanks to us."

"Light isn't free."

"It's pretty damn close." Michael reached for Ian's cigarette and took a deep draft. "General Electric and the Metro-Vick fellas and us boys over at Siemens have been price-fixing for the past couple of years. Pooling information, too. About everything, really. Stalin's right to call us all spies. We had a nice little cartel going—nobody undercut anybody else, Russia got electricity, and we made a buck or two. But the Iron Man will probably seize our plants now and send us packing. It's cheaper than paying for it."

"Then what will you do?"

The familiar smile turned in on itself. "Sell what I know," Michael said, "to the highest bidder."

IAN WAS to remember that when war broke out six years later—and Roosevelt suddenly needed spies.

CHAPTER 10

The November dark had fallen by the time Ian reached Mena House. Golden light spilled from the windows staring out at Giza, but the Great Pyramid rose implacably cold in the desert night, its massive white blocks faintly luminous. He had found no official cars waiting at the Khan el-Khalili Bazaar when he'd taxied there from Shepheard's, so he'd hired a driver to get him to Mena House. Concertina wire and checkpoints stopped them half a mile from the hotel. Ian showed his papers and set out to walk the rest of the way. He moved quickly, his head down.

Nazir's warning had forced the only possible decision that afternoon: if the Fencer had orders to kill, Ian must tell Churchill what he knew. Then he and Hudders would talk to Roosevelt's man, Sam Schwartz.

Marshal Stalin, Nazir had said, *knows a killer is waiting in Tehran. The same man who snatched Mussolini from the sky. Our network has told him this. Stalin comes to Tehran with an army around him, and if our network cannot save him, we will all die, Fleming.*

Ian had neglected to tell Nazir that his killer was right there in Giza. It would save a world of trouble if he could flush out the Fencer tonight.

He reached the end of the drive and hesitated. Strains of music fil-tered from the hotel: orchestral background, not dance tunes. That meant the delegations were still at dinner. There would be a number of ceremonial toasts, since the Chinese were parting from them tomor-row. The dinner would be protracted, which would give him time to compose his briefing.

He turned aside from the front entrance and followed the line of the building as it descended the hillside. Mena House was laid out on sev-eral levels, with multiple entrances, following the terrain in such a way that at least three floors were technically at ground level. Ian took a path that brought him down to his floor, found the entrance, and made for his room.

This end of the hotel was far quieter. He shut the door behind him with a sense of relief. His bed had been turned down, his dressing gown laid out. He picked off his cuff links and undid his tie. While his bath was running, he poured himself a drink. To his disappointment, no pale blue official telegram had been shoved under his door in his ab-sence. Alan Turing had no more information to offer. Ian would sound like a fool when he briefed Churchill. He had not a shred of proof to support what he meant to say.

The bathwater was scented with orange and clove. He sighed as he slid into it, reached for a writing tablet he'd left on the commode, and propped it on his knees.

You mean to tell me, 007, that you expect His Majesty's Government to alter its whole course of action in the final hour—when the war hangs in the balance? Dammit, man, we've flown halfway around the world to meet Stalin tomorrow!

—I'm afraid it can't be helped, sir. The Fencer expects you to walk into his trap. The surest way to foil his plan . . .

No pun intended. Ian crumpled his sheet of prose and began an-other, aware that the water was cooling and his Scotch was growing warm.

Dear Hudders,
Meet me at the PM's villa as soon as you get this.

Johnnie

Fifteen minutes later, he was swinging down the sanded path in a fresh dress uniform, his dark hair slicked back behind his ears. He hadn't eaten since breakfast, but his nerves were too raw to stomach food. At Eton he'd broken his nose on the playing field and an indifferent doctor had fused the cartilage with a metal plate. Whenever Ian was under stress, the plate let him know. Pain was flaring along the bridge of his nose and behind the sockets of his eyes. He closed them for an instant. With the shuttering of sight, sound was suddenly amplified.

The strains of music from the hotel, several hundred yards behind him. The ripple of the swimming pool, at the edge of the lawn on his left. The rustle of the breeze in the fronds of a date palm, waving just off this sanded path.

He stopped short, eyes fluttering open. The air was dead calm. There *was* no breeze tonight. Which meant . . .

He started to turn just as the knife pierced his back with a force that sent him stumbling. Instinct helped; that slight shift in posture at the moment of attack deflected the thin steel into his shoulder blade and saved his lung. He flung his arm backward, groping for his assailant, and fell to his knees.

Applause burst from the Mena House ballroom. Churchill must have said something witty.

Pain seared through Ian's shoulder. The man was on him immediately, one gloved hand clamped across his mouth. He would pull the knife out of Ian's back and slit his throat in a matter of seconds. Ian thrust an elbow viciously into the man's rib cage, trying to twist out of his grasp. There was a grunt. But the hand on his mouth only tightened.

He could feel the man's free arm rising. *The knife,* he thought. But he was wrong. Something hard and metal came down on the back of his skull. Ian's world cracked wide.

IT HAD NOT been difficult to lure Michael Hudson into the waltz, Pamela reflected, once she found him standing by himself near the entrance to the lounge. The music and the servicemen ringing the wooden floor weren't officially part of this final night in Giza, but once the stuffy dinner broke up and the various members of the delegations began drifting away to their rooms, she'd been mad for some sort of diversion—anything but her empty bed and another dose of chloral to bring on sleep. Pamela had walked alone to the lounge, her head lifted. She would be unassailable. Beyond criticism. She would not hear them if they called her back. Someone would stand her a drink and charm her. Someone would play the game.

One cigarette and a drink into the night, she'd glimpsed Michael.

She leaned now against his encircling arm, her half-lidded eyes fixed on his. He was a superb dancer. Had Pamela been asked what she meant by this, she'd have said he didn't think about his feet and he made the point of the whole exercise the greater glorification of Pamela. He certainly behaved as though there was nobody but themselves in the room; his eyes never wavered from hers, and his hands made her body respond in exactly the way he intended. Pam couldn't help but enjoy herself. For all his breeding and charm, Averell Harriman was an uneasy dancer. Ed Murrow didn't have time for it. Was it any crime to amuse herself with Michael, who took to music like a cat? All these men pretended to love her—said they would give the world for her . . . but they left her alone in the end. She hated being alone. *Randolph.* Ave. Now Ed. Expecting her to waste the best years of her life while they ran off on their adventures.

The best years. She loved this war. It was the most exciting time she could ever imagine. None of the old rules applied. Everyone snatched at sensation because they might die tomorrow. When the killing was done, it would be the risk-takers who'd won. The people who seized their chances with both hands. The ones who didn't bother with guilt. Pamela's mother had put the fear of God in her as a girl, but she learned early that fear was just another name for guilt, and she'd chucked both when she left home. She was one of the winners.

Michael's face was very close to hers. The intensity of his gaze was making her restless. He was ten years older than she was, but twenty years younger than Ave. She wondered what he was like in bed. Her gaze wandered to his mouth. His lips parted and he drew a rapid breath, as though winded. The music stopped.

"Walk me home," she murmured. "I'm so tired of all these people."

He steered her through the group as instinctively as he'd waltzed. The faces around her seemed to fall back, an indistinct halo to their charmed circle; Pamela kept her easy smile fixed on her face and murmured nothings at the others. She must be tight. How much champagne had she drunk? Or was she intoxicated by Michael? She could feel his hand in the small of her back. Her evening cloak—one of Ave's furs—slid over her bare shoulders. She nestled her chin in the softness and closed her eyes. *Lord.* She would see Ave tomorrow. She hoped she could manage to feel something.

The desert air was chill and a vault of stars arced overhead. She shuddered and leaned into Michael as he steered her down the sanded path. *It was going too fast. They'd be there too soon.* She stopped short and made him face her. Went limp in his arms. Of course he bent his head and kissed her. Probing. Hungry. Bending her head back to find her throat, the cleft at her collarbone, intent on the breast curving below. The fur cloak wrapped around both of them.

"My room," she breathed.

He lifted his head, gathered her in, hurried them both down the path.

And so neither of them noticed the clawed and painful marks in the sand, the spray of pebbles in the garden bed, the scuffs where the heels had been dragged in a wavering sketch toward the date palm—or the dark gouts of Ian Fleming's blood.

GIL WINANT NOTICED.

He never drank to excess, and he had piercing eyes that were used to working in the dark. Too many nights in the past year he'd jumped into a bomb crater, pulling back timber and brick rubble where there'd once been a house.

"Looks like somebody's butchered a pig here, Sal."

He came to a measured halt on the sanded path, Sarah Oliver shivering in her evening dress beside him.

"Arabs don't eat pork."

"Sheep, then."

"Or fatted calf. For a prodigal son. Bloody hell—do you think Randolph's turned up? And Pamela's murdered him?"

Gil drew Sarah toward the PM's villa. "Come on," he said gently. "You're cold as ice and you need your sleep. We've all got a big day tomorrow."

THE MOONLIGHT moved slowly across the uneven stone of the Great Pyramid. It picked out the edges of the hewn stone blocks and the Bedouin stillness of the snipers positioned among them. A jackal threw out its high-pitched cry. One of the snipers shifted painfully, his muscles cramping from the cold.

Michael Hudson moved his right leg from the warmth of Pamela's bed to the floor, careful not to make a sound. He waited for the space of several heartbeats, then slid the rest of his body from beneath the covers. Her steady breathing was unchanged. She slept facedown, her cheek turned away from him, her burnished hair spread across her pillow. One silken arm reached toward him. But she hadn't held him close in sleep; Pamela was anything but possessive. It interested Michael that a woman so voracious in her pursuit of men felt so little need to hold on to them. Pamela was beyond his usual experience. She'd enjoyed him like a good glass of wine or a satisfying meal, as if there'd always be another waiting for her.

A thin line of moonlight knifed through a gap in the heavy draperies at the window. She'd told him she hated the sight of the Great Pyramid, that the curtains were always drawn in her room. It didn't matter. The moonlight was like a pencil torch—it illuminated enough so that Michael could navigate.

He pulled on his trousers and quietly slid his arms into his shirt. Then he drifted toward Pamela's desk. A sheaf of papers, scrawled in her somewhat childish hand. *Letters.* What was she telling people about the conference?

He scanned them quickly. One to Beaverbrook. Another to Murrow. *Madame Chiang has the most divine frocks, but her husband never gives her the time of day . . . Mr. Roosevelt really* is *a cripple! He has to be lifted out of his wheelchair . . . The son isn't half as good-looking as his pictures make him out to be . . .*

She shifted in her sleep—the arm she'd flung across his pillow collapsing like a furled wing. He watched, his breathing suspended.

She slept on.

He moved from the desk, crouched down near the wardrobe, and began to ease the door open. He was looking for anything—a transmitter, a radio, a codebook with a German name.

He had a bet with Ian Fleming that there was nothing to find. And a deep personal reason for hoping he was right.

CHAPTER 11

The slender opium pipe was of black lacquer, set with silver and spinach jade. The silver was engraved with cranes in flight and had been chased by a master craftsman; the pipe was several centuries old. When it was no longer needed, it lay on a black lacquer rest. Carved in the base of the rest were three convex circles. These held the opium paste.

Chiang lay on a couch in his Mena House suite. He wore a dark blue silk robe embroidered with scarlet dragons. His eyes were fixed on the ceiling of the room, tracking visions through clouds of yellow smoke. There was nothing dreamy about the pinpoint pupils.

With his lean, regular features, his black hair silvering at the temples, his elegant frame, he cut a dashing figure by day; but in the evening, May-ling thought, shed of his Western uniform, he was magnificent.

In a bloodless and terrifying way.

When he was drugged like this, stilled by his visions, Chiang seemed at once dead and alive, like a demon-god of ancient times. Opium freed his deepest self, just as Western clothes shrouded it.

May-ling sat in her composed fashion in the main salon, legs tucked beneath her and teacup cradled in her hands. She had left the room in darkness, content to gaze at the Great Pyramid flooded with moonlight. It had been a good day. She had got free of him, and enjoyed her-self, and though her legs were tired from climbing countless stone steps, her hands still tingled as she held the porcelain cup. Remembering the touch of Elliott's fingers on hers.

"Wife," he sighed, the voice no more than a whisper, a faint thread of sound, like a summons from the spirit world.

Almost she did not answer it. She was never entirely sure he recog-nized her in the grip of opium. But when the summons came again she set down her cup.

"Husband," she whispered, as she knelt by his bedside. She allowed her eyes to adjust. He was surrounded by flickering candles, their light unnaturally bright after the glow of the moon.

The pipe lay on its rest. His hands were folded slackly at his hips, but he lifted the right one and set it lightly on her shoulder, allowing it to slide like a falling leaf to her elbow.

"So beautiful," he murmured. "Like rarest celadon."

The voice was childlike with wonder; and she, who had never borne a child, felt her heart soften toward him.

"My concubine," he crooned. "My whore."

His eyes were still fixed on the ceiling, but he gripped her arm pain-fully now. She stiffened and tried to pull away. His head whipped around like a snake's.

"You are hungry for Roosevelt's son. You'd open your legs if he asked. You shamed me through Cairo today, dallying and laughing and swinging your hips."

"No," she cried. And wrenched her arm free.

"Kwang followed you." He spat the three words. His bodyguard. A Kuomintang veteran.

"Kwang lies."

"He knows shame when he sees it. He called you whore."

"And you let him?"

He sat up.

The first blow was for the pipe. The flat of his left hand sent the precious thing skittering against the far wall.

The second was for May-ling.

She flew backward into the doorframe, hitting her skull hard. He was upon her in seconds, fingers clenched in her hair. He dragged her to the far side of the room and discarded her with the broken silver and jade. A fragment of lacquer bit into her palm.

"I renounced my wife for you," he said between his teeth. "My concubines. And this is how you repay me. You parade like a slut before the leaders of the West. My enemies laugh at me."

"The dishonor is yours," she said clearly. She studied the pieces of shattered jade, not his face. "You believe a liar rather than your wife. Another man would have killed Kwang for his insolence."

She expected a second blow. But to her surprise, Chiang laughed softly. "What would that get me? Nothing."

May-ling looked at him directly then. "That's what it's always about, isn't it? *What you get.*"

"Yes." He crouched down beside her. "And you have given me nothing. All these days in Cairo. All your smiles and swinging hips. I have no secrets I can sell. What good are you, wife?"

CAIRO AND TEHRAN

SATURDAY,
NOVEMBER 27, 1943

CHAPTER 12

C ommander. Commander Fleming."

There were weights on Ian's eyelids, pennies for a dead man. He struggled to obey the Voice and raise them. But the light that penetrated was painful, and his vision was blurred. He closed his eyes again.

"He should do for a bit, now," said the Voice. "When he's alert, give him something for the pain. He'll have a head on him."

"Good." A second man, vaguely familiar: "Leave some instructions for my housekeeper."

"And I'll call again tomorrow. Don't hesitate to get in touch if there's anything—"

Ian was aware of a door closing. One voice would stop badgering him, at least.

Somebody crossed the room in a casual way. Ian could feel a presence looking down on him. It reminded him of Mokie. When he was young. Ill with fever. That detached, speculative look, hands in his pockets, as though Ian were a dead fish washed up in the Arnisdale gravel.

He opened his eyes and scowled into Alex Kirk's face.

It was neither a pleasant nor a repulsive one. The American ambassador to Egypt was fastidious, well groomed, pleasure-loving; his skin was smooth and carefully tended. It was possible, Ian thought, that he plucked his eyebrows. Not a stray hair anywhere. His tie was of an exquisite silk, expertly knotted. It was rumored that he liked young Egyptian boys.

"There you are." Kirk drew up a chair and seated himself by Ian's bedside. "Headache?"

"A snorter." The double vision was leveling out, which he found reassuring. "Somebody coshed me."

"And stabbed you in the back."

"I know." He squinted and gazed around an unfamiliar room. "Where am I?"

"My villa. My gardener almost fell over you this morning. Right around sunrise. We figured this was the best place to bring you."

Ian's mind groped its way back through a fug of half images and hallucinations. He had crawled out of underbrush. Or had he dreamed that? He remembered severe thirst and the heat of fever. Sand beneath his elbows. The conviction he was dying in the Sahara. He had fetched up near a stone fountain, driven there by the scent of water.

"Why not the PM's villa?" He tried to raise his arms, felt a stab of pain, and settled for lifting the left one. No sign of gravel burn, but then he had been wearing a dress uniform last night. "I crawled there. I'm sure of it."

"You made it to the PM's garden. Must've come to sometime after the attack and tried your damnedest to reach civilization. Until you passed out again."

"Concussed?"

"Sure. You also lost a lot of blood. Scalp wounds are a helluva mess, not to mention the cut in your back. The doctor's swell news is that the knife didn't reach your lung. Or anything else you might need."

Kirk spoke soothingly, but Ian was unconvinced. He ought to be in the British villa, not the American. Apprehension curled in his gut.

"What time is it?" He tried to sit up, whistled *bloody hell* between his teeth, and settled cautiously back onto the mattress.

"Little after ten-thirty."

"I have to get dressed."

"Fleming." Kirk smiled apologetically. "Relax. The planes already left. You've got no particular place to go."

"You can't be serious."

"'Fraid so."

"*Bugger.* All of them? The PM? Miss Cowles?"

"Gone."

"Your people, too?"

"Yep. Sorry."

So Hudson had flown out a few hours ago. Without a hint of what was happening. He'd watch President Roosevelt roll straight into a Nazi killer's trap. Churchill, too—Ian hadn't even warned his own people! Christ—he hadn't sent so much as a memo to Grace or Ismay or, God help him, his chief, Rushbrooke—and now they were all flying, ignorant as babes, straight into their destruction. And it was his fault. Everybody would die—Hitler would win the war—and it was *his fault.*

He tried to sit up again and settled for a stream of foul language.

"Your boss, old Rushbrooke, thought you ought to stay here," Kirk explained. "I guess you're gonna be weak for a while. Your orders are to lie around for a few days, then head back to London."

"No," Ian said firmly. "That's what he wants. To get me out of the way."

"Who? Rushbrooke?"

Ian glanced at Kirk. "The man who did this."

"You mean you recognized the guy?"

"It was dark. And he came from behind. *My killer.*"

Kirk's eyebrow rose. "You're not exactly dead, buddy."

"That's the oddest thing about it."

Kirk placed a cool hand on his forehead. "You running a fever?"

"I'm entirely sane," Ian snapped. "Be a sport, Alex, and give me a hand."

Kirk supported Ian's good left shoulder and helped him ease to a sitting position. Ian's teeth were gritted against the pain, and sweat stood out on his forehead.

"I thought there was more to this than Rushbrooke let on," Kirk said. "He told the rest of the delegation that you'd come down with bronchitis. Seemed a bit cagey to me. If you were mugged and robbed— why not just say so? It's not like it was going to happen to anyone else. They were all leaving."

"I was robbed?"

"Your papers and money are missing. Even though the place had more guards last night than Fort Knox. I figure you were rolled by an enlisted guy. Nobody else could get in or out of this place. But that's why you're alive, Ian. Nobody'd kill a man for his passport and spare change."

Ian did not argue with the ambassador. He said nothing about Nazi agents or a plot to assassinate the Big Three. Bletchley's decoded traffic was classified as ULTRA, and only a handful of people were allowed to see it. Kirk wasn't one of them.

Ian's head throbbed. He wanted to cut it off and lie down again in peace. It was tempting to accept that he was sidelined, out of combat, done with this.

Do you mean to say, 007, that you allowed yourself to convalesce in comfort while Hitler murdered the only hope for victory in this dreadful war?

You lay back and let the Nazis win?

"I appreciate all you've done, sir." He turned the wretched granite of his skull carefully toward the ambassador. "But I have a few more favors to ask, I'm afraid."

"Shoot."

"I need my passport replaced as soon as possible. I need some cash. And I absolutely must send a cable."

FOUR HOURS LATER he had managed to stand, swallow some morphia for the pain, vomit it immediately, and keep down a plate full of English breakfast. Eggs, broiled tomatoes, some sort of fish. Flatbread and blood oranges. Black coffee. It was the coffee that helped more than anything. Kirk had put brandy in it.

"I don't know how I'm gonna explain this to your folks," the ambassador said gravely, staring through the louvered shutters of his villa. "Folks," apparently, stood in for His Majesty's Government. Kirk was late for a luncheon he was hosting for some Egyptian ministers aboard his Nile houseboat, but he was wasting time talking to Ian. "I think you're nuts. I'll tell anybody who asks."

"If I die honorably in the line of duty," Ian said, "no one will blame you."

The ambassador tossed a wallet full of money and a passport on the bed.

Ian glanced at the passport picture—his own—and the name on the papers.

"Who in bloody hell is James Bond?" he demanded.

Kirk shrugged. "Search me. Probably some poor guy who died chasing Rommel. It's the weekend, Fleming. Your embassy can't just gin up a passport on short notice. The official seals on that thing have to say *London*. They cobbled something together from your delegation snapshot and some old docs in their files. Be grateful. They did you a favor.

Your ambassador, Lord Killearn, made a point of saying he knows your brother."

"Everyone does," Ian said.

"Yeah, well—he can't be any tougher than you are. There's not much money in that wallet, by the way. Banks are closed on the weekend, too. I think you got the sum total of the British embassy's petty cash."

"Go to your party, Mr. Ambassador."

"Most guys in your shoes would jump at a vacation." Kirk turned in the doorway. "Particularly if they think they oughta be dead."

He was shrewder than he looked. But Alex Kirk hadn't grown up with the ghost of a hero in his pocket. He didn't know what it was like to ask for commando training and get a briefcase instead. He'd never carried a secret bigger than himself. Every hour Ian wasted in Giza brought Winston Churchill and Roosevelt closer to death. Sick leave, on those terms, was treason.

Ian thanked the ambassador for his kindness, pocketed the wallet, the passport, and the rest of the morphia. Then he set about composing his cable.

By three o'clock Kirk's Signals people had sent it on to the American embassy, Tehran. It was addressed to Sam Schwartz. Roosevelt had told Ian to remember the name. It seemed like the right time to do it.

THE BRITISH and the Americans had left from the desert airstrip in Giza, with their cars and their bodyguards and their chiefs following behind in separate transports. But Ian needed to hire a pilot: a lone fellow in a small plane capable of crossing fifteen hundred miles of Arabian Desert and the Persian Gulf. He might find him in Cairo, but first he must find Nazir.

The Fencer had tried to silence Ian. *But he had not killed him.* Unconscious, bleeding, alone in the dark—Ian ought to have been finished off. Instead, he was alive.

He found this troubling and strange. It was one of Alan Turing's much-vaunted contradictions, but so far it failed to explain anything.

Did Hitler's prize agent hate to kill with his own hands? Or was he keeping Ian alive out of vanity—to prolong a secret contest? Ian thought perhaps Nazir would know.

The Russian had given him a card engraved in beautiful flowing Arabic with a French translation beneath; the address of his antiquities shop was on the reverse. The Mena House driver who'd agreed to take Ian to Cairo grunted when he saw it. He glanced at Ian assessingly. Was he familiar with the NKVD chief's name? Part of Nazir's intelligence network?

They drove north through the late afternoon, the sun setting over the desert on Ian's left hand. Within half an hour they had reached the Nile. Wooden feluccas with their heavy centerboards were anchoring for the night, furling patched sails of Egyptian cotton. Brown boys with wide trousers hitched above the knees waded with fishing nets in the shallows, calling like birds across the water. Ian's driver crossed the ancient river and Gezira Island, where the six-furlong track and the golf course were oases of green in the fading light. Then into the narrow streets and clustered houses of Old Cairo. Prostitutes, remarkable because unveiled, lingered in the doorways behind the old train station.

The driver jogged left, jogged right. Slowed to a crawl as donkey carts struggled for position ahead and behind. The driver leaned on his horn. There was a camel. Another camel. An official car with a siren parked askew on the narrow paving, and three men in uniform with their arms outstretched.

"This is the shop, *effendi*," the driver said with a gesture. "But I do not think we should stop. See, trouble. The gendarmes."

"Wait for me," Ian said, and handed him a British pound. In war, hard currency was treasure. The man would wait.

He eased himself painfully out of the backseat and made his way to the police. He was as weak as Alex Kirk said he would be. Stars burst before his eyes. He would find a pilot in the bar at Shepheard's and drink on the deal. Then he would take morphia and sleep most of the night while they crossed the Arabian Peninsula.

One of the police—he had a square-jawed face and pronounced nose over a full bottlebrush mustache—said something in Arabic and held up his hand. This was universal for "Halt," and Ian halted. He tried English; Egypt had been in British hands long enough that the police must speak it.

"The shop. My friend owns it. What has happened?"

"The shop is closed."

"But I must speak to my friend. It is urgent." Ian drew some piastres from his pocket and placed them in the policeman's open palm. "War business. Will you send him out to me?"

"What is your friend's name?"

"Nazir."

Mirth bubbled faintly in the policeman's dark brown eyes. He pocketed Ian's offering. "I regret to say your friend cannot speak to you this afternoon."

"Is he being detained?"

"He is dead, *effendi*."

Ian took a step backward. "When?"

The man shrugged. "He was found three hours ago."

"How did he die?"

The policeman's eyes were already moving past Ian to the crowd that refused to disperse. Ian dug in his pocket for more piastres.

"His throat was cut," the man said. "This Nazir dealt in many beautiful things. Many stolen things, you understand. From the tombs in the desert. It is not surprising someone killed him."

No. Not entirely surprising. But Ian found himself remembering the urbane chuckle of the gray-haired man with the saffron pocket square, who had taken his vodka martini shaken, not stirred. He had been so thoroughly alive twenty-four hours ago. So thoroughly at home in Shepheard's bar.

"The girl," Ian said. "His granddaughter. What happened to her?"

The policeman studied Ian with contempt. "I know nothing of any girl. Your driver is blocking the street. You will move along, *effendi*?"

CHAPTER 13

The President's DC-4 was nicknamed the *Sacred Cow,* and at the recommendation of the President's doctor, it flew a low-altitude route from Cairo to Tehran. Roosevelt was not entirely well. The idea that he might be ailing was a closely guarded secret. Of his staff, only Sam Schwartz knew. He'd flown the same low-altitude route the day before Roosevelt, and radioed approval.

He was waiting at Gale Morghe Airport outside of Tehran at three o'clock that afternoon when the *Sacred Cow* touched down. Gale Morghe was an air base held by the Soviets and it was in good condition. Schwartz had fifty American troops standing at attention, ready to roll into Army jeeps for Roosevelt's escort into the city.

When the cabin door opened, he raced up the steps to help with the President's ramp. He would roll the wheelchair down himself, walking backward, so that his body shielded FDR's at every step. The President's armored car had arrived an hour earlier. It was already waiting beside the plane.

"Hello there, Sam."

Roosevelt lifted his hand. He was still sitting with a blanket over his knees beside one of the cabin windows. Cadaverous Harry Hopkins was opposite, stubbing out a cigarette. Elliott and John Boettiger held down the back of the plane, while General Marshall was up front, close to the Special Air Mission pilots who manned Roosevelt's craft. He'd been amusing himself during the eight-hour flight with navigation.

"Mr. President," Schwartz said. "Good trip?"

"We're here in one piece. Whaddya think of this place, Sam? Is it crawling with Germans?"

So the President had talked about the alleged threat with his closest aides and family. Schwartz felt a ripple of misgiving. Roosevelt was following his own agenda.

"Not so's you'd notice," he temporized. "I thought I might brief you on the ride into town."

The plane's propellers were slowing to silence; the copilot came aft to help Schwartz position the ramp. Everyone waited until both men had lifted FDR into his wheelchair, and laid the lap robe across his knees. Tehran was surrounded by mountains—capped with snow this last weekend in November—and the air was far colder than Cairo. Schwartz backed carefully down the ramp, his feet finding position from long practice, and halted in the lee of the open car door. It was a relief to see the President screened by something stronger than Schwartz's back. Marshall and Hopkins joined them; Elliott and Boettiger got into the car behind. Doors slammed and the first of the Army jeeps moved off, ahead of Roosevelt's car.

"Where are we going, Sam?"

"The American legation, Mr. President. Louis Dreyfus has moved into a hotel, and it's entirely at our disposal." Schwartz had inspected the whole place yesterday, extending the security cordon and doubling the number of men on guard. Part of his Secret Service detail was working its way through the occupied city, on the hunt for German agents. He hoped none of them got a bullet through the brain. "I've deployed a hundred American troops in pitched tents on the embassy grounds. Just in case."

Roosevelt whistled. "You're not fooling around."

"When I got here yesterday," Schwartz said, "this Russian general named Arkadiev was waiting for me. He's a big cheese in Transport, I guess. Anyway—he took me through his embassy and managed to drop some hints on the tour. Says a bunch of Nazi paratroopers landed in the hills outside the city a few weeks back. The Sovs rounded most of 'em up, but a few slipped through the net."

"Paratroopers." Roosevelt flashed his shark's smile. "What are they doing here, Sam?"

"Nobody'd give me a straight answer, sir. But the Russians seem to think they're gunning for all of us."

"From what little I know of Uncle Joe," Roosevelt mused, "he wouldn't leave Moscow if he truly thought he was at risk. Too much of a homebody. And too superstitious."

"Just say he's a coward and have done," George Marshall barked from the front seat. "Stalin is sure he's going to be shot one of these days. He's shot everybody else. Wouldn't be surprised if he fails to show up at this circus."

"He's already here, General," Schwartz said. "A day earlier than planned. So I think we can say this Nazi threat isn't half as bad as the Russkies would like us to think."

CHURCHILL'S ENTOURAGE touched down at Tehran's Doshan Tappeh complex—where the young Imperial Iranian Air Force had once trained and flown. British airmen now ruled the runway. Since the joint Anglo-Soviet invasion of the country two years before, the Iranian pilot school had been shut down, the pilots decommissioned, and the fleet of Imperial fighter planes sawn in half. Sarah Oliver knew all this, but few others in her father's orbit understood anything about the country they had just entered.

Sarah had spent months working in aerial reconnaissance, and she was a practical woman. She understood that the Russians had seized northern Iraq to control its oil fields, and that the British Army had taken the south to secure their land route to India. But it was an uneasy partnership. Both Stalin and Churchill mistrusted the deposed shah because he was a Nazi sympathizer. His son, Mohammad Rezā Shāh Pahlavī, was new to power. They trusted each other even less.

Sarah was wearing her WAAF uniform and riding in the backseat of an open car with her father. His bowker—a homburg without the usual depressed crown—was in his lap. He was fiddling the brim with his hands. A cold breeze ruffled his white hair. An airman from Doshan Tappeh was driving, with Walter Thompson—her father's devoted bodyguard—seated next to him. Still, Sarah felt exposed. There were so many checkpoints on the way into the city. They were drawing up to another one now—and a crowd had gathered. As the official car with the fluttering flags slowed to present its papers, she saw it was a Soviet-manned checkpoint. They would not be simply waved through this one.

The car stopped and the crowd surged forward. It was entirely male. Tribesmen from the provinces, in every kind of native dress.

Hands touched Sarah's shoulder. Her arm. Hands probed her legs and lap. She gripped her handbag firmly between her ankles and glanced desperately at her father. Winston was reaching out of the car, shaking hands, smiling his broad smile and snorting in English, "Good show! Good show!" while the Russian soldier took his time with the papers. Anyone might shoot Father through the heart. Or toss a bomb into the open backseat. That was how the German Gestapo chief—Reinhard Heydrich—had died in Prague last year. Sarah slipped her hand under Winston's arm, protective, seeking comfort from the solid wool sleeve of his Chesterfield coat. *Mother will never forgive me if*—

Panic rose in her throat.

"Fatal to show fear," Winston growled sidelong.

Her heart skipped a beat. Then she turned resolutely to her side of the car and reached out with both gloved hands, greeting the Persians with a blinding smile.

"Sorry to disturb you, Mr. President."

Schwartz hesitated on the fringe of the legation's main reception room. What passed for the U.S. foothold in Tehran was a cramped and slightly shabby building in a small compound in the northern part of the city, where the wealthiest Iranians lived in beautifully designed mansions behind walled gardens. The Shah's summer palace was here, and many of the government ministers' homes; farther north, beyond the wooded grounds of the Russian and British Embassies, the mountains rose massive and sheer against the bluest of skies.

The Russians had been sending ambassadors to Persia since the 1580s. England had maintained diplomatic relations almost as long. The two powers struggled for influence and control over Persia throughout the centuries, a violent contest of espionage known as the Great Game, in which scores on both sides died. The current Anglo-Soviet Occupation was a rare moment of coordinated effort in a long history of murder between rivals. The Russian and British embassies, side by side in a walled compound, were palatial and imposing. At times it felt as though the real center of power was *here,* not in the orbit of young Mohammad Rezā Shāh Pahlavī.

The United States was renting a far less impressive place a mile away, and their official representative, Louis Dreyfus, was an envoy, not an ambassador. Diplomatic relations had only existed between Persia and America for about eighty years. To each other, they were both remote and fabled lands that just might not exist.

Schwartz saw immediately that Roosevelt had company. Averell Harriman looked like a movie star—Gary Cooper, perhaps, although he was a good decade older than the actor. Both men shared a rugged American style that suggested the wide-open spaces of the West. Harriman's jaw was more pugnacious than Cooper's, and at fifty-two years of age, he was uninterested in sharing the limelight with anyone besides the President of the United States or Joseph Stalin. The considerable power and fortune he'd inherited were less interesting to Harriman than what they could buy: *influence.*

"Sam!" Roosevelt grinned at him; it was an invitation to enter. "You remember Ave Harriman."

"Ambassador," Schwartz said. "I understand you flew in on Marshal Stalin's plane."

"Along with the Kremlin guard." Harriman glanced sidelong at Roosevelt. "He's surrounded by generals and NKVD people and he's got his Foreign Minister, Molotov, to talk dirty for him. His security chief, Lavrentiy Beria, is walking about two feet behind him wherever he goes. Two feet behind Beria is his personal bodyguard—although some say he's Beria's personal assassin. Lavrentiy brought his kid along, too. I guess it's never too early to start the son off in the family business. And don't get me started on the three thousand NKVD troops Stalin's shipped into the city. We're calling it the Second Occupation."

"There's been some rumor about German paratroopers," Roosevelt said. "Heard anything, Ave?"

Harriman hesitated, then laughed. "Talk to a Russian, and you'll get five different conspiracies in five minutes, Mr. President."

Roosevelt's gaze shifted to Sam Schwartz. "Ave tells me Uncle Joe thinks he's too tired to have dinner here tonight. But apparently the real reason is he doesn't want to leave his compound. Afraid of being shot in the streets. Can a man with such a reputation for ruthlessness really be that much of a chicken, Sam?"

"Even with three thousand men at his back."

"There's a reason he's still alive," Harriman said cautiously. "Call him yellow if you like—but the Marshal's no fool."

"I tried to get Winston to come over for dinner, but he tells me he's lost his voice and is going to bed early with a glass of Scotch and a volume of Dickens," Roosevelt persisted. "So if you'd care to join me, Ave, we'll see whether the State Department cook is worth his salary. I've got my son Elliott here, and John Boettiger. They'd love to hear all about Moscow."

Harriman dropped his gaze. "I'm deeply grateful for the invitation, sir, but—well, I think it's my duty to remain available in the event Premier Stalin . . ."

"I understand." Roosevelt turned his wheelchair away from Harriman and winked roguishly at Sam Schwartz. The look said quite plainly: *Pamela.* "Tell you what. Why don't you take Molotov a message from me? My official answer to Uncle Joe's invitation to bunk down in his quarters. Tell him I'd love to accept the offer, but I'm in a bit of a bind. Winston's invited me to stay at his place, too. The young Shah has offered me the run of Golestan Palace. Don't want to offend anybody. Suggest to Mr. Molotov that his boss meet me here tomorrow after lunch. See what excuse he comes up with next."

"Will do, Mr. President." Harriman moved swiftly across the room and shook FDR's outstretched hand. It was clear, Schwartz thought, that he wasn't going to risk another invitation to dine in a room full of men. "I'll stop by the British embassy and send in my regards to the Prime Minister, too."

"He has a nasty cold."

"That's too bad. He's not getting any younger."

"None of us is, Ave," Roosevelt offered benignly. Like so much of what the President said, the simple phrase carried an underlying note of mockery.

SCHWARTZ WAITED for the legation's main door to close and for the thrum of a high-powered car engine carrying Harriman into the night. Then he turned to Roosevelt.

"Let's have it, Sam."

The Secret Service chief handed him a folded cable. "This was waiting for me when we got back from the airport. Alex Kirk's people sent it, but it's from that Royal Naval Intelligence guy you talked about a few days ago. Fleming."

"He's down with bronchitis."

"And a knife in the back."

Roosevelt's eyebrows soared. He adjusted his pince-nez and read swiftly through the text. Then he peered at his Secret Service chief. "Why have I never heard of this Fencer?"

Schwartz looked slightly apprehensive. "I'd never heard of him, either, until Mussolini's rescue. The people at Bletchley Park turned up his name in their German traffic. They guard those intercepts like King George's balls."

"Rightly so. Knowledge is power, Sam." He snapped the pages of the cable. "Fleming says this Fencer is behind the Nazis who've scared Uncle Joe shitless."

"He also says they mean to kill you, sir."

Roosevelt lifted his shoulders irritably. "Let 'em try."

"Easy for you to say," Schwartz retorted. "It's my head if they do."

"I wonder why Winston hasn't told me about this?" Roosevelt mused. "He must know. Fleming's in his shop. But instead we got some bullshit about bronchitis. Why lie?"

"Maybe Mr. Churchill was afraid you'd turn tail and go home," Schwartz said bluntly. "Or maybe he doesn't trust Fleming."

"Huh." Roosevelt handed the paper back to Schwartz. "And now he won't come over for dinner. Down with a volume of Dickens and Scotch, my ass! The whole thing stinks. If I'd known . . ."

"Yessir?"

"If I'd known about Fleming this morning, I'd have delayed takeoff long enough to talk to him. I don't like this bit in the cable." He shook it at Schwartz. "About how the Fencer may be one of us. If Joe Stalin gets wind of a traitor among his allies, he'll never trust another word we say. We need Stalin, Sam. We've got to have his trust."

"The whole Fleming story sounds like a bunch of who-shot-John," Schwartz said. "What do you know about him, Mr. President?"

Roosevelt looked suddenly tired. "No more than you do. He's been trailing along behind his chief and Churchill at every one of our joint conferences over the past two years. Likes the ladies. And they like him. When he does offer an opinion, he's not stupid. Hudson—our OSS man—knows him best."

"Thank you, sir. Will there be anything else?"

They looked at each other for the space of several heartbeats.

"What would you do, Sam?" Roosevelt asked thoughtfully. "Sit on Fleming's cable—or confront Winston with it?"

Schwartz shook his head. "That's not much of a choice, sir. Sit on the cable, and you could be target practice for Hitler's boys. So do we move into the British Embassy—or shack up with Stalin?"

CHAPTER 14

The pilot was called Dutch and nothing more. He was a genial Jewish air rat from Poland who'd fled the German invasion in '39 and had knocked around North Africa ever since. He told Ian that when one place got too hot for him, he flew to another. There was always somebody who wanted to hire a set of wings, whether he was in Casablanca or Tripoli or Addis Ababa or Cairo.

Joe, the Swiss barman at Shepheard's, had sent Ian out to Payne Airfield, the massive complex that had suddenly bloomed under American hands, in the desert an hour northeast of the city. It was a major Allied Air Transport command, shipping cargo and troops in and out of Egypt. Ian found Dutch drinking coffee in the mess. By that time, it was seven o'clock in the evening and Ian's bandaged shoulder blade had stiffened to a vise. He could not lift his right arm. His bludgeoned head was pounding methodically with his heartbeat, as though Big Ben had taken up residence in his skull.

"Tehran?" Dutch asked, his voice unexpectedly high and light, but overlaid with Poland like treacle on a tart. "It'll cost you, mate."

"I want to be there by dawn."

Dutch took a slow sip of coffee. "Night flying? Over the Arabian

Peninsula and the Trans-Jordan? Crash in those parts, you don't just walk out. Got a death wish, Commander Bond?"

"Ever since I was a boy," Ian said. "You?"

He was trembling all over at this point in the night, barely holding himself together. More than the pain and lethargy that swept over his body, it was the fear that made him shake. Nazir had been knifed to death. His throat slit. That simple phrase encompassed a slew of garish images in Ian's mind. A severed carotid. Blood sprayed in an arabesque across the wall. Had it been the same hand, the same knife, that plunged into his back?

Then why was he still alive?

The question—Turing's contradiction—tolled like a bell through his brain. The endless boring clang would drive him mad. Nazir was the only one who knew what Ian knew. Nazir was dead. Ian had been spared for the pursuit—and he suddenly understood it was his own madness driving him forward, his need to prove something that should not have to be proved. *His worth.* To his brother. To Eve. To a man who had been dead for more than twenty-five years.

You actually believe, Bond, that the Fencer knows your mind? Understands what drives you? That this is a personal contest—between you, a Chocolate Sailor in His Majesty's Wavy Navy, and the most dangerous agent Hitler has ever known?

You're drunk, 007. Not to be trusted.

Not just that, sir. I'm completely absent without leave. Defying direct orders. Terrified to the point of incontinence.

Shitting yourself, in other words?

And completely buggered.

He and Dutch decided on a price of forty-two pounds, seven shillings, which was all Ian found in the wallet Ambassador Lord Killearn had given him. They would refuel at RAF Habbaniya. This was the sprawling and raw complex built by the Royal Air Force on the west bank of the Euphrates. It was the principal Allied airfield in Iraq and a favorite stop of American Lend-Lease transports delivering aircraft to the Soviet Union.

"If we leave in an hour," Dutch said, "we should touch down at Habbaniya by two a.m. Provided the Old Sow holds up. That should get you to Tehran by daylight."

The Old Sow was a Polish R-XIV two-seater parasol wing recon plane, with a two-hundred-twenty-horsepower radial engine and fixed landing gear. There was a machine-gun port in the tail that a third passenger could use, if they'd had a third passenger.

"It was in for repairs the last day in August 1939," Dutch told Ian. "And I was the mechanic. Three days later I'd put the engine back together and the Germans were in Warsaw. I liberated the Sow and flew to Romania that night. Not like she could beat the Luftwaffe in aerial combat, anyway. A lot of good men died trying. By the end of the week, my country had ceased to exist and it was an easy decision to keep flying south, with the birds, for winter."

Dutch filed a flight plan with the Americans while Ian found a girl who could mix a stiff drink in the airmen's lounge. He took two morphia pills and bought a packet of sandwiches. Lamb on flatbread, of course, with some kind of yogurt. The metal plate in his nose radiated pain. Within minutes of consuming his first sandwich, the morphia had kicked in and his right arm felt like a helium balloon. It threatened to levitate. He blew his nose and felt light-headed, as though his cranium might lift off, too.

Dutch came back. He carried Ian's bag like a porter, and Ian followed him out onto the tarmac. The air was cool and dry off the desert, and but for the landing strip lights, the night was like pitch. Dutch gave him a leather pilot's cap that strapped under the chin and a set of goggles. The cockpit was open. There was no second leather flight jacket. Dutch handed him a rough wool blanket. Ian tucked it under his bad arm and tried to pull himself into his seat. He discovered that the morphia had rendered his good left arm as wobbly as gelatin. Dutch heaved from behind and Ian tumbled headfirst into the cockpit. It was a labored business to right himself and settle his legs. As soon as he had managed it, he was overcome with acute claustrophobia.

Dutch was extending his hand to a slight, muffled figure standing on the tarmac in the darkness—no more than a boy, Ian thought—who sprang up on the wing and moved past him like a cat to the machine-gun port in the tail. The fellow settled himself into the narrow seat and blew on gloved hands.

So they did have a third passenger, after all—one who possessed his own cap and goggles and leather jacket, and who apparently knew how to train the barrel of a weapon on a swiftly moving aerial target.

"Is that really necessary?" Ian shouted at Dutch, but by that time the propeller was turning and the pilot's head was wavering in front of his as the plane bumped its way down the strip. The Sow surged forward and lifted uncertainly into the air.

Ian glanced down.

Egypt retreated like the perpetual mirage of old tribal fires flickering. The fires were hotel lights and airports and highways now—but still tribal, Ian thought. *His* tribe. He felt intensely lonely. His teeth were chattering from wind and cold. He struggled to wrap the blanket around him and waited for it to warm.

"HOW'S DARLING KATHLEEN?" Pamela asked brightly. "Dashing about like a Tolstoy heroine, charming all the Russian men?"

Kathleen Harriman was Averell's daughter and his official hostess in Moscow—his wife was too rooted to her life in New York to play that role. Kathleen was a couple of years older than Pam, and they'd been good friends in England. Pam had found her useful in cultivating Ave; and Ave had used his daughter as cover for his affair. He'd rented a house for the two girls outside of London when the bombing got serious—and visited often. Kathleen loved Ave more than anybody on earth; and his current wife wasn't her mother, anyway. Kathleen did not confront Ave when he dallied with her friend.

Breeding, Ave would have said if Pamela asked. His Kathie had breeding.

It went without saying that Pammie did not.

"She's well," he said. "Working as a reporter, in fact, while she helps me out in Moscow. She's writing great stuff. But surely you've had letters?"

"A few," Pam replied. Very few. She suspected Kathleen's affection for her had waned. Someone else had written to alert her, perhaps. Rumors about Ed. Or one of Pam's other men.

"But tell me about *you,* sweetheart," Averell said, as he sank down into the love seat beside her. "Tell me about London! I miss the place terribly. And all the old gang."

It was nearly midnight, and the two of them had long since finished dinner—a small affair of a few tired people gathered around the British ambassador's shining mahogany table. Winston, true to his word, was in bed with Dickens. Sarah and Gil Winant put in an appearance—Gil was an old colleague of Harriman's from London, and always treated him as a friend. Sarah was less predictable. She knew her father valued Harriman and winked at his affair with Pamela, but she resented the mogul's presumption on her brother's behalf. This was one of those inexplicable emotions so common in siblings. Sarah had no great love for Randolph, but her loyalties were divided: between her father's pragmatism and her brother's humiliation.

Dinner was an uneven affair—Gil talking shop, Pamela uttering bright commonplaces, Sarah mostly silent. She pushed her food around on her plate without eating much, responded absently to the ambassador's studied small talk, and excused herself on the grounds of exhaustion immediately after dinner. Gil lingered, hoping to share Harriman's hired car back to the American legation, but after ten minutes of awkward waiting he allowed a British staffer to drive him home.

Pamela was sorry to see Winant go. She valued the safety of numbers, these days, in Averell's company.

She was wearing the turquoise evening gown she'd shown off in Cairo; Ave had paid for it, after all—he deserved to get his money's worth. She was nursing a glass of port and smiling at him dreamily over the rim of her crystal glass. Hoping to forestall any painful questions. The British ambassador had left them to themselves. Apparently he had a great deal of work to do with the Churchills in town.

"It's very dull, really," she murmured. "I volunteer at the servicemen's clubs. We just started them—a couple of places where the boys can relax for a bit, have a cup of tea, read a scandal sheet and talk about something other than war for a change. It's exhausting work, running the whole show—but so worthwhile. The boys are pathetically grateful."

"Boys always are, where you're concerned," Harriman said. He lifted her chin and stared into her vivid blue eyes. "Age becomes you, Pammie. You're more confident. More fully the woman you were always meant to be."

"I'm only twenty-three," she said defensively.

He smiled, and kissed her.

She tried to respond, parting her lips and leaning into his embrace, but she sensed he was unmoved. Whatever had stirred between them in the first months of meeting—more than two years ago, now, she thought with slight surprise—was utterly gone. When she had met him at Chequers that day in late March, she hadn't expected to be so bowled over by his magnetic charm. She'd given birth to Little Winston six months before. Randolph had spent her hours of labor in the bed of another woman. Averell was not yet fifty, then. His hair was jet black. He wore the rumpled, careless clothes of the very wealthy, who never need to impress. There were dark circles under his eyes because he worked too hard, but his sudden smile felt like a gift, rarely bestowed.

Three weeks later, after a party at the Dorchester, Pamela found herself sheltering in Ave's apartment at three o'clock in the morning. Wave after wave of German bombers were flying over London. Nearly five hundred that night. They watched the flames go up all around them and fell into a frantic bout of lovemaking, tearing at each other's clothes. It was, Pamela told herself, the survival instinct. The Dorchester was considered the safest building in London, but Pamela had no desire to be safe. That was the start of her life of dancing on the grave's edge.

"How's Little Winston?" Ave asked now, releasing her with a faintly sardonic lift to his mouth. He was grayer, more lined, she thought. The three decades between them were increasingly obvious.

"Thriving. Nanny stuffs him with so many good things, he doesn't know what war is."

"Then he's lucky. You wouldn't believe the scenes I've witnessed in Russia, the past few months." His expression darkened. "Makes you feel that a lifetime will never be long enough to atone for the things you've always taken for granted. Food. Heat. The assurance you won't be killed when you're forced to go hunt for either."

"How dreadful for you," she murmured.

He studied her. "You missed the point, Pammie. It's terrible for the *others*. Never for *me*. I've been safe all my life, and only lately have I learned to despise myself for it."

"Lord! You sound like Gil Winant," she said petulantly. "As though you weren't enjoying every *minute* of this war! It's the most glorious time of our lives, Ave!"

"Pamela. Haven't your new friends taught you about suffering?"

"My new friends?" she faltered.

"I hear you've been running around with the CBS news boys. Ed Murrow," Ave said neutrally. "Seems to me he takes nothing for granted. Except possibly his wife."

She felt a chill finger her spine. "Don't be silly, Ave. We're just good chums. That's all."

He offered her his sudden audacious smile. "Let's not lie to each other, my dear. Our time together is so short as it is."

"Averell—" She clutched at his sleeve, suddenly terrified. If he cut off her rent in Grosvenor Square—if he stopped telling her all the delicious gossip she knew so well how to sell—

"Ambassador," said a voice from the doorway.

Pamela glanced over and saw Michael Hudson. He still wore his overcoat and held his hat in his hand. He had clearly come from the American legation, and at such an hour . . . She searched his face for some hint of the trouble, but his expression was carefully wooden. He refused to meet her eyes. She might have been invisible. Some other woman kept at great expense by Averell Harriman. Was it only last night he'd carried her up to her room in Giza?

Damn. Now she would have to explain to Michael—

"The Soviet Foreign Minister—Mr. Molotov—has arrived at our embassy. He's asking for you," Hudson said.

IT WAS A FEW MINUTES after midnight, somewhere over the Trans-Jordan, when they picked up the pair of Messerschmitt Bf 110s, the heavy night fighters of the Luftwaffe. The German planes announced their presence with a strafing burst that fell harmlessly short of the Sow but got Ian's attention all the same. He had been dozing before the staccato fire punctuated the steady throb of the propeller. The Messerschmitts came in from the north, off the Mediterranean, dividing their attention and killing force as they bore down on Dutch's tail.

Ian could not have said at that moment, with the wind whistling through the wings and the Sow suddenly diving and bucking, what model plane the Germans were flying. He merely recognized a silhouette familiar from a hundred glimpses of aerial combat in the Battle of Britain a few years before. The Bf 110s were terrifying planes, equipped to locate and kill anything in darkness, heavy and indefatigable as sharks. The Sow looked like a child's kite in contrast.

To his shock, there was answering fire from behind his back. He craned to look over his shoulder and saw the boy in the gunner's seat crouched over his weapon, wheeling and turning with the Messerschmitts like a falconer. Tracers from all three planes lit up the sky around him like festival lights on Guy Fawkes Night. The Germans strafed the Sow again and Ian instinctively ducked as bullets raked the left-hand wing. He cried out. The night was full of noise: the machine-gun bursts from the Sow's tail, strafing fire from the Messerschmitt on Ian's right, a high-pitched scream from their tail gunner (was he hit?), and a continuous stream of Polish profanity from Dutch in the cockpit.

Dutch dove steeply and the ground spiraled toward them. Ian felt his gorge rise and squeezed his eyes shut against the torque of gravity. Tracer bullets were streaming by his head like firecrackers, one every three seconds. He braced himself, hands gripping the edge of the cockpit, against the slamming impact of earth and metal. Another burst of fire from the tail. So the gunner wasn't dead, at least.

The Sow pulled out of the dive and immediately flipped back on herself. Now they were diving upside down. Ian opened his mouth in a guttural yell. Their gunner, impossibly, was still firing toward the belly of the Bf 110 above them. A spatter of German bullets grazed Ian's right shoulder, tearing away shreds of Dutch's blanket.

A compression wave shuddered the Sow violently to the left, and then Ian heard the *crump!* as one of the Messerschmitts burst into flames. The Sow's gunner had hit an engine.

Dutch righted the plane and flung it sharply down to the left, away from the disintegrating Messerschmitt. Ian peered out of the right side of his cockpit and watched the enemy plane drop in pieces to the indistinct terrain of Trans-Jordan below. Ian's teeth rattled with gunfire. Bullets pinged across the Sow's nose, and for a heart-stopping number of seconds the propeller cut out.

They were falling.

Gently, it is true—falling without spiraling, Dutch fighting to keep his nose up—but the sensation of slipping out of their proper realm in the sudden silence of the dead engine was horrifying. Ian thought far too late of such things as parachutes. Was Dutch wearing one?

The remaining Messerschmitt whined vilely over them. Dutch could no longer maneuver. They were going to die, in a fireball in midair or in a heap of flattened metal on the ground.

And in a few hours or days Winston Churchill would be murdered. Shot to death in a Tehran street or blown to bits as he reached for Stalin's hand. Hitler would win the war. Because Ian Fleming was no hero. Just a useless desk jockey in a make-believe war.

The machine-gun burst, when it came, was shockingly loud in his ears. It came from the gun in the Sow's tail, and the Messerschmitt answered almost immediately.

Dutch's gunner cried out again; shrapnel, Ian thought. Was the gunner dead? He craned upward at the looming bulk of the Bf 110 nearly upon them. It seemed to check in midair, hesitate, and then slip sideways into a stall. A column of smoke, and it was gone.

Dutch was fighting the Sow for control now. The stream of Polish invective was more urgent, more pleading. He was trying to keep the nose up, keep lift under the wings, so that when they crashed it was in the semblance of a landing. Ian was breathing heavily, his heart pounding. His brother Peter would have a parachute in this situation. If Dutch had one—and if he had any brains at all—he'd bail out and leave his passenger to the Sow's fate. But as Ian was thinking this, the propeller coughed to life. It sputtered. Died again.

"Come *on!*" Ian yelled.

He thought the gunner echoed him.

The propeller caught.

Dutch lifted one arm silently in triumph and turned his plane toward Iraq.

———————

"WHERE DO YOU think those Germans came from?" Ian asked him hours later. Rommel's Afrika Korps had surrendered in May, under Italian command. Most of the men who'd served in it were killing time in a POW camp in Mississippi.

"Greece," Dutch said flatly. "More likely, Crete. They still run the show there, and sometimes they throw a few fellows up on fishing expeditions over British territory."

Dutch's luck had held out that night. He'd found a tailwind sweeping across North Africa that carried him over the Iraq border. It was exactly one twenty-seven a.m. by Ian's watch when the Sow began to lose altitude again and the faint lights of Habbaniya airbase floated up on the horizon. Ian's feet were blocks of ice in his thin leather shoes, and his ears were ringing. He had dozed fitfully, unable to entirely trust the dodgy propeller, certain they would crash before much more time was out. His limbs had stiffened with cold, but there would be coffee in Habbaniya.

When Dutch had bucketed to a stop on the fine British runway, Ian could not unbend from his seat. He almost told the pilot to leave him— he would wait out the refueling—but without asking his permission, Dutch lifted him under the armpits and hauled him to a crouching position. "Swing your leg onto the wing," he said. "Do it now, you motherfucking bastard, or I swear I'll drop you on your head."

Ian half crawled, half fell from the cockpit to the ground. After a few seconds, he forced his aching body upright.

"That bandage has soaked through your jacket," Dutch said casually. "Blood's frozen. You might want to give it a look in the canteen."

Habbaniya was an extensive new British base, the pride of the RAF Iraq Command. It was a principal link in the air route chain among the Allies, a transfer point for war matériel and basic supplies from the U.S.

through North Africa to the Soviet Union. The RAF ran maintenance units here for much of the Middle East. There was an aircraft depot, a hospital, some barracks for Iraqi recruits, and bomb stores. There were even swimming pools, movie screens, sporting fields, tennis courts, and riding stables. Habbaniya had its own water purification plant and power station. It drew water from the Euphrates to sprinkle the very British lawns.

Ian cared nothing for all this in the early-morning dark, moving instead like an automaton to the warmth and light of the airmen's lounge. He was aware, suddenly, of Dutch's gunner following a few paces behind him, diffident and solitary, as boy soldiers had learned to be in this war. Ian stopped short and turned. He held out his hand.

"That was some rare shooting," he said. "Thank you for saving all our lives tonight."

The gunner came to a halt and simply stared at him. Under the harsh and episodic airstrip lights, his face was a composition of shadow and bone, hollows and bleached places, punctuated by the goggles that deflected any attempt to meet his eyes. As Ian watched, the gunner raised his right arm. Ian saw that it was spattered with blood; the leather sleeve was gaping and torn.

"Good God, you *were* hit," he muttered, reaching for the boy.

With his left hand, the gunner unstrapped his helmet and whipped off his goggles. A cascade of platinum hair slid over one cheek.

Ian's eyes narrowed. He stepped closer.

The gangly kid who'd downed two Messerschmitts was the girl he'd last glimpsed on the ramparts of the Citadel, in a saffron-colored scarf. Nazir's granddaughter.

Fatima.

"I HAVE SUMMONED YOU," Molotov told the two men waiting on his pleasure in the salon of the Soviet Embassy, "to inform you that under no circumstances will Premier Stalin leave the safety of this compound tomorrow, or indeed at any time prior to the end of this conference."

He stared ponderously at Averell Harriman and Archibald Clark Kerr, as though daring them to object. Harriman glanced at Clark Kerr—he was the British ambassador in Moscow, and, like Ave, he'd flown in on the plane with Stalin yesterday. Clark Kerr looked resigned; he'd had a year longer to get used to Stalin's caprice than Ave had.

"It's the American location that's at fault, I gather," Clark Kerr said. "The Premier can have no objection to walking next door to our embassy?"

"None whatsoever. But you must know, my dear ambassadors, that our security forces have learned there is to be a violent public demonstration—whether tomorrow or the next day, I cannot say—instigated by Hitler's agents in this city. Iranian peasants screaming for Russian and Western blood. Screaming to expel the Occupiers. The Marshal will not expose his precious person to such Nazi . . . indignities."

Clark Kerr smiled faintly, as though such a fantasy was no more than he had expected. "Prime Minister Churchill has been living with Nazi indignities for more than four years. He goes to bed with them, Mr. Molotov, and wakes up with them again in the morning. It's hardly a reason to stay inside."

"It is not for himself that Stalin fears, but for the people of Tehran, you understand. Possibly these ignorant peasants are of no consideration to the British. You have long sacrificed the many to preserve the few. But if innocent blood is spilled because of Stalin's presence, the Premier will not be able to live with himself."

"Then it'll be the first time in his life," Clark Kerr muttered.

Harriman kept his gaze trained on Molotov. He was trying to decide whether the man believed what he said or he was deliberately bullshitting them. "I will inform my President that Premier Stalin declines to meet with him after lunch tomorrow."

"But no. It is the *location* of the next meeting that is inconvenient, not the meeting itself. If the President likes to come *here,* of course . . ."

"I will convey your message." Harriman bowed. "And now, as it is very late, I will take my leave, Mr. Secretary."

"Not yet," Molotov retorted. "Clark Kerr may go, it is obvious, he has only to walk three paces and he is on his own ground. But you, Mr. Harriman—you must see the rooms we have prepared for Mr. Roosevelt. *Then* you may tell him what a fool he is to remain in that American hovel!"

CHAPTER 15

They had waited out the snowstorm until late the previous afternoon, when the clouds breaking up over the mountains revealed a sun so close to setting that movement was pointless and they'd agreed to stay put for the night. All five of Skorzeny's men, from the nineteen-year-old Fuchs to the veteran Braun, had grown leaner over the past few weeks of survival training. He'd kept them busy with reconnaissance exercises and hunting and hand-to-hand combat tests that sharpened the wits. If they were snowbound much longer, Skorzeny thought, boredom would set in. *Quarrels.* They had learned one another's stories by heart now, and knew every dream or vanity the others nursed in secret. With inactivity came a sense of being trapped, and the men would begin to voice their fears. The crimes they'd committed. The nightmares that threatened to drive them mad. None of them had reached that nadir yet; he intended that none of them would.

New orders helped. The transmission Fuchs had received in the early hours of the previous morning—the message from their Control in Cairo—had been short and to the point. *Infiltrate.* The training phase of their operation was over; it was time to move into action.

Skorzeny had roused them at first light that morning and broken camp. They'd eaten the last of the roasted ibex scraps and washed their mouths out with snow. He'd sent them in pairs—keeping himself for last, with Fuchs and the radio—through the ironwood trees and the suddenly monochromatic landscape. In a few short weeks they had internalized all he'd taught them. Richter no longer tramped like a prizefighter through the underbrush; Lange's eyes were constantly roving to record the slightest movement ahead. They fanned out, separated by hundreds of yards, so that if one pair encountered a hostile force, the rest would not be taken. They serpentined noiselessly through the leafless trees. The snow was slick and their progress incremental; it was important to set each foot carefully before the other, testing the ground underfoot for loose stones. In their field grays, they must be indistinguishable, Skorzeny thought, from a herd of Persian gazelle.

He intended to shepherd them to the base of the mountains and then rest. Two of the men—Hoffman and Braun, he thought—he'd send to reconnoiter. He was supposed to contact the Nazi agents in Tehran who ran a safe house in the southern part of the city, but after the NKVD reception party at the drop zone and the loss of thirty of his men, he'd decided to improvise for a while. Somebody—Berlin or Tehran—had blown his boys, and he would not deliver himself into their power so quickly again.

He needed a modest place on the very edge of Tehran's outskirts. A lonely place, more mountain than town. He needed food and shelter. And surprise.

Ahead, the trees were thinning. Light increased. Skorzeny knew this place. They were coming to the headwaters of the Jajrood River.

There was a muffled curse behind him—the single word, *Scheisse*—and then the tumbling sound of a body pitched headfirst and out of control.

Skorzeny pulled his gun and turned.

Fuchs was rolling down the hillside, the unwieldy radio pitching him over and over, unable to slow his momentum with his scrabbling hands. As Skorzeny watched, the compact body slammed heavily into a tree trunk, one leg headed downhill, the other trailing behind. There was a crack and groan. Fuchs came to rest.

He was lying on the radio pack like a beetle turned on its shell, blinking dazedly at the sky. All around them, the silence of the forest renewed—but it was a listening silence now, Skorzeny thought.

He imagined the other men halted halfway down the hillside. Staring wordlessly at one another. Wondering whether to turn back or bolt.

"Your leg is broken," he told Fuchs.

Then he lifted his gun matter-of-factly and shot the boy in the head.

DAY FOUR

TEHRAN

<small>SUNDAY,
NOVEMBER 28, 1943</small>

CHAPTER 16

M ichael Hudson was too junior to rate a room in the American legation where Roosevelt and his party stayed. The official U.S. envoy, Louis Dreyfus, had commandeered half of the Park Hotel— Tehran's finest—for the President's entourage. Hudson caught a few hours of sleep there and a ride in one of Dreyfus's cars to the legation the next morning.

The first man he met was Sam Schwartz.

He was familiar with him by sight. But the two men had never had much reason to speak. Hudson walked up to Schwartz, who handed him a cup of coffee. Then he drew him slightly apart and muttered low in Hudson's ear.

A few minutes later, Schwartz welcomed Averell Harriman with another cup of coffee. Amid all the noise of the ambassador's arrival, Hudson slipped unnoticed back out into the street.

This time, he took a cab.

GRACE COWLES had finished her breakfast. For such an exotic place as Tehran, it was sadly anticlimactic: an expatriate cook's attempt to reproduce Britain in the heart of Persia. They were dutifully served broiled tomatoes, so out of season that they looked like dead salmon, with fried eggs and streaky rashers of bacon. Grace ought to be thankful—the food in London was so stringently rationed it had been months since she'd seen real bacon—but her mind was not on her work. There'd been a letter for her in the embassy pouch. *News from home.* As usual, it was uniformly depressing. Her sister Audrey, who was barely sixteen, had gotten into trouble. Which meant that some soldier on leave had either seduced or raped the wretched girl. Audrey would say nothing about the father, however much Grace's mother beat her. She was ruined now and would have to leave school.

Another casualty of war, Grace thought.

Men, she thought.

She lifted her eyes from the sickening breakfast plate, with its dried smear of egg and flaccid tomato. From this makeshift breakfast room— hastily converted from a lady's morning room before the Prime Minister's delegation arrived—the wide windows offered a staggeringly beautiful look at the world. Today it was sunlit, fringed with pines that Grace knew would scent the air with resin. There would be the smell of snow, too, off the heights of the mountains that ringed this extraordinary city. If she had thought about it at all in her hurried progress in Pug Ismay's service, she had expected Persia to be hot, like Egypt. With palm trees. It was *Persia,* after all, a word that made one think of rugs and camels and men in turbans. But that was British stupidity. The lovely old embassy sat snugly behind its walls in a lap of green, the pines rising grandly. It was the most restful place Grace had seen in a very long time.

And when they laugh at my dedication, she thought bitterly, *they never understand this. Work has saved me. I am no one's plaything. No war casualty. Or any man's.*

"Grace."

She peered over her shoulder and felt her heart skip a beat. "Mr. Hudson."

He was halfway through the breakfast room door, one hand grasping the lintel. His hair was mussed and he was not smiling.

"Have time for a walk?"

She glanced at her watch. "I don't think so. Pug—"

"And I'm due back at the ranch for a briefing. Five minutes, Grace. *Please.* We should talk."

THEY CHOSE the back garden, where paths of crushed stone wound among the trees and the distant plash of water suggested an unseen fountain. Another day, Grace thought, she would like to find it. If Pug could spare her.

"Did he send you some sort of crazy cable?" Michael asked abruptly.

"Who?"

"Ian. I hear he was *attacked* the other night in Cairo. With a knife. That's why he stayed behind. It wasn't bronchitis at all."

"I know," Grace said. Rushbrooke had told Ismay. Ismay had told her.

"Why didn't you say something?" He stopped short on the path and glowered at her. "He's my best friend."

She hugged herself defensively. "Because I was informed it was a security matter, Mr. Hudson. And however matey you may have become with *some* members of the British delegation, you are not, after all, a British subject."

"Matey," he repeated.

"Much less cleared for our intelligence."

"Come off it, Grace." He grasped her by the elbows and shook her slightly. "This isn't intelligence. This is *Ian.* You're punishing me because of Pamela."

"I don't know what you mean."

"You needn't bother. She was tucked up quite nicely with Harriman last night."

She stepped backward, safe from his reach. "If you've quite finished, Mr. Hudson—"

"Michael. For Chrissake, I'm Michael." He ran his fingers through his spiky hair. "Look—Ian's already shared his story with the rest of the world. He sent some long rigmarole about an assassination plot to Sam Schwartz. Schwartz is—"

"The head of Roosevelt's Secret Service. I know." Strange, Grace thought, that Ian hadn't sent the cable to Hudson instead. But perhaps the matter was urgent enough to go straight to the top. In which case— "Why exactly are you here, Mr. Hudson?"

"Because you need to tell your people. About Ian. That this whole cable is . . . is some kind of *spy story* he's made up."

She stared at him, brow furrowed. Was it possible Michael was drunk? Not at this hour of the morning, surely. Had he even read the cable—or merely heard about it secondhand, from the Secret Service fellow?

"Are you saying," she attempted, feeling her way, "that you know . . . Ian *lies* . . . too?"

His harassed expression softened. "Oh, God, Grace—I'm so sorry. Is that why you stopped seeing him?"

She shrugged, her gaze falling to the ground. "I couldn't trust him. He'd tell me he was working late. Or engaged in an operation overseas that was frightfully hush-hush. When all the time, he was just with that . . . female dispatch rider. With the motorbike."

It sounded pathetic even to Grace's ears. *Jealousy.* Disillusionment. Duplicity. The usual ration from Ian Fleming. She'd been warned off him by nearly every girl she knew, before she'd agreed to see him.

"Muriel," Michael said.

"I'm sorry?"

"The dispatch rider. With the motorbike. She delivers his supply of cigarettes when she has time. It's a custom blend, you know—from Morlands."

"Your point?"

"Just that Muriel's an old flame. She's known Ian forever. It doesn't mean a thing to him, sweetheart. She doesn't, I mean."

Grace flinched. "That's even worse. It means we're all just bodies. Ian's incapable of caring for anyone but himself. Would you call that arrogance, or something more pathological?"

"I'd call it self-protection," Michael said. "Something to do with his mother."

"Oh, Lord—not *that* old chestnut."

"If he doesn't give his heart away, he can't be hurt."

"Then he'll never win hearts, either," Grace said crisply. "Certainly not mine. But you seem more forgiving, Mr. Hudson. I suppose men ignore the ways they fail each other."

"Not exactly." He raised his arms in a gesture of futility. "He doesn't lie to me. Not about important things. But the guy writes *stories,* Grace. Spy stories. About adventure heroes. That's what this cable's all about. He's been doing it ever since Mokie died."

"Mokie?"

"His dad." Michael began to trudge along the gravel path. "It's how he deals with—with his nerves, I guess. When things get too tough. He escapes into fiction."

"The way you do, by playing music," she suggested.

He glanced at her, his expression arrested. "Why do you say that?"

"I hear it," she faltered. "In the sound. The pain and . . . and the grief—"

"I play show tunes, for Chrissake."

"Not always." She hurried on, aware she had trespassed and he might not forgive her. "Don't they say the most desperate actors usually try comedy?"

"The point is, Ian goes off into a dream world where fiction is fact," Michael said impatiently. "*And* he drinks too much. We joke about all that Scotch he carries around, but seriously, when you look at what he consumes . . . Nerves, again. Last week he told me somebody at the conference—*one of us,* Grace—was spying for the Nazis. Now he's convinced the guy is going to kill us all."

She made a small sound of protest. He stopped short and grasped her shoulders urgently.

"When we were at Eton, he was almost sent down for printing a smutty story about his house master and circulating it anonymously throughout the school. He hated Slater because the guy was a sadist who liked to draw blood. But Ian's prank nearly cost him his place and, incidentally, threw suspicion on everybody else in his house. I think Johnnie liked that—watching the others squirm."

"But in the end, he owned up to it, didn't he?"

Michael glanced at her, surprised. "He told you about it?"

"No. But Ian Lancaster Fleming would never be the sort of scrub who would let another boy take his blame."

"Actually, you're right." A grudging silence. "But try to understand, Grace," Michael said. "Ian's not entirely . . . *reliable.* That's why I meet up with him at every one of these conferences. I want to make sure he's on a tight leash when the President's around. He's never been sent out into the field, either—Rushbrooke is afraid he'll make a complete ass of himself and go to pieces. Don't get me wrong—Ian's damn good at coming up with Ops. When we were kids, he was the mastermind of every stunt we pulled. But there's a reason he's permanently tucked behind a desk. He needs to be under a grown-up's eye."

Grace drew a shaky breath. "Are you suggesting that besides being a liar and a cad, Ian Fleming is *potty?*"

"I'm suggesting that after a guy's been whacked on the head hard enough to bleed, we might want to give him some time before we swallow what he says," he retorted.

They walked on. The morning was growing late. She ought to turn back. Pug would be looking for her, and Michael was expected at the American legation—

Ian had sent his cable to the American legation.

Suddenly, she was awash in dismay. He *did* tell stories. He loved detective films. There had been that one, last summer, they'd seen in London—*The Thin Man* . . . Nonsense, of course, with a terrier and martinis. But then there were the bones hidden beneath the floor . . .

"If Ian's unreliable," she demanded, "why is he still employed? And in such a sensitive intelligence position?"

"Because he's been shielded," Hudson said quietly. "For years. By me. By his brother Peter. You know his dad was a friend of Churchill's, right?"

That conversation in the Signals Room at Giza. The PM signing Ian's yellowed scrap of paper. *Shielded.* "Why are you telling me all this?" she asked.

"Because he's a loose cannon." Hudson rolled his eyes. "And he's not in my shop. He's in *yours,* Grace. You're the only person I can talk to, in your delegation."

Other than Pamela, she thought. But there was no point in stating the obvious. Michael needed somebody in the chain of command. Somebody like Pug, who had Churchill's ear.

"I'm concerned about the damage he could do," he persisted.

"What kind of damage?"

"Harriman's called a meeting of the President's advisors to discuss Ian's *Nazi threat*. Which means Schwartz shared the cable. For all I know, Roosevelt's read it by now."

Dismay turned three times and settled like a dog in her stomach. But she said nothing.

"So I repeat, Grace: Did he send this espionage crap to you? Has Ismay read it?"

"Yes," she muttered. "And naturally—*yes*."

Hudson closed his eyes, as though willing a higher power to give him strength. "Then you might want to pass this on. Ian's cable has the U.S. delegation in such a snit, Harriman says we all ought to move in with Joe Stalin for the duration of the conference. Think about the security implications of *that*, Grace. And how Churchill will feel when you're all shut out of our party."

CHAPTER 17

Dutch spent several hours longer than he'd expected at Habbaniya, so that Ian and the girl could get medical attention. Ian's stitches were intact but seeping blood; a medic painted him with iodine and applied fresh bandages.

Fatima had pieces of German steel in her left arm.

"It is of no importance," she said impatiently, as the medic picked at the shrapnel with a pair of surgical tweezers. "Nothing hit bone."

"Where did you learn to shoot like that?" Ian asked.

She lifted her eyebrows coolly and ignored the question.

He left the clinic and found Dutch beside his plane, examining the propeller with an RAF mechanic.

"Where'd you pick up the girl?"

"I knew her grandfather," Dutch said.

Ian noted the use of the past tense. News of murder traveled fast.

"Where'd she learn to aim a gun?"

"In an NKVD training camp, of course," the pilot said. "They've got a strict up-or-out system. Hit your targets or die trying."

"NKVD? That girl? She can't be out of her teens."

Dutch grimaced. "Communists don't believe in childhood. Try to get some food or sleep, Bond. I have some repairs to make before Tehran."

Ian made his way to the airmen's lounge. The door from the tarmac was unlocked, but the place was utterly deserted at three a.m. There was a pot of stone-cold coffee that still managed to smell burnt. He went around the bar counter and used his good arm to rummage among the higher shelves. There were bottles of Bass and Guinness. A half-empty fifth of bourbon. And another, surprisingly, of—

"*Vodka,*" Fatima said behind him. "I would like a martini. Shaken, not stirred."

"I don't think you have a choice," he replied, without glancing around. "There isn't a shaker in the place. Much less ice."

"That's where you're wrong. That brute of a doctor used an ice pick on my arm."

She was smiling crookedly. There were dark hollows under her eyes and her child's skin was almost transparent with a mixture of exhaustion and what Ian suspected was grief. She spoke English with a heavy accent but great precision. She was wearing borrowed khaki clothes that looked vaguely military but lacked any insignia. A field uniform for an operational girl.

"Who killed your grandfather?" he asked her gently.

"I don't know. But when I find out—" She glanced away, toward the silhouette of Dutch's plane.

"You weren't there?"

"I had gone to the market. I found him when I returned. On the floor. You saw him?"

Ian shook his head.

"His throat was slit. The Egyptians, they do this sometimes, for sacrifice—with sheep or goats, not men. I dropped my basket. Vegetables, oranges, bread. They rolled into the blood on the floor. God forgive me, I tried to pick them up—"

Ian handed her the vodka.

She tipped the bottle straight into her mouth and drank it like water, like she was overcome with heat on a summer's day. "Then I packed a small bag and left him. I did not run, because he trained me in such things. You run, you draw attention to yourself. I walked very fast through the streets of our quarter, and I went veiled, like a good Egyptian woman. I turned into side streets and doubled back on my trail as he taught me, and I do not think anyone was following. So I went to Dutch."

"Why?" Ian asked. "Why come to Iran, Fatima?"

She set the vodka bottle carefully on the bar. It was nearly empty.

"Because you know, and I know, that my grandfather was hunting a German agent. Someone has to finish the job."

"And avenge him?"

"That, too."

"He shared his work with you? Wasn't that dangerous?"

She shrugged, and winced as her arm twinged. "My choice, not his. I do not ask why you are in Dutch's plane, Mr. . . ."

"Bond," he supplied. "James Bond."

"Men are expected to fight and women are told it is *dangerous*. You are hunting him, too, no?"

"The Fencer?"

"Or Butcher. Whichever you like." She met Ian's gaze and shrugged slightly. "He is a killer. Call him anything else, you give him power. You give him a story to tell, a myth to wrap himself in. He becomes a monster of fear and greatness, harder to fight. But this Butcher? He is just good with a knife."

"You're better with guns," Ian said quietly.

Fatima smiled again—that heartbreaking, crooked smile.

She was unlike any woman he had ever met. How many had he known well, however, besides his mother, Eve? And even Eve he did not begin to understand. There had been a fearless girl he had loved briefly in Geneva and a clutch of cousins he'd known in Kitzbühel. His old lover Muriel, who skied like an Olympian and wove her motorbike through the London bombs as though they were raindrops. He was drawn to women who flouted convention. Who flouted fear. But he expected them to desire and need him.

Fatima needed nobody.

It was a challenge, this brittle indifference she wore. It intrigued and alarmed him. She had been schooled by brutal circumstances and pitiless teachers. There were stories of endurance she could tell. And yet she was here—barely twenty, a gossamer thinness. Weariness about the eyes. She remained. She could teach him what no other woman could: how to risk and die.

He walked behind her across the tarmac an hour later when the Sow was ready to fly, uncertain whether anyone who had drunk so much would be capable of mounting a plane's wing. But she seemed unaffected by the vodka or her bandaged arm, allowing Dutch to hoist her up. She skittered across the body of the plane to the gunner's seat, camouflaged once more in her goggles and flight jacket. She did not look at Ian as he stood on the tarmac, staring at her. She was already examining her gun mount. Dawn was breaking.

Three hours later, they landed in Tehran.

"THE DETAILS ARE SKETCHY," Averell Harriman said, "but hairraising. Our Russian friends tell me that a squad of German commandos parachuted into the foothills outside the city about three weeks ago. Soviet security forces rounded up all but six of them. Molotov says they're true believers, like all Nazi Special Forces. Hell-bent on completing their mission. And their current whereabouts are unknown."

They were gathered around the breakfast table in the American legation, a litter of stained coffee cups and soiled plates in front of them. Harriman and Schwartz, Hudson and FDR. Elliott Roosevelt and John Boettiger were not included, because they were family, not staff. Gil Winant was already at the British Embassy. General George Marshall was sitting a little by himself, toying with a piece of toast, a skeptical expression on his face. Harry Hopkins was at Roosevelt's right hand. He had eaten nothing, but had smoked three cigarettes to ash.

There were pomegranates in a bowl in the center of the table. Most of them had never seen pomegranates before and had no idea what to do with them. Michael Hudson was the exception. He had split open a fruit and was digging at its seeds with the tip of a knife.

"The mission being . . . ?" Marshall asked.

Harriman shrugged. "Raise a little hell around the conference, I guess. Molotov didn't really say."

"Can we talk to the guys they captured?" Sam Schwartz demanded. "Find out what they're planning?"

"I should have been clearer." Harriman refilled his coffee cup. "When I said the Krauts were rounded up, I meant they were killed."

"Or executed," Hudson observed, "after digging their own graves."

Harry Hopkins cleared his throat. "That sounds like sympathy for the Enemy, Mr. Hudson."

"Does it? My apologies, sir. But I think it's worth remembering that we're dealing with the Soviets. Who'd butcher their own mothers if Stalin told them to do it."

"I think that's a bit—" Harriman began.

"Hear, hear," Marshall intoned.

Hudson waited for silence. "We should be careful before we believe what the Russians say. Who knows if these Nazi commandos even exist? They haven't shown us a single German." He glanced at Roosevelt. "It seems damned convenient, Mr. President, that there's nobody left to interrogate. Molotov's ginned up a bogeyman."

"Why?" Roosevelt wondered genially. He was at ease in his chair, a cup and saucer balanced on his carefully crossed legs. "You know him best, Ave. Any ideas?"

"Molotov's just the front man," Harriman said. "We already know Uncle Joe refuses to step outside his embassy's door. There's a lot of bad blood between the Persians and the Russians, Mr. President, and it's not only about this Occupation. This so-called Nazi plot helps Stalin save face."

"In other words, he wants us to move over to that compound," Schwartz interjected. "Accept his hospitality. Or Churchill's."

"And piss off the fella you don't take to the dance," Marshall interjected. "Don't get caught between the Lion and the Bear, Franklin. Fool's game. Stay here."

"With respect, Mr. President, I agree," Hudson said quickly. "Move into Stalin's embassy, and you put yourself entirely into Soviet hands."

"There's no love lost between you and the Russians, is there, Mr. Hudson?" FDR was smiling his shark's smile. His teeth were bared, but no emotion reached his eyes. His face was creased with exhaustion; he wasn't sleeping well in the series of strange beds he'd inhabited lately. "Winston has been pressing me to accept his hospitality. But I hate to give Uncle Joe the idea that we're ganging up on him."

"Gil Winant won't like it if you offend Churchill," Harry Hopkins said. He was frowning; he was as fond of the PM as Gil was.

"Winston will understand," Roosevelt retorted. "Like a loyal dog, he always trots back. What exactly is it that scares you about Stalin's shop, Mr. Hudson?"

"Thugs monitoring your every move," Michael said frankly. "If Lavrentiy Beria is in the Soviet embassy, the most deadly intelligence network in the world is there, too. There's a reason Stalin chose Tehran for this conference, Mr. President."

"Which is?"

"Because Beria has got one of the best NKVD spy networks already in place. His son was part of it for the past two years."

Schwartz raised his hand.

Roosevelt nodded at him.

"If Soviet intelligence is as crackerjack as Hudson says," the Secret Service chief suggested, "shouldn't we believe what they're telling us about the Nazis?"

This unexpected reversal stopped the conversation dead.

Marshall looked at Harriman. Who looked at Roosevelt.

"Mr. Hudson?" Roosevelt queried.

"They're more interested in you, Mr. President, than anybody else in the world right now," he said. "You're meeting Marshal Stalin for the first time. You're about to negotiate the invasion of Europe. The future of the Balkans. The fate of Poland. *He wants to know what you think. In the privacy of your own bedroom.* No sitting president in your shoes would place himself in the hands of such an enemy."

"He's our ally, Mr. Hudson," Roosevelt reminded him.

This time, the silence was profound.

It was a matter of faith in government circles that Stalin was a friend to the United States. Somebody the President could work with. A sagacious and capable guy. But Hudson had followed the Great Terror of 1938. Lavrentiy Beria had made sure that Stalin's rivals were accused and tried and shot for their crimes. Thousands had disappeared overnight into the gulags. Stalin's boys made the Gestapo look like Judy Garland's Lollipop Kids. Hudson doubted Roosevelt had an inkling of this, and it was no time to explain it to him. Roosevelt was still studying Michael's face. "Does your friend Fleming agree with you?"

Hudson glanced up quickly. "I couldn't say, sir. We never discussed Mr. Stalin."

"I read his most recent cable. It tracks with the Russian story. He thinks these Nazi commandos want to assassinate all of us."

The men around the table stirred restively.

"I think it's possible Commander Fleming wrote that in an impaired state, sir," Hudson said. "He was recently hit in the head, not to mention stabbed in the back. He lost blood. He can't have been thinking clearly. And his story is . . . well . . . a little fantastic. In my opinion."

"What story? What cable?" Harriman demanded.

He pushed back his chair and threw his napkin on the table, a potentate denied his empire. "And who the hell is Commander Fleming?"

CHAPTER 18

They shook hands with Dutch at the edge of the airstrip, their duffel bags at their feet. Ian was down to one spare uniform. Two of his jackets were bloody; one had a gaping slit over the shoulder blade. But he wouldn't be wearing military clothes for the next few days, anyway. The farther he got from Cairo, the more of a deserter he became.

"You're headed back to Egypt?" he asked the pilot.

"Soon as I spend your money." Dutch held up Ian's pound notes and grinned. "Wine, women, and song. If Tehran's too hot for you two, just ask for old Dutch at the Park Hotel. I'll be holed up there for the next few days if you need a plane out."

"Kind offer," Ian said. "But right now I could use cab fare. Lend me a fiver?"

Dutch handed him the bank note. He gave another to Fatima. "For those Messers you downed," he said. "I'll miss your hand on the gun, girl, flying home."

Ian saluted the Pole and watched as he ambled off, studying the aircraft scattered around the British base with a jewel thief's eye. One of these days, Ian suspected, a plane would go missing from some godforsaken strip in the Middle East, and the Sow would be left in its place.

"Cab fare?" Fatima asked him mockingly. "You are a British officer, Bond. Tehran is your town. Surely you don't intend to *pay* for anything?"

"I'm not a Communist," Ian observed, "so presumably I'll have to. We British think it's bad form to exploit the downtrodden, you know— although I'm sure Stalin was anxious to keep that fact from you. This fiver won't run to the Park Hotel, but with luck and the exchange rate, it should get me through a few days. Where do you intend to go?"

She shouldered her bag with her good right arm. "To my people."

"You have family in Iran?"

"Now Nazir is gone, I have family nowhere."

Ian considered this baldly. Fatima was young and alone in Persia, in the middle of a world war. It wasn't a pretty picture. Unless you'd seen her fire a gun.

"So there's a local NKVD network?"

Her green eyes were amused. "We are allies, Commander. Not friends. There is a limit to what I tell you."

She didn't have to confirm what he already knew. Nazir had got his information about the Fencer from his NKVD colleagues in Persia. The local Soviet network must have considerable resources in this part of the world; Stalin himself was from the Caucasus region of Georgia, just north of Iran's border. Soviet operatives had been active in this land for centuries. NKVD Tehran would have sources. Knowledge of the city. Arms.

All things Ian might badly need in the next few days.

"What if I could use an ally more than a friend?" he asked Fatima.

"Call the American Embassy."

"There isn't really one in Tehran. Besides, I'm not sure I can trust them."

"This is nonsense," she said impatiently, and began to walk away from him. "I don't have time to waste, Bond, and we expose ourselves like idiots. Anyone may see us. Good luck."

"Fatima—"

She stopped in her tracks, her back still turned to him.

"Someone in the Allied delegation in Cairo tried to kill me. Just like your grandfather."

"Then why are you still alive?"

Good girl. She'd seen the contradiction as soon as he had.

"That's one of the questions I'd like to answer."

"I repeat: *Good luck.*" She stepped forward.

"Fatima."

She sighed in exasperation, dropped her bag, and wheeled on him. *"What?"*

"I knew too much. I might have told Churchill. Roosevelt. Ruined his plans. The Fencer thinks he stopped me—because I didn't show up yesterday on a British plane."

"So?"

"So he's jolly well pleased with himself. Thinks I'm tucked up in bed at Mena House, eating ices, while the fate of this sodding war hangs in the balance. He's free to kill the Allies in one fell swoop—"

"I do not understand this. *One fell swoop.*"

"In a single deadly blow. The point is, if I mean to catch him, I must stay hidden. He can't know I'm here. I can't saunter into the British Embassy and order drinks all round, or I'll get coshed again. This time, he'll make sure I'm dead."

She stared at him intently. "You will not catch him. Because I will do it first."

"I hope like hell you do," Ian said. "But I know some things you don't, Fatima. I know the delegations. American. British. The Fencer's one of us. You haven't even caught a glimpse."

He watched her consider this. Himself, as an asset she could use.

"Your people know the ground," he persisted, "and the Russian end of things. The NKVD must want me involved, old girl, because they told Nazir to contact me."

She looked away from him; they both remembered the episode of the saffron scarf. Her fingers grazing his, around a flaring cigarette.

"Wouldn't it be clever," Ian said, "to pool our resources and make fools of them all?"

THE MAN IN THE WHEELCHAIR rolled carefully down the ramp from the American legation to the waiting car. It was pulled up at the rear of the building—safely hidden from a reporter's camera or an unfriendly pair of eyes. Sam Schwartz was standing by the open rear door. Elliott stood beside him. Roosevelt grinned at both; his cigarette holder was clamped at a rakish angle between his clenched teeth, and his fedora was set precisely on his gray hair. When his chair reached the two men, Elliott moved behind it and braced the wheels. Schwartz extended his strong right arm. With an effort, Roosevelt forced himself upright. His useless legs offered no sensation and they were as wayward as two rolls of rubber. With practiced care, Sam helped his chief duck into the rear seat.

The military driver saluted the President and slid behind the wheel. Elliott took the front passenger seat; Schwartz and his gun sat next to the President. The small walled compound that housed the American legation had a rear service gate; this had already been opened by Schwartz's people, two of whom were standing at attention as the simple black car rolled by. Roosevelt lifted his hand in acknowledgment.

"Sir," Schwartz said, "now would be the time to remove your personal effects. If you don't mind."

"Mind? This is the most fun I've had since Groton." He was positively gleeful. In the front seat, Elliott broke into a smile.

Roosevelt removed his hat, his spectacles, and the cigarette holder. Schwartz handed him a wool scarf to wrap about his collar, muffling the lower half of his face, and a soft newsboy's cap to pull jauntily over his head. He also offered him a fake dark mustache, already slathered with spirit gum. FDR pressed it gingerly to his upper lip.

"How's that look?"

"Preposterous," Schwartz said, "but anonymous."

In fact, his chief looked completely unlike the occupant of the President's official car, who at the same moment was waving grandly from the rear of the presidential limousine with fluttering American flags on the hood. That car moved at a stately speed, along with an entourage of Secret Service visibly brandishing weapons, several jeeps full of American servicemen, and three additional vehicles transporting Harriman, the Russian translator Chip Bohlen, Michael Hudson, Harry Hopkins, and George Marshall. They were all probably exiting the compound's *front* gate at that very moment.

One hundred American troops remained behind, their tents pitched in the legation's courtyard, to guard a bird that nobody in Tehran knew had already flown. It was essential, Schwartz thought, to let the world believe Roosevelt was still staying there—as essential as moving him, now, to the Soviet Embassy.

Elliott turned in the front seat. "Ready to brave the Nazis, sir?"

In reply, Roosevelt slid a nine-millimeter revolver from his coat pocket. "More than ready, son."

"Outrageous," Churchill growled.

He had taken lunch on a tray in his bed, nursing his bronchitis with champagne. It appeared to be growing worse, which vexed him immeasurably—to be coughing and inchoate when he had meant to be eloquent was a cruel twist of fate. Now Pug Ismay was down with the vile disease as well; the British delegation was dropping in the traces when it most needed strength.

Churchill liked working in bed. The embassy in Tehran was so deliciously Old England that he might have been at his beloved Chartwell rather than in Iran. But he had set aside his dispatch box at Pamela's entrance. She had come to inquire if he would like a hand of bezique—

charming in her cream-colored serge dress with a flared skirt and a collar high as a nun's. She had stopped short, however, at the sound of engines in the central courtyard below. A convoy of cars, motorcycles, and jeeps filled with Secret Service men brandishing Thompson submachine guns had just roared through the compound's gatehouse.

"It's the Americans." She peered through the draperies of his window. He watched her head swivel from one side to the other, following the motorcade. She stood on tiptoe. "They're pulling up in front of the Soviet Embassy. I gather they turned down our invitation." There was an unexpected note of relief in her voice that, in other circumstances, Churchill might have noticed.

"Apparently our accommodation was *inadequate* for them. Inadequate!"

"Well, there are rather a lot of us already. I say, Papa"—she liked to call him that; it was a mannerism she'd adopted once she started living with the Churchills during her pregnancy three years ago—"somebody's pretending to be Roosevelt. He's just got out of the President's car, and they're all laughing at him. The Secret Service chaps, I mean."

Churchill swung himself out of bed, a comic figure in his old-fashioned nightdress, and joined her at the window. The Russian Embassy—he still thought of it as Russian, although it had been Soviet for over twenty-five years—was a beautiful Czarist building, a perfection of triangular pediment, broad steps and Doric columns that reminded one inevitably of the Parthenon. A regiment of French windows with Palladian fanlights gave on to the wide marble front terrace. A circular sweep of drive led up to it, through the pines that dotted the green compound Stalin shared with his British neighbors. By day, it was filled with birdsong, and the snowcapped heights of the distant Lesser Caucasus filled the horizon.

There were at least thirty men milling around the sweep at the foot of the embassy's steps with guns dangling from their hands. Standing near Franklin's car, in a hat and spectacles remarkably like the President's, was a fellow Churchill recognized. He could not quite remember his name.

"A decoy," he said hoarsely. "Clever, that. If anyone had tried to kill Franklin, they'd have got this fellow. Courageous of him."

"So where's Roosevelt?"

"Being carried by his bodyguards into the rear of the Russian Embassy, I'll wager."

Pamela slipped her arm around Churchill's shoulders. "Try not to mind, darling. Americans don't mean to be beastly and offensive. They simply can't help it. They're like rude children playing at soldiers—they've no notion how deadly serious it all is."

Churchill squeezed her hand. "They won't have to live with Stalin when this is all over. We will."

Pamela was a rare comfort—she understood so much without having to be told. It was the reason so many men adored her, he thought. She never criticized, never argued; she accepted and supported the people she loved. She was as bracing as a stalwart nanny, but far nicer to look at.

She reminded him, more than he dared say, of his mother, Jennie. A brilliant political hostess, and a target of scandal in her day. Another unofficial power in the politics of her time. Pamela would go far, with or without Randolph.

"Do you believe this story of German agents?" she asked.

He frowned. "What story?"

She shrugged. "Molotov sent for Ave after dinner last night. Now the Americans are moving into the Soviet Embassy. There's a rumor going round that Roosevelt's got the wind up. Some Nazi plot or other. I thought you might tell me if it's true."

Harriman, Churchill thought in exasperation. He wasn't bound by the limits the British government imposed on its public servants. The bloody Yanks had no real intelligence service. They understood so little of the secret world: How a brilliant deception could camouflage truth. Or a brotherhood bound by silence could safeguard an empire. They shared everything, as though it were enough to take a drink with a man to trust him. And they talked too much—especially to women. As though the ladies couldn't make four from a pair of twos.

"I wonder you didn't tell me of Molotov's summons before you turned in," Churchill growled. "I should like to have known of it."

"Ave came back here afterwards," she murmured, "and then it was far too late. You were snoring, Papa. I should have thought Clark Kerr would have mentioned it. Ave said he was there."

"Clever child." He patted her shoulder. He *had* been briefed by the British ambassador at breakfast that morning. But he was more interested in what Pamela knew than in answering her questions. "Did Harriman believe the story?"

"Yes," she said. She was looking out the window at the courtyard again. "But I'm not sure why. That's why I asked what you thought—because you'd *know*."

But I do not tell you everything I know, my dear, he thought. "There is a good deal of uncertainty regarding the source of those rumors," he said cautiously. Nothing about Bletchley or Engima traffic. Pamela wasn't cleared for ULTRA.

"But this man," she persisted. "This . . . Fencer. He's supposed to be one of *us*. How can you bear it? Knowing that somebody—either in our group or Roosevelt's—is a traitor?"

He stared at her. "My dear girl, is *everyone* talking about it?"

"Not really. But you know, Papa—people tell me things." She looked suddenly helpless and young. Like a kitten. "They just do. As though they were talking to themselves and have forgotten I'm in the room. Take that jolly Yank, Mr. Hudson. We had a drink or two in Cairo. He's a friend of Commander Fleming's. Why *did* Fleming stay behind in Giza, Father?"

"He came down with bronchitis," Churchill said distinctly. "You're not to suggest anything else, mind. Regardless of other people's questions. This is very important, Pamela."

"Because the traitor is still with us?" She pressed her hand against his cheek. "Papa, darling—please. *Tell me.* I so hate to think I'm stupidly in the dark, when the danger . . . Papa, *whom do you suspect?*"

Churchill removed her hand gently from his face. Her breath was coming quickly and her blue eyes were wide with apprehension. She was fearful for someone. But whom? He knew she cared for Harriman, but surely she had no reason to *fear* for him. He could not be guilty of treason. He was . . . Harriman. One might as well suspect the Princess Elizabeth.

And Harriman had not been in Cairo when Fleming was attacked.

"Don't worry your pretty head," he soothed, squeezing her hand. "I daresay it's all Russian lies, intended to get poor Franklin into their clutches. I could wish he'd shown better judgment—and remembered his *true* friends."

CHAPTER 19

The NKVD safe house was in the southern part of Tehran, within the gates of the Grand Bazaar, a vast covered market that was the largest of its kind in the world.

"They say that twenty thousand people walk through this place each day," Fatima murmured.

"Who does?"

"My friends. That is why they live here. If you do not wish to be seen, wrap yourself in a crowd."

That had been Nazir's philosophy, too, Ian supposed—settling himself like a benign spider between the alleyways and leaning mud-brick houses of Old Cairo. But Nazir had been seen. And eliminated. The crowd had not saved him.

"We must get out of these clothes." With his height and his uniform, Ian was instantly identifiable as Royal Navy Reserve. If he ran into some of the British Occupying Forces, they'd be certain to ask his name—and why he was there. Fatima had pulled a shawl from her bag and thrown it over her bright hair. She was less obvious than Ian in her stateless khaki, but an oddity nonetheless; although he counted a number of people in Western clothes and a babel of foreign tongues, she was the only woman he'd seen in trousers.

He walked protectively beside the girl, closest to the street. Instinct, on his part, not something she wanted. "Have you been to Tehran before?"

"Never. But Grandfather made me learn the direction. If anything happened, I was to find Arev, in the Grand Bazaar, above the gold sellers' corridor, at the Sign of the Camel. He made me learn this by heart."

"Arev?"

"I was only told his first name."

"As I only learned Nazir's. And yours."

She flashed her crooked smile. "When we find Arev, please to call me Siranoush. Otherwise it is possible he will kill us."

"He dislikes Fatima so much?"

"Siranoush is my real name. Fatima is . . . *was* . . . something to use in Cairo."

"Siranoush. I like it. What does it mean?"

She shook her head slightly and looked, if anything, embarrassed. "Never mind. Siranoush, for Arev, will be a sign. You understand?"

"*Bona fides,*" Ian said. "Tells him you're on the up and up. That you are who you say you are," he added, when she looked puzzled.

"Up and up," she repeated. "I like that. It is hopeful, no? *Siranoush is on the up and up.*"

The bazaar was as soaring and inspired as a cathedral, Ian thought. The stalls were laid out under beautiful stone arches that called to mind the Byzantine Empire, the floors flagged and the walls covered in mosaics. Oil burned in heavily wrought lamps suspended from the ceiling, and shafts of sunlight penetrated from Moorish windows set high in the stone vault. It felt to Ian like a sacred space—but for the cries of merchants hawking their wares.

They were surging with the crowd through the Perfume Bazaar. Ian was conscious of eyes on his back. He walked stiffly from his wounds. He stuck out. A stranger. An Occupier. An Infidel.

The clouds of scent wafting from the stalls on every side were clouding his senses. He hadn't eaten much since his skull was bashed in, and the combination of morphia and whiskey he'd ingested over the past forty-eight hours had done nothing for his head. It was throbbing abominably. He glanced behind him, with a sickening sensation of a trap closing.

"Gold sellers," he muttered. "It's a different corridor, surely?"

"So many things are on offer here," Siranoush faltered. "There are even schools within the bazaar. Guesthouses. Banks and moneylenders."

And if there were signs, Ian thought, they were all in Farsi. The flowing script painted on the plaster meant nothing to him.

Hands pressed against his thighs, multiple hands, patting him rhythmically. He glanced down: a covey of children, brown eyes staring up at him unblinkingly, repeating one word over and over.

"They want money," Siranoush said.

His sensation of claustrophobia surged. He had only a fiver to his name and somehow, at some point, he would have to buy his way out of this country. He grasped the girl's good arm and led her rapidly down the corridor to the point where another crossed it, and turned blindly left. He was walking too fast. People would notice. What had Siranoush said, back there in Habbaniya? *You run, you draw attention to yourself.*

They hurried through the spice corridor. Turned right into the rug and carpet stalls. Kept going, and found themselves among lamps. Alabaster. Spices. *Chickens.* Impossibly, there was an entire corridor of goats. The smell was, if anything, more comforting than the perfume.

"Here," Siranoush breathed. "To the left—quickly!"

And into the soft quietude of men counting coins.

Robed figures were seated at tables with abacuses. Ian heard the clink of coin against coin and wondered why the pack of children did not find their way here. Some mark of respect, perhaps, not accorded to Occupiers. The gleam of gold flashed beneath the brazier lamps and was reflected in the eyes of the dealers. Fingers moved swiftly, a blur of exchange and sale. Ian felt his racing heart grow calmer. His steps slowed.

Trust an Englishman to relax in a bank.

"The Sign of the Camel," Siranoush whispered.

He glanced around. It was a dromedary, in fact, with two humps and a tasseled harness, in mosaic, set midway up the eastern wall. Its mouth was open in a blaring howl and its yellow teeth showed. For an instant, he thought they were made of gold. Beneath the sign was a man with an abacus. Above it, there was a stone gallery with several dark archways leading into shadow.

Siranoush had seen it, too. Without a word, she made her way to the foot of the stairs, Ian following. There was no one about. He glanced over his shoulder. Only the moneylender sitting beneath the mosaic dromedary was watching them. At his feet was a small boy, curled up like a dog. As Ian watched, the moneylender spoke a single word. The boy sprang up and ran off.

Because of them?

Siranoush was already halfway up the stairs. Ian mounted them two at a time. Once on the gallery she hesitated. There were too many archways, too many paths.

"It'll be the one above the camel," he murmured.

She glanced down at the moneylender's head, and turned left through the nearest arch. Ian followed her.

And felt the cool metal cylinder of a pistol abruptly against the base of his skull.

He stopped short and did not turn around. After a few seconds of heart-stopping silence, he put his hands in the air.

"Jesus," Sam Schwartz muttered as one of the Soviet Embassy's numerous staff strode past. "Have you noticed the heat that guy's packing?"

He spoke in an undertone to Michael Hudson. They were standing in the hallway outside Franklin Roosevelt's suite. The President was lodged on the ground floor, so that no awkward arrangement of wheelchair ramps was required. The only drawback to the quarters was that Roosevelt was isolated. His relatives and staff were placed upstairs.

That fact had not escaped Michael Hudson's notice.

Schwartz had his hands shoved into his trouser pockets, the tails of his suit jacket rucked up around his wrists and his legs spread, gangster style. It was an image he intended to convey to the Russian guys all around them—a deliberately Cagney look he figured they'd recognize. They had to have seen at least *one* American movie. He felt like loosening his tie and knocking back a strong drink after the tense and hurried drive from the legation, but even though his chief was safe, he couldn't afford to relax yet.

Within five minutes of their arrival at the embassy, Joseph Stalin had appeared in Roosevelt's doorway. He was in uniform, complete with medals and marshal's peaked cap. Franklin was seated in his wheelchair, but at roughly five-foot-six, Stalin was short enough that the difference between the two men was far from humiliating. Roosevelt extended his hand. Stalin bowed over it in a courtly—almost Czarist—fashion. He'd brought his translator, a tall fellow in his late twenties with immaculately groomed black hair and tailoring that suggested Savile Row. There was no time to summon Chip Bohlen. The solid wood door had closed and the murmur of voices came dimly to those standing guard outside in the corridor.

"There's another one." Hudson nodded slightly toward a waiter opposite them, a napkin draped over his forearm and a jug of ice water firmly grasped in both hands. "They're all NKVD. Harriman says Uncle Joe shipped three thousand of his best into Tehran for the conference. That's insane, Schwartz. Three *thousand* secret police! How many have the Brits got? How many have we?"

"Couple hundred, total," Schwartz returned grudgingly.

"So we're surrounded by thugs in white aprons. You can see their uniforms trailing out beneath. And the gun holsters under the armpits. There have to be fifty strongmen masquerading as servants in this place."

"I guess they think we won't notice." Schwartz rocked on his heels. The waiter with the pitcher of ice water was singularly expressionless. Either he understood not a word of English or he understood it far too well.

"They want us to notice," Hudson said grimly. "It's an implicit threat, Schwartz. You've just delivered the President of the United States into the hands of the Russian secret police. And left the cowboys in tents back at the legation."

"You're a little ray of sunshine, aren't you, Mike," Schwartz said admiringly. "You realize I take orders from Mr. Roosevelt, just like everybody else?"

Hudson rounded on him. "We're talking about a man who can't stand up without help. Much less run. They've got his son here—Elliott would make a great hostage—and an entire conference to waste, negotiating their terms. You realize that if anything goes wrong—if Stalin gets his balls in a sling or decides he doesn't like the tone of FDR's conversation—there's absolutely no way you, or any of your Secret Service clowns, can save him? Uncle Joe will have you shot in the line of duty without a thought. And blame it on his imaginary Nazis."

Schwartz's expression hardened. "Secret Service clowns, eh? I've been protecting the President since you were in short pants, buster. Don't tell me how to do my job."

"I'm sorry," Hudson muttered. He raked his fingers through his hair—a mistake, as he'd pomaded it that morning. "I shouldn't have said all that. I'm just . . . jumpy as hell. I don't like this place."

Schwartz clapped a hand on his shoulder. "It's all the rumors flying around. Nazis gunning for us, these boys . . . And Fleming's a friend of yours. So I guess what he says, you take to heart. His cable sure backed up Molotov's story. That's enough to make anybody jumpy."

"Here's something I don't understand, Schwartz." Hudson lowered his voice, his eyes on the sphinxlike NKVD waiter. "Stalin doesn't share *intelligence*. He doesn't share anything. So why are Stalin's boys pushing this story? Why trot out Molotov to give Harriman a tour of the splendid facilities? Why feed Ian Fleming a fairy tale?"

"Show of good faith for the new allies?"

Hudson shook his head. "These guys want control. They want to dictate terms at this conference of ours, and if things go wrong—if Roosevelt or Churchill ends up dead—they'll score twice if they blame it on Hitler. All Stalin has to do is *stage* an assassination and announce the sad news to the rest of the world!"

Schwartz's hands came out of his pockets. They were balled into fists. "You think we've been set up?"

"Brilliantly," Hudson muttered. Then he moved toward the gun-toting waiter. "Can we get a couple of glasses of water here?"

The man nodded. He'd understood every word.

THERE WERE five of them, which Ian took as a compliment. They could not possibly have known his right arm was almost useless and he was unable to fight his way out of a girl's knickers. While one of them pressed the pistol muzzle above his left ear, another swung out of the shadows and punched him hard in the gut. He doubled over and crumpled to the floor, which had one advantage—it displaced the gun muzzle—but a serious drawback: he was curled in a fetal position while his opponent kicked him in the head. He made the stupid mistake of warding off the blows with his left hand and got his fingers battered.

Incongruously, he was transported back to Durnford: a chill day, possibly his second year, well after Mokie was gone. Shrill cries of in-

vective and support, from the ring of boys in for the kill. Hudders taking bets on the side with marbles as collateral. Himself, groveling in the
mud of an inner courtyard. The smell of earth and rain. A savage on
his neck, scrabbling at his ear with dirty fingers. Some sort of bitter
dispute between ten-year-olds he was foreordained to lose. And a can-
ing, afterward.

Peter would manage better, he thought. God knows 007 would.

Both of them had training. Ian would have to make it up.

He could hear Siranoush speaking urgently—not screaming like a
girl, he thought, with a fairly disembodied admiration, but *talking* to
their assailants in a firm and rational manner, even if her voice was
raised. She was delivering a stream of words in a language he did not
recognize. It was certainly not Arabic, but he wasn't entirely sure it was
Russian.

Armenian, he thought suddenly, remembering a peddler in the Por-
tobello Road.

Nazir was Armenian. So's she.

The booted blows at his head suddenly stopped and he was hauled
abruptly to his feet by a wrenching hand on his right shoulder. His
unhealed knife wound screamed. He felt stitches rend. He wavered,
trying to focus on the small, pinched face of the ratlike man in front
of him.

Man? He was nothing more than a boy. With thin shoulders and a
bad haircut. Half Ian's age. Barely as old as Siranoush, in fact. The rest
of the emaciated band hovered behind him. None of them could possibly be old enough to shave.

Ian's humiliation surged. Not only was he deskbound in wartime,
he was on the *far* wrong side of thirty.

"Siranoush," he murmured, glancing at her. "Introduce me to our
genial host?"

"That is Arev," she said clearly, in English. "Arev, this is Commander James Bond. You will please to stop killing him now."

CHAPTER 20

*P*amela had struck one of her cherished poses—standing by a window in a black-and-gold evening dress, left hand supporting her right elbow. In her right hand she held aloft a cigarette lighter—a lovely thing of ebony and gold that Ave had given her, from Tiffany in New York. She was ignoring the cigarette. Smoke curled unnoticed along her cheek and drifted into her hair. It would smell vile in the morning, but she didn't care. She was bored and she had begun to hate everything about this trip with Papa. She had expected it to be more glamorous. She had dressed so carefully—thinking of Stalin, whom she was *certain* she could charm—but he had not included her in the invitation to dine that evening at the Soviet Embassy.

Sarah had been left out as well. The two women endured a tedious four courses with the British ambassador's wife and various lesser satellites. Sarah had barely listened to the chatter and had spoken as little as possible. She seemed remote, distracted. Which meant that Pam had been forced to *more* than carry her end, answering inane questions about Little Winston and his progress—as though she were his nanny, not his mother. A two-year-old's *bowel* movements? As dinner conversation? She was utterly wasted on these people.

She crushed out her cigarette and turned back toward the fire.

"Care for a drink?" she asked Sarah carelessly. The ambassador's wife had pled a headache and escaped to her private rooms after dinner, leaving them alone in the salon. Wretched manners, Pamela thought, but perhaps the woman suffered from an inferiority complex. She was plain enough.

"No, thank you." Sarah closed the novel she was reading and rose from her chair. "It's after ten. I think I shall retire."

Pamela surveyed the bottles on the drinks cart. A soda siphon. Whiskey. An indifferent sherry. What she wanted was a sidecar—or, barring that, pink gin. She wanted a silly little drink in a dark corner of Café de Paris, with Snakehips Johnson playing the latest tunes and Ed Murrow's hand on her thigh.

"Not waiting up for Winant?" she murmured, as she poured herself two fingers of whatever she could find. "He *shall* be disappointed."

"Don't be vulgar, Pamela."

"Oh, dear." She looked pityingly at Sarah. "Is Mrs. Oliver the Vaudeville Queen attempting to take the high road? Don't make me laugh."

Sarah picked up her bag and wrap. "When are you going to ask my brother for a divorce?"

Pamela took a stiff pull of her drink. "When I see him next. Whenever he gets leave."

When Ed finally tells Janet.

"I'll be counting the days."

Sarah swept through the doorway of the salon without a backward glance. It was the actress's classic exit—on a good line. But Pamela didn't have time to applaud.

She gathered up her fur stole and evening bag and almost ran in her dance slippers to the embassy's front hall. There was a porter there, writing something under a beam of light. He glanced up. Flushed dull red at the sight of her.

"Would you be *very* kind," she breathed, "and summon a taxi for me?"

"A taxi, miss—ma'am? But . . ."

"It's rather urgent, you see."

They wouldn't catch *her* waiting up for Ave. The good little woman sitting by the fire. She would have some fun if she died for it.

SAM SCHWARTZ hadn't liked Michael Hudson's hints this afternoon. The notion that he'd been gulled into placing the President of the United States in enemy hands was unnerving. He struggled against the fear it might be true. He considered himself to be well endowed with street smarts. A canny guy. He'd come up through the ranks of the Army, then a look-see with Hoover's FBI, and finally the Secret Service, which he loved and which had rewarded his competence and loyalty. He was alive to the presence of evil in the world—but in his experience, it generally came from a fella with more firepower than brains. Hudson's ideas were more complicated. He was a Yale man like so many of the new OSS people, and in some ways Schwartz thought he spoke a different language. He saw wheels within wheels, where Schwartz just saw . . . a truck.

And Hudson's whole take on things—the undercurrent of conspiracy—made Schwartz intensely uneasy. He preferred an enemy he could face to one he was expected to outmaneuver.

When the Big Three convened that night for their first official dinner, he and Hudson were both shut out of the dining room. Schwartz immediately took a chair in the corridor and resigned himself to several hours of waiting. Hudson prowled, his hands shoved in his trouser pockets. At least four NKVD men pretending to be waiters were arranged around the hall. They never spoke to one another, nor did they speak to the Americans—but, like haunted portraits, their eyes followed wherever Schwartz or Hudson decided to go.

"You've got a room in this place, right?" Hudson asked.

"Upstairs." Schwartz shrugged. "On the same hall as Colonel Roosevelt, Mr. Boettiger, and Mr. Harriman. The Chief's down here. Easier on the wheels."

"Leahy? Marshall?"

"At your hotel."

Hudson snorted. He strode down the hall and back, his glance flicking contemptuously to the spurious waiters. Abruptly, he crouched down by Schwartz's chair. "Have you checked this place out yet?"

Schwartz doubted the NKVD goons could hear them. But he made a show of removing his pack of cigarettes from his pocket all the same, and offered one to Hudson, who produced a lighter. They bent their heads toward each other.

"I ran my fingers around the baseboard of the President's room," Schwartz murmured.

Hudson emitted a particularly nasty laugh, as though Schwartz had said something dirty. One NKVD guy turned and fixed his gaze on them.

"I need a diversion," Hudson said softly, "without disturbing the President. Help me out?"

"Sure." Schwartz blew a stream of smoke toward the ceiling, which was vividly painted. They might as well be in Rome, he thought, or any of those places where nymphs danced in the clouds and angels threw spears into the devil's horns. The old Russians had done themselves proud. Or the old Persians. Hard to know who'd owned this palace originally. A whole lot of money had gone into it, regardless. Schwartz figured the nymphs and angels had been painted in blood. The more he saw of the Old World, the gladder he was that his grandfather had gotten the hell out of it.

"When?" he murmured.

"Anytime you like."

He rose from his chair, slapped Hudson on the shoulder, and stretched his arms over his head. The same NKVD guy—a hooked nose and a thatch of wheat-colored hair, eyes so light they might have been agates—glared at the two Americans. He's the chief, Schwartz thought. Prizefighter, by the look of him. The rest of these goons take their orders from him.

The man was holding yet another silver salver of ice water as though waiting to be summoned into the dining room. Condensation beaded the pitcher's surface, a mist of cold. He had a napkin draped over his left arm.

Schwartz sauntered toward the guy. He held out his pack of American cigarettes. "Have one, Comrade," he said loudly. "Free. Like most things in life—for a good Communist."

No reaction.

Schwartz took a drag on his cigarette, his eyes narrowed at the pseudo-waiter, hand still extended as though offering the pack. Without warning, he choked. Coughed. Rolled his eyes to the ceiling and scrabbled at the Russian's coat. The pitcher of water flew upward into the man's face just as Schwartz fell heavily against him. Schwartz had been a wrestler in college, and he made sure his center of gravity hovered right around the man's groin.

The Goon Chief doubled over, shaking the water out of his eyes and howling something in Russian. Schwartz slid into a heap at his feet. Two of the Russians came to the injured waiter's side.

"Jesus!" Hudson collided with the fourth as he headed in the opposite direction. "A doctor," he said distinctly. "I'll find a doctor."

He pelted down the corridor in the direction of Roosevelt's suite.

Schwartz did his best to look like he was dying. He writhed on the floor, spitting and gasping, his hands at his throat and his feet in the air.

He might buy Hudson ten minutes.

It took Michael less than that to find what he was looking for.

The microphones, he figured, were embedded in the walls or floor of Roosevelt's suite. Probably behind the massive wardrobe thrust up against one wall or concealed in the overhead chandelier. He didn't need to find them. All he needed was the listening post.

It would be close to Roosevelt's rooms—above, below, or beside them. He'd ruled out above—too much traffic upstairs with the rest of the Americans staying there. Roosevelt's suite was in a corner of the building; on both sides were formal reception rooms with no sign of Stalin's translators busily scribbling anything. That left Hudson with the basement.

He made immediately for the staircase at the end of Roosevelt's corridor. No one followed. But the place was crawling with NKVD; he'd have to seem anxious and confused if he ran into any of them. His feet slowed as he reached the last step.

The embassy's lower level was a service and support area—offices, storage rooms, communications equipment. The corridor in front of him was lined with closed doors and bisected by a second hallway. The electrical feed from the hidden microphone might run through Roosevelt's bedroom floor to the room directly below it, or into the embassy's Commo and Signals Room. Hudson would have to look for both.

Where was Lavrentiy Beria tonight? The secret police chief was not included in the cozy dinner upstairs. Where was his son? Hudson had glimpsed the eighteen-year-old kid among the Soviet officials gathered to welcome Roosevelt earlier that day. He knew a little bit about Sergo Beria. The boy had graduated from a scientific academy; he spoke German, Georgian, Russian, and English. For the past two years he'd been part of the NKVD cell here in Tehran. A few months ago, Beria recalled his son to Moscow for fresh orders. It was no accident, Hudson thought, that Sergo had flown with Stalin to the Tripartite Conference. A spy who spoke English was essential.

There was no one in the corridor in front of Hudson. But he could hear voices in the distance, a guttural Slavic rumble. He did not have much time.

He quietly turned the knob of the first door in the hallway. A storeroom. Uniforms. Shoes. He went on and turned another two. Office supplies. Medical supplies. A large room ranged with typewriters that he guessed was for clerical workers. Canned goods. He reached the cross passage and hesitated. He hated blind corners.

Look anxious and confused. He swung into the side hall as innocently as possible.

Three men stood in the corridor, staring back at him. Only one wore a waiter's uniform. The other two were in dark suits.

Soviet diplomats.

"Doctor?" he called urgently.

Without pausing for a reply, he turned the knob of the nearest door and peered inside. Nothing.

The three men lunged toward him. The NKVD man was reaching for his gun.

Hudson reached for the door opposite.

Pay dirt.

A single lamp floodlit a bare desk. He saw a pad of paper. A silhouette in earphones, transcribing something.

"Doctor?" Hudson said loudly.

The silhouette swiveled and pulled off the headset.

Sergo Beria.

A hand gripped Hudson's shoulder painfully and jerked him backward.

He pivoted and nearly fell into the muzzle of a gun.

"Hey," he said indignantly. "A guy's sick upstairs. I need a doctor. *Doktor,*" he added, with more emphasis, leaning in to the waiter's face.

The guy bared his teeth and thrust his gun close to Hudson's ear.

"You must go." This, from one of the Suits. He was barely a foot away. Although his features were devoid of expression, his manner was menacing. "It is not permitted. *Go.*"

"But he's having a fit." Bewilderment. Helplessness. "Right outside the dining room."

"You will show me."

The Suit made a slight movement with his head, and the NKVD gun was lowered. "Come."

Without touching Hudson, he suggested that Michael was entirely in his power as they marched back up the corridor and stairs. Hudson said nothing. They passed Roosevelt's suite and swept into the hall outside the dining room.

Schwartz was smiling benignly in a chair, his tie loosened and a glass of vodka in his hand.

"Hey, Mike," he crowed, "where you been all this time?"

THERE HAD BEEN eleven of them at dinner that night, but the party felt smaller. The three heads of state, of course; two ambassadors to the Soviet Union; a translator for each man; and Harry Hopkins. Churchill had brought Anthony Eden, his Foreign Secretary. Stalin had Molotov at his side. Only the three who counted really talked—and their translators. The rest crumbled bread and murmured appreciation for the quality of the food. A surprise, given the privations the Soviet Union had endured. Nobody said this out loud.

Roosevelt excused himself early that evening. He felt sick to his stomach, although he would never broadcast that to Stalin. He grinned and lifted his hand and allowed Chip Bohlen to say all that was proper in Russian to Uncle Joe. Then Harry wheeled him out of the room and down the corridor—Sam Schwartz was nowhere in sight—to his private apartments.

"Nice of you to give Winston some time alone with the Bear," Hopkins said.

"Bohlen will take notes on everything they say. Get me a basin, Harry, will you?"

He vomited into his own shaving cup. Hopkins hovered gauntly, saying nothing. "Jesus, I'm sorry," Franklin said.

"That's okay. You done?"

He nodded. Hopkins took the basin away. Roosevelt heard the sound of running water and a toilet flushing from the bathroom. Good old Harry. He'd been with him from the start. Whenever he needed someone to be his legs, it wasn't his Vice President or his Secretary of State—it was Hopkins, traveling to London to reassure Churchill, or to Moscow, to glad-hand Uncle Joe. The whole business would be harder when Harry was gone.

Hopkins handed him a handkerchief from his own pocket. Like most things Harry wore, it wasn't particularly clean. Franklin wiped his mouth anyway and sighed.

"I guess the Nazi commandos poisoned you," Harry joked. "I'll call a press conference and make Uncle Joe's day. You okay?"

"Better, now."

"Want some water?"

"That'd be grand."

He drank it down and removed his spectacles, pressing his fingers onto his eyes. "Aside from making me sick as a dog, I'd say the dinner went well."

"Uncle Joe sure hates the French," Harry said.

"And the Germans."

"Don't we all. But Stalin wants to tear apart both countries when the shouting's done. I loved it when Winston said he *couldn't conceive of a civilized world without a flourishing and lively France.* He'll start World War Three if Stalin ever threatens what really matters—Bordeaux, Champagne, and Burgundy."

Franklin smiled. "Some people think we started *this* war over Polish vodka."

A knock. Hopkins crushed out his cigarette and went to the door.

"Sam," Franklin said, with a feeling of relief. His bodyguard's absence had been troubling him obscurely, a question on the fringes of his mind.

Schwartz crossed the room quickly, a dispatch box in his hands. During this protracted trip, Roosevelt's official business was flown in to every city he visited, for review and signature; Schwartz must have brought today's packet from the legation's diplomatic pouch.

"Put it down on the table, please."

"Certainly, sir." Schwartz deposited the box, sliding a single sheet of paper from the interior as he did so. With an eloquent grimace, he gestured toward it. Then he put his finger to his lips.

Frowning, Roosevelt took the sheet.

CAREFUL, it said in a scrawl of block capitals. HE'S LISTENING TO EVERY WORD YOU SAY.

CHAPTER 21

I like what you've done with the place." Ian's eyes roamed over the stone walls of the bazaar's upper chamber. It was lit by two small windows set high near the ceiling, one of a warren of rooms connected by tunnel-like passages. An oil lamp burned on a broad wooden table and a few high-backed chairs were ranged against the walls. A samovar was steaming in the corner, and for an instant he was swept back to London and the Bohemian studios of his mother's friends, the stout talk of world revolution that was such a persistent cliché of the Thirties, the overheated atmosphere and the clouds of pungent smoke. Always there had been a samovar in a corner, a nod to the host's Red sympathies.

Arev had led them swiftly into the NKVD headquarters, which was blocked off from the bazaar's broader humanity by massive wooden doors hinged and locked in iron. Every few yards the greeting party passed an armed sentinel, who saluted their leader. None of these women or men—Ian saw both—wore the NKVD field uniform of sage-green wool. No rank was obvious, except for that lightning-swift salute for the boy swaggering ahead.

It feels more like a rebel band, he thought, than an arm of the Soviet state. He should consider the possibility that Nazir and Siranoush had deceived him about their allegiance, for reasons of their own. For the moment, however, he brushed conspiracy aside and tried to concentrate on the passages, in case he needed to retrace his steps. Hopeless, of course. If events turned against him he would die here in the bowels of Persia, and his body would be discovered weeks later at the bottom of a cistern.

They had fetched up in this room at last, Siranoush standing mutely by Arev's side and Ian flanked by two of Arev's men. In front of them, seated at the broad table in one of the high-backed chairs, was someone who at last looked like a commander. He had Arev's hooked nose but was altogether much fleshier. His grizzled hair and mustache were ragged and untrimmed. He was missing the index finger of his left hand. He did not acknowledge them, but continued to scan a sheaf of papers on the table before him.

A ferret was crouched on his shoulder.

From time to time, he reached up with his mutilated hand and fondled its head.

"Thank you," he said at last. This was a reply, Ian realized, to his muttered *I like what you've done with the place.* "It is sufficient to our purpose."

He held the papers to the flame of the oil lamp and tossed them, burning, to the stone floor. No one moved. He rose and poured a glass of tea from the samovar.

"Barer dzez, Siranoush. *Vonts ek?"* he said, offering her the glass.

She took a sip of it. *"Vochinch."*

He did not offer Ian a drink. He launched instead into what sounded like an interrogation—entirely in this language that was unfamiliar but just might be, Ian thought, Armenian or Kazakh or some other tongue of the Caucasus. One word was thrown repeatedly in his general direction: *Angliatsi.* Englishman?

Siranoush remained self-possessed. Unruffled. She drank her tea between answers.

The men at Ian's side moved closer. He felt claustrophobic, hemmed in by these watchers as he'd been in the bazaar—at any second he might crack from the tension and bolt for the door.

Bond waited for the precise second when the partisan chief's back was turned, then swiftly grasped his guards by the neck and smashed their heads together. They fell senseless at his feet. Two more were swiftly upon him, but he . . .

He'd probably get a bullet in the back.

Ian kept his eyes on Siranoush. She seemed controlled and impassive, a different girl from the gunner with the crooked smile. Doubt coiled in his gut. Could he trust her?

Suddenly the commander—for he must be a commander—wheeled and pulled a knife. The ferret dove off his shoulder, chittering, and vanished in a blur. The guards grasped Ian's shoulders, forcing his arms backward. He drew a sharp breath as his wounded shoulder screamed.

The commander walked toward him, knife foremost. He slid the blade under Ian's chin.

"You are Bond?"

"James Bond," he agreed. His passport was one of the first things Arev had taken from him.

"Did you talk, Mr. Bond?"

"In general, or on a particular occasion?"

The knife jibbed against his throat.

"It's just that talking's rather a habit of mine. Difficult to break."

He was speaking in his toniest drawl, all Eton and Sandhurst. The British *pukka sahib*. Whether the commander understood the words or not, he caught the sneer in Ian's voice.

The knife snicked his skin.

"You betrayed Nazir. *You talked.* He died. Yes?"

"No." Ian glanced over the commander's shoulder. Siranoush's green eyes were watchful. She expected to see his throat slit right in front of her. But she wasn't particularly pleased about it, Ian thought. That was comforting.

"Our friend meets with you. He trusts you with our secrets. Pouf! His throat is cut and thirty years of work in Cairo betrayed. Yes?"

The knife pressed wetly into his skin.

"No," he croaked. "When I left Nazir he was alive. I was attacked myself before I had a chance to speak to anybody. By the time I regained consciousness, Nazir was dead. I assume the same man attacked us both."

"Then why are you alive, Bond?" The commander grasped Ian's hair and wrenched his head back. The knife snicked a little deeper.

I have no idea, Ian thought. The contradiction, again. Turing's exception that was supposed to explain everything. Only it didn't.

Siranoush said something in her language. Urgency in her voice.

The commander looked at her. He smiled unpleasantly and turned back to Ian.

"You hear what she says? *A man cannot knife himself in the back. He cannot smash his own skull.*" He released Ian and stepped back, uttering a terse command in that foreign tongue. The men grasping Ian unfastened his uniform coat. The commander walked slowly around him as though appraising an indifferent horse. Ian felt his broad hands lifting his shirt. The same hand probed the back of his skull. He winced.

"True, insofar as it goes," the commander said grudgingly. "Tell me, where did you meet Nazir? In his shop?"

"At Shepheard's Hotel."

"In the Long Bar?"

"Yes."

The man muttered something like a curse under his breath. He came around to face Ian. "The Swiss was there? The barman?"

"Joe's always there." Ian wished he could massage his neck or stanch the trickle of blood, but his arms were still held in a vise.

"Of course. Because he's a Nazi spy." The commander said it carelessly as he set down his knife. He snapped his fingers. From the shadows at the corner of the room, the ferret streaked upward to balance on his shoulder. He lifted his mangled hand to caress it. "But he will not be much longer. Arev, my son—take our guests to their rooms. They will want to change their clothes."

IAN WAS GIVEN a dark suit, abominably cut, and a white dress shirt. From the weight of the fabric and the overall style, he concluded these were of Soviet make.

"Arev says you're too tall and too pale to dress like an Irani," Siranoush translated, amused. "It's enough to get you out of that uniform."

"I could be court-martialed for not wearing it."

"Only if you're caught."

He must not be caught.

She rejoined them in a drab wool dress. Her bright gold hair was pulled severely into a bun. There were circles under her eyes, and Ian thought, not for the last time, how frail she seemed. As though she had been denied sleep from an early age.

"Arev says you are to be trusted, Bond," she told him.

"What does that mean?"

"Not very much."

Could he come and go at will? Wander into the Park Hotel, where Hudson had planned to stay, and ask loudly for his friend? Even if Arev and his pack of NKVD dogs allowed Ian out of their sight, he'd be running a risk. Too many of the Americans lodged with Hudders would know him. Bump into even one of them, and he could kiss his rogue operation goodbye.

"Russians never really trust anybody," Siranoush added, "and the NKVD is beyond Russian."

"Particularly when they're Armenian," Ian suggested.

She threw him her crooked smile. "Come. Zadiq is waiting."

"Zadiq?"

"Arev's father. Also his boss."

The young man did not react to this exchange; he did not speak English, Ian realized. But he led them back along the passages to the room where they had met the man with the ferret. Two of the high-backed chairs were drawn up to the wooden table now, and Zadiq had spread out a map.

"Here, here, and here," he said, stabbing the heavy paper's surface. "That is where we found them. Thirty Nazis. Special Forces. And all their matériel."

Ian leaned over the table. Tehran sat in the northern saddle of the country, not far from the Caspian Sea. Between sea and city were the Elburz Mountains. He noticed, as if for the first time, how close the Soviet Union was—just the Caspian separated Iran from Russia. Less distance separated both from what had once been Armenia.

Zadiq had pointed to the foothills north of the city, on the fringe of the Elburz range. "They dropped here, south of Tochal. That peak. We were waiting for them."

"You knew they were coming?" Ian asked.

"We turned two German agents a year ago," the commander said simply. "They preferred to help us rather than die. A few weeks ago they gave us the drop zone coordinates."

"Nazir said that you missed a few."

Zadiq's expression turned ugly. "You should do so well, Bond. A half dozen men escaped. No more. We will find them in the end."

Ian held the man's gaze. "Berlin must know that they came to grief."

"Our double agents blamed the failure on a drunken traitor. Another German. I regret to say that he was turned by the English."

"Allies *do* come in useful, don't they?" Ian murmured.

"In moments," Zadiq conceded. "Each of our agents accused the English spy independently of the other. That carries truth in Berlin. Sadly, we do not expect your Nazi traitor to live much longer."

"Probably better that I don't know," Ian said.

Siranoush was frowning. "Are you tracking the Germans who slipped through our fingers?"

"Our agents are in radio contact with them," Zadiq said dismissively. "We do not think the paratroopers suspect that these two Germans were turned."

She made a small sound of protest. "Then you *must* know where they are! You can locate the transmission signal, surely?"

"How like a woman," Zadiq retorted. "Such foolish questions. These Nazis are constantly on the move."

"What do you know about the Fencer?" Ian asked. The code name dropped like a weight in the middle of the table. "These are his men, I gather?"

"Ah." Zadiq's black eyes flicked over him appraisingly. "We do not know who this Fencer is. Or where he operates. And if the paratroopers are talking to him"—he shrugged—"we cannot listen. We do not know the Fencer's frequency."

Ian looked up from the map. It was an Enigma frequency. As he well knew. Bletchley suspected the Soviets had never broken Enigma codes. But . . . "Nazir said that you intercepted the Fencer's operational plan to kill the Big Three."

Zadiq held up his hand. "We intercepted *Berlin's* communication of Operation Long Jump to our German double agents. The Fencer was mentioned, yes. But of his personal radio transmissions, we know nothing. If he is directing these surviving men—what remains of his team— we are blind and deaf to their orders."

Ian considered this rapidly. The Fencer must be sending out reams of code right now, to Berlin as well as the paratroopers hiding out near Tochal.

Which meant Alan Turing ought to be intercepting the traffic.

"I think," he said carefully, "I might be able to help you. Could someone take a message to the British Embassy?"

———

PAMELA KNEW NOTHING about Tehran. She was accustomed to the men in her life managing such things as taxis and fares and destinations and drinks. But she was feeling mutinous and desperate to get away, so she hurled one word at the driver: *Casino.*

He drove her to the finest hotel in Iran.

The Park had been open only three years. It was the brainchild of Abolhassan Diba, an Iranian with royal blood in his veins, a Sorbonne education, and a considerable fortune in Swiss bank accounts. Diba was an engineering titan intent on modernizing his country. He replaced camels with trucks, plows with tractors, dirt with asphalt. The first telephone exchange in Iran was established by him—and the first Western-style five-star hotel.

You could get a good, stiff drink at the Park, one reason the Armies of Occupation loved it.

A liveried doorman swept open Pamela's cab and offered her his hand. She exited with her usual grace and stood blinking on the pavement, transported for an instant to Mayfair, years before the war, free of sandbags and rubble and blackout shades. This was how life ought to be. A pang of nostalgia and self-pity pierced her. Then she gathered her furs more closely about her shoulders, lifted her chin, and gave the doorman a dazzling smile.

By the time Michael Hudson walked into the Park Casino, Pamela was tossing dice with Mr. Diba.

BOURBON AND RYE were unknown in Iran, so Hudson fetched himself a Scotch, with a mental nod at Fleming. Pamela hadn't noticed him yet, too absorbed in the novelty of this streetwise game and her suave partner. Diba was dark and protective; he was immaculately tailored and entirely in command of his world. From the lovely flush on Pamela's skin and her effortless peals of laughter, Michael guessed she was tight. It was the right hour for it. What was she doing here? Had Harriman brought her?

Of course not. Harriman was still going over his notes from the Tripartite Dinner with the translator, Chip Bohlen.

Michael threw back his Scotch and set down the glass. Leave Pammie alone for another ten minutes, and she'd follow Diba home.

He strode across the room and eased his shoulder into the space between Pamela and her neighbor. She had a Pass Bet down and was feebly palming the dice as though they would bite her. The need to appear elegant had clearly superseded any gambling drive Pamela might have had.

"You can't just drop them on the table like that," he scolded, reaching for her wrist. "You have to hit the opposite wall of the table when you shoot the dice. Shake them like a martini, darling, then unleash them like a tennis ball."

"Michael!" she squealed, and threw her arms around his neck. "What are you *doing* here? I thought you were at that stuffy dinner."

"I happen to be staying here." He glanced with just the right amount of amusement at Abolhassan Diba. "And I'm astounded to find you playing anything so American as craps."

"I've never played it in my life," she said roundly, "but there's a first time for everything."

Pamela's words to live by, Michael thought. But all he said was "Would you be so kind, Mrs. Churchill, as to introduce me to your friends?"

He encompassed the entire group surrounding the craps table, as though she hadn't been clinging to the potentate's arm.

"Of course!" she cried. "Mr. Diba, Michael Hudson. He's with the American delegation to the Tripartite Talks, so we're great chums. Mr.

Diba is the owner of this hotel, Michael. And these"—she glanced vaguely around and waved one gloved hand—"are his people."

Diba shook Hudson's hand, retaining it for a moment longer than necessary. "We are honored, Mr. Hudson, that your remarkable President chose Tehran for his meeting. We are unfortunately situated here, as I'm sure you are aware—with oil fields both the Germans and the Russians want. We regard the presence of your leader—and yours, Mrs. Churchill"—this with a nod to Pamela—"as our greatest safeguard against dismemberment by wolves."

A bold statement for a man whose city was occupied by the Soviets, but Abolhassan Diba radiated security. He probably paid off English and Russian alike, Hudson thought, as the necessary price of doing wartime business.

"Never mind the nasty wolves." Pamela patted her new friend's hand. The gesture was at once so alluring and so bracingly like a nanny—her signature style—that Hudson felt a ripple of laughter in his gut. An Iranian prince like Diba could never have met anyone like her. Already, Hudson could tell, Diba was mesmerized.

Hudson offered Pam the dice. "Try again. This time, do it the way I showed you."

She mimed the movement in the air before him, lips pursed and eyes twinkling roguishly. He was transported that quickly back to her bed, the dim golden light and her body arching above him. He closed his eyes for a second, drawing breath. When he had opened them, the dice had hit the far wall and bounced back. Three and four—a seven. Exactly what she needed.

Pamela glanced at Diba. He bowed, and gestured to the stickman, who moved a pile of chips across the table. Pamela squealed and lifted her arms above her head. Her sable stole slipped to the floor.

"Congratulations," Hudson said drily. "Now, quit while you're ahead. Will you excuse us, Mr. Diba? Mrs. Churchill promised me a dance."

"But of course." Diba inclined his head, reflexively courteous, but his dark eyes remained fixed on Pamela's angelic face. She turned the clutch of chips in her fingers like a toddler with a new toy.

"It has been *such* a pleasure, meeting like this," she murmured to Diba. "I hope we'll see each other again before I have to leave Persia."

"I shall ensure that we do," he replied.

Hudson slipped the stole over Pamela's shoulders and steered her away from the craps table. "You're a dangerous woman, you know that?"

"Why? Because I like taking chances?" she demanded defiantly. "I must cash in my chips."

"Okay." He located the grille of the caisse and led her to it. She hesitated for an instant, unwilling to give up her hoard. Like a magpie, Hudson thought, with a bright bit of foil. That was Pamela's instinct— to collect treasure and turn it over in her hands. The men who offered it were much easier to part with.

The cashier passed a wad of rial notes beneath the grille. Pamela's eyes widened. "I'd no idea I'd won so much!" she breathed. "Look, Michael—hundreds and hundreds!"

He thumbed through them quickly. "That's about five pounds, Pamela, at the current exchange rate."

"Oh." Crestfallen, she slipped them into her purse. "At least I have cab fare back to the embassy."

"Let me escort you."

She glanced up at him, and to his surprise, an expression of fear flickered across her face. "I can look after myself, thank you."

"What's the matter?" He ran his hand gently down her arm.

"It's nothing. I'd just . . . prefer to be alone."

"Because of Harriman? Is he having you followed?"

"Don't be silly." She clutched her stole more closely around her in a protective gesture.

He frowned down at her. "What, then?"

"Michael—" She hesitated, her nubile form stiff with indecision and dismay. Then her chin lifted and her blue eyes looked guilelessly into his own. "The other night—when we . . . in Giza . . . Why were you searching through my things?"

CHAPTER 22

*E*lliott Roosevelt caught a glimpse of Pamela with the OSS fellow as he swung through the doors of the Park Hotel, but he had no intention of stopping to talk to them. He knew Pam Churchill was a whole lot of trouble, and he had enough of it on his hands. His first marriage had lasted only a year; he was extricating himself from his second—the war hadn't done wonders for connubial bliss. But that suited Elliott just fine. He loved planes and everything to do with flying, and a protracted war was the perfect excuse to stay in the air and a continent away from his wife and kids. The war had freed up all kinds of attractive women, and with the threat of death hanging over them daily, they were always ready to waste a few hours on FDR's son. Elliott had been damned lucky in his Pop. He'd hated prep school—hated the rules and the ridiculous expectations, all the Republican kids derisively chanting his last name—and he'd refused to go to college even after Pop had gotten him into Harvard. But Elliott figured he could trade on his war record and access to top circles when the fighting was over. There was money to be made in air route expansion after the war, and Elliott knew how to make it. The trick was not to worry too much about rules. Influence was everything.

You scratch my back, he thought, and I'll scratch yours.

He kept his head down and walked swiftly past Pamela and the Intelligence guy, making directly for the hotel elevator. From the back, he'd be just another man in an Army Air Corps uniform, and there were enough of them in Tehran right now to sell. He punched the call button and the cage descended; when it halted at ground level, the operator slid open the heavy grilled door. His right hand fingered the elegant card of scented paper he'd slid into his pocket that afternoon. It had been delivered to the American legation, where nobody was staying anymore, but Louis Dreyfus made sure all official papers were sent over to the Soviet Embassy several times a day. Elliott had read it in plenty of time.

Room 318, it said. *Midnight. I will be waiting for you.*

A slight thrill of anticipation as the elevator lifted. He gave the operator a few coins. He hadn't bothered to calculate what the local currency was worth.

She answered his knock almost immediately, as though she'd been waiting by the door. As exquisite as he remembered—a porcelain princess in a silk robe.

"May-ling," he murmured.

She drew him quickly inside.

He stood awkwardly for an instant after the door closed, uncertain—as he rarely was—of his next move. Should he be passionate? Sweep her into his arms? They had never been alone like this—shut into a private room—and he had no script for what came next. He took a tentative step toward her.

She turned swiftly and led him into her suite's sitting room. Her maid was there, arranging teacups on a tray.

Disappointment crashed over him.

She said something sharp and incomprehensible in Chinese and the maid bent double in obeisance, scuttling in the direction of what must be the bedroom.

May-ling was offering him tea.

He took the cup and looked at her fully for the first time. Her dark eyes were smudged with sleeplessness, and there was a purplish bruise high on her right cheek.

"Please, Elliott," she said softly. "Sit down."

He took one of the easy chairs.

She curled herself like a cat on the suite's couch, and reached for her own teacup. Poise. That was the quality May-ling had. She made Elliott uneasy.

"What are you doing in Tehran?" he asked abruptly.

Her eyes flicked up at him. She took a deliberate sip of tea. "I had nowhere else to go."

"But—I thought you and the Generalissimo were headed back to China."

"My husband has already arrived. I was not permitted to accompany him." Her voice was impersonal, almost remote. She set down her cup and rose from her seat.

Mesmerized, Elliott watched May-ling approach him. Swaying, graceful, like a reed in the wind. She lifted his tea from his hands and placed it on the coffee table. Then she slid into his lap and put her arms around his neck.

"I have been banished, Elliott, because of you," she whispered. Her lips moved over his cheek as she spoke; the sensation was intoxicating. "My husband says he will divorce me. That I have shamed the name of Chiang by pursuing you in public. I will no longer be the uncrowned empress of China, Elliott. You are all I have, *darling*."

"But—" He drew a shaky breath, bewildered. "He's out of his mind! What can I possibly do, May-ling?"

She stared deep in his eyes, her own tragic. "Marry me," she said.

DAY FIVE

TEHRAN

Monday,
November 29, 1943

Grace Cowles paid off her taxi in Khordab Avenue, at the northern edge of the bazaar. She hurried across the broad avenue in the direction of Golestan Palace. The hour was still early—not yet seven o'clock—and there were street sweepers in long white tunics and trousers poking at the gutters near the palace in a desultory fashion. The scent of coffee and horse dung and charcoal from street braziers, the whiff of snow from the high mountains just visible in the distance, hung tantalizingly on the air. Sunlight cut through the branches of bare trees. It was beautiful, she realized. Foreign and yet less exotic than Cairo, because the chill reminded her of London.

Golestan meant *rose* in Farsi, Pug Ismay had told her when they passed the palace on the way in from the airfield. He was full of odd information like that. The Rose Palace. It was actually a complex of buildings too numerous for her to distinguish, each more elaborate than the last. Four hundred years old, covered in gold mosaics, with pools of water and hidden gardens. The young Shah did not live there now; he had his own modern place in the north of the city. Such a waste, Grace thought. Like abandoning the Tower of London for a Mayfair flat.

She hurried across the street, clutching the lapels of her army jacket against the cold. Ian's message had mentioned a park. There was a greenish space in front of Golestan that qualified. It was absurd that she had run out of the British Embassy and motored south through the waking city to meet a man who must be mad. Or at least a deserter.

The sudden news that Ian was there—*in Tehran,* when he'd been ordered back to London—had shocked Grace to the core. She'd held his handwritten message for the space of thirty seconds, staring sightlessly at her own reflection in her bedroom mirror. Then she had nearly gone to Pug. But telling Pug the truth would have meant Ian's arrest. The end of his career. Grace had decided she should talk to him first.

That's your weakness, she thought. Stop trying to save him. He doesn't want to be saved.

She fetched up on a gravel path cutting diagonally across the park and slowed her steps. Ian had stressed the need for absolute secrecy, and although she was pretty sure he was engaging in what Hudson generously called "fiction," she should not draw attention to herself. She ought to look like any other stroller—a woman in British uniform, alone at that hour of the morning in the middle of the Persian capital! Impossible.

She caught sight of his profile—broken nose, compressed lips, arrogant fall of black hair across the brow. He was wearing an ill-fitting civilian suit and tossing unleavened bread to pigeons near a central fountain, his sensitive fingers tearing the stuff into scraps. She strolled up to him and stood for an instant in silence. The pigeons stretched out their necks and lifted their wings irritably. "Where did you get those abominable clothes?" she said. "And what the *hell* were you thinking, summoning me here like a bellboy?"

He glanced sideways, his mouth quirking. "You may despise me, Grace, but you've never let me down yet. No tip for the bellboy, however. I've only got a fiver to my name."

"You've deserted, haven't you?" she said contemptuously.

"Gone underground, more like."

"Chasing your Fencer?"

He dusted bread crumbs from his fingers. "Clever girl."

"That cable of yours dropped like a mortar in the middle of the delegation. There are all sorts of rumors running round. That one of us is a traitor. That there are Nazis hiding in the hills. Or that you dreamed it all up."

"Who's casting me as a liar?"

She did not answer him directly. "You *did* take a nasty knock on the head, Ian. You might be . . ."

"Call me James. My new passport does."

"James what?" she demanded, startled.

"Bond, actually. Short, British, and to the point."

Grace stared at him. "You really believe it, don't you? That this play-acting is real? Michael said it was a habit of yours. I didn't want to listen."

"Michael said *what* was a habit of mine, exactly?"

"Making things up." Her voice was acid. "He used the word *fiction*. I was content to simply call you a liar—and have done."

He turned toward her. "It's time to let go of the past, Gracie. Your resentments. My failures. Did I ever truly *lie* to you?"

"You let me think . . ." She swallowed. It was too humiliating to say out loud. *You let me think you loved me. You let me love you.*

"My sins were ones of omission. They usually are. All my life I've found it easier *not* to do than to do." He walked slowly toward a park bench, guiding her with a hand to her elbow. They sat down. His blue eyes were probing, but Grace's guard was firmly in place. "This trip to Tehran is an attempt to change that. I owe you an apology. Not for my lies—but for all I never said out loud."

She shrugged. "Call it what you like. You deceived me . . . *Bond*.

And from what your friend says, it seems to be a pattern. Tell me why you called me here so that I can get back to Pug. Not all of us can be absent without leave."

"Are you going to tell Ismay about me?"

She hesitated. "That depends."

"Don't. You'll be the death of me."

"Don't be so dramatic!"

"I've got no choice. *I know why the Fencer is here.* Hiding in plain sight in the Allied delegations. That alone is reason for murder."

She sighed and folded her arms.

"If you don't believe me, go back and signal Turing."

"About what?"

"Operation Long Jump, Grace. The German plan to assassinate Winston Churchill. And Franklin Roosevelt. And Joseph Stalin."

"All of them?"

He nodded. She could detect no spark of insanity in his eyes. No suggestion he was delusional. "You're serious."

"Dead serious."

"Turing *told* you this?"

"No. I had it from a dead man—a Russian contact in Cairo. His throat was slit the same night I was coshed and stabbed."

Grace reared back. In all her bitter talks with Hudson, she'd lost sight of that fact. Ian *had* been attacked. It might have been for his wallet, of course—a violent act he'd magnified into something more . . . She rose hurriedly from the park bench.

"I ought to turn you in to Pug," she said rapidly. "I'm a fool not to, and if you come a cropper, it'll be me they dismiss."

"Please," he said. "If the PM dies, you'll never forgive yourself. There's too much at stake, Grace—*the whole war*—"

He made no move to touch her. Just kept his eyes fixed steadily on her face.

"I'll signal Turing," she said.

To the steel-hearted citizens of Stalingrad • The gift of King George VI • In token of the homage of the British people . . .

Churchill ran his fingertip over the script engraved on the Sword's blade. It was a purely ceremonial piece—a stunning bit of trumpery he'd commissioned in Sheffield. But grasping the hilt took him back to his days in Africa, the feel of a horse—restive in anticipation of battle—and the strain in his biceps as he lifted his right arm high. There would never be a cavalry charge again in his lifetime. The tanks he himself had invented had replaced the warhorses of old. Including the men who'd ridden them.

Pity, how time makes fools of us all.

This was not a cavalry officer's weapon, of course; it was modeled on a two-sided Crusader's sword. But he liked the heft of the four-foot steel blade and the feel of the hilt bound in gold wire. It fitted his hands. The hilt's pommel was rock crystal and the cross guard was silver—shaped like a half-moon, with leopard heads at each tip. The leopards were washed with parcel-gilt, their teeth bared in menace.

At Harrow he'd been a champion fencer—All England—a fact most people had forgot, if they'd ever known it. He swung the Sword high over his head and opened his jaws wide. A warrior's face. Then he thrust brutally through his imaginary foe's neck—and ended with the tip of the blade buried in the carpet.

The momentum almost toppled him.

Churchill glanced around for the scabbard. He'd ordered it in Persian lambskin—a nod to this historic meeting in Persia itself—and had specified that the supple leather must be dyed scarlet. Stalin, after all, was a _Red._ At the top of the scabbard the Wilkinson swordsmiths had engraved the royal arms, the crown, and King George's cypher—his scrolling initials. Five silver mounts ran the scabbard's length; three of these were set with gold stars. Each star held a bezel-cut ruby.

It was a sumptuous, an archaic bit of swagger to strap around one's waist. It appealed to every fiber in Churchill's imperial being. He suspected it would appeal to the pirate in Stalin, too.

From the moment the Soviet leader had confirmed he would meet with his Allies that November, Churchill had been searching for some sort of grand gesture. An act that would solidify the respect and need among all three Allied leaders. He'd hit upon commissioning this Sword of Stalingrad. A symbol of Russian endurance—and German horror.

Hitler's forces had spent two hundred days fighting for Stalin's city. When the bloodletting was done, three quarters of a million German soldiers were surrounded and six entire German divisions wiped off the map. Four hundred thousand Soviet troops had died in the nine-month battle, and tens of thousands of civilians had perished from violence and famine. Stalingrad was a byword for nightmare—in Berlin above all.

Churchill intended to present his Sword to Stalin that night at dinner. But he was feeling unsettled and uneasy. Nothing about this Tripartite Conference had gone as he'd expected—starting with the Chinaman's appearance in Cairo and Franklin's inexplicably distant behavior now. Churchill had imagined that his prior acquaintance with both Stalin and FDR, and his ready flow of conversation, would bridge any awkward differences. He had cast himself as conference host, in short—but that role was already taken. Stalin had usurped it by taking Roosevelt into his camp. It was Churchill who was the odd man out—when he'd expected to run the show.

The Sword of Stalingrad felt over the top, suddenly. Excessively showy. Would offering such a florid trophy make him look ridiculous?

There was a tap at his door. He slid the Sword carefully into its scabbard and reached for his dressing gown. It was a little after ten in the morning, but he was not yet dressed. Too old to alter his habits now, even in a strange country—and it was his habit to work in bed during the morning hours. He never appeared in public much before luncheon.

"Come in!"

He expected Pamela.

But it was Sarah's face that hovered near the door.

"Father," she said, "is Dr. Wilson about?"

"Lord Moran," he corrected absently. Wilson, his private physician, had been elevated to the peerage that year with the rank of baron and a title. "He must have shown his face at breakfast, my dear. Is he wanted?"

She nodded swiftly, slid into his room and shut the door firmly behind her. "It's Pamela."

He frowned. "Has she come down with this wretched bronchitis?"

"I don't know," Sarah said impatiently. "She didn't wake when her tea tray was brought. I'd have said she was simply sleeping off her usual rag. But the tray was still outside her door just now, untouched. We knocked and called—"

"And?"

"We can't wake her up." Sarah hesitated. "I think she *took* something, Father."

THE MAN IN THE WHEELCHAIR had dressed and breakfasted in his room hours ago. Harriman had warned him that Stalin was an early riser. Roosevelt had been reared by a mother of strictest social propriety. *Never sleep later than your host at a house party.* That went for politics and war. *Never be caught napping.*

He was rolling along a path in the Russian Embassy's withered garden, the wheelchair rocking and bucking as Sam Schwartz thrust it by brute force through the gravel. "Did you find the microphone?"

"No, sir," Schwartz said. "I'm guessing it's wired beneath the flooring under your bed. With pinpoint holes in the wood for reception. Not obvious to a casual eye, and the bed's too heavy to move."

Not that he would be trying, Roosevelt thought—but yes, the bed was a hundred years old, a magnificent Empire piece. "And Beria's son is the scribbler?"

"Once I knew what the kid looked like," Schwartz said, "I noticed him entering Uncle's Joe's quarters this morning with the wake-up samovar and rolls. I figure he pulls up a chair and respectfully tells the Great Man what you've said over the past twenty-four hours."

"Which means he's a direct line to Stalin," Roosevelt said thoughtfully. "Anything I say in the privacy of my own room goes by the back door to Uncle Joe. We can use this, Sam."

The wheelchair came to a halt. Schwartz appeared to be admiring a particularly fine specimen of cypress. "Disinformation, sir?"

"In a manner of speaking. Whatever I say in that room, just play along, okay? We've got to sound sincere. And if you need to tell me anything off-script, pass it on a piece of paper. That's the British Embassy we're looking at, isn't it?"

"Yes, sir."

"If I need to talk privately to Winston, I'll just roll next door."

They surveyed the neighboring building for an instant from the height of the Soviet back garden. Through the lattice of bare tree branches and the knifing boughs of cypress, they could make out a cluster of figures ranged around the entrance portico. A dark van was pulled up to it, and as they watched, two figures in white clothing hurried up the British Embassy steps.

"If I didn't know better, I'd say those were medical people," Roosevelt said. "Have you got a light, Sam?"

Schwartz came around the side of the wheelchair and bent over the President. Roosevelt's long cigarette holder mimed an arabesque in midair. The two white uniforms were back: each on either end of a stretcher. An indeterminate body lay between.

"Too slight to be Winston," Roosevelt said comfortably, through his smoke. "That's a relief. I was afraid he was the one vomiting this time."

"Sir?"

He looked up at Schwartz. "Helluva bodyguard *you* are. Don't you know I was poisoned by Nazis last night?"

"WHAT HAS HAPPENED?" Grace demanded, as she hurried into the embassy's main foyer. It seemed crowded with people. She had paid off her cab at the compound gate, shown her papers to the guards, and walked up the long drive to the British legation. She hadn't expected a greeting party, particularly one that stank of anxiety. Churchill, she thought. Dear God. He can't be—

"My sister-in-law has been taken ill," Sarah Oliver said steadily. "Those people are known to the embassy. Some sort of private clinic Dr. Moran located. I wonder, Miss Cowles, if you could help me? I should like to place a trunk call—only I'm uncertain how, in this wretched place."

"Of course," Grace murmured. She led Sarah through the scattered groups of people, all muttering in subdued voices, to the Signals Room. This was a dreary cubby stashed behind a trompe l'oeil door off the grand staircase's lower landing—a windowless mezzanine, quite undetectable from the exterior of the building. It had probably been a service cupboard when the embassy was a private palace. Now, in anticipation of the conference, it had been augmented with three additional lines and the mint-green Bakelite of the Secraphone.

She offered Sarah a chair. "I expect you'd like to call Home."

The actress gave her a strange look. "Not just Home, but *home,* Miss Cowles. I must speak to my mother."

Grace took down the number Sarah dictated. "This will require at least an hour. Shall I fetch you when the call is put through?"

"You're very kind. Someone will know where to find me."

Sarah rose and turned toward the door.

"I hope Mrs. Churchill is soon better."

Sarah stopped short, her hand on the knob. "The silly little fool tried to kill herself," she said.

CHAPTER 24

They have made contact." Siranoush grasped Ian's coat sleeve and pulled him determinedly down a narrow passage in the heart of the NKVD warren. There was little light here in the stone tunnel, and he was pressed close to the girl's body. It felt too whipcord thin to be believed. He grazed her hip and imagined spanning her waist with his hands. Instead he raised his left palm—it was still painful to lift the right—and smoothed it down her back. He felt her skin shiver.

She twitched her hair as though annoyed. "*Bond.* Arev tells me your woman is beautiful, though her clothes are ugly. Me, I think English girls are cold."

Of course Arev had watched him at Golestan. Trust only went so far. "So are English men," Ian observed.

"That is not what I hear. In your public schools, you have great passion for one another, no?"

Again, that Siranoush smile. She was hoping for a reaction.

"God give me strength," he said, then pulled her close with his one good arm and kissed her.

For an instant, it was like drowning. No air. No possibility of surfacing. He had dropped off Dancing Ledge into the shock of the Channel, like the boy he'd once been.

Then she broke away and stared at him, her breath coming in gasps. He could just see the gleam of her eyes in the dimly lit passage.

"Bastard," she said through her teeth. And whipped around the passage's next turn.

He followed, sirens singing in his ears.

The tunnel ended in bars.

The cell was lit by an iron lamp filled with coals from Zadiq's brazier. Four men were inside—two sitting at a table and two standing over them with guns pointed at their heads.

On the table was a wireless transmitter.

Ian came up with Siranoush, his mouth close to her ear. "They can transmit in this place?"

"You forget," she said. "We are very near the bazaar roof here. The ceiling is wood."

The two men at the table were, Ian guessed, the turned German agents. He had imagined them going about their lives in Tehran, ostensibly normal citizens, with occasional offerings of intelligence to Zadiq. This was naïve, of course. Ian knew from his work with the Double-cross Committee—the British group that handled turned Nazi agents in Britain—that the Enemy could never be trusted, even if they cooperated. It was enough that they had bought their lives with their treason; freedom could come after the war.

He wondered if freedom was even a concept Zadiq understood.

The commander was holding a gun. His son held another. Their weapon of choice, Ian noticed, was the old Czarist service revolver, the Nagant M1895. Standard issue for the NKVD. It was a 7.62mm double-action model that fired seven bullets. The great thing about the Nagant, Ian had heard, was that its breech was gas-sealed, making it far more powerful than anything the West had. This also meant that the Nagant could be effectively silenced. He would not like it leveled at his skull.

As the commander's eyes slid toward Siranoush, one of the men at the table—Ian could not see his face, but his hair was gray and his hands were trembling slightly—spoke up wearily in German. A language Ian immediately understood.

"They are coming," the prisoner said. "To Tehran tonight. They ask for shelter."

The Nagant wavered. Zadiq, Ian saw, was motioning to Arev. The boy must also speak German.

"Shelter?" he repeated. "Not tactical support?"

"Then the attack is *not* to be tonight," Siranoush broke in.

The second prisoner swiveled a birdlike head. "They wait for in-structions." His voice was unctuous, oily, difficult to place. Neither Ira-nian nor German; an East European, Ian thought, in Hitler's service. "They wish to lie low. To be ready when the time comes. It will be any day now. What do we tell them?"

Zadiq did not reply. He motioned with the gun to Arev. The boy lifted the transmitter from the table and backed toward the door of the cell. His father followed him with the lamp. The two Germans were left in darkness.

"We must plan," Zadiq said in English as he turned the bolts of his cage and joined the others. "It will be a delicate business."

A delicate business. There would be directions to transmit—to a safe house the NKVD controlled. Bona fides to exchange. The German radio operators would have to be taken to the safe house and guarded, so that the place looked plausible when the paratroopers arrived that night. And the NKVD presence would have to be considerable—although to-tally hidden. Otherwise, the turned agents might seize the moment to make a break for it, rather than betray the Nazi soldiers.

A delicate business indeed.

"What do you want most, Zadiq?" Ian asked.

Siranoush turned and stared at him. They were walking briskly behind the commander toward his conference room.

Zadiq snorted. "What *you* want, Bond. To stop this madness. Before my leader dies."

"That's not all I want," Ian replied. "Capture these men, torture them if you like—kill them, even. But the real player is still out there. *I want the Fencer.*"

"You'll take what you can get." Zadiq placed the lamp on his conference table; Arev set the transmitter down beside it. Siranoush was speaking low and fast in Armenian to the boy, who was staring in his unfriendly way at Ian. "You're lucky I include you."

"I think we can do better. I think we *must*."

"Nothing is better than saving the Marshal's life."

"There's something you don't know." They were all standing in the center of the room, unwilling to be the first to take a chair. Even Siranoush looked taut as a wire. Her fists were slightly clenched by her sides. Had he really kissed her? What had he been thinking?

"The Fencer is one of us," Ian said.

Zadiq's head shot around, as though a killer were somewhere in the shadows of the room.

"He's a member of the Allied delegation," Ian amended. "We're fairly certain. Our Signals intelligence intercepted traffic that suggests he was right in the middle of our counsels in Cairo. We have to assume he traveled here with us."

"One of you British," Zadiq said slowly.

"Or Americans."

"You let him near Stalin?" The NKVD chief lunged for him, his Nagant lifted high. He was going to smash Ian's skull.

Arev grabbed Ian's arms and pinned them behind his back. He ducked his face instinctively to avoid Zadiq's gun, and felt Siranoush's hair against his skin. She had slid between him and the NKVD commander.

Like a fury, she thrust out her arms and shoved Zadiq backward.

She was shrieking in Armenian. Ian had no idea what she was saying, but it stopped Zadiq cold.

He set his gun shakily on the table. Then he pulled out a chair, sank into it, and put his head in his hands.

Arev released Ian, who tentatively rubbed his right arm. He still had too little strength in it. He would never be able to throw a punch or fire a gun and hit his target—in the next few days, at least. He was a sitting duck if he met the Fencer alone.

"You say this killer is one of us," Zadiq said. He lifted his head and stared at Ian. "That he meets with our leaders every day. Churchill. Roosevelt. Iosif Vissarionovich. He could murder them right now."

"He won't." Ian took a chair at the table. After an instant, Arev and Siranoush sat down. It felt safer—more controlled—to say these things with a table between them. "He wants it to look right. It must happen in public. Hence the paratroopers. He wants an obvious attack and victory for Nazi power. Or maybe he plans to blame it on the Iranians, and give Hitler an excuse to invade the oil fields. I don't know. Either way, he wins."

Zadiq shot to his feet. "We must tell Stalin. Beria."

"We can't," Ian said gently.

Zadiq reached for his gun and leveled it at Ian's face. "If I say nothing, my life is forfeit, Bond."

"And I have Churchill to save." With effort, Ian ignored the Nagant. "Listen to me, Zadiq."

The gun's firing pin was unusually long. The Armenian cocked it.

Siranoush said something quickly under her breath. Arev answered her. Ian kept his eyes on the trigger.

"Capture the paratroopers," he said calmly, "and the Fencer will know. We'll bugger his plans. But he won't stand down. He won't give up and go home. His targets are here."

"So? Beria has three thousand men in this city."

"The Fencer's *inside the conference.* Sitting next to Stalin. With his hands on Roosevelt's wheelchair. He'll find a way to kill them, Zadiq, even if we take his paratroopers away."

"Then we have already failed."

"Not if we bag them *both.* The Fencer *and* his men."

Arev muttered something under his breath.

"Let the paratroopers feel safe," Ian persisted. "Let Long Jump go forward. Track the signals between the Fencer and his team, and shut them down at the last possible second. Once we know who the Fencer is."

Zadiq smiled at him ferociously. "You forget, Bond. We *cannot track* the signals. We do not have the Fencer's radio frequency."

Ian pushed the Nagant's barrel aside. "We have something better. A woman named Grace Cowles."

"—DASHED UNFORTUNATE," Lord Leathers mourned as he sipped his cocktail. "Such a charming gel. Still, I daresay the nursing home will put her right."

Michael Hudson murmured a commonplace and began to edge toward the British Embassy's foyer. He had stopped in for lunch at the invitation of Sarah Oliver—she'd asked most of the American delegation, since they, like so many of Churchill's entourage, were cooling their heels while the principals talked. It was Gil Winant who met him at the door, however—with the news that Sarah would not be joining them. She had gone with Churchill to the clinic where Pam's life hung in the balance.

Very little was being said about the incident. Even Winant had no details to share. Hudson got the impression a scandal was being contained.

He caught sight of Gracie mounting the staircase in her neat uniform and immediately excused himself to Leathers.

"Miss Cowles!" he called.

She turned on the landing and peered toward the voice in the crowd. "Mr. Hudson."

He hurried up the stairs. "What happened here today?"

"Why do you ask?"

Her voice was deliberately neutral. Hudson shook his head slightly and said, "Because I saw Pamela last night. Christ, I was probably the *last* person to see her. It was nearly one a.m. when she left me."

Grace knit her brows and glanced over her shoulder. There was still a crowd of people milling about the foyer, talking and laughing among themselves. "Come," she said, and led him to a door on the landing, set seamlessly into the woodwork. "We can be private here."

It was the Signals Room, Hudson saw. She closed the door behind him and offered him a chair. "Did you arrange to meet her last night?"

"God, no." He ran his fingers through his hair. "I went looking for a nightcap at my hotel—the Park; most of us Americans are staying there—and ran smack into Pam in the Casino. She'd picked up the hotel owner somewhere. She was high as a kite."

Grace pursed her lips. "I gather she and Mrs. Oliver had a bit of a row last evening. Mrs. Oliver blames herself—but everyone's on edge. It's the atmosphere. All these Russian soldiers looking over one's shoulder."

"Yeah," Hudson agreed. "But tell me. What happened to Pam? She was fine when I put her into a taxi. Tight, but then, she's almost always tight. I told her to get to bed."

"We think she took chloral," Grace said. "There was a bottle by her bedside. She often has trouble sleeping. But she must have taken—a stronger dose last night."

He whistled. "And Mrs. Oliver thinks it was deliberate?"

"That's nonsense, of course," Grace said briskly. "Mrs. Randolph must have mistaken the amount. You say she was drunk. Perhaps she dosed herself twice."

Hudson did not immediately reply. He was studying Grace's face with a troubled expression.

"There's no reason on earth for Mrs. Randolph to make away with herself," she said.

"I hope like hell it wasn't because of me."

"Don't flatter yourself," Grace said harshly. "Do you really think she would end it all, for love of *you*?"

He felt himself flush. "Of course not. I meant—I hope I didn't . . . drive her to it."

Grace raised an eyebrow and waited.

"She just asked me straight out," Hudson explained. "What I'd found in her room. And I told her, you see."

"You searched her room," Grace said. "After I *forbade* you to do it?"

"I had to, Grace."

"No, you didn't. You just couldn't help yourself." She moved quickly for the door, clearly done with him. "You're nothing but a spy."

"Of *course* I'm a spy," he retorted, angry now. "Half the delegation are spooks of one stripe or another. What war are you fighting, anyway?"

She stopped short and took a deep breath. "And you think you found something she'd kill herself over?"

"Well—I found this."

He reached into his coat and pulled out a German codebook.

CHAPTER 25

When Michael left her, Grace went in search of Pug Ismay. The Military Chief of Staff was closeted with Churchill, however—as he ought to be, she thought with irritation. They had, after all, come to Tehran to negotiate the timing and location of the Allied invasion of Europe. That night's dinner at the Soviet Embassy would be a strategic minefield. Pug was not invited to attend, any more than he had been last night; Roosevelt's military advisors were similarly in exile. Which meant the PM and the President would have to face the wily Marshal Stalin on their own. Pug would naturally want to coach his man.

What would she have said to General Lord Ismay, in any case?

It has come to my attention that the Prime Minister's daughter-in-law is a traitor to the Allied cause.

Oh—and by the way—Commander Fleming has deserted.

Damn these personal complications! What the *hell* was Pamela thinking? Was cold hard cash so irresistible, even at the expense of her father-in-law's career—Good God, his standing in *history*?

Traitors were shot in time of war. But Pamela would be cosseted and sheltered because she'd tried to do away with herself, Grace thought cynically. After a long period of contrition in a quiet nursing home in

Devon or Cornwall, she'd sally back into town with a clutch of new evening gowns and a string of men willing to pay for them.

Did she think of no one but herself?

Grace's footsteps slowed. She was giving vent to something deeper than indignation at the betrayals of Pamela Churchill, and much more personal. She was feeling rage. The woman got endless chances at love and happiness—and she squandered them all. Without the slightest regard for the people who cared about her.

Like Michael.

Grace had seen it in his face. He'd hated what he'd found in Pamela's bedroom. Probably because he'd enjoyed his time there so much. The woman had no right to toy with hearts as carelessly as she did. Destroying the integrity of good, honest fellows—

Who searched through women's lingerie at the dead of night, Grace thought wryly. *Enough.* There was no way to make a hero of Michael Hudson.

The man she really needed to talk to was infuriatingly out of reach. She glanced at her wristwatch and calculated the time in England. Two o'clock in the afternoon here, eleven-thirty in the morning there. Alan Turing ought to have received her message by now. She had to make a decision about Ian Fleming. Keep his secret—or turn him in to Pug.

She almost ran back to the Signals Room, hoping for a few stuttered words from the Prof.

"So AFTER I got sick last night," Roosevelt said, "Churchill and Stalin decided the future of *Poland*?"

"I wouldn't go so far as that," Harriman amended. "They were talking about borders. Recognizing that the Germans have completely swallowed the country, including the Free City of Danzig, and that the situation will have to be put right."

"Sure. But it's too bad I couldn't have a say in the conversation. Did it occur to them I might care about Poland?"

"As I say. Nothing was *decided*. Mr. Churchill simply dropped some matches on a map of Europe. Showing where the future borders might be, and so on." Harriman shifted in his chair uncomfortably and glanced around the President's bedchamber. He'd been ambassador in Moscow for only a few months, but he'd been informed when he walked into the post that his embassy was bugged. He assumed this one was, too. How detailed did Roosevelt want to get? Did he *understand* the Soviets had no compunction about eavesdropping on private conversations?

"How many Polish Americans do we have in the States right now, Ave?"

Harriman cleared his throat. "No idea, Mr. President."

"Five or six million. And most of them vote *Democratic*. If I run for a fourth term next year—"

"Their concerns will be your concerns. I understand."

Was he running for a fourth term? It seemed fantastic to Harriman— this visibly aging paralytic who had already shocked history by refusing to say goodbye at the end of eight years. He'd been serving now for more than ten—a decade of economic chaos and physical violence that made everything previous seem tame by comparison. And if FDR was elected a fourth time, next fall? Harriman wondered if the country could survive it. The Imperial Presidency. The Democratic Dictatorship. People would grumble. They'd begin to think Roosevelt would have to die in office before they'd get rid of him.

Die.

His thoughts flitted away to the girl in the hospital bed he'd seen only a half hour before. What if that were his Kathleen, lying white-faced and still, her hair a damp mat against the sterile pillow? Pamela was out of danger, the doctor had assured him, in a stream of Iranian-accented French; but it had been a tricky business. A mess, Harriman thought to himself bitterly. A fucking mess, as only a woman can make it. There will be questions. From Winston. From Franklin, too, if he starts to think about the implications. If she starts to talk. Jesus, I wish I'd never had anything to do with her.

"Ave?"

His gaze returned to the inscrutable eyes behind the polished lenses. "Sir?"

"Where exactly did he put them?"

Harriman frowned, momentarily at sea.

"The matches," Roosevelt said patiently. "Where did Churchill put them? There's no mention of it in Bohlen's notes."

"He dropped them in the middle of Eastern Germany," Harriman said quietly. "He thinks that part of the world should go to the Poles. Uncle Joe is sticking to the Molotov-Ribbentrop Line."

"The one he established with Hitler, back when they were in cahoots?"

"Yes. If Churchill's going to give the Poles land on their western border, Stalin's going to take it from them in the east."

"Well—I'm not sure I disagree." Roosevelt reached thoughtfully for his cigarette holder. Harriman dove for his lighter. "Uncle Joe is worried about Germany coming back to bite us in the ass. He wants to see the country broken up so it's not a military threat in the future. Giving some of the terrain to Poland makes sense. I'd support it. What do you think, Ave?"

"I think Churchill wants to take good news back to London." The Polish Government-in-Exile had set up shop there under General Sikorski. "And I think we need to look at both sides."

"Of course." Roosevelt lifted his brows expressively. "We're certainly not going to cave to Winston, after all, at Uncle Joe's expense. The British Empire is finished. It's our friends in Russia we have to think of now."

Was he posturing for him, Ave wondered, or for the microphones in the walls?

HARRIMAN EXITED the President's suite with relief when Harry Hopkins knocked on the door. He would have liked to call his daughter Kathleen, back in Moscow, to make sure she was all right. But the embassy line would be monitored and he wasn't sure he wanted to hand Stalin's goons the latest gossip about Pam Churchill. It could be used against him in future.

What he wanted was a real drink. He'd get one next door, at the British Embassy. He might even find Sarah Oliver there—and it was time he confronted her.

Harriman strode down the hallway under a gauntlet of NKVD eyes that failed to faze him in the least. He commanded respect and fear all over the world; no one would lift a finger against him. He had moved in a bubble of invulnerability for as long as he could remember—insulated from the realities of pain or love, loss or grief—even of world war.

CHAPTER 26

*I*t was nearly four o'clock when Arev came to him in the small cell lit by a single lamp, where he had been talking, in a friendly fashion, with the two German agents Zadiq owned body and soul. Ian did not think of this as an interrogation. He had no love for the Nazis, he hated what German bombs had done to his London and the people who lived in it, and he would continue to use every wit he possessed to bring Hitler down. But he enjoyed speaking German. He had liked any number of the Austrian girls who had beguiled his youthful summers in Kitzbühel. Most of them had been Jewish—wealthy daughters of Viennese merchants with summer homes in the Tyrol. In the past few years, he'd helped a few of them get out of Austria and set up new lives. They were still trying to get cousins, sisters, and elderly parents to England. But communication across enemy lines was difficult.

He did not mention all this to the turned radio operators. He ignored the entire issue of their race or allegiance. He talked instead of hiking in Austria and the freshness of the air among the tall black pines.

Very subtly, however, he drew them out regarding Iranian mountains. The terrain and the weather. The skills a man would require to survive for weeks alone and hunted on foot. He suspected the six paratroopers might be in dubious condition when they arrived that night in Tehran.

Siranoush was with Arev when he interrupted Ian. Although the boy might have spoken to him in German, too, Ian suspected he did not want the German agents to overhear what he had to say. So Siranoush told him in English.

"Your English woman," she said, with a toss of her hair. "She is wandering the bazaar. You told her to find you there, yes? To make contact?"

"In the Perfume Sellers Hall," Ian said, rising to his feet. He had been sitting on the floor and his back and arm were numb. *Foolish.* If the Germans noticed how stiffly he moved, they'd realize he was vulnerable. *Drop your gun, 007. We know you are incapable of using it in your condition. Fire it now and the ricochet will only kill us all . . .*

"You're sure?" he said to Arev. "You recognize her?"

The boy nodded.

"He remembers the way she smiles," Siranoush said with contempt.

"Ave!"

John Gilbert Winant was sitting alone in a small study at the rear of the British Embassy. The narrow, draped window overlooked the wintry parterre outside. He had pulled a book from the shelves, Harriman guessed; the binding was identical to the rest of the old calf lining the room. The gold light of an alabaster lamp fell across his chiseled profile and turned it iconic: the face of an Abe Lincoln, minus the beard. A coal fire was burning in the hearth beside him and the small room was an island of quiet. That was like Gil, Harriman thought; he carried an aura of peace and introspection with him wherever he went.

They were profoundly different people. Harriman loved activity, bustle, the center of things. Winant loved the country, a view of hill-sides or dense forest, the quiet of birdsong. And yet he cared deeply about his work in London, Harriman knew; cared about the substance of his responsibilities far more than the fame his job brought him. They were both in their early fifties and their backgrounds were not dissimilar. Harriman had gone to Groton and Yale, Winant to St. Paul's and Princeton. But they attacked life from opposite poles. When Harriman gave Roosevelt advice, he talked tactics and strategy. How to wrestle the most concessions from a crafty opponent. Winant spoke of ideals: the integrity of American actions, and the decency of the world they wrought.

He was a philosopher poet, Harriman thought. And the idea came to him, unbidden: *No wonder he loves Sarah and not Pam.*

Strange, that they were connected by two women in the Churchill family. But even there, they had nothing really in common. Gil, Harriman guessed, had gone off the deep end. Gil was in love.

"What are you reading?" he asked.

"Walden," Winant replied. "For about the fifth time." He closed the book and turned the spine toward Harriman. "Funny how old Henry David comes back to haunt you, even in the oddest of places. A British embassy in the heart of Persia. He'd be embarrassed, probably, to find his maunderings here. This place isn't really his style."

"Nor the company," Harriman replied.

"True." And then, as if the observation naturally led his thoughts to another, Winant said, "I'm sorry about Pamela. I'm glad she's on the mend."

Harriman glanced at his drink. Some of Churchill's considerable supply of Scotch. He took a sip—not for Dutch courage, but to buy an instant. Then his eyelids drooped a little, shuttering his thoughts. It was a characteristic look, one his daughter and Pam would recognize. Ave on the hunt. Ave the predator. There was nothing, really, but Robber Baron blood in his veins.

"She's the reason I've been looking for you." He sat down next to Winant.

Gil dropped the Thoreau on the table beside him and turned slightly toward Harriman, his fingers laced over one knee. "Yes?"

"Pammie said some strange things. When I saw her this morning, at the clinic."

"She wasn't herself," Winant said carefully. "I wouldn't place too much importance on it."

"I have to." Harriman tossed back the remainder of his Scotch with a sigh. "She told me why she tried to kill herself."

Winant's interlaced fingers tensed. Harriman watched the flesh go white, then flush with blood as Gil relaxed.

"You don't think it was an accident?"

"She never suggested it was. She clutched at my hand and said she couldn't face me. That she had no plausible explanation to give."

"Oh, Lord. This isn't about her affair with Ed Murrow?" Winant said.

Harriman went rigid. So that was true. She *had* been two-timing him. He'd suspected as much before he even left London. But once he was safely across Europe—isolated by war and weather in Moscow—she hadn't lost a night's sleep before she'd gone public with her new boyfriend. If Gil knew—Gil, who was so unworldly he'd probably never even been to one of Pamela's famous parties—then the entire world was laughing at Harriman.

But all he said was: "That's not what she was talking about. No. This was about some sort of codebook found in her things. A German one. She said it had been discovered while she was in Cairo and she was going to be accused of spying for the Enemy."

Winant practically gaped at him—like one of those tragedy masks, Harriman thought. "A codebook? Pamela? Are you suggesting she's been . . . that all these months, in Winston's back pocket . . . that the Nazis have been paying her? Jesus."

"No. That's not what I'm suggesting."

Winant waited.

"Pamela says she has no idea how the thing got into her drawer. She says this OSS guy on the trip—Hudson—went snooping and found it there. Never mind what he was doing in Churchill's villa. That's a security breach, to start with. But Pam says the codebook is a plant."

"A plant," Winant repeated.

"To incriminate her."

"Pamela thinks she was framed?"

Harriman nodded slowly. "Do *you* see the girl working for Hitler? Come on, Gil—seriously? Party-girl *Pam*?"

"Nope," Winant replied. "But who would do such a thing? And why?"

Harriman studied him, almost pityingly. "She told me she had a bit of a kickup with Sarah last night. Says the woman hates her."

Winant raised his brows. "They aren't naturally compatible. You know that."

"Pam was a wreck. Said it was a deliberate plot to ruin her marriage and destroy her place in the Churchill family. She's afraid she'll lose Little Winston, even."

"Are you telling me she thinks *Sarah* put the codebook in her room at the villa?"

"And led Hudson straight to it."

"That's preposterous!"

"Is it? Pam's edged Sarah out a bit, wouldn't you say, in Winston's affections?"

"Sarah's his *daughter*, Ave. To Churchill, blood will always be thicker than water."

"Which is probably why Pamela tried to kill herself last night," Harriman said, with mounting frustration. "Think of it—if she were publicly accused of *treason*? In the middle of this war? She'd be burned alive in Piccadilly. Of *course* she took too much chloral at bedtime.

Because you're right, Gil—in any contest between Sarah and Pam, Sarah's the one Winston will believe."

"Maybe Pamela has lied once too many times," Winant said quietly.

"Hell, yes," Harriman agreed. "She's a competent little fibber. But think about it, Gil. Sarah's a WAAF. She works aerial reconnaissance. *Intelligence.* Who else is likely to have access to a German codebook?"

IAN WAS CAREFUL not to startle Grace Cowles. She was halfway down the main hall of the Perfume Sellers Hall, her nose hovering uncertainly above a glass bottle, the stopper held aloft in her right hand. She looked unfailingly English, he thought—not just the neatly pressed uniform and the sensible shoes, but her sleekly controlled hair. That nose, for instance—aquiline as a countess's, from this viewpoint; it might have stepped down from a Gainsborough portrait.

He strolled over and touched Grace's elbow. "What are you sniffing?"

"Attar of roses," she said briskly. "Far too overwhelming for a decent girl. It conjures a French love nest. Very Left Bank."

"This one conjures an opium den," Ian observed, with a flacon to his nose. "What ever happened to bay rum and vetiver?"

"Lilies of the valley for me," Grace said sedately.

"That's exactly what I should have said," he replied. "Which means we'll take the attar of roses."

Arev had exchanged his five-pound note last night in the Money Traders Hall. Ian pulled a hundred rials from his pocket and offered it to the perfume seller.

"How foolish," Grace chided. "I'll never wear it."

"Certainly you will. On your Paris honeymoon." He waited while the seller wrapped the bottle in brown paper. "Don't smash it on your way back to England, mind. Pug will have to torch his plane. Would you like some almond paste?"

"Not at all."

"Coffee, then? Tea?"

"Real tea would be divine."

"I'm sure we can find some version of it."

He mooched along companionably beside her, trying to look for all the world like just another European in Occupied Persia. "Talk to me as we go," he murmured, "in a normal tone of voice. Nobody will give you a second look."

"Turing's wired back."

"And? Does he vouch for me?"

"He's placed the Fencer in Tehran. Says the fellow sent out one coded message last night—to Berlin. Requesting permission to proceed."

"Was it granted?" Ian demanded.

"Yes." Grace's voice was strained. "Turing says Berlin gives the fellow anything he wants."

"Did the Prof get a location? A time?"

She shook her head. "A second message was sent on the same frequency about an hour later. He's not sure where this one went. All it said was: *Long Jump. Operational. Proceed per instructions.*"

That would be for the Nazi paratroopers, of course. A short burst that would be largely undetectable in the greater scheme of Signal things, but for Alan Turing.

"We need details," Ian muttered. "The blow could come at any time. Tell the Prof that he's to drop everything else or Churchill will die."

"I'll tell him. He knows how serious it is. *You're* on the job."

She met Ian's gaze squarely. There would be no more talk of desertion or fiction or insanity or Ismay. "I'd like a fix on the Fencer's location," he said. "Turing couldn't narrow it down closer than Tehran, I suppose?"

Her brows knit. "He said the burst came from the center of the city. Rather near where we are now."

"Did he?" Ian's heartbeat accelerated. The Park Hotel. Where the Americans were staying. The embassy district was too far north.

He should find Hudders and set him to watch his people. But he couldn't walk into the Park and expose himself if the Fencer was staying there. Too risky. Perhaps Grace . . .

"Are you listening to me, Ian?"

"What? Sorry." He turned back to her with a start. She had led him to a tea seller.

"My treat."

Grace held up two fingers to the peddler. "There's something you should know. Your friend Hudson found a German codebook in Pamela Churchill's bedroom. He was stupid enough to avoid normal channels and confront her himself." The tea peddler busied himself with tall glasses. "Pamela tried to kill herself last night. A double dose of chloral."

"Christ," Ian muttered. "I'd have said she was too . . . *invested* in living to pull a stunt like that."

"Funny, isn't it, that one always chooses monetary terms to describe her," Grace observed dispassionately. She handed him a glass of tea. "Don't worry. They found her in time."

"Did Hudders say what kind of codebook it was?"

Grace blew on her steaming drink. "He *showed* it to me. I suppose he thought I'd never accept an accusation like that without proof. It was a simple one-time pad."

"Was there a wireless?"

"Not to my knowledge."

Ian's abdominals clenched. It sounded damning. The bursts from the city center, possibly the Park Hotel, where Pamela had gone last night . . . Pamela's ties to Averell Harriman, a man powerful enough to fence with the world . . . the German codebook Hudson had found in Giza. But Grace had not been informed of all the details. She could not know—Hudson would never have told her—that if Pam were transmitting to Berlin from that room in Churchill's villa, she ought to have been using an Enigma machine. That was the code Turing had broken. A simple one-time pad was anything but proof of guilt.

Carefully, he set down his cup. His mind was racing. "Does Michael know I'm here?"

"I didn't tell him. I haven't told anybody. You said secrecy was vital."

"I did." He leaned toward her impulsively and kissed her cheek. "Nothing so precious as a discreet woman, Grace. Keep mum. I'll talk to Hudson myself. Tell him to find me here as soon as possible, will you?"

CHAPTER 27

He had hoped to present the Sword in the middle of the afternoon, so that the gift would not dominate the dinner hour at the Russian Embassy, but poor Pamela's illness had made a general muck of things and the schedule was unavoidably delayed. The lunch meeting among the three principals had been moved back, so that they gathered at three o'clock to take up the issue of Overlord.

The discussions had not gone well, in Churchill's opinion. Stalin was adamant that the Allied invasion of Western Europe must take place by May, and must be launched from England across the Channel into France. He had no notion how difficult such a seaborne invasion would be—or how brutally the Channel had devoured any army that attempted to cross her. Churchill had argued for the Mediterranean as the point of attack, with a land assault north through the Balkans. But Roosevelt seemed to be leaning toward Stalin's point of view. Roosevelt controlled the main part of the Allied invasion force. And that meant, to Churchill's dismay, the American preference would probably prevail. His personal ability to use England's influence to England's long-term good was failing. He felt outnumbered. Uneasy. Irrelevant.

Roosevelt had drawn him aside at one point that afternoon and whispered to him bluntly: "I'm going to try to get on Uncle Joe's good side, Winston. I know you won't mind if I pretend to be a little hard on you, now and then. It doesn't mean a thing."

Idiotic words, in the midst of a tense and delicate negotiation about the future of a global war. They should have decided beforehand what their joint position would be. But Roosevelt had resisted his attempts to plan. Churchill understood, with desolation in his gut, that Roosevelt had no need to stand with him anymore. Franklin had learned from the past few years—from Churchill's wisdom and long experience. He was ready to cast aside his mentor now, and act alone.

The afternoon talks ended without a decision. Overlord would be raised again tomorrow, and the day after that. But Churchill suspected the decision was already privately made. They would not be attacking through the Balkans.

It was six o'clock, therefore, before the three delegations could be mustered in force, in the Russian Embassy's large conference room—a beautiful elongated oval, rather like a race course, lofty and lined in cypress paneling—for the Sword of Stalingrad.

Honor guards of British and Soviet troops were ranked down both long sides of the room, and a hush prevailed, rather sacred, as though a Holy Relic were about to be unveiled. Stalin stood on a dais with his generals beside him. Lavrentiy Beria, short and solid and grimly bespectacled, hovered behind the Marshal's back. His son, Sergo, was nowhere to be seen.

Churchill was still nursing his voice. He cleared his throat noisily as he waited outside the conference room, and took a nip of whiskey from the flask he carried. He was wearing a dark blue Royal Air Force commodore's uniform. This was a conscious sartorial choice. At the moment he glorified Stalingrad, he intended everyone in the room to remember the RAF boys who had died over the English Channel, vanquishing Hitler's Luftwaffe in the Battle of Britain.

There was a Soviet military band set up somewhere and it had launched into "God Save the King." He lifted his chin and marched ceremoniously into the long room, a lieutenant following him with the Sword. "God Save the King" segued into "The Internationale." Churchill halted before Marshal Stalin, bowed, and took the scabbard from the lieutenant.

"I am commanded to present this Sword of honor as a token of homage of the British people," he said. Homage. Good lord. What a choice of words. As though this man were God. The Press will have a field day.

He placed the Sword firmly in Stalin's outstretched hands.

The Russian pirate let his eyes run the length of the scabbard. Then, to Churchill's surprise, he kissed it and said something in Russian.

"You have the thanks of the Russian people," said his translator, Valentin Berezhkov.

Churchill felt his eyes grow moist. He had been afraid, these last few days, that the entire effort would be for naught—that Stalin would place no value on the gift or the emotion behind it—but he could see, now, that ritual was important everywhere, among Communists and aristocrats alike. How else to elevate the loss and pain of war, if not with the trappings of *glory*? He had always known how to strike the right chord—in speech or gesture—that could render the common-place historic. It was one of his gifts. In the Marlborough blood. A relic, like the Sword, of a vanished power.

Stalin offered the Sword to Roosevelt, who was seated—as he was throughout the public events of this conference—in a straight-backed chair. A bit of theater that preserved the illusion the President could come and go at will. The wheelchair appeared only in the private corridors of the embassy. Stalin was keeping his allies' secrets.

Roosevelt unsheathed the Sword in a debonair fashion, and examined the writing engraved on the blade. "Truly," he said, "they had hearts of steel."

The translator translated. Stalin threw back his head and laughed. Inappropriate, perhaps—but *Stalin* in his native tongue meant *Man of*

Steel. Perhaps he thought Roosevelt was making a pun. Never mind. Roosevelt sheathed the blade and returned it to Stalin.

Which was when it happened. In front of the entire assembly—the gathered members of three delegations, several hundred strong—Stalin turned and casually handed the Sword of Stalingrad to his old friend, Marshal Kliment Voroshilov, who was standing on the dais near him. Voroshilov clutched at the unexpected burden and grasped it upside down. The Sword clattered out of the scabbard and struck his foot, bouncing off the dais to the parquet floor.

There was a gasp—from whom?

A titter, quickly converted to a cough, from the far right of the room.

Churchill flushed to the roots of his hair, glanced at Stalin—who was smiling strangely—and then bent to pick up the trophy. Voroshilov was ahead of him, however, spluttering in his guttural way. He dove for the Sword and the scabbard, clapped them together with unseemly haste, and scurried back to his place on the dais.

And that was that.

Someone in the delegations began to applaud. The band played a Russian folk tune—sad and plaintive. Churchill bowed again, feeling overblown and idiotic. He hoisted himself up onto the dais and bent over Roosevelt's chair.

"That fellow," he said, with a nod toward Voroshilov, "was never trained for cavalry."

"But he's damned good at a stab in the back," Roosevelt murmured.

So he saw Stalin's smile, too, Churchill thought. And flushed, if anything, more deeply.

"SHE HAS RETURNED, that English woman, like a fool in love," Siranoush announced, as she handed Ian a bowl of stew.

He was sitting at Zadiq's conference table, poring over a map. He was famished, but the scent drifting up from the bowl was dispiriting. "Lamb, again."

"With eggplant," she said encouragingly. "It is called *khoresht bademjan,* Arev says, and he gets it from a woman who cooks in the bazaar. You should eat it. I do not know when last you ate."

"But my friend." He set the lamb stew aside and rose. "I must go speak to her."

"If she is a proper woman she will know how to wait." Siranoush sat down with her back to the fire. It turned her tumbled hair to shot silk. "She is an operational risk, Bond. Wandering the bazaar twice today with her nose in a perfume bottle. In her ugly English uniform. There are German agents everywhere in Tehran, and they will see your fool. She draws attention."

"She doesn't realize. Not all of us grew up in the bosom of the NKVD," he said lightly.

To his surprise, Siranoush turned her head as though he had struck her.

"Some of us had no choice," she said.

GRACE WAS looking for him this time, if only out of the corner of her eye. To Ian's practiced gaze she looked self-conscious, too aware of her movements among the perfume bottles, as though she were running through a rehearsal. He glanced around for Hudders in a neighboring aisle, but there was no lanky American in civilian clothes examining spices or walking sticks. He approached her in a leisurely fashion and waited until she had seen him. She smiled perfunctorily.

"How odd that we should meet like this, Commander Bond, twice in one day!" she exclaimed. "Among the perfume sellers, too!"

Siranoush was wrong. Grace had never been a fool. Not even in love.

"Was the attar of roses disappointing?"

"It's lovely, of course," she said, "but I think I shall make a gift of it. I want something fresher for myself—perhaps orange water. I believe it's one of the specialties here."

"Where's Hudson?" he murmured, as he watched her swoop and flutter among the bottles.

"Couldn't come. The PM presented the Sword and the known world was packed like sardines in the neighbor's best room."

"Of course. I'd forgotten about the ceremony." Ian shoved his hands in his pockets with forced ease. "What now?"

"There's a dinner, but Hudson mayn't be going. I'll try to send him here later, but I can't promise. I'm supposed to be on Signals duty. For your Professor. He won't talk to a regular embassy staffer."

"If Hudders can't get away tonight, tell him to try in the morning," Ian said. "In the meantime, tell him to watch Harriman like a hawk."

She stared, a bottle of perfume suspended in midair.

"It can't be too difficult. They're both Americans."

"Harriman?" she repeated. "Because he sleeps with Pam Churchill? By that logic, you could suspect half the men in England."

"Cat," he said.

THE DINNER went from bad to worse.

Only Stalin and his interpreter, Berezhkov, were there to represent the Soviets; Molotov was indisposed. Churchill wondered briefly if he'd eaten the same stuff that had made Roosevelt sick the night before. His bronchitis was so bad he could taste very little and had almost no appetite. He made a show of pushing his food around on his plate and concentrated on the wine, of which there was far too much. They were all half drunk. That would serve Stalin's purposes very well, Churchill thought acidly. Whether he felt outnumbered by his allies or strangely resentful of the ceremony that had just been enacted, the glorious Sword put into his hands, Stalin was vicious this evening. He offered up barbed comments through his interpreter that only the enforced good-will of his guests prevented from being received as insults. He was par-ticularly cruel to Churchill—almost as though by offering the Sword of Stalingrad, the PM had deliberately embarrassed his host, who had nothing to offer England in return.

I am a duke's grandson, Churchill thought, showing up a barbarian warlord from Georgia. I should have known how he would take it.

But he hadn't, and in retaliation Stalin threw his vile pronounce-ments in Churchill's face. *Just because Russians are simple people,* his in-terpreter said blandly, *does not mean that we are blind and stupid as well. We can see what is before our faces.* How to respond? Should he utter a hearty "Of course! Naturally! No one would suggest . . ."

And what on earth was he expected to reply to this? *You nurse a se-cret affection for Germany. You wish to see a soft peace. A negotiated sur-render. You wish your friends to survive with their dignity intact. As for me—I believe that fifty to a hundred thousand German officers of the Commanding Staff must be liquidated . . .*

Liquidated! It was outrageous. Perhaps this was why Molotov was absent; no Foreign Minister worthy of his portfolio could sit by while such despicable jokes were uttered.

Franklin's son Elliott was at dinner this evening—a strange conces-sion, to admit family when military chiefs were absent. He had downed at least four glasses of red wine and his face was beet red. A weak and anxious smile was fixed on his face. "Kill 'em all," he agreed. "The Nazi swine."

Churchill's frown deepened and he reached for his wine, feeling the edge of a black depression knife across his brain. There was no basis for trust in the room. No possibility of *working* with such a man.

Roosevelt was grinning determinedly, as though the conversation were all in jolly good fun. Churchill darted a glance at his old friend over the rim of his wineglass and detected a look he had last seen on the playing fields at Harrow, the sort of expression two bullies share when they're enjoying a joke at a third boy's expense. I'm Third Boy, he thought morosely, and so is England now we've exhausted ourselves in this war. These two will carve up the globe between them and ask us to thank them for it.

"Now, now, Marshal Stalin," Roosevelt cried in the gayest of voices, "surely we can agree to shoot just forty-nine thousand. It looks better if the number's odd."

Stalin made a show of laughing. As though so many more corpses in the tally of carnage was a better tribute than a trumpery sword.

Churchill's rage reached its tipping point.

"Criminals must pay for their crimes," he said furiously, "and so must individuals who commit barbarous acts. But the cold-blooded murder of soldiers who fought courageously for their country will never be tolerated. In accordance with the Moscow document, *which I myself wrote* and both your countries signed, the guilty must stand trial at the place where their crimes were committed. But wholesale slaughter in the name of political expediency? Never!"

He threw down his napkin, pushed back his chair from the table, and stalked from the dining room. Had they forgotten the Moscow Declaration so soon? It had been ratified only a month ago. It outlined a reasoned approach to justice and retribution in the postwar world. Trials, not firing squads. A United Nations, not a witch hunt.

Behind him, he caught the murmur of Stalin's voice. And then his interpreter's.

"You see? He *loves* the Germans who have brought his country to its knees!"

And to his rage and shame, he heard Roosevelt laugh.

CHAPTER 28

*I*t is not enough," Zadiq said.

"Turing is monitoring his transmissions." Ian managed to hold on to his patience. "My friend at the embassy will monitor Turing. We'll know almost as soon as those Nazi paratroopers when and where Long Jump will go off."

"It is not enough."

"Why not?"

Zadiq was looking not at Ian but at his son, Arev. The boy asked something in Armenian and Zadiq answered. Arev shot out of the room.

"We must know the frequency ourselves. We must know immediately when the Fencer communicates. The risk to Iosif Vissarionovich is too great."

"But the Fencer transmits in code," Ian pointed out. "Turing is the only one who's broken it."

"Then he must give us that, too," Zadiq insisted stubbornly.

Ian went very still. So that was the point: The NKVD wanted Bletchley to share its crown jewels. The technology behind Turing's bombes and his cryptanalysis. The breakthroughs made by the Government Code and Cypher School during four brutal years of torpedoed ships and drowning men. The NKVD wanted access to ULTRA—the most secret intelligence Britain had ever known. And Zadiq was the instrument. Playing roulette right now with the British intelligence officer who'd stupidly betrayed Turing to him.

Ian.

The stake? All their lives.

Not just the Big Three, anymore.

His life.

Ian suspected Zadiq had met with Lavrentiy Beria, the NKVD chief, by some secret route of his own. Slipped out of the bowels of the Tehran Bazaar while Ian ate lamb stew with the beguiling Siranoush. Which meant Beria knew everything Ian had shared about Operation Long Jump. He knew the Fencer was one of the Allies. He knew that Churchill and Roosevelt and Stalin would be killed before they all left Tehran. Beria could work with British intelligence to save all three—or he could let the dice fall.

Beria could ignore the Fencer and the Nazi threat.

He might even allow himself to think of a future without Stalin. A Russia where Beria was King.

In the meantime, it would be enough to see what Ian Fleming was worth. How much of ULTRA England would squander, in order to buy his life.

What had his superiors always told him?

Too great a risk to send you into the field. You're too valuable. You know too much.

He understood, now, what they'd really been saying: *We will not barter with your blackmailers.* They would expect him to do the honorable thing—and die by his own hand.

Dulce et decorum est pro patria mori . . .

He watched with sick finality as Zadiq pulled out his Nagant.

"Come," the Armenian said, motioning toward the corridor that led to the turned German agents' cells. "You will walk ahead of me, please."

He could rush Zadiq right there and force him to shoot. Seek the bubble reputation at the cannon's mouth. But it bothered him that no one would ever know. He would simply disappear off the face of the earth. A deserter, in the official record.

A raw wound, in his family's.

Surely, Mr. Bond, you won't take death sitting down?

He would play for time a bit longer.

THE FAKE Russian waiters were good at moving furniture. They'd filled the large conference room with round tables that were hurriedly draped and set with flatware. Chairs for a hundred were placed around them and ashtrays set out. The delegations were dining together tonight, and the Soviet military band continued to play. People milled around, checking place cards. The room was uniformly male, except for Grace Cowles.

She had no intention of eating in the Soviet Embassy. She would be fixed at her post in the Signals Room, desperate for a message from Bletchley. But it was imperative she find Michael Hudson—and he ought to be here. She craned on tiptoe, searching the room, then felt a hand in the small of her back.

Damn him. She never saw him coming.

"Hello," he said. "You're in uniform. Don't tell me you're working?"

"War is hell," she said lightly.

"You must have time for a drink, at least."

She shook her head resolutely. She had to stay sharp for Alan Turing. "But I'd like to talk to you, if you've a moment."

He understood. His gaze briefly searched the oval room and then he touched her elbow. "Let's take a turn around the garden. It's a bit chilly in the dark, but no one will be listening there."

She wondered if he suspected the Soviet Embassy was bugged. She allowed him to weave her through the crowd and out the French doors that lined the far wall. There was a terrace beyond, with a stone balustrade and steps down to the lawn.

"That must have been a ballroom once," she said, as she glanced back at the conference–cum–dining room. For an instant she could imagine it: Women dressed like Anna Karenina. Hussars and diplomats. Candlelight softening the lines on their faces.

"And this used to be a garden," Michael added. "Like Stalin's world used to be Russia. It's only going to get drabber."

The paths were unlit and uninviting; the garden was obviously untended. She hesitated on the scant gravel, shivering.

"Cigarette?"

She waited for him to light it and then let the smoke roll over her tongue and into the Tehran night. "It's about Ian," she said.

"Flem? You've heard from him?"

"I've seen him."

Michael went very still. His expression was suddenly blank. "*Here.* Ian's here?"

"Well, not in the embassy. He's met me in the bazaar. He's wearing civvies and lying doggo, and he's quite definitely absent without leave. He's even using a false name."

"He was ordered back to England."

"He hired a pilot and flew east instead."

Michael swore softly under his breath and inhaled deeply. Their clouds of smoke met and mingled.

"Without telling anyone, Grace? You didn't know his plans? Nobody in the British delegation knew?"

"Nobody. He says he kept mum for security reasons. That if he was *thought* to be safely out of the way, he'd live longer."

"The usual drama." His mouth twisted in a semblance of a smile. She caught the glitter of teeth in the darkness. "He's hunting the Fencer, I suppose?"

"Yes."

"Single-handedly? Pigheaded fool. Why didn't he—"

Michael broke off and dropped his cigarette angrily underfoot, crushing it into the stone.

"Contact you?" Grace reached impulsively for his sleeve. "He is now. That's why we're talking like this."

"And?" he demanded. But his anger had faded.

Grace glanced over her shoulder. The dining party was seating themselves. Golden light spilled through the French doors and left vivid splashes on the garden steps. "Go to the bazaar. The Perfume Sellers Hall. He'll be watching," she said. "Call him Commander Bond when you see him."

"Bond," Michael repeated. "And he wants me now? Tonight?"

"I told him you have the dinner. But it's incredibly urgent, Michael."

"Did he say anything else?"

"And you're to watch Ambassador Harriman like a hawk," Grace said. She still felt uneasy and exposed. As though Stalin himself were listening.

"Am I?" Michael returned ironically. "Flem's up to his old spy tricks again, isn't he? I hope it's worth a court-martial."

Her brow furrowed. Her cigarette had burned down unnoticed; she dropped it hurriedly at her feet. "You still think he's imagining things?"

"Sure. That's what Ian does. Escapes into his fantasy world. I mean, seriously, Grace—*Averell Harriman*?"

"But Pamela's codebook . . ."

"You told him about that?"

She didn't have to admit it. Michael sighed.

"I'll go see him, Grace. But promise me something in return. Stay away from Flem from now on. He'll get you in too deep."

"But—"

"You'll attract too much attention if you keep slipping out to the bazaar. I have a plausible reason to go there—I'm staying at the Park, and nobody will notice if my taxi drops me a few blocks away. If this thing blows up in all our faces, I want you to be in the clear."

Nice of him, she thought. But her uneasiness deepened. The whole conversation was too fantastic, like the attack on Churchill Ian Fleming was convinced would come. She hugged herself suddenly against the garden and all its works.

Was she a fool? Was Ian really mad?

"Should we tell somebody about all this? Pug, or—"

"Not on your life," Hudson said. "Let's go in. You're dying of cold."

CHAPTER 29

They herded Ian at gunpoint down a long and narrow stair, Arev in front and the two Nazi agents behind him, with Zadiq bringing up the rear. Zadiq had placed two of his most trusted subordinates between Ian and the Germans, to prevent them from acting together on a whim. Ian's hands were bound behind him.

Of Siranoush, there was no sign. Would she even be told what they'd done with him? Or would Zadiq say Commander Bond had turned tail and run back to Egypt like a coward?

The staircase ended at a door that led out into an alley. It seemed to be used for donkeys and camels unloading goods in the bowels of the bazaar. There was a nose-curling stench of animal urine, feces, and rotting hay. A truck covered with a tarpaulin completely filled one end of the narrow space.

He was forced into the back of the lorry along with the Germans and two of the NKVD men. It was pitch-black until one of Zadiq's people placed an oil lamp between himself and the edge of the lorry opening. The double doors were then swung closed and bolted from outside.

Ian studied the other four faces. The Germans kept their heads down. The gray-haired one was twitching faintly.

Zadiq and Arev were driving.

Ian thrust his back up against the lorry wall and felt the vibration of the engine roll throughout his body. His hands were going numb. The taut position of his right shoulder blade should have been excruciating. He realized, however, that his knife wound was slowly healing. The thought gave him a flicker of hope.

The lorry lurched and rolled forward.

"Where are we going?" he asked aloud.

Zadiq's men did not answer. But the gray-haired German glanced up at Ian briefly. He understood English. Or perhaps he was simply expecting Ian to speak German, as he had in the man's cell. That gave Ian an idea.

"Wie heißen Sie?" he asked.

"Erich," the other said. *"Und Sie?"*

"James."

"Engländer."

"Yes," he agreed, in the man's tongue. Zadiq's guards failed to react, but they were watching the conversation all the same. "Any idea where we're going?"

Erich shrugged. "I am thinking it is to the safe house. Where we told the paratroopers to come. We will be expected to welcome them so that all looks correct. So they do not suspicion anything."

"You've been there before?"

"But yes." He smiled mirthlessly. "It was my house, you see, before we were taken by these *russische Schweine.*"

Of course. Zadiq had intercepted Erich's communications, tracked where they came from, and arrested him with his partner.

That partner—whose accent had sounded vaguely East European to Ian—was staring at him now. "I thought you were one of them," he said. "Not cattle like us. Maybe you still *are* one of them—put back here to spy. Don't talk to him, Erich. It's a trick."

"I wish it were." Ian studied the man warily. "Where is this safe house of yours?"

"In the southern part of the city." Erich shot his partner a look. "It is nothing, Tomàš. If he were with them, he would know this, already."

Tomàš. The man was Czech. Possibly of Sudeten origin, if he had joined the Nazis. And they were all headed south—farther away from the British Embassy and its targets.

"Do you know when your friends are expected to come down from the hills?"

"We were told to say 2200."

"Erich!" hissed Tomàš. "Shut up, you fool!"

"He would know," Erich repeated patiently. "If he is one of them, I am telling nothing of importance. And if he is not—still I am telling nothing. We gave them directions. Bona fides. They will not suspect."

His voice died away on these last few words, and he dropped his head again. Erich obviously was haunted by his multiple betrayals. At the way he was saving himself, by luring these men to their deaths.

War is bloody, Ian thought. But he felt a distaste for Tomàš and Erich, regardless. They probably had thought it would be easy to sell a few secrets to Zadiq. Play both sides of the field. Wait for the Germans or the Russians to come out on top. They were agents in Occupied Persia, after all—and anyone with a secret to sell was a fool not to seek the highest bidder.

But this couldn't be easy.

It was cold-blooded murder.

And they didn't have the comfort of viewing the paratroopers as enemies. Like Ian did.

He turned his head slightly and studied the most vigilant of the NKVD escort. He was slightly older than the boy Arev—in his twenties, perhaps—with closely cropped black hair and a nose that had been frequently broken. His left fingers were stained yellow by nicotine, but his gun barely wavered in his right hand, despite the lurching lorry. He'd let Ian and Erich talk freely. Which meant he wanted to hear what they had to say.

There are three of you and only two of them. When the lorry stops, 007, kick out with your legs and smash the oil lamp. Utter darkness. Flame, perhaps, on the NKVD agent's leg. He's shrieking. His men are fighting. Your hands aren't free, but your head is. Use your weight and height. Use your skull if you must. When the door is unbolted, leap out into Zadiq's face.

And then?

He'd be shot to death.

Or he'd hobble away into an unknown part of the city, an obviously escaped prisoner with no Farsi to his name. He'd be arrested and eventually turned over to the British Embassy, if he lived so long.

Roll the dice either way, he'd be shut out of Zadiq's plans. No paratroopers. No idea when the Fencer meant to kill Churchill and the others.

Unacceptable.

He leaned back against the lorry wall and closed his eyes.

SIRANOUSH HAD washed her hair and dressed carefully for this meeting. She was wearing a frock she'd admired in Cairo; Nazir had bought it and given it to her as a gift. It was silk and very dear—silk was almost impossible to obtain, now that there was war. Except for a dealer in precious antiquities. A man who knew the value of every material that came under his hand. A man who knew how to haggle for what was precious.

Nazir had haggled for her, she thought, as he might have for a fragment of Nefertiti's head unearthed in the Egyptian sand. She had never been his granddaughter and he knew nothing really about her, but he had found her in the NKVD camp in Yerevan, a scrawny orphan of fourteen, and coveted her like the collector he was. Like a man with an eye for perfection.

He had given her a new name once he bought her. *Siranoush.* It meant *Creature of Beauty* in Armenian.

She could barely remember being anyone else.

She thought of the old man now with vague nostalgia and not a little hatred. As was true of some connoisseurs, Nazir was inclined to peculiar tastes. Siranoush had fulfilled all of them. Fantasies. Crudities. He had enjoyed each infinitesimal variation, and had enjoyed most, perhaps, the perversions from which he rescued her himself. The time he had tied her wrists and ankles to a bed in a suite at Shepheard's Hotel, and then sent a series of strangers in to ravish her. The time he had sold her in a game of cards to a man whose throat he cut just at climax. He liked to think of himself as God: Creator, Seducer, Rapist, and Savior.

Father, Son, Virgin, and Holy Ghost.

She was glad he was dead.

But she wondered, now, if she still existed.

Without the old man's eyes on her, she felt increasingly invisible. Remote behind opaque glass, beating her hands to break out.

She smoothed the silk over her hips and sighed. Then she bit her lips to bring color to the flesh—strange, how pain animated everything—and went down into the bazaar.

MICHAEL HUDSON idled among the perfume bottles. Grace had said the Perfume Hall—he was sure of it. But maybe she was smarter than he thought. Maybe she'd lied to him on purpose.

He thought fleetingly of the earnest face, drowning in the dusk of the Soviet garden. No. Gracie didn't lie.

He smiled faintly as he considered her. She wore her heart on her sleeve. He excited her—in ways she couldn't fathom, and probably couldn't trust. And so she said more than she should. She'd told him Ian was operating alone and was in civilian clothes. Nobody from the embassy behind him. He was out on a wire, teetering above the ground, and the slightest push would send him plummeting to earth.

Michael had known Ian long enough to appreciate his uncanny grace. His extraordinary luck. His facile charm. He could slip through fingers, balance on any tightrope, land on his feet like a cat. But there was a limit to nine lives.

Michael needed to find Ian. Before he hurt himself or anyone else.

Commander Fleming ought to be watching the bazaar right now. All Hudson had to do was show up. Look obvious. Wait for Ian to stroll over and say: *I told you Averell Harriman was a wrong'un from the start.*

Only it was not Ian whose heels were clicking swiftly toward him across the ancient mosaic floors. With the sixth sense of the born spy, he turned just as the girl launched herself into his arms.

"Darling!" she cried, kissing him full on the mouth.

He was aware of a ripe body pressing against his. His groin surged to life. He stared dazedly into the flowerlike face hovering beneath his own.

"It's been so long!" she breathed. "And I've been so lonely. Tell me you've *missed* your Siranoush!"

HE TOOK HER out to the street and began walking, aimlessly, toward the Shah's empty palace. She stared straight ahead, the darkness punctuated by passing lights, her face sporadically illuminated. Her hair was a river of platinum. She was a magnificent creature, Hudson thought. And totally uncontrollable. He would have to work carefully.

"Siranoush," he said aloud, savoring the word. "Don't you think it was ill advised to approach me in such a public place, in such a headlong manner? I enjoyed it immensely—don't get me wrong, but—"

"I do not understand this *headlong*," she said impatiently. "You are looking for Bond, yes?"

"You know him?"

"We made contact in Cairo. The night he was attacked. You knew he was attacked, yes?"

"I heard. Eventually. Also that he was ordered to return home."

"He flew with me to Tehran instead."

"He *would*." Hudson pressed his fingers against his eyes, feeling a dull throb of pain at his temples. "Military transport would never do—it'd have to be hot and cold running blondes. Have you been with him ever since?"

She shrugged dismissively. "He was taken away tonight. By my people."

"Taken? Where?"

"I do not know. They no longer trust me."

"Because you've been with . . . Bond?" he guessed. "You're tainted by association?"

She gave a little shrug, her eyes still not meeting his. "It is not important. What matters is that you find him."

"I thought we were all supposed to be Allies," he muttered in frustration. "What do *your people* want with my friend?"

"Something to do with codes. Intercepts."

Turing, he thought. "German codes?"

"Probably." She glanced at him. "I do not think they mean to kill Bond. Not yet. But they will hurt him until he gives them what they want. And then . . . They took two German agents, too. Radio operators."

"Why?"

"Long Jump," she said. "They are to ambush a group of paratroopers who have been hiding in the hills."

Hudson's brows shot up. "And these Nazis have no idea their friends have been turned. So tonight . . ."

"The German radio operators will lure six men to their deaths. In order to save your President's life."

Hudson laughed brusquely. "So *your people,* as you call them, have known all along where the last few commandos were. Not exactly the briefing Molotov gave us. Just goes to show. Never trust a Russian."

"Then it is just as well I am Armenian." She flashed a rare smile. "Bond thinks Stalin and the others will die, whether we trap the paratroopers or not. He is sure the Fencer will go ahead with his plan—he is a member of the delegations, and has perfect access to his targets. How can he fail?"

"It'd be a first," Hudson admitted.

If he was startled by her casual use of a code name few people knew, he did not betray it. "Why was Bond taken prisoner tonight? He's no threat to *your people.*"

"A disagreement. Bond wants to use the paratroopers as bait. Let them launch their operation—and follow them to the real leader."

"The Fencer." How like Flem, Hudson thought. Ian had stumbled stupidly into a snare—and nobody in his chain of command had any idea where he was. He'd made himself a hostage. He was a liability to Britain now. Whether he divulged anything about Turing or the codes Siranoush had mentioned, Naval Intelligence would cut him loose.

Unless Ian could pull off the impossible.

Trap the Fencer. Save three critical lives.

They had reached the empty gardens of Golestan Palace, and Hudson's feet slowed. Should he tell somebody at the British Embassy what he knew—or keep Ian's secrets?

"He has courage, this Bond," the girl said with a trace of wistfulness. "But he is naïve. It is very English, yes? To be forever the schoolboy?"

"It is." Hudson grasped her arm. In her frail silk dress, she was shuddering with the November cold. And something else. Fear?

"Don't worry," he said. "I'll find him."

THE GERMAN named Erich was passive, Ian knew—he seemed to accept his fate as the lorry rolled to a stop in the darkness. But it surprised him that the Czech, Tomàš, was equally resigned. Tomàš was younger. More impassioned. A truer believer, Ian guessed, in Hitler's cause. If anybody was going to be a hero tonight, it would be Tomàš. But as the heavy steel doors were unbolted by unseen hands, the Czech merely studied the lorry floor. One of the guards had forced him to kneel, hands bound behind his back.

The other guard had his gun trained on Ian.

The doors swung open. Arev's pinched face, peering above the edge, and Zadiq behind him. His Nagant covered all of them.

"Aussteigen," Arev barked. Get out.

Tomàš was hauled to his feet and forced to descend. Then it was Ian's turn. He thrust himself upright by levering his bound hands against the lorry wall; he refused to be tossed around like a swaddled baby. A maniac in a straitjacket.

A helpless hostage.

He moved at a crouch toward the lorry opening. He could see very little of the street beyond; the southern part of the city was generally impoverished, the houses small and leaning together along fetid alleyways. There was a strong smell of cat. A hand grasped his left shoulder; he was pulled off the lorry and landed hard, on his left side, on the ground. It was unpaved mud, wet and stinking against his cheek. Someone kicked him in the ass. He tried to roll to his feet and was hauled upright, struggling. They would fight his impulse toward self-sufficiency as soundly as open rebellion.

He was hustled a short distance through a door. Tomàš was standing in what looked like a kitchen, head bowed, Zadiq a few paces away. Behind Zadiq was the welling blackness of a doorway; the only light in the room was from the head guard's oil lamp. Ian was thrust toward the kitchen table and stumbled into it. Arev or one of the guards had pushed him, and he wondered, idly, if they hated him because he was English, or because of Siranoush?

Where was she now?

Erich jostled him and fell heavily onto the table.

"Warten Sie," he breathed.

Wait.

Ian did not betray that he had heard.

The door of the safe house closed behind them.

And at that moment, a face loomed out of the darkened doorway behind Zadiq and a rifle was punched forcefully into his back.

On impulse, Ian shoved himself sideways and felt Arev tumble to the floor. Swearing in Armenian.

Tomàš slammed his skull into the nearest guard's nose. The man fell back, howling in pain. And there were other faces now, rolling through the doorway, bodies in field dress and helmets with rifles raised.

Nazi paratroopers.

"Lassen Sie Ihre Waffe," one of them commanded.

Zadiq dropped his gun. His black eyes glittered and his teeth were bared in a grimace. He was not the kind, Ian thought, to go quietly.

"Your friends?" he murmured to Erich.

"Ja. We were supposed to tell them to be here at 2200 hours. But we told them twenty-one. We thought they would like time to prepare."

His voice held the satisfaction of a simple man.

CHAPTER 30

When he was finally able to slip away from the formal dinner, Elliott Roosevelt was lucky to find a phalanx of taxis pulled up before the diplomatic compound's guardhouse. He'd excused himself from his father's table with the idea that he was bound for the men's room. Franklin had probably lost sight of him immediately in the crowd surging through the Soviet ballroom. The President would be closeted again that evening with Stalin and Churchill. Elliott figured he had a few hours before he'd be missed.

He was sweating freely despite the bone-chilling cold. He'd drunk too much. Once he'd settled himself in the taxi and directed the driver to the Park, the warmth of the car made his skin clammy to the touch. Coffee was what he needed. But the thought of it made him sick.

It was his wretched nerves, Elliott thought, that were upsetting his stomach and making him drink so much. May-ling had rattled him badly last night. He'd been forced to pick her up off his lap and set her squarely on her feet, facing him. *I can't marry you, Madame Chiang,* he'd said with a terrifying sense of entrapment, *because both of us are already married.*

He made no mention of his pending divorce. The last thing Elliott Roosevelt wanted was a crazy Chinese prima donna clinging to his arm as he flew out of Tehran. May-ling was beautiful, sure—but she wasn't much of a sport. Too refined. And too . . . Christ, too foreign! He'd spent the past few years building his chops as a war hero, and right as he was set to cash in on the deal, he'd be ostracized for marrying outside of his kind. Nossir Bob, that wasn't Elliott Roosevelt's plan. Nosiree.

To do her credit, May-ling was all cut up about the idea of a divorce. She bowed her perfectly molded head and dropped her almond-shaped eyes. She spoke of the dearness of her Methodist faith and the shame such a scandal would visit on her family. Elliott guessed it'd be no picnic for *her* to marry outside of her kind, either. Which was when he saw a glimmer of hope.

"If I tell the Generalissimo that you were nothing but a perfect lady in my company," he suggested, "maybe he'll take you back."

She had glanced at him wistfully and shaken her head. "Chiang has been dishonored. Merely your word cannot change that."

Jesus, he thought. The guy's not gonna want to fight me, is he? Make a hell of a headline back in the States.

Elliott's taxi pulled up beneath the lighted portico of the Park Hotel. He could assume that most of the American delegation was still working their way back from the Soviet dinner, but nonetheless he made a point of keeping his head down as he entered the foyer. His pulse was throbbing painfully, and he was afraid, for an instant, that he might throw up. Despite his best instincts, he veered away from the elevator and into the bar.

"Coffee," he said tersely. "Black."

It was scalding. He downed the cup in two gulps, anyway, and felt immediate relief.

Better seize the bull by the horns, he thought, before this wears off.

MAY-LING WAS FULLY DRESSED TONIGHT, and her maid opened the door to Elliott. She did not efface herself as she had last evening, and May-ling did not order her to go. The sitting room was filled with bandboxes and hats waiting to be packed into them; with Vuitton trucks compartmented for shoes; with handbags lying carelessly on chairs; and dresses cascading across the sofa. There was nowhere to sit.

So Elliott stood, swaying slightly, as May-ling studied the floor. Her role was to oversee the packing; it was the maid whose hands busily fluttered among the cashmere sweaters and silk cheongsams.

"You're leaving," he said.

She shrugged exquisitely. "You gave me no choice. Having shamed my husband, I am now an embarrassment to *you*."

"Gosh, I'm sorry, May-ling. I never meant to—"

"That is immaterial."

She would not meet his eyes. Elliott felt like a worm. "Where will you go?"

"To Shanxi."

"Where's that?"

"*China.*" Her voice was scathing; it was clear she regarded Elliott as worse than hopeless. "The Red Army headquarters is there. I will give myself up to Mao Zedong."

Elliott stepped toward her impulsively. "You can't mean that! It's madness for a woman like you . . . Mao is your husband's enemy."

"You know that?" At last she raised her eyes to his. "I thought you Americans believed this nonsense about our *united front* against the Japanese."

"The Communists will torture you," he said hoarsely. "They'll want to know every last thing about Chiang's military structure and the Kuomintang's movements in western China, the Generalissimo's plans for Mao once the war's over . . ."

"Then perhaps Chiang will come for me," she said simply.

Elliott stared at her, aghast. "*That's* your plan? To give yourself up to the Enemy, so your husband will dash to the rescue?"

"He will not want me to tell Mao what I know. Chiang understands the value of information."

Elliott ran his hands over his face. He was feeling clammy and sick again. He wished he could sit down.

"If I could bring him some information," May-ling murmured, with that same wistful air, "some priceless piece of news he could never learn elsewhere—it is possible he might forgive me. I might save myself."

Chiang understands the value of . . .

"May-ling."

"Yes, Colonel?"

"The Generalissimo wasn't invited to this Tehran Conference . . ."

"That is correct. Only Cairo."

". . . because the conference is not about the Pacific War. It's about Europe."

She looked bewildered. "Why do you tell me this, Colonel?"

"Stalin wants the Allies to open a second front against the Germans. He wants us to invade Europe in the next six months. Would Chiang be interested in information about that?"

"I do not know," she murmured.

"If I told you the place and time we're going to attack, would he take you back?"

May-ling frowned. "How could you know such a thing?"

"Because my father's deciding when and where the invasion happens," he retorted. "Nothing will be decided without his say-so. He commands most of the troops. And once the war in Europe is over, those troops can help Chiang get rid of the Japanese—before Mao does it for him."

"That is true," she admitted. "He would give much, I think, to know of this invasion."

"If I tell you about it—will you give up this crazy idea of turning yourself in to the Reds? Will you go home to your husband?"

She bowed her head submissively. "Yes, Elliott. I will."

He glanced at the maid. "Send the girl away."

May-ling spoke a few sharp words to the maid in Chinese.

Elliott shifted a pile of handbags and sank down onto a chair. He mopped his face with a white linen handkerchief his mother, Eleanor, had embroidered with his initials. He waited until the bedroom door closed behind the girl.

"Now, listen, May-ling. The invasion is set for the middle of May. We're going to launch it from the Adriatic, with the full Allied force driving north through Yugoslavia . . ."

CHAPTER 31

The call from Turing came through at one twenty-six a.m.

Grace had fallen asleep in the embassy's Signals Room with her head lying on her arm. Nearby, an ashtray overflowed with half-smoked cigarettes. She had sent the usual diplomatic operators home when she'd taken over at eight p.m., telling them it was a special case. War business. Now the building was silent and the room was chilly. When the persistent ring of the Secraphone roused her, she discovered that her arm had gone numb. She forced herself upright, shaking the tingling limb, and reached for the green receiver with her other hand.

"Emb-b-b-bassy Tehran?" The voice was tinny and howling, like a gramophone played through a cyclone.

"Speaking."

"Turing here. For Grace C-C-C-Cowles."

"Go ahead, Mr. Turing."

"No news, I'm afraid," he said without preamble. "The whole b-b-bloody channel's gone silent."

"Does that mean . . . the operation is under way—or that it has been called off?"

"Means they're not b-b-bloody talking about it."

Grace hesitated, at a loss. She must ask the Prof *something* while she had him on the line. "Did you find out where that second burst went? The one that wasn't for Berlin?"

"I t-t-told you. Channel's *dead*."

Then so is Churchill, she thought despairingly. "You'll call if anything changes?"

"Won't. Fellow's g-g-got the wind up. Tell Fleming g-g-good luck."

"Thank you," she said, but he had already rung off. She stared blankly at the Secraphone in her hand.

She had no news, no hope, to give to Ian. How could she tell him that even Turing had failed?

Was the Fencer's sudden silence, Grace wondered, the result of Pam Churchill's suicide attempt? The British Embassy had made every effort to camouflage Mrs. Randolph's illness, but whispers had circulated. If the Fencer truly was a member of either the American or British delegations—and if Pam was working with him—he would know she had lost her nerve. He'd wonder what she'd confessed. He'd feel hunted, on his guard. And more likely to act as soon as possible.

Or, Grace thought with a sudden chill, what if *Pamela herself* is the Fencer? And when Michael confronted her, she tried to take the easy way out?

That might mean that Operation Long Jump was called off.

She needed to talk to Michael. He must have met with Ian by this time. Why hadn't he called? Now it would have to wait until morning.

Morning. When the three men most worth saving could be riddled with machine-gun fire.

Grace shivered, and took herself off to bed.

DAY SIX

TEHRAN

Tuesday,
November 30, 1943

arah Oliver was finishing her breakfast in the embassy's morning room when Pamela appeared in the doorway. Her face was pallid beneath her hat, despite the distracting wisp of black veil that swept over her eyes. She wore no lipstick. Sarah had never seen her without it before, and the absence of color seemed to magnify her drained appearance, as though Pamela were a watercolor sketch someone had left out in the rain.

"You've been discharged! Thank heaven," she said, by way of greeting. "Would you like some tea? Shall I ring for another cup?"

"No, thank you," Pamela said. "You might put something in it— and then everyone would think I was mad again."

"I?" Sarah frowned at her. "Why should I put anything in your tea? You don't even take sugar."

"No. I don't. I'm very careful about what I take. Regardless of what some people say." She deliberately drew off her gloves, her gaze fixed not on Sarah but on her fingertips. "I am exceedingly careful about my things, too. I always know what's supposed to be in my drawers and what isn't. But you couldn't have known that, Sarah. We've never really known each other, have we? No matter how many homes we share. I suppose that's why you did this. You feel justified in hating me."

Sarah set down her tea. Her hands were controlled, but still the china gave off a faint ring as the saucer met the cup. "What are you talking about, Pamela?"

"I think you know."

"I assure you, I don't."

"Ave hasn't mentioned it?"

Sarah rose and walked toward her. Pam stood rigidly in the doorway, still swathed in her fur coat. "Are you all right? Do you need to lie down?"

"And take another dose to make me sleep?" Pamela suggested mockingly. "No. I've slept enough. I need a public apology, Sarah. I need you to tell Papa that you lied. That I would never betray him or England. Then I need to get the hell out of this *wretched* country."

She turned and groped her way almost blindly into the hall. Sarah watched Pamela mount the stairs and disappear from view. Then she hurried across the foyer to the opposite wing of the embassy, where the official conference rooms were. Gil Winant would be in one of them.

"I KNOW you are adamant in believing the assault must come from across the Channel and strike at the heart of France," Churchill was saying, as he stood by the conference room window. "But there are so many competing alternatives! We might sap the Germans' strength by forcing the Italian campaign on to Rome! Or *compel* Turkey to enter the war! We might blockade or seize the islands of the Aegean! Only consider, Franklin—that archipelago taken, we might open transport lines through the Dardanelles and Black Sea into Russia itself!"

"We're not invading Russia," Roosevelt said, "and as I recall, the Dardanelles were an Allied grave once already."

Churchill's shoulders hunched a trifle. He *had* been the architect of military disaster at Gallipoli during the First World War. But the essential strategy even then had been correct. He refused to pick up

Roosevelt's bait. "That part of the world secured, we might then make forays across the Adriatic, to aid Tito and his partisans in Yugoslavia. Or send an expedition to the Adriatic's head—and march north through the Ljubljana Gap and on to southeastern Hungary. Good God, man—the Nazis would not know where to fight us off first!"

"If we spread ourselves too thin, and start brushfires all over the map, the Nazis will beat us with one hand behind their backs. Remember: I've got a hell of a war going on, myself, all over the Pacific. I can't throw men and arms across Europe, too. This effort has to be focused and forceful, Winston. It has to end Hitler."

Churchill was silent; he knew as well as Roosevelt that a massive assault across the Channel into France would require the concentration of forces and matériel. If the blow was struck, it must be struck hard. But—

"Uncle Joe wants us to draw as much of the German Army as possible away from the Eastern Front," Roosevelt went on. "He wants Overlord. Overlord as it was outlined at last month's Moscow Conference. And he wants it launched as soon as possible."

"I fail to comprehend why *all* alternatives are unworthy of consideration." Churchill knew he sounded peevish; was it his cold, or his unhappiness? "At the very least, such joint operations as I've suggested might pave the way for Overlord. Ensure our success when once we breach the Channel defenses in Normandy. And that need not be so soon as May. It might well be . . . next year, perhaps."

"It worries you, doesn't it? Going back into France?"

Churchill shot Roosevelt a look. The man had never seen an entire army pulled off a French beach by a flotilla of simple fishing boats. He'd never watched the flower of his generation—good men, blood brothers like Val Fleming—die useless deaths in French mud. Churchill would willingly stand alone before a German firing squad, rather than consign an army to trench warfare again.

"You told me in October," Roosevelt persisted, "that the Germans were building guided missile launch sites in Pas de Calais and the Cherbourg Peninsula."

"Yes. Rockets capable of striking London."

Roosevelt pulled his cigarette holder from between his teeth and exhaled a cloud of smoke. "Don't you want to get your boys over there and beat the crap out of them?"

Churchill turned away and stared bleakly through the window. "And who is to command this Overlord?" he inquired. "Your man, I suppose?"

"SHE WAS accusing me of something, Gil."

Sarah and Winant were standing together in the small library where he'd talked to Harriman the previous day. Winant was reading a different book this morning, but the view and the peace were the same.

"One of our fellas searched her room." He raised his hand placatingly as Sarah began to protest. "Don't ask me why. I'm not in the OSS chain of command. But he must have followed a damn good hunch, because he found what he was looking for. Pammie had a German codebook in her drawers."

"That's absurd," Sarah retorted. "Pamela? A spy?"

"She denies it, too," Winant said drily. "She told Ave you must have put it there. To get her in hot water."

Sarah took a step backward. "Hot water? That's *treason*, Gil. She could be . . . tried for that. She could be . . ."

"Executed," he agreed. "Make a hell of a splash, wouldn't it?"

"I'd never do such a thing."

"I know."

"But Ave believes it?"

"If blaming you puts Pamela in the clear? Sure. He'll give it a thought."

She sank down onto the sofa. Winant sat next to her. Sarah stared at her knees, brow furrowed. "She must truly think I hate her."

"Don't you?"

"Not in that way. Not to see her killed. But there's something else, Gil. We assumed she'd tried to end it all yesterday, with that dose of chloral. It didn't make sense at the time. It makes even less now."

"Ave thought she couldn't face the music."

"Nonsense. Pamela's as tough as nails. She as much as accused me just now of murder—all sorts of insinuations about putting things in her drink. Which means, Gil, that *she didn't do it*. Someone else gave her more than she wanted."

"In her own tooth glass?"

Winant sounded skeptical.

"It's not as though she's alone in her bedroom very often," Sarah snapped. "But that's not what I meant to suggest. I think she took her usual bedtime dose from the bottle on her nightstand—but it was a *second* dose. Someone had given her a first. Without her being aware. Perhaps in a drink. Something that disguised the taste."

"Champagne," Winant said. "She's generally got a glass in her hand."

Sarah's head lifted. "She went out that night. After I quarreled with her."

"Drinking?"

"In the Park Hotel bar."

Winant moved swiftly, Sarah following, from the small study at the rear of the embassy to the wide foyer at the front entrance. A porter sat there, on guard, as he always did.

"Excuse me," Winant said in his usual self-effacing way, "were you on duty here two nights ago, by any chance?"

The porter looked from Winant to Sarah, standing behind him. The Prime Minister's daughter. A slightly scared expression crossed his face; he was, Sarah thought, probably little more than eighteen.

"No sir, Mr. Ambassador, sir, I was not."

"It's all right, Perkins," Sarah said. "We wondered if anyone saw Mrs. Randolph Churchill when she returned that evening."

Perkins's expression eased. He reached for a telephone in a cubby set into the wall by his station. "I'll just ask in the mess, shall I?"

They waited out the murmur of conversation.

Perkins replaced the receiver. "It was Morrow, ma'am, who helped Mrs. Randolph out of her cab."

Winant's eyes narrowed. "Did she *need* help?"

"I couldn't say, sir. Morrow will be out directly to speak with you."

Morrow was older and tougher-looking than Perkins, but he flushed scarlet when Sarah asked him about Pamela.

"Sound asleep like a baby in the backseat of the car," he said. "I had to shake her. Meaning no disrespect. I'd never have touched her, ma'am—knowing it to be a liberty—if she hadn't been so hard to rouse. Paid off the cab and helped the lady up the stairs, I did—all the way to her room. Though I'm not supposed to desert my station. I didn't think she'd make it there, otherwise."

"Thank you, Morrow. I'll repay you for the cab fare."

"That isn't necessary, ma'am." He went, if anything, redder. "It's an honor to do for one of the Churchills."

"All the same—" Sarah broke off, and turned to Gil. His hand was extended, carefully official for the watching porters. "I'll say goodbye now, Mrs. Oliver. Thank you for your hospitality."

Her brows knit faintly. "You have an appointment, Mr. Winant?"

"At the Park Hotel. And there's no time to waste."

CHAPTER 33

*I*an was lying in the fetal position on the floor of the German safe house. He'd been bound and gagged and thrown into a windowless storeroom. Eight inches from his face were the staring eyes of the NKVD operative who'd trained a gun on him in the lorry so unwaveringly last night—the one who'd kept the oil lamp upright while he listened to Erich and Ian talk. There was a large and ragged hole in his chest where the paratroopers' bullets had torn away the flesh around his heart. The storeroom was dark, but Ian could still make out the gleam of the man's dead eyes and the stench of his blood.

He had not slept. The noise from the far side of the wall—the main room where Zadiq was forced to watch his son be tortured during the long hours of the night—made the idea of sleep obscene.

Ian tried to inch away from the corpse, but his limbs were too numb. He was as heavy and useless as a beef carcass suspended from a butcher's hook.

Zadiq was sobbing now. Exhausted words spewed out in English and Armenian. Did the bastards realize he didn't speak German? That the brutalities they were practicing on Arev could never force his father to confess in a language they would understand?

And then he heard Erich's voice. The German agent was foolish enough to try to intervene. Ian hadn't heard him or his partner Tomàš in hours. Had they been sent out of the safe house?

Had they met up with the Fencer?

His blood quickened suddenly at the thought. Then his excitement died. If the paratroopers could contact their Nazi handler without the use of a radio, there was nothing for Alan Turing to intercept. Nothing for Gracie to report. Nothing that might spur a hunt for a missing Commander Fleming.

Your prospects for survival were always dim, Mr. Bond.

It was possible that Zadiq would have killed him in the end; but it was certain the Nazis would.

He heard the tramp of booted feet cross the uncarpeted lino floor. The storeroom door was pulled open. The searing stream of daylight hurt his eyes. He squeezed them shut, gagged mouth in a rictus.

He was hauled to his feet, which failed to support him. He fell to his knees and toppled sideways onto the Armenian's corpse. Two men lifted him now and dragged him passively from the storeroom and into the normalcy of a November morning. He cracked his eyelids, willing himself to endure the light and take in the scene. Three of the paratroopers were seated at the kitchen table. One of them had made coffee, but there did not seem to be much food shared between them. Their helmets were off and their rifles were stacked on the floor nearby.

Arev was suspended by his wrists from a ceiling rafter. His hands were bent at a bizarre angle, as though the wrists were broken. He was naked, and strips of his skin had been flayed from his buttocks, his ribs, his groin, and his face. Ian slipped on a wad of flesh discarded on the floor and saw too late that he had trod on Arev's scrotum. The boy had been castrated during the night. Gouts of blood trailed down his legs.

Ian glanced at Arev's face. The painful thinness of the skull seemed unspeakably poignant now—because it screamed of his youth. All the years he had yet to grow. Ian saw that he was either dead or unconscious. The paratroopers seemed indifferent to the boy now, so perhaps Zadiq had given them something they valued.

Ian looked around for the NKVD leader.

Zadiq, too, was naked.

He was seated awkwardly in a kitchen chair whose seat had been hacked out, so that his genitals dangled through the hole. His legs were tied to the chair legs, and his arms were stretched behind him and tied to the chair back. Ian could see the strain in his shoulders and the hideous vulnerability of everything else. The hair on the man's chest was grayish white, sparse, pathetically aged. Zadiq's head was hanging and he did not lift it as Ian was dragged across the room.

One of the paratroopers—Ian thought it was the first he'd glimpsed last night, an apparition with a gun in the darkened doorway—held a length of chicken wire in his right hand, the kind used for temporary fences in the field. It was tacked to a piece of wood maybe eighteen inches long, a sort of makeshift paddle. As Ian watched, the paratrooper swung it sharply under Zadiq's chair. The chicken wire tore at the man's dangling genitals. Zadiq screamed.

There was a second chair near the NKVD commander. The bottom had been hacked out of it, too. Ian guessed sickly who it was for.

He'd regained enough use in his legs and arms to struggle, at least, when they began to tear off his clothes.

"Ambassador Winant! It is an honor, sir, to welcome you here."

Abolhassan Diba rose from his chair behind the handsome pear-wood desk and offered his hand. He spoke French—almost his first language, Winant guessed. He knew very little about the Iranian business magnate, other than that he had been educated, like so many aristocratic Persians, in Switzerland and France.

French was the universal diplomatic language. Out of courtesy, Winant fell into it immediately.

"The honor is all mine, sir. To receive me without proper notice—no appointment—"

"It is nothing," Diba said. "Please—if you would consent to take a seat."

Winant had tracked his elusive quarry from the Park Hotel—which Diba owned, but only frequented at meals or during the evening night-club hours—to this office building a few blocks to the north and west. At six stories, it was one of the highest buildings in Tehran, and Winant was surprised to see an elevator waiting in the lobby. They were rare in Persia. The lift operator informed him that Diba had been the first entrepreneur to bring them from Europe to his country.

"I hope you are finding the Park Hotel comfortable, Ambassador?" the man inquired politely.

"Perfectly. It's a lovely place."

"You have everything you require?"

"And more." Winant clasped his hands over his knee, a characteristic gesture. "I regret that I have been able to spend so little time in your beautiful establishment. But the duties of the conference . . ."

"I understand. Perhaps when this dreadful war is over, you will pay a visit to Iran solely for pleasure."

"I hope I may. But it is about the conference that I have come to speak to you this morning," Winant said. "I am presently serving as ambassador to Great Britain. I divide my time in Tehran between President Roosevelt and the British Embassy, consulting with Prime Minister Churchill. Are you aware, Mr. Diba, that the Prime Minister brought several members of his family with him?"

An expression of hauteur descended on the handsome face; the black brows lifted imperiously. The French became, if possible, more formal and florid. "I am. I had the very great pleasure of making the acquaintance of Mrs. Randolph Churchill a few evenings ago. I shall not soon forget so divine an experience."

My God, Winant thought. He thinks I'm an asshole. That I'm here to tell him no Persian should presume to talk up a lady like Pamela.

There's diplomacy, for you.

"I'm relieved to hear it," he said, with conscious warmth. "You may be of immeasurable service to the government of Great Britain, Mr. Diba—and to the Churchill family."

"If I may assist you in any way—"

Winant summoned his most respectful French. "You are undoubtedly unaware that Mrs. Randolph Churchill has been decidedly unwell in recent days. In fact, those closest to her fear that she has been deliberately poisoned."

"Ambassador Winant, I hope you are not suggesting—"

"Not by anyone at your magnificent hotel, of course," Winant added, with a placating gesture. "But perhaps by . . . someone she encountered there."

"I am desolated to hear of it," Diba returned. He rose from his chair and came around the pearwood desk. His hands were folded behind his back, and he began to pace before the electric fire—another innovation he'd probably introduced to his country. "Is Mrs. Churchill in any danger?"

"She was discharged from a private nursing home this morning, and we have every reason to believe she is on the mend."

"May I inquire what poisoned her?"

"Chloral," Winant said. "Probably administered without her knowledge, in a drink."

"She took only champagne in my presence," Diba said. "Pol Roger 1928. A favorite vintage of Prime Minister Churchill's, I understand. I had it brought from the cellar by one of my personal assistants. And uncorked, I might add, by that same man at the craps table. He poured it out for us under my eye. I certainly suffered no ill effects from drinking it."

"So, unless the poison was put into the bottle in France itself . . ."

"Mrs. Churchill cannot have been sickened in my company."

"The idea is so ridiculous, Mr. Diba, that I did not for one second consider it," Winant said. "But I still hope you may help me. When you parted from Mrs. Churchill, did she go directly into a taxi?"

"I cannot say. She encountered an acquaintance, you see, who claimed a dance, and swept her away from the craps table."

"Ah," Winant said.

Diba looked at him piercingly. "I imagine you are familiar with the gentleman, as he is a member of your delegation."

"Is he, indeed?"

"Yes. I cannot quite recall the name. You understand, it was mentioned only a few times in my presence. An introduction . . . from Mrs. Churchill to myself . . ."

Winant waited, a benign smile of inquiry on his face.

"A river," Diba said suddenly. He snapped his fingers in a thoroughly Gallic gesture. "Yes, that is it. The man had the name of a famous river. Not Thames, but . . ."

"Hudson," Winant said.

Disappointing. He already knew Michael Hudson had talked to Pamela that night. It was Hudson who had confronted her with the German codebook.

"And you know of no one else? You did not observe Mrs. Churchill at any other point in the evening?"

Diba shook his head regretfully. "I did not. The press of business . . ."

"Of course." Winant rose and offered his hand to the Iranian. "Thank you for your time."

"It is nothing, Ambassador. Tell me—" Diba hesitated. "If I were to dispatch a bouquet of flowers to Mrs. Churchill—it would not be regarded as an impertinence?"

"It would be regarded, Mr. Diba, as the very highest mark of esteem," Winant returned.

THE CROWD assembled in the *zurkhaneh* was entirely male. Although the covered wrestling arena was only a few blocks from the Park Hotel, it was centuries distant in both style and substance. *Koshti,* or wrestling, was the most cherished sport in the Caucasus—and every Iranian province had its own type, rooted in folklore and tribal custom. The Mazandarans preferred *loucho*; the Golestans, *tourkamani* style. In this place, however, it was *Pahlavani* wrestling that ruled. It was no accident that *Pahlavani* wrestling was named for the Shah's tribe, or that it was considered the "official" wrestling school. For years, it had been a religious practice as well as a contest. Religion and dictatorship, Siranoush reflected, went hand in hand in Persia.

She was no stranger to wrestling. It was as common in the town squares and fields of Armenia as it was in Iran. But in the sepia-toned memories of her childhood—increasingly fragmentary and elusive— the grappling men were usually in bars. Knocking over chairs and breaking heads. In Iran, wrestlers were the mercenaries of the diplomatic world. The equivalent of Nazir's pit diggers. They took money from all comers. Sold their knowledge and their fists. They carried messages and guns for anyone willing to pay, no questions asked.

Here in the arena, they were kings. And she was an interloper.

There were serving women, of course, moving among the men. But even their eyes swept Siranoush with disapproval. The men were more vocal. She descended the sloping aisle between the ranks of seats, toward the sunken octagonal pit, where two young wrestlers—naked above the waist, sweating profusely and swaying—fought for submission. She ignored the catcalls, hissing, and guttural insults. She did not speak Farsi. Ignorance—and her obvious Western dress—might protect her.

She was looking for Dutch.

The Polish pilot still had a room at the Park Hotel. She had left a

note for him at Reception only forty minutes ago. But it was the hotel
bartender—who had an eye for a pretty blonde—who told her where
Dutch went most days. He was gambling on *koshti* with Bond's money
and doing quite well for himself. In fact, the bartender suggested, he
might stay in Tehran indefinitely.

She raked the crowd, looking for the Pole. Easier than it might
seem, because the *zurkhaneh* was divided into specific sections: athletes
sat on one side of the sunken pit; musicians on another. The audience
was confined to a third.

Dutch was gray-haired and clean-shaven, and he insisted on wearing
a Polish Air Force cap that was as threadbare as the Shroud of Turin.
She picked out the cap first, in the third row of seats up from the pit's
edge. Like most of the men, he was looking at her instead of at the
wrestlers.

At that moment, a pair of hands seized her by the shoulders and
turned her roughly around. A young Iranian, obviously drunk. His fingers slid up to the nape of her neck and seized her hair in a painful grip.
With a grin and what was probably an insult, he dragged her back toward the door.

She had been trained for stupidities like this.

She allowed herself to be dragged for a few seconds, then twisted
like an eel and kicked the man hard behind his knee. His leg doubled
beneath him. He let go of her.

She turned and looked for Dutch.

He had torn himself away from whatever bet he was nursing and
leapt for the aisle. Before her bruiser could force himself upright, Dutch
had reached them. For an instant, she thought he might slug the man
in the jaw. She caught his wrist in midair and said, "Mistake."

His eyes grazed hers.

"You'll bring the whole place down on us."

He nodded once. And then they ran.

"BOND'S GONE MISSING?" he repeated, as they settled down with drinks in the Park Hotel bar.

Twelve minutes and a world away from the Tehran *zurkhaneh*. Siranoush sipped her martini and felt some of the tension ease from her chest. They were both drinking vodka. Nobody in Cairo liked it, and most of the Westerners she'd met had barely heard of it. Vodka was Russian. Polish. *Armenian*. Dutch had ordered an entire bottle and had tossed back several shots. The two of them understood each other.

"Not missing," she said. "I know where he is. I just don't know *where* he is."

Dutch laughed. "Clear as mud."

"My people took him away in the night. To a safe house. They left me behind. They should have been back by now—somebody should have returned. They haven't. I need to find the safe house."

"And?"

"I thought you might know where it is."

Dutch poured himself another slug. "There are probably a dozen NKVD places in this town. If there aren't fifty. Fatima, my dear— wouldn't you just rather fly back to Cairo?"

She tasted her vodka. "This is a different kind of house. It used to belong to the Nazis."

Dutch pushed the shot glass aside. "Then stay away. Far away."

"We turned them."

"You never really turn a Nazi, darling."

"Dutch," she said, pouring him another shot of vodka, "you know people."

"On four continents."

"Wrestlers, for instance. They're the tough boys of Tehran."

He simply looked at her over the rim of his glass.

"The tough boys work for whoever pays. You've made a lot of money, lately. From wrestling."

He sighed. The air was filled with vodka fumes. "You expect me to go back into that lion's den. The *arena*. Now that you've thrown them all meat."

"I expect you to ask questions." She smiled at him brilliantly. "One of those wrestlers knows where Bond is."

CHAPTER 34

Otto Skorzeny needed to clear his head.

It was late Tuesday afternoon and they had come down from the hills on Saturday. There had been a little food in the isolated farmhouse the five of them had taken at gunpoint that evening at dusk; an old woman lived there alone with a herd of goats. They'd forced the woman to give them goat stew and what bread she had in the place. It was only two rooms, and the goats held down one of them. But it was isolated, and that was all Skorzeny cared about. He'd waited until midnight to be sure the old woman had no son who might walk through the front door. The fact that she didn't bought her another twenty-four hours.

Skorzeny would not let her out of his sight, and he refused to allow his men to go in search of food. It was essential, he thought, that they all lie low.

On Sunday, Hoffman killed one of the goats and Skorzeny forced the old woman to roast it over her open fire. She wailed and berated them in her foreign tongue until Hoffman pulled his gun and threatened to shoot her. That night, to Skorzeny's relief, the Fencer made contact.

Long Jump. Operational. Proceed per instructions.

He had unstrapped the radio pack from young Fuchs's back Saturday after the boy was dead. Fuchs's body he'd dragged farther under the tree that had proved the death of him. The snow had already formed a well around the trunk, and Fuchs would lie there, frozen, for the rest of the winter. Skorzeny was the only Enigma-trained trooper left among the five of them. When he emerged from the trees near the Jajrood River and rejoined his men, none of them asked about Fuchs. They knew a gunshot when they heard one.

The tension and fear had been building in them ever since. They were too well trained to question him directly, but he'd caught each of them averting their eyes. If the Fencer hadn't given them the green light—a reason to radio their German contacts and storm the safe house last night—Skorzeny might have had a mutiny on his hands.

He tossed the dregs of his coffee down the safe house kitchen sink and turned back to the men bound in their chairs. There had been too many hours of groaning and blood with too little to show for it. He would have to interrogate them himself.

DAY SEVEN

TEHRAN

WEDNESDAY,
DECEMBER 1, 1943

CHAPTER 35

*H*ow's the President's stomach?" Hudson asked.

"Seems A-OK," Schwartz replied. "He hasn't eaten much, of course—just pushes the food around the plate. Says the spices in all these Oriental countries are playing havoc with his system. But it's nothing a little good straight whiskey can't put right. He should eat more with the Brits and less with the Russians."

Hudson laughed. "Ain't that the truth. I'll be glad to see the back of this part of the world."

"Me, too," Schwartz said. "At least we'll be home for Christmas."

Christmas. There was a scent of snow from the Caucasus on the air. Hudson and Schwartz were strolling around the withered back garden of the Russian Embassy during a break between final conference sessions. Both men were smoking, and the good scent of tobacco mingled with the clean smell off the mountains.

"Seriously, though," he said. "Is it possible Mr. Roosevelt was poisoned that first night he was here?"

Schwartz glanced at him sidelong. "Dunno. If he was, they didn't try too hard. And what would be the point?"

Hudson shrugged. "Uncle Joe gets a leg up on the Poland question. He wants part of East Prussia, I hear, so he can get an ice-free port.

Roosevelt's got a lot of voting Poles back home. Sideline him in the discussion, maybe Stalin gets what he wants."

"You've got a very suspicious brain, Mike," Schwartz said admiringly. He took a drag on his cigarette. "Could be right. But I know for a fact the President plans to raise the Polish issue with Uncle Joe tonight."

"Better hope he's got no appetite for dinner afterwards." Hudson kicked a piece of gravel into a dormant fishpond and watched it skitter across a thin layer of ice. "Then what?"

"We go home."

"Just like that? Drive right out the gate of the embassy compound, and wave goodbye as we pull up to the plane?"

"More or less. What's eating you?"

Hudson hesitated. He wanted to know Schwartz's plans. But he didn't want to tell him about Ian being in Tehran or his conversation with the NKVD girl, Siranoush. If he reported what she'd said about Nazi paratroopers, Schwartz might go talk to his opposite number in the British Embassy. And then Hudson's ability to control what happened would diminish rapidly.

"Just wondered if you'd heard any more about that Fencer guy the Sovs were all het up about."

"We both know that was bullshit. Just a way to claim bragging rights for averting disaster—and convince the President to move in with Uncle Joe and his microphones."

"Yeah," Hudson faltered. "Only . . ."

Schwartz came to a stop and tossed away his cigarette. "Only what? This place giving you the heebie-jeebies?"

"Something like that." Hudson stuck his hands in his pockets against the cold. His shoulders were hunched. He looked more than ever like an elongated bird—a heron, perhaps. "This is Franklin Delano Roosevelt we're talking about. The greatest president the U.S. has ever known. You can't be too careful with cargo like that. So maybe you err on the side of caution."

Schwartz clapped Hudson on the shoulder. "That's the Service's first rule, buddy. We take nothing for granted."

"And tomorrow—"

"We trot out our presidential double and send him off with all possible fanfare at 0900 hours. Motorcade, adoring NKVD troops, flags of three nations and a twenty-one-gun salute from the Kid Shah. We carry FDR himself to a plain sedan and I drive him by the back road to the *Sacred Cow*. Works like a charm."

Hudson frowned. "You mean you're driving the two of you alone? You got no protection?"

"Sure. Nobody'll look at us twice. They'll all be riveted on the car they *think* has the Old Man."

Unless they know he's not in it, Hudson thought. He hoped Schwartz hadn't shared his plan with half the delegation. But he wasn't about to teach the Secret Service chief his job.

"Sam," he said, "is there any chance you'd let me ride in that car?"

Schwartz studied him for a long moment. "You really *are* worried, aren't you?"

Hudson nodded.

"Know how to pull a trigger?"

"Of course."

"Then I'd never deny you the chance to serve your country. You can ride shotgun. Be waiting at the back gate of the embassy compound at 0830 tomorrow morning."

"Thank you," Hudson said. "I won't forget it."

"Keep this close to your vest," Schwartz warned. "A plan's no good if the whole world knows."

So he's figured that out, Hudson thought. And hoped it wasn't too late.

———

THE WRESTLER'S NAME was Mostafa, Dutch said, and he spoke enough French to make himself understood among the foreigners who had sprung up overnight in his country. He had listened to Dutch's questions and, more important, to the rials Dutch had offered. Then he took the rials and meandered slowly among the athletes waiting in their section of the *zurkhaneh*. Two of them—older men with families to feed and long memories—thought they knew where the former Nazi safe house might be. For enough cash, they were willing to show Dutch.

"You're an expensive girl, Fatima," he told her. "I've gone through a quarter of my winnings in the past hour. The gods of wrestling bestow, and the gods take away."

"Then let's hope it's the right house," she said.

Now, looking at the run-down shack from the far side of the street as the wrestlers accepted Dutch's cigarettes and murmured in their sibilant Farsi, she wondered for an instant if the safe house was even inhabited. The windows were shuttered and no smoke came from the tin pipe on the roof that served as a chimney. "They're sure," she muttered to Dutch doubtfully. "This is where the Germans lived?"

Dutch lifted his shoulders. "There are a lot of Germans," he reminded her, "even in Occupied Tehran. Who knows if they got the right ones?"

They were standing on the broken paving stones that fronted what appeared to be a closed factory. Something to do with rugs and weaving, Siranoush thought. She had veiled her bright head and now stood suitably a few paces from the knot of men, with her face slightly downcast. She'd forced Dutch to stuff his tattered Air Force cap into her handbag before they'd climbed into the taxi with the wrestlers and wound their way through the poorer parts of the city.

"What do you want to do?" he asked her now. "Ring the doorbell?"

She was about to reply when they heard the scream.

It was a man's voice, high-pitched in agony. A scream that was forced from the body and ended in a gasp.

Siranoush stared at Dutch, her pupils dilating.

"*Gówno,*" he whispered.

A Polish expletive even Siranoush did not understand.

THE MOST SENIOR of the five paratroopers was named Otto Skorzeny, Ian learned. He carried the rank of colonel and moved with such consummate assurance that it was unsurprising he and the men he commanded had survived the drop into enemy hands a few weeks ago. He spoke German with a Viennese accent and the right side of his face was fantastically scarred from cheekbone to jaw. It looked as though somebody had once tried to slice his face in half.

"You're a fencer," Ian muttered at one point, when the pain exploding from his groin was too much for his clenched jaws. It made a change from the raw hatred that spewed forth from his mouth in English whenever the length of chicken wire tore at his scrotum. He was sweating profusely, and the moisture mingled with the spatters of blood that covered his thighs. Clenching his fists, he'd dug his fingernails so tightly into the flesh of his palms that these, too, were streaked with red.

"Yes." Otto brought his face close to Ian's. He had a glorious mustache that was probably a point of pride and an attempt to distract the eye from the livid scar that carved a trailing half-moon through his cheek. "You fence also? What is your weapon?"

"My brain," Ian gasped.

Otto threw back his head and laughed.

"And now let me ask you again, Commander Bond. How many in Mr. Churchill's party travel armed?"

"I don't know," Ian said. He clenched his teeth. It was just another type of birching, after all. He'd endured Pop and he would endure this.

The chicken-wire rod swung viciously upward. He screamed.

This time, the pain knifed through his stomach and he knew he was going to be sick. He retched, black dots swarming in his vision. Otto forced his head down. It was a difficult maneuver when a man's arms were tied behind the back of a chair. But Ian's eyes cleared. He stole a second to glance at Zadiq. He thought the NKVD commander had slipped into unconsciousness about an hour ago. Zadiq was still bound to his chair, and his skin was goosefleshed. A pool of blood was congealing beneath his seat. Ian retched again.

Otto tugged impatiently on his hair.

"Churchill carries a pistol," he muttered.

"And the others? There are soldiers? Bodyguards?"

"Of course. A couple of pretty girls. You'll like killing them."

Stupid answers. Banal. Nothing worth dying for. But he would die in the end, anyway, and the small child in his brain was begging for relief.

Otto pulled his head up. *"How many* bodyguards?"

"Just the one," Ian said. "His driver has a gun, too."

The door to the front room was ajar, and he could hear the German boys playing cards and talking. He concentrated his anguished mind on their words. Parsing out the language. They wanted food and drink, and Otto had ordered no one to leave the safe house on pain of death for desertion.

"One bodyguard. You know how many men watch the Führer when he takes a piss?" Otto asked softly. "Eight. Never mind how many put him to bed. I'm glad you're starting to answer me, Commander. But I don't believe a word you say."

The chicken wire flashed again.

"Colonel!"

Erich's voice from the doorway. Excited. Urgent.

Otto glanced over his shoulder. "What is it?"

"The radio. It's beeping."

The wooden rod slapped hard against Ian's scrotum. He felt something burst—and went howling into black.

MUCH AS SHE disliked the Soviet Embassy, Grace went looking for Michael Hudson there a little after three o'clock in the afternoon Wednesday. They had unaccountably missed each other yesterday and Grace had never been able to ask what he'd discussed with Ian. Whether there were plans. She had visited the bazaar herself twenty-four hours ago, dawdling among the perfumes until she suffered a sick headache, in the hope of telling Ian about the Prof's call. About the Fencer's channel going silent. About how they were all *buggered* and she kept flinching at the sound of backfiring cars on the Tehran streets, certain it meant the murder of Churchill.

But Ian hadn't surfaced yesterday. Grace was worried.

She found Hudson standing in a smoke-filled salon with perhaps a dozen other members of the delegations, nursing a whiskey and a cigarette.

"Miss Cowles," he said formally, and murmured a word of apology to one of Anthony Eden's sub-secretaries, a fellow Grace knew by sight but not by name. "Were you looking for me?"

"Yes, Mr. Hudson," she returned in her most professional manner. "I have a message for you from the Prime Minister."

He bent his head toward her as they strolled placidly from the salon.

"The air is far fresher outside," she observed. "I'm sure a quick jog along the drive would do you good."

"I was just about to suggest the same thing."

They nodded to the uniformed NKVD guards at the front entrance and received an unsmiling stare in return. Outside, the cold slapped Grace's face.

"Brisk," Hudson said.

"Winter," she replied. "I went back to the bazaar both yesterday and today. There's no sign of Ian."

He glanced at her sidelong. "I thought I told you to leave Ian to me. I don't want you mixed up in this, Grace. It could be damaging."

"I had a message for him."

"I'd have taken it."

"Never mind!" she said impatiently. "Aren't you afraid something's happened to him?"

"He's probably out playing spies with his new friends."

"Michael—this is serious. Ian was waiting for my news. He wouldn't have missed our meeting."

His footsteps slowed. "What was so important?"

She bit her lip, hesitated. "You mentioned Alan Turing once. Said he wasn't very reliable."

"I said he was odd. I could have said crazy."

"So you know Turing has been intercepting the Fencer's coded messages?"

Hudson nodded.

"Damn Ian," Grace muttered. "You're not cleared for it. But I suppose at this point . . . I spoke to Turing last night. He says the Fencer's gone silent. Right when we expect him to strike. Ian needs to know who the man is, *where* he is—and the whole show has shut down."

"Including Ian. No wonder you're worried." Hudson stopped short. They had almost reached the British Embassy. "Look, Grace—I have a pretty good idea where Ian is, and I'm pretty sure he's safe."

She took a step toward him. "You're joking. Why didn't you tell me?"

"Because you're *not cleared for it*." He managed a wry smile. It would now be their joke. All the white lies they told each other. "I talked to my NKVD liaison last night. Ian was harboring with one of their splinter groups. Rogue operators. They took him to a safe house. Beria's people will keep him there for the duration of the conference. They don't want a guy like Ian popping out of the woodwork right before this show is over."

"Why not?" she said. "Doesn't Ian's story about the Nazis tally with the Russians'?"

"A little too much," Hudson said drily. "Did you know they've been running the surviving paratroopers all along, through some turned radio operators of theirs? Knew exactly where they were. Could have picked 'em up at any time. But they've been holding them in reserve. Probably plan to unleash them at the last moment, so they can gun them down in public and have the glory of saving Churchill and Roosevelt."

"That's . . . that's abominable."

"That's Communist Russia."

"And you think Ian mistook this plan for a serious German plot?"

"Sure. With a little help from Turing. Of course the Fencer has gone silent—he's probably just Sergo Beria sending messages from the basement! The NKVD orchestrated this whole sham from beginning to end. Only they didn't count on Ian surfacing in Tehran. The loose cannon. Beyond their control."

"So they bagged him." Grace glanced back at the Soviet Embassy. "Bastards."

"Uncle Joe doesn't play nice."

She tried to follow his train of thought. It made overwhelming sense. But there was a snag somewhere—a problem . . .

"What about Pamela?" she said.

"Pamela?"

"The codebook. That you found in her things. If the Fencer's nothing more than Beria's son, why does Pamela have a German codebook? And not even an Enigma one?"

Michael lifted his arms in a gesture of futility. "Search me. But I'm sure Ian could invent an explanation. Come on, Grace—let's get out of here. Can I buy you a drink at the Park Hotel bar?"

CHAPTER 36

The first thought that penetrated Ian's mind was that he must have died. Death was the only explanation for the surreal blend of pain and Siranoush's voice. The pain was real, but the voice must be a hallucination. The fact that Siranoush was speaking German deepened his conviction. She spoke too many languages as it was. There ought to be one she hadn't mastered.

His mouth suddenly watered as the tantalizing smell of lamb stew from the bazaar hit his nostrils. The warmth of it filled his mind. He struggled to lift his head and open his eyes. Tried to croak her name. *Siranoush.* His mouth and tongue were swollen. His arms were still bound, the limbs deadened from lack of blood, and he could not touch his face. He sensed, however, that his eyes were swollen, too. The slight movement he made in his effort to lift his eyelids awakened the excruciating wounds in his scrotum and penis, and he whimpered aloud.

No one answered.

He forced his eyes open, one at a time.

The light in this back room was dim. The door to the front was firmly closed. Next to him, Zadiq was breathing like a man whose lungs were filling slowly with fluid. Otto was nowhere to be seen.

Then he heard the Nazi colonel's voice, raised in flirtatious laughter.

Siranoush. She was laughing, too, and it came to Ian with sickening despair that he had been duped by all of them—by everyone he'd trusted—and that the girl was a liar and a bitch. Otto had forbidden all contact with the outside because Otto knew Siranoush would come to help them. It was prearranged. She'd brought dinner.

She would feed Ian's enemies and watch him die.

Cutlery scraped earthenware plates. Men sighed with satisfaction after a long pull at a bottle. Someone gave forth a belch. The pain in Ian's groin was maddening. He would scream until he blew himself out like a candle.

Not in front of that girl.

"Danke, Fräulein." Erich's voice. He was still there, then. He yawned audibly. Yawned again. Tomàš said something Ian couldn't catch, and the rest of the Germans roared.

He thought suddenly of Mokie: his father's face, blurred in memory and gradually replaced by the set image of a photograph. It captured nothing of his soul. Mokie had known exactly what death was like. Not glorious. Balls torn to shreds. Please, dear God, he thought, in a variation on the old theme, help me to face death more like Mokie.

There was a crash from the front room. A chair had toppled over. None of the Germans was speaking anymore. The only sound was a persistent snoring.

The door to his death chamber eased open. She was standing there. Staring at him. A look of horror and pity on her face.

"Bond," she whispered. Then she came swiftly to his side. She had a knife in her hands. She cut the ropes at his arms. He tried to move them while she freed his legs, but they fell to his sides like planks of wood.

"Otto," he ground out.

"Drugged. They're all drugged. I put it in the food."

"Erich. He didn't . . ."

"Betray me to them? No. Maybe even *he* wants out."

She glanced over her shoulder as a man's shadow filled the doorway.

God help us, Ian thought. Then he saw who it was.

"Dutch," he gasped.

"I'll help you get your shirt on." The Polish pilot was sweating profusely, and his hands shook. "*Skurwysyn*—what have they done to you?"

More Polish obscenities as he saw Zadiq.

"*Kurwa!* We'll never get trousers on these two." He glanced around the storeroom. "Blankets. There must be blankets."

"Out there." Siranoush tossed her head toward the front room.

Dutch disappeared from Ian's view. He closed his eyes for an instant; Siranoush was cutting the bonds on Zadiq's arms.

"We'll have to carry them out one at a time," Dutch said.

"Arev?" Ian asked.

"Dead," Siranoush said brusquely.

She'd freed Ian's legs. He tried to move his feet. The mere twitch of his thigh muscles sent agony spiking through his abdomen. He had to stand up and free himself from the chair, but his mind skittered away from the pain.

Dutch lifted one arm, then the other, as he eased Ian's shirt onto his back. Ian was still weak; but sensation was returning. From his shoulders to his fingertips, he throbbed with blood.

Dutch gripped him beneath the armpits. "Swear if it helps," he said. "Now. On the count of three—"

"No," Ian said clearly. "Get Zadiq out first."

"AMBASSADOR WINANT?"

"Yes?" He poked his head out of the conference room. He and Anthony Eden, Churchill's Foreign Secretary, were fine-tuning the proposal for postwar Poland's borders. Stalin demanded the frontiers respect the Molotov-Ribbentrop Line of 1939—which had been guaranteed by Hitler—because it returned Ukraine and White Russia to the Soviet Union. The British government preferred something called the Curzon Line, which dated from World War One and gave a bit more land to the Poles. Roosevelt wanted the Poles to gain territory to the West, land taken from Eastern Germany. He'd ordered Gil Winant to talk to the Brits. If anybody could broker compromise, Winant could.

Gil lifted his brows at the uniformed NKVD officer standing before him. The man inclined his head. "You are requested on the telephone line."

He followed the soldier to the embassy switchboard—the obvious nerve center for communication, as opposed to the secret one below stairs that Michael Hudson had found. A young woman offered him a receiver. He put it to his ear. The woman remained standing, staring at him, as did the NKVD officer. Both were probably ordered to listen to his conversation. He turned his back.

"Winant speaking."

"Good evening, Mr. Ambassador."

"Mr. Diba! What a very great pleasure, sir."

"As it is for me." Diba switched immediately to French. "I regret to disturb your conferences, Mr. Winant, but I have encountered a slight problem at the Park Hotel. There is a young British woman in uniform sound asleep in a chair in the lobby. We do not believe she is one of our guests."

Winant frowned. "Is she a member of the Occupation Forces?"

"I do not think so. When I arrived here for my usual luncheon, I observed her in the hotel bar. I will add that I noted her particularly, because she was in the company of your American friend. The one named for the river."

"Where is Mr. Hudson now?"

"Certainly not in the Park Hotel." Diba hesitated; Winant could almost feel him thinking down the telephone wire. "We have tried to rouse the young lady. She remains quite insensible. In view of that—and a similar incident involving another young Englishwoman—I decided to call *you,* sir, rather than the British Embassy."

"I see." Winant thought quickly. He would find Sarah and take an embassy car. "Get some coffee into her, Mr. Diba. I'll be there as fast as I can."

ZADIQ HAD NOT regained consciousness, and his breathing was labored. Ian guessed he was in a coma and envied his near-death state. It allowed Dutch to throw a blanket over Zadiq's body and lift him like a large sack of potatoes. He turned carefully and made his way through the room full of snoring commandos.

"Water?" Siranoush said.

Ian lifted his head.

She held a cup to his mouth and he felt the liquid seep between his lips. It dribbled over his chin. He tried to raise a hand to wipe his mouth—and found that he could. He grasped the cup and drank by himself.

Then he looked at her. "Is there a car?"

"A taxi. We paid it to wait."

"Where do we go?"

"Back to the bazaar."

Ian shook his head. "Zadiq needs a doctor. So do I. We go to our embassies this time. You, too—and Dutch. You'll be safer there."

"Can you stand?"

Ian met her eyes. No tears of pity there—just ice-cold determination. "I can try. Let me hold on to you."

He grasped her shoulders and clenched his teeth. The blood from his torn genitals had congealed on the wood frame of the gutted chair. Like a bandage, he thought. Tear it free in one go. He bore down with his hands on the girl's frail shoulders and forced his thighs to lift him.

The dancing dots of pain swam again in his vision. Siranoush, unbalanced, took a step backward. He swayed and moaned but did not scream. The blackness cleared. He stood upright by himself.

He swaddled himself in the blanket she gave him and said, "Let's go."

They shuffled slowly into the front room. The time it took seemed endless. They were horribly noisy. Exposed. At any moment, Ian thought, one of the men would wake and with the reflex born of years would reach instantly for his gun.

Otto was sprawled across the table, his head in his arms. Ian was tempted to take the knife Siranoush had used to cut his bonds and plunge it into the man's back, but she was guiding him carefully along the wall, well away from any of them, and he did not have the strength to fight her. Or the strength to plunge a knife.

The house's front door eased slowly open. Dutch's head peered around it, and he seemed about to speak. But there was a small *pop!* as though one of Pamela's Pol Roger bottles had blown its cork, and Dutch forgot whatever it was he had intended to say. With an expression of astonishment, he crumpled suddenly to his knees. Then fell face forward to the floor.

A neat black hole was burned through his back.

Ian looked from the dead Pole to the man in the doorway.

"Hudders," he said. "I've been wondering when you'd get here."

CHAPTER 37

Michael Hudson had a gun trained on them—a High Standard HD .22 caliber pistol, the usual OSS issue. It had an integral sound suppressor—a silencer. Wonderfully effective for killing a man in broad daylight.

He shoved Dutch's body farther into the room with his foot and closed the door. The Polish pilot lay like a bundle of old clothes in the entryway. "How long have you known?" he asked.

"Since I heard about Pam Churchill's German one-time pad," Ian said. "You and I both know the Fencer uses Enigma codes."

"My mistake."

Ian drew breath. It hurt to expand his lungs. "Pammie knew you'd searched her things back in Giza. You were afraid she'd tell Churchill. So you spiked her champagne in the hope she'd die. When she survived, you were forced to frame her—and produce a plausible reason for a suicide attempt. But it was the wrong evidence, Hudders. You couldn't produce an Enigma encoding machine. I'm sure you've got one in your hotel room at the Park—but you needed it for this operation. So you showed Grace the one-time pad."

He shrugged slightly, his head down. "I didn't know you were here in Tehran, Johnnie. Or that Grace would tell you about Pamela. I tried to get you out of this. Why didn't you go home?"

"Because I never do what I'm told."

Michael stepped deliberately over Dutch's body and set his gun down on the table with a sigh. "No. You don't, do you? It's the pin-striped pants all over again."

Ian closed his eyes. He was still leaning heavily on Siranoush. "I wish it were. I wish there were some reason to stand with you, Michael. But we have different loyalties now."

Michael shoved his fingers through his hair. "Stand with me! Nobody stands with me. That's what those pants were all about, Johnnie. You made a fool of yourself then, and it's exactly the same now. You think you've betrayed me—but I'm the one who's going to walk out of here alive."

"You betrayed yourself," Ian retorted harshly. "Quite early in the game. You allowed me to *live,* that night you coshed and stabbed me in Giza. The Fencer ought to have killed me. It was a contradiction I couldn't figure out. Alan Turing's basic rule of code-breaking. *The contradiction that holds the key to everything.*"

"I guess I never wanted you hurt."

"Because it would have been killing a bit of yourself," Ian said implacably. "I know. Stupid of you, Hudders, to hold on to any kind of feeling. It's a luxury your sort can't afford."

Hudson's face twisted briefly. Regret? Grief? "*My* sort. The ones who are really running this war," he said. "As opposed to the Ian Flemings—who just think they do. You live in a fucking fantasy world, Johnnie. You always have. You like to think you break the rules, but you've never broken any that matter. You've never killed a man just because you could or watched the best hope of a nation explode in flames. You don't have that kind of power. You're a hero of the old school. And you're going to die a ridiculous death. Do you know what a waste I think that is?"

"Probably for the best." Ian ignored the grief for both of them that was turning his heart over. "I'm not fit to live in your world."

"No. I've known that for years." Hudson's eyes roamed over the sleeping Nazi commandos. "What happened here? Chloral?"

"Barbiturates," Siranoush said crisply. "Much more effective."

Hudson inclined his head. "I'll have to take some lessons from you, sweetheart. Come here and give me a kiss."

She did not let go of Ian, but he felt her stiffen beside him.

"Siranoush," he said slowly. "She's the Kitten?"

"Of course." Hudson smiled faintly. "She was right there on the inside of the NKVD operation. And along the way, she'd picked up *you*. She kept me informed. But I didn't know Commander Bond was my old friend, Ian."

"Yet she couldn't let me die, either," Ian said. His grip tightened on her rib cage.

"She's a woman. Emotion's her weakness."

"Don't be so bloody patronizing. She's worth ten of you."

Hudson set down his gun and lifted Skorzeny's head. He pulled back one eyelid. "How much of that stuff did you give them?"

"I don't know," Siranoush said woodenly. "Perhaps too much. It had to be . . . enough."

Hudson allowed the colonel to slide to the floor. Then he pulled out Otto's chair and sat in it. He sighed. "Christ, what a day. We'll have to make coffee and start getting it into them, or they'll be no use at all. Put Ian down and get working on it."

"I can't sit, old thing," Ian said, before Siranoush could move. He was swaying as he leaned on her, and he doubted she could support him much longer. He summoned his ebbing strength to face Hudders; he would not appear weak. "My arse is out of commission. Which reminds me—did you kill Zadiq, too?"

"If you mean the bloody corpse in the taxi, I didn't bother. He won't last till midnight. What did they do to you, Johnnie?"

For a second, Ian almost thought Michael cared. "If you're a very good boy, I'll let you have a look," he said.

"He needs a doctor," Siranoush burst out. "He has lost too much blood. There will be infection—fever—"

Hudson frowned. "That's not possible tonight. The last conference dinner is about to start, with kisses and fanfare and bullshit no one will read in the morning. We need to sit tight and get our rest. Stir up the troops and push through to the end."

"Long Jump?" Ian asked.

"Sure. Everybody says *ta-ta* tomorrow." Hudson grinned—his old, familiar look of mischief. "Gonna be quite a send-off, Flem."

SARAH OLIVER and Gil Winant were pacing the floor of a private dining room in the Park Hotel with Grace Cowles between them. Abolhassan Diba had informed the Tehran police—because, as he explained to Winant, he could not allow the Park's guests to be drugged in his bar. Winant had called the British and Soviet Embassies, asking for Hudson, and had been unable to locate the man anywhere. He was not in his room at the Park Hotel. He seemed to have left Grace Cowles in the lobby and vanished into thin air.

The Signals officer's head was lolling like a broken doll's, and her eyes were closed, but she was no longer a dead weight, and from time to time she made a faint moaning sound that suggested she was doing more than dreaming.

"She got less than Pamela, didn't she," Sarah said.

"Probably just the one dose. Pamela took a second in her bedroom. Which raises a question," Gil replied. "Was Grace just meant to sleep—and was Pamela meant to die?"

Sarah shook her head. She had kicked off her high heels and was walking the carpet in her stockings, aware of both increasing tiredness and panic. She and Gil were supposed to attend the final Tripartite

Dinner tonight. Their absence from the Soviet Embassy would be noticed. Hers could be put down to a headache. Gil's was a diplomatic breach that bordered on a political insult.

"Either, probably," she said. "It's the coward's murder weapon—let God choose. The chloral is just a passive agent. It sets off a chain of events that may or may not end in death. Like the man who administers it."

"I wouldn't call that cowardice."

"No?"

"It's a supreme act of egotism. Any man who believes he's an agent of Fate is convinced he controls the future."

"Does that sound like Michael Hudson?"

Winant pursed his lips. "I wouldn't have thought so yesterday."

"Then he's very plausible," Sarah suggested. "Which means he's clever enough to subdue his egotism to a greater end. But what's the point, Gil? Why poison these women?"

He did not immediately answer. He was convinced that Pamela's drugging had been attempted murder—because she had caught Michael Hudson spying. Had he really found a codebook in Pamela's drawer in Giza? Or was the whole story a lie?

What Winant could not explain was the decision to drug Grace. What did she know—or what was she capable of doing—that threatened Michael Hudson?

"You say she works for Pug Ismay?" he asked Sarah.

"His personal assistant."

"So she must know a good deal about the PM's plans."

"Absolutely. Lives in Pug's back pocket. Sends out all his intelligence. She's worked Signals most of the conference—it was she who connected me to Mummy when I was forced to call home with the bad news about Pamela."

"Signals," Winant said thoughtfully. "Any idea how she came to know Hudson?"

"She's an old flame of Ian Fleming's. He and Hudson were always palling around."

The girl stumbling between them suddenly lifted her head. Her lips parted. In a slurred voice that was almost unintelligible, she said, "Ian."

Sarah and Winant stopped walking. Grace's eyelids were fluttering.

"Quickly," Sarah said. "More coffee."

"It's stone cold."

"Does it matter?"

They eased Grace onto a sofa. She was definitely awake—staring blearily before her, dazed at the strangeness of her surroundings. "My head," she moaned.

Sarah cupped one hand behind the girl's neck, and with the other held a cup of coffee to her lips. Grace tasted it and grimaced. But she held on to the cup with one hand and helped Sarah guide it.

A few seconds later she said, "Where am I?"

"The Park Hotel," Winant said.

Grace closed her eyes. "Am I drunk?"

"You had a drink. We think it was drugged."

"That's mad."

Gil met Sarah's eyes. Sarah shook Grace gently and said, "Who bought you the drink?"

"Michael." Her eyes opened. "Michael. He was with Pamela, too."

"Good girl," Winant said. "You're thinking again."

"Oh, God!" Grace gestured away the cup and tried to force herself upright from the sofa. "Ian. I told him everything about Ian."

"Fleming should be back in England by now," Sarah soothed.

"What time is it?" Grace was still struggling to rise.

On impulse, Winant reached out and helped her to her feet. "It's nearly seven o'clock."

"Which means it's four-thirty in England."

"Thereabouts," Sarah said.

Grace's eyes were wide open now. She began to walk unsteadily toward the dining room door, her arm clinging to Winant's. "He wanted me out of the way. In case Turing cabled."

"Who?" Winant asked, bewildered.

"The Fencer. *Michael.*" She clutched at his arm. "I've got to get back to the embassy."

THEY LAID Ian on his stomach across a couple of chairs. Hudson began to rouse the unconscious paratroopers while Siranoush attempted to bathe Ian's wounds. She used hot water and gauze she took from a dressing kit she had found in one of the Nazis' packs. There were iodine tablets in the kit, too, and she dissolved one of these in a teaspoon of hot water and painted it on Ian's torn flesh. She gave him a knife with a wooden handle she discovered in a kitchen drawer, and he put this between his jaws like a dog. When she touched him, he left deep tooth marks in the wood.

"You should have listened," she whispered. "You should have stayed out of all this."

"But then we should never have met," he gasped. "Only think how tragic that would be, Kitten."

"My name is Siranoush."

"Ah. So *something* you told me was true."

He could feel her tense as she worked above him, and for an instant he was afraid she would deliberately hurt him. But she governed her temper. The searing pain of the iodine dissipated and he was able to breathe again.

"How did you meet Hudders?" he asked.

"Years ago. Before the war. He knew Nazir."

"Nazir being the sort of man to play both sides."

"Nazir played only his own. He was a Soviet, remember."

"And you? What are you playing at, Siranoush?"

The gauze moved with deliberate pressure, regardless of the cost.

Gentleness would never have got the job done. She was that kind of woman. Despite everything, he could admire her. The inner certainty that kept her alive.

"I want revenge."

"Against us? The Allies?"

"No, no." She shook her head; he glimpsed a fall of blond hair. "I like the Allies! Someday I will live with Hudson in America."

"So that's the lie he told you."

"But first I must revenge my parents. My mother died in the Gulag. My father—God knows where. We were left, my brother and I, in the NKVD camp. Stefan was shot for stealing bread. He was only eleven years old. I could not save him. I could not . . . And I . . ."

"Grew up angry."

"I was sold to Nazir. When I was fourteen. That was six years ago."

Ian considered this. *Not* her grandfather, then. The exchange of money for the life of a girl suggested something far beyond repugnant.

"You want to kill," he said. "And Nazir is already dead."

"I made sure of that. It was many years in coming."

The knife blade to the carotid artery. What had she said? Her market basket rolling to the floor. Vegetables smeared with blood.

"And now? Who do you kill now, Siranoush?"

She was silent. Her fingers probed at his exquisite agony.

He did not repeat the question. He already knew her answer.

CHAPTER 38

The final dinner was over, Churchill thought with a sigh, and what had they accomplished tonight or any night, after all? The Allied invasion would go forward in May, too early and in the wrong place. Stalin had grudgingly agreed to discuss elections in the Baltic states, but he'd gone on and on about the *right kind* of Poles in postwar Poland. Meaning, of course, Communist partisans—not Sikorski's Government-in-Exile Churchill was supporting in London. Eden had proposed the Curzon Line as a Polish frontier, without gaining much of a reaction. Stalin talked instead about Germany—how it must be completely dismembered when the war was over. It was a personal grudge, Churchill thought. Hitler had stabbed Stalin in the back. And in return, Stalin would wipe every last German from the face of the earth.

It had all gone very much as Uncle Joe wanted. Germany would be atomized, France stripped of her colonies, and the rest of Europe prevented from forming an alliance or federation. The Soviet Union would be the sole power on the Continent.

And Britain, Churchill thought, would remain an island on the edge of darkness.

Winston was frustrated and distraught. Stalin's dream would never bring peace to Europe. It would merely give Europeans a grudge. A reason to hate. A battle cry for the next millennium.

He hoped Franklin knew it.

Roosevelt had listened, indeed, more than he'd talked. Winston guessed he was reserving judgment until he decided whether Russia or England would win the argument. But he seemed to be betting on Stalin. Winston was feeling more beaten and ill than he had since leaving England, as though the bronchitis was devouring his lungs. Tomorrow, his plane would fly back to Giza and he would sit in the Egyptian sun for a few more days, hoping his aging body would mend.

There was a tap at his bedroom door.

He downed the last of his whiskey neat and hunched himself forward in his chair. When he exhaled there was a wheeze deep in his chest like the deflation of a tire. He remembered that sound from his wretched father's final days. The death rattle.

He rose and surged toward the door, wrapping his depression around him with his dressing gown. If he were fortunate, it would be Pamela standing there: Pamela, with her winsome face and her daring frocks, with a bottle of Pol Roger waggling in her hand. But no: Pamela was greatly changed since her brush with scandal. She seemed to be avoiding him.

He pulled open the door.

"Father."

"Sarah." She was white-faced and exhausted; this trip had taken the stuffing out of her.

"You were missed at dinner, my dear," he growled. "Marshal Stalin had made a place especially for you at his table. He's a dull dog at the best of times and you'd have had heavy work of it, but—"

"Can you spare a moment?"

He frowned at her heavily. "I'm on my way to bed."

"Only, there's been rather an important communication. In the Signals Room."

"Of course," he said. "I'm just coming."

GRACE COWLES was seated in a small conference room on the embassy's ground floor. She had traded stale coffee for ice water and had changed her uniform; the fuddled look of a few hours ago was gone. Gil Winant had taken another chair at the table. He was still wearing his overcoat. There was no fireplace, and the room was freezing. Churchill had traded his dressing gown for one of his famous jumpsuits—his preferred form of battle dress.

"Alan Turing attempted a Secraphone trunk call while I was absent this afternoon, Prime Minister," Grace began. "A colleague in the embassy tried to take down the message, but Turing preferred to speak directly to me. Unfortunately, it was over three hours before we successfully made contact."

"Deserting your post, Cowles? Not bloody like you."

"I am aware of that, sir," she said. "I take full responsibility for my dereliction of duty."

"Nonsense," Sarah Oliver interjected. "She was drugged, Father—rather like Pamela."

"Had I remained at my post," Grace countered, "rather than allowing myself to be carried off to the Park Hotel, I should have avoided the entire incident—and received Turing's call."

"But instead, your experience has allowed us to pinpoint a pattern," Winant said. "Which is immensely valuable."

"I was told you'd received an important communication!" Churchill exploded. "I left my bed on the strength of it. Get to the point, Cowles, if you please!"

"Yes, sir." She glanced at a sheet of notes. "Professor Turing has been intercepting and decoding German Enigma signals exchanged over a specific frequency, which he believes to be used by an agent known only by his code name, the Fencer."

"Chap who's supposed to be gunning for all of us."

"Yes, sir. As you are aware, Turing contacted Commander Fleming of Naval Intelligence with the news that the Fencer appeared to be a member of our Allied delegation. Fleming asked Turing to track the Fencer's signals. Today Turing intercepted a communication with Berlin. It stipulates that simultaneous attacks against Mr. Roosevelt, Marshal Stalin, and you, sir, will be attempted tomorrow, at approximately 0900 hours."

"Bloody cheek." Churchill looked from Cowles to Winant and Sarah. "We're all scheduled to depart from this compound at that hour, and make for the airstrips. I suppose the fellow means to bottle us up at the compound gate. Toss a bomb or two into the cars. He shan't get far—Stalin will see to that! Three thousand of those ruddy NKVD soldiers the Marshal's got, just straining at the leash."

"Father." Sarah reached for his arm. "Gil says—and I do believe he's right—that under no circumstances must you be here in the morning. You should pack up and leave for the airstrip now. Even if the plane waits until dawn to take off, you'll be among British forces. You'll be splendidly safe."

"Turn tail and run, like a thief in the night? What would Roosevelt think? I don't have to ask about Stalin—the man would regard it as an insult."

"I would like permission, sir, to inform President Roosevelt of the threat myself," Winant said. "I intend to urge him and his Secret Service chief, Sam Schwartz, to take similar precautions—depart tonight for the American legation or the Park Hotel. If each of you leave from a different spot, a joint attack should be impossible."

"Franklin's not likely to bolt, Gil," Churchill retorted. "Won't want to lose face in front of his precious host. Won't want to embarrass Uncle Joe. Even if we shared the details of ULTRA with Franklin—and I should like nothing better—he's got no reason to trust in Turing. Don't suppose the Prof has any idea who this Fencer *is*? Now, *that* would decode something!"

For the first time in several minutes, Grace Cowles spoke up. "He's beginning to have an idea. We all are. But there's no hard proof."

Churchill scowled as he looked at their faces. "Proof, eh? What was that you said earlier—about Cowles being drugged? At the bloody hotel? Had a drink in the bar, I suppose, like poor little Pammie. Who bought you the drink, Cowles?"

Her color was heightened. "I regret, sir, that I cannot tell you that."

"Can't—or won't?"

"I have no proof of guilt, sir. Only strong suspicion."

"And the fellow's too highly placed." Churchill nodded. "Public embarrassment if you're wrong. Rank pulled. I understand."

There was a brief silence.

"Father," Sarah said, "you must protect yourself. You're too vital to the war effort to play at being heroes."

"I never play, my dear. Winant, answer me this: We've agreed the Fencer fellow is one of us?"

"Yes, sir."

"And thus privy to our most secret councils?"

"He is."

"And if we run for the airstrips in the middle of the night, what do you regard as the most likely eventuality?"

Winant glanced around the table. "We defeat his plan. We prevent an attack. We save the lives of the three men most critical to Allied victory."

"Perhaps," Churchill temporized. "But we also leave the bugger free."

There was a silence.

"Free to report back to Berlin on everything he's learned here. Having failed in his primary task, he will want to buy favor with a gift of extraordinary value. What would you regard, Ambassador, as the most critical piece of intelligence the Fencer could carry to his Nazi masters?"

Winant sighed heavily. "The date and location of the Allied invasion of Europe."

"Overlord." Churchill thrust out his jaw and glared at all of them. "It is already a perilous undertaking. A Channel crossing toward a fortified landing, heavily defended by the Enemy. Countless thousands of lives will be sacrificed—we know this for a certainty—even with a measure of surprise. If we allow the *precise details* of Overlord to fall into Hitler's hands, we lose more than that. We lose the war."

Sarah spoke up. "Couldn't we arrest our suspect and detain him indefinitely?"

"On what charge? Have you found a wireless in the man's possession? Chloral in his pockets?"

Winant cleared his throat. "The suspect in question, Prime Minister, has in fact disappeared."

"Well, then." Churchill pushed back his chair. "We shall have to obtain proof of the fellow's treason. I suspect there should be plenty of it tomorrow around 0900 hours. Sarah, my dear, would you have Thompson roused? Send him to me."

Walter Thompson, the PM's bodyguard, had saved Churchill's life more times than he liked to count.

"And Winant—please inform Mr. Schwartz of our discussion. Tell him that we intend, as Englishmen always do, to stand firm."

THE FINAL DAY

TEHRAN

Thursday,
December 2, 1943

CHAPTER 39

*O*630 hours.

He spent the night lying on the floor on his stomach, with a German bedroll unfurled beneath him. Siranoush had split his undershorts to expose his iodine-painted wounds to the air—impossible to place a blanket over them, anyway. Otto had taken the bedroom as a right of rank; Hudson had sat up in a chair all night, sleeplessly waiting.

At around three p.m., Ian asked the question he'd saved for the wee hours.

"When did it all change, Hudders? When did you leave us behind?"

There was a silence. Perhaps Michael was asleep.

After a few moments, Ian wondered if he'd even voiced the question out loud.

But then Michael said: "I didn't leave you. You let me go."

"Let you go?"

"Like that day off Dancing Ledge. When I dropped down to the bottom. I could see you kick out for the surface. Away from me."

"I came back," Ian said. "I came back and saved you."

"Not when it mattered," Michael said. "Not when I was really drowning. Those years in New Haven. And after."

"I didn't know. You didn't tell me." It was like Hudders, he thought, to make this *his* fault. He knew how Ian was driven by guilt.

"You never bothered to ask." In the dim light of the safe house, Michael's head lifted. "You didn't have to. You've always had a place in the world. Eve and Peter and the rest. You *mattered*. I was just extra."

Ian might have protested. Argued. But the self-pity behind Michael's words seemed suddenly sick.

"So you joined Hitler's family?" he asked. "Seems a bit extreme."

"Hitler joined mine," Michael retorted. "Make no mistake, Johnnie. I control this party. I have for years."

Poor fool, Ian thought. And asked him nothing more.

Michael was gone when Ian woke at dawn. He was stiff from lying on the floor on his stomach. He felt nothing of the winter cold, however. He was sweating and shuddering at once as he thrust himself upright on his arms.

Fever.

His mouth was parched, and the outlines of the room dilated and contracted before his eyes. He saw the paratroopers begin to rouse, rolling monstrously from their bedrolls. And then a face loomed over him. Bloated and almost unrecognizable. He fell back heavily to the ground.

"Too hot," Siranoush whispered.

He lifted an eyelid, but the bloated shape had gone. His entire pelvic area throbbed. He let out a groan.

"Here." She was back, pressing a cool cloth against his forehead and neck, what little of his face she could reach. "Take some water."

He struggled upward again. She dribbled some water between his lips.

"Now. Two morphia pills."

"Where did you get those?"

She smiled in the piratical way he loved. "They were in your uniform pocket. Zadiq gave them to me when you changed clothes, back in the bazaar."

He swallowed the pills with more water and then sank back onto the floor. His mind skittered away into feverish dreams.

"The sod'll die soon enough," he heard Otto say from the bedroom doorway. His voice came to Ian amplified and distorted, a run-down gramophone.

Siranoush did not answer.

0800 HOURS.

When he awoke again, there was a strong smell of coffee. His fever was unabated, but his pain floated somewhere above him in a bubble of helium. The pain was a distraction like a persistent fly, but he could swat it aside from moment to moment and force himself to concentrate. To comprehend his hallucinations. The Germans were eating fresh bread—Michael must have fetched it—their jaws working stolidly as cows. They muttered jokes he could not hear or stared in an unfocused fashion at the floor in front of them. The light seeping through the shuttered windows was much stronger now.

Coffee at his elbow.

"Try to drink," Siranoush whispered. "It may help."

"With what?"

"You have to stand."

"I can't," he hissed back.

"You must. He has plans." She glanced over her shoulder; Ian followed the direction of her eyes.

Otto. The Nazi colonel was in high spirits, slapping one of his boys on a meaty shoulder. Maybe it was the distortion in Ian's head or the angle at which he lay, but each of the paratroopers looked gargantuan. Inflated. The sort of brawn generally reserved for sideshows, in England.

"Is he going to hit me again?"

"I don't think so. It doesn't matter anymore what you know." She was half kneeling beside him; Ian cocked his head sideways.

"Because *the sod'll die soon enough*?"

Her eyes met his, flicked away. "I have to go. Please—will you drink the coffee?"

"Then I'll have to pee." He grimaced and hoped the effect was comic. "You have no idea how agonizing the thought seems."

"If you will try to stand," she said patiently, "I'll walk you to the WC now."

He nodded. She was right. He had to get off the floor. To die like a paralyzed animal would be humiliating.

Very well, Mr. Bond. For England and His Majesty's Secret Service—

He thrust himself upward on his hands. Then, more shakily, brought first one leg and then another to a kneeling position. He swayed, suspended there with his torn flesh dangling, but the morphia dulled the edge of the knife slicing through his groin and colored the stars exploding before his eyes. He drew a shuddering breath and reached for Siranoush's arm.

She helped him to a half crouch. He swore fluently. She eased him upright. He wrapped the blanket like a shroud around himself, and with one free hand, took the coffee.

Siranoush slid her shoulder under his right arm—had he once found that knife scratch painful?—and helped him shuffle toward the water closet.

"It's today, isn't it," he said, as she stood with her back to his, blocking the doorway. "Long Jump."

"Yes."

"Where's Michael gone?"

"He didn't tell me. I have only my orders."

"Which are?"

"To kill Stalin, of course."

"And then? You run away to America with your Fencer hero?"

She did not reply.

"He didn't give you an escape plan, did he?"

Ian was stalling. He had to pee—but he was terrified of the searing pain he knew would come. "Do you still have that piece of wood?" he asked. "The one you gave me to bite?"

"Of course." She disappeared momentarily. When she returned, she murmured, "Reach behind you. Carefully."

He felt for the knife handle and clenched it between his teeth. It was pitted already from last night's ordeal. He closed his eyes and emptied his bladder into the filthy bowl of the German safe house.

"Bond," she said urgently. "Bond!"

He shook his head to clear it. He had crumpled by the base of the commode, clutching it for dear life. Probably blacked out momentarily. There was blood mixed with the urine in the bowl, and he did not think that was a good thing. Unless, of course, one expected to die in the next few hours. Then it was immaterial.

He had dropped the knife in falling, and it was lying by his left hand on the floor. He palmed it.

Siranoush grasped his shoulders. He forced himself to stand. Wrapped the blanket around himself, hiding the knife in the folds.

"Could you possibly find my trousers?" he asked carefully. "If I must go to my execution, I bloody well won't go debagged."

"What is this *debagged*, please?"

"Without my pants."

She managed a smile. When she left him, he slid the knife into his right sock. He had a bad moment, bending over, when he thought he might not stand up again. It passed.

"Siranoush," he said, as she helped him into his trousers, "why are you so kind to your enemy?"

"Because I do not love Hudson anymore. And we are both about to die, Bond."

———

0830 HOURS.

Franklin Roosevelt allowed himself to be shifted from his wheelchair to the backseat of the embassy car. When Schwartz had settled the President, Elliott stood for a moment by the open car door and peered at his father. When he grinned, there was something about his mouth that reminded Franklin of Eleanor.

"That's the most ridiculous fake mustache I've ever seen," Elliott said.

"You can have one if you like," Franklin offered. "I've got three more in my pocket."

Elliott saluted his Commander in Chief. "Save them for Halloween, Pop."

Schwartz waited for the President to flash his grin, then slammed the car door. Elliott stepped back. Schwartz slid behind the wheel. Franklin waved to his son and tried to tamp down his excitement. Sneaking like a covert operator from the embassy compound made him feel like a boy again. It was as good as playing cowboys and Indians in the long grass, long ago, when he had never thought of such things as wheelchairs.

Schwartz let in the clutch and the car rolled forward. They bucketed over the gravel drive and turned away from the compound's front entrance, where already crowds were gathering beyond the guardhouses, across the street from the iron gate: Iranians from the provinces in tribal dress; impromptu bands playing the dulcimers, drums, and long-necked lutes of traditional Persian music; tumblers turning handsprings in the street; beggars with blighted eyes and tin cups. They had assembled because the Great Leaders of the West were leaving Iran today and they were happy to see the back of the Invaders. But they would not be seeing Franklin Delano Roosevelt. Only his Secret Service double.

Schwartz came around the bend on the unpaved back drive and slowed as he approached the compound's rear gate. A lanky figure was lounging against it, head down as he consulted his wristwatch.

"There's Hudson, by all that's grand," Roosevelt said, craning forward to look over the front seat.

Schwartz grinned and waved at the OSS man.

Hudson hurried to unbar the gate and swung it open.

He lifted his hand to his hat as the car passed through. Then he closed the gate and ran up to where Schwartz waited, motor idling.

"Good morning, Mr. President," he said. "I'd never have known you in that mustache."

Roosevelt held a finger to his lips. "Call me Frank," he said boisterously. "I'm nobody's leader now."

SIRANOUSH WAS GONE.

Otto and his men were dressed in a miscellany of Persian tribal clothes that Hudson must have collected at the bazaar. The colonel ceremoniously returned Ian's passport and wallet to him, tucking them himself into Ian's suit pockets, since Ian's hands were still bound. Then he ordered two of his men to drag Ian to the back door of the house, which was flung open. Two lorries were parked in the alley beyond: Ian recognized one as the NKVD vehicle he'd ridden in a few nights before. The other was Tehrani. A dozen goats were penned in the open back.

Otto and two of his commandos jumped into the NKVD lorry. Ian was lifted, his teeth gritted at the careless manhandling of his body, and tossed into the rear with the goats. His wrists and ankles were still bound, but no one had thought to pat down his socks.

He heard the remaining two paratroopers climb into the cab and start the engine.

With a groan, he rolled to his stomach and then to his knees. The lorry lurched in and out of ruts, tossing him like a bale of hay. The goats were interested. They crowded against him, strong-smelling and inquisitive, their uncanny devil's eyes staring through him. A few nibbled tentatively at his clothing and his hands tied behind his back. He knew goats from his boyhood at Arnisdale, and he did not fear them. But why bring them at all? Why *two* lorries, if it came to that? There was plenty of room for all of them in the NKVD one.

Knees planted, ankles bound, Ian craned his head to peer over the roof of the cab. Otto was driving ahead of them, bowling along in his stolen vehicle and his peasant's clothes. Although he might be the kind to die for the Führer, Ian thought, he was not likely to do so for Michael Hudson. Even if Hudson *was* the Fencer. Which meant that when the violence came, it would not come from Otto.

Two lorries. Because the Nazis needed one for killing. And the other for escape.

The situation is dire, Bond. The Kitten is under orders to assassinate Stalin. The Fencer means to get Roosevelt. And YOU, 007—you will take the fall for Churchill's murder . . . When the shots ring out or the bomb goes off, it will be Ian Lancaster Fleming, deserter, *whose body they find in the wreckage . . .*

It was a nice touch. Winston Churchill, killed by the son of one of his oldest friends. Hitler would love it.

Get the knife, 007 . . .

Arms still pinned behind his back, he began to wriggle his wrists. He swatted a goat's nose in the process. Felt teeth beneath his fingers. The ropes were wet. They would be hemp in this part of the world. Edible. Inviting, even, to a local ungulate.

Ian held himself as still as possible in the rolling lorry bed. The flutter of tongues and noses against his hands resumed. How much time did he have? How much rope would the goats eat? He tried not to calculate his chances.

0840 HOURS.

When the guard at the compound gate challenged her, Siranoush barked a command at him in Russian. It was a phrase she had heard often in her NKVD camp. *Shut up, pig. Don't you know who I am?*

He had no idea who she was, but he took one look at the flowing blond hair, the glimpse of silk beneath her coat, her flawless skin—and came to attention. He held his gun on the girl and said, in a more tentative tone, "Identify yourself."

From the bodice of her dress she drew her papers. The boy—he was younger even than Siranoush herself—paled a little when he saw the special identification she carried.

"SMERSH," he whispered. "I have heard rumors. But never have I met . . ."

"Be glad," she said. SMERSH was the counterintelligence section of the NKVD. Few Russians knew it existed, but those who did were terrified by the name. The acronym stood for *Death to Spies*. SMERSH operatives had one job: to kill those who betrayed Stalin. "May you never have reason to meet us, Comrade."

He swallowed hard. "You wish to speak to . . ."

"Lavrentiy Pavlovich," she said clearly.

He let her pass.

It never occurred to him to search her.

Siranoush kept her hands in her coat pockets as she strode up the embassy drive. It was a cold morning, this second of December, and her fingers were chilled. Her right hand gripped the butt of her gun. It was Arev's old Nagant M1895.

ONCE OUTSIDE the center of Tehran, the idea of civilization vanished abruptly and gave way to a treeless plain, barren at this time of year, the road to Gale Morghe airstrip spooling out in front of Schwartz. There were no other cars. A vague suggestion of hills, dark on the horizon. The occasional herd of Persian gazelle. Schwartz kept the sedan at a steady forty-five-mile-per-hour clip, the noise from the engine loud enough to make conversation difficult. When he glanced in his mirror, he saw Roosevelt dozing, his hat off and his head lolling. In the passenger seat beside him, Hudson was more alert, glancing through his window from time to time like a tourist confounded by lack of subject.

"Looking for something?" Schwartz yelled.

"Caracal," Hudson said.

"What?"

"A caracal. Type of cat. Like a lynx or a cougar. They're native to this place."

"Ah," Schwartz said. They were coming up on a bend in the road, and he knew Gale Morghe wasn't far now—a matter of a mile and a half. There was no one ahead and no one behind. A hundred yards up ahead there was a turnout from the road. He had just seen it when he caught the flash of Hudson's hand reaching into his breast pocket.

He had almost turned to look at him when he felt the steel cylinder against his right temple.

"Pull over," Hudson shouted.

Schwartz hesitated. "You really want to do that, Mike?"

"I said, *Pull over.*"

"Okay. If that's how you want this to go," Schwartz bellowed. He pulled the wheel hard and fast to the right. The car squealed and spun in a tight three hundred and sixty degrees, the movement so sudden and vicious Hudson was unprepared. His gun wavered toward the roof, and Schwartz abandoned the wheel, allowing the tires to follow their ordained momentum. He grasped Hudson's wrist with both hands and slammed it hard against the car's dashboard. The gun flew out of Hudson's grip.

Schwartz jammed on the brakes and felt the car skid sideways. They were facing the wrong way on the road. Correction: he'd spun roughly five hundred degrees.

Hudson sprang for his neck.

"Mike," Schwartz gasped as the hands closed around his throat. "You don't want to do this."

"Let him go," Roosevelt said. "Let him go, or I'll shoot."

He had pulled his personal revolver from his coat and had it jammed, now, in Hudson's neck. Never mind that he was clinging to the back of the front seat as a climber clings to a cliff edge, using all the strength of his fingertips to pull his body forward; his paralyzed lower half had not cost him much. He was grinning ferociously at Sam, and there was such a look of elation in his eyes that Schwartz merely reached for Hudson's slack hands and removed them from his windpipe.

"Thanks, Mr. President," he said. "How about I take care of that thing for you now?"

0850 HOURS.

"This woman begged to see you in person, Iosif Vissarionovich," Beria said. He was standing before the great desk in Stalin's embassy office. There were papers scattered all over it—he recognized his son's handwriting. Translations. Transcriptions. Nothing really worth reading. Abuse of himself, of course—it amused the Americans to ridicule him in his own hearing. Toward Stalin they were respectful. He wondered how Sergo felt, writing down the insults leveled at his father. Conjugating them in two languages.

"Why?" Stalin asked. His flat, hard gaze traveled indolently from Beria to the girl standing two yards behind him. She was stiff and expressionless, the gun she had carried in her coat pocket held steadily to her own head. Sergo's finger was on the trigger. He and the girl were roughly the same age, and it would be interesting, Beria thought, if he told his son to kill her. A demonstration for the Marshal of what family loyalty could do.

"She says—"

"I am an officer of SMERSH, Excellency," the girl interrupted.

Beria glanced at her. Two spots of color were burning now in her cheeks.

"So?" Stalin offered indifferently.

"I worked with Colonel Zadiq before his murder last night."

"Zadiq is dead?" Beria asked tonelessly.

"He was tortured by Nazi commandos he was attempting to intercept. His son also was killed. A useless woman, I was left behind in the NKVD headquarters."

"How do you know this?"

"Zadiq told me the location of his safe house. When he did not return, I went to the place. I found him dying."

"Beria," Stalin interrupted. "Do I give a shit about the death of an NKVD officer?"

"No, Excellency."

"Then why do you bore me with this bitch?"

Beria glanced at the girl. Then at his son. Sergo's hand was trembling. The weight of the gun held aloft, perhaps, for so long a time. Or the weight of what it could do.

"You are boring us, bitch," Beria said.

The girl had the stones to smile faintly. She looked straight at Stalin, and it seemed to Beria that if looks were a knife, Iosif Vissarionovich would be bleeding by now.

"Zadiq had only enough breath for a few words," she said. "'*Long Jump*. 0900 hours. The embassy gate.' I do not know, of course, what it means. But I know, from his blood, that it is a matter of life and death."

There was a short silence.

Stalin grunted. "The time?"

"Five minutes to nine." Beria was looking at his son. Sweat had settled like mist on Sergo's forehead. Anxiety for the girl? He should tell him to kill her. It would be good for the boy. Put some steel in his veins. He was too much his mother's son.

Stalin slapped his desk. "Then we go. You first, Beria. You can shield me with your body, eh?"

"It would be my honor, Iosif Vissarionovich." Beria inclined his head.

"Cocksucker," Stalin said genially. "I'll ask Churchill to drive through the gate first. With his little Sarah, who refused to eat at my table. No loss if they're blown to bits, eh?"

He stopped short as he passed the girl. She was staring at the place where he'd been, her lip bitten between her teeth. Sergo still held the gun to her head. But his hand was shaking so badly, now, that if he'd actually cocked the thing, it might have gone off.

Stalin stroked his finger down the girl's cheek. "You did well, bitch. Spread your legs once or twice and you'll go far in SMERSH."

Her head turned as swift as an adder's, and Beria saw, then, the hatred in them. Her lips parted, and for an instant he thought she would curse. Or spit.

"Fortune preserve you, Iosif Vissarionovich," she whispered, "because your friends never will."

Stalin threw back his head and laughed.

GRACE COWLES had been unable to eat that morning. She had risen early and sent a coded cable to Alan Turing. *Fleming missing. Believed taken or killed by Fencer.*

It wasn't as though Turing could do anything to help. Grace simply needed to tell someone who understood the few words. By the time Turing replied, she would already be in the air. Clutching her knees in Lord Leathers's plane—which still smelled of Ian's Laphroaig. Gazing down at the hills and forests of Iran as they sped away from her, wondering if he was alive.

Ten minutes before they were scheduled to load up in cars and brave the compound's gate—all but a few of them utterly unaware that an attack was coming—Grace slipped by the porter at the embassy entrance and hurried down the drive. The British military police manned one side of the compound entrance, the NKVD officers the other. Two guardhouses flanked the gate itself, and visitors to the embassies reported to one or the other before being admitted. Identities and appointments were verified via phone lines connected to the embassies themselves. It was all very modern.

Grace rapped on the guardhouse's rear door. A cautious face appeared around the edge of it—wearing a helmet and battle gear instead of the usual uniform.

"Yes, miss?" the guard said impatiently.

"I . . . I wanted to . . ." Why had she come, indeed? To reassure herself that everything was normal? That Turing was inventing things? That Michael had been right all along—not a traitor but a true friend, who knew Ian Fleming was lost in his own fiction?

"You've been warned," she said to the guard. "About the possibility of attack."

"Mr. Thompson sent down a message an hour ago," the guard explained. "We're double-staffed and on the alert. There's a couple of jeeps full of snipers, too, stationed both directions along the road."

Thompson was Churchill's bodyguard. Of course he would have informed the gate staff. Grace was useless here.

"I'm glad to hear it. Good luck."

She glanced at her watch—five minutes to nine, and nearly time for the first cars to depart. She must hurry. Her luggage—

Then the sound of a lorry horn, wildly blowing, assaulted her ears.

She turned and peered through the bars of the gate at the street outside. Impossible to detect the military jeeps full of snipers in the crowd that had gathered—both sides of the road were lined with colorful groups of people, men and women and children, clapping their hands and shouting in various dialects, in Arabic and Farsi and even French. There were music and small pops as children tossed lighted firecrackers in the air. Any excuse for a celebration.

How horrible, she thought suddenly, if they're hurt by this—

The horn blared again. She looked to the left, where an ordinary lorry approached. Behind it, careening out of control, was another vehicle, probably headed for market. Its lorry bed was filled with goats.

And a man.

He was in torn and filthy clothes, but Grace saw immediately that they were Western, not Persian. And he was hanging over the side of the lorry's cab.

Grace's pulse quickened. Even upside down and from the rear, she recognized those shoulders. That head.

The guards ran pell-mell out of the gate, rifles leveled. The NKVD soldiers, too, were moving.

"Don't shoot!" she screamed. "He's a British officer!"

THE GOATS had done their work. When the last frayed edges of the rope parted from his wrists, Ian reached for the knife hidden in his sock and slashed at the bindings on his ankles. The fact of his fever and his wounds could not be ignored. His hands shook, and his vision was blurred. His body from the waist down throbbed relentlessly, and the friction of his trousers on his raw backside was both maddening and banal in its familiar pain. But he would not lie down and take the death Otto had planned for him. He would not die a traitor.

Ian lurched forward through the forgiving goats and grasped the edge of the cab. He could see the former NKVD lorry ahead of them—they would not yet have noticed he was standing with his hands free. There were only two men in the cab below. The point was to keep the lorry from arriving at its destination—he felt sure it must be the British Embassy, because they were rolling through a tony section of Tehran, the preserve of the wealthy and the foreign. There were people lining the sides of the road now, and up ahead he could see what looked like a massive stone gate.

He should try to take out the driver first. By the time the passenger reacted, the lorry would be out of control. It might crash, and if there was a bomb hidden somewhere it might explode and kill them all. But it would not kill Churchill.

He peered over the side of the cab and realized that it was not a British lorry—the driver of this one sat on the left. Fortunate; Ian's left hand was the only one he could trust. He edged in that direction, swaying with the movement of the vehicle. The driver's window was open, and his arm rested casually on the edge. Summoning his giddy body, Ian leaned over the lorry's bed, knife raised. He plunged it as forcefully as he could into the man's left biceps.

The arm was flung upward with a howl. Ian pulled out the knife blade and plunged it again, this time into the cab—and into the man's neck.

The lorry swerved and the horn blared; the driver had fallen forward onto the steering wheel. Then the lorry turned violently in the opposite direction. For an instant it was possible it would somehow find balance. But the tires were old. Ian was thrown back among the goats and huddled there on his hands and knees, feeling the slow-motion whirl of the lorry as it began to overturn. The animals were bleating with terror, scrabbling on their cloven hooves as the world upended. A horn grazed his temple. Then they were all tossed like garbage into the air. The last thing Ian saw was the ground coming up to meet him.

"DON'T SHOOT!" Grace cried again, but the NKVD troops did not understand her, and as the lorry overturned and slid, metal groaning under the impact of the road, a rifle shot rang out.

There was a muffled *crump*. A millisecond's hesitation. Then the engine of the still-sliding truck exploded in a ball of flame. As Grace dove for the withered grass behind the guardhouse, a single lorry door arced upward and struck the iron bars of the compound gate with a resounding clang.

"SO WHAT WAS supposed to happen here, Mike?" Sam Schwartz inquired as he stood by the President's car in the turnout of the Gale Morghe road. "Were you going to shoot us both? Did I die first, then Mr. Roosevelt?"

Hudson said nothing. His hands were cuffed behind his back and his legs were bound securely with Schwartz's necktie. He was sitting in the dirt by the side of the road, staring at his knees.

"Or did you plan to make it look like I'd pulled the whole stunt?" Schwartz persisted. "Murdered the President and then killed myself?"

Hudson glanced up.

Schwartz nodded, sure of himself. He was suddenly insanely angry. "You calculating bastard. You didn't figure on an old Secret Service guy outsmarting the Ivy League, didya? OSS asshole. Wheels within wheels. But I saw the *truck*."

"You were warned about me," Hudson said.

"Gil Winant told me all about it last night. But he needed proof. So I explained the deal to Mr. Roosevelt and he was game. It's a big risk, shooting craps with a president's life—but Mr. Roosevelt hates a traitor, Mike. He wasn't about to skip town early and let you scuttle back to Berlin with the dirt on D-day. He put his gun in his pocket and his smile on his face. And we both let you into our car."

"What now?" Hudson asked.

Schwartz squinted at the horizon. The faint sound of an engine drifted out of the distance on the morning air. "We wait and see who shows up. I figure you didn't plan to walk out of here after that murder-suicide. Got a ride coming?"

Silence.

Schwartz strolled over to the car and thrust his head into the back. "How we doing, Mr. President?"

"Just grand, Sam. Just grand."

"I think we'll be pulling out of here in a minute or two."

"Wouldn't want to keep the *Sacred Cow* waiting."

"No, sir. You just sit tight and keep your head down, all right?"

Schwartz slapped the roof of the car and straightened. His eyes narrowed again as he peered back down the road. A truck was coming. He pulled his Thompson submachine gun from the floor near Roosevelt's feet and propped it on the roof. The entire body of the car was between him and the approaching vehicle, and Roosevelt was lying flat on his back on the car seat.

The truck was slowing as it approached the turnout. The driver wore Persian tribal dress, but his face was a Westerner's; a livid scar ran crudely from his left temple to his jaw. Schwartz watched the man take in Hudson's figure huddled by the side of the road. Then the truck started to accelerate again.

"Germans?" FDR asked softly from below.

At that moment, the driver raised his left hand from the wheel and aimed a pistol at them. A second gun snaked from the passenger window and a shot rang out. Schwartz squeezed his trigger and let the Thompson dance.

The truck veered and swayed under his concentrated fire, but as he watched, the driver pulled back his arm and put his head down. The truck sped up. Schwartz kept it in his sights. He fired another round.

"Sam."

He glanced down.

Roosevelt was sitting upright, staring through the back windshield at Michael Hudson.

He was sprawled like a dummy in the dirt, killed by a single bullet to the head. That would have been from Scarface's pistol, Schwartz thought. He let him go—the truck was too far to reach now, anyway—and walked over to Hudson.

He was staring up at the sky, his face in death more than ever like a hawk's.

"With friends like these . . ." Schwartz said softly.

After an instant, he bent down and closed Michael's eyes.

GIZA

SATURDAY,
DECEMBER 4, 1943

*H*e was resting earlier," the nurse said, "but I think he may be awake now. Remarkable how a few days in that wretched Persia can wreak such havoc! The poor Prime Minister is in a very bad way, what with pneumonia taking hold, and as for *this* fellow . . ." She leaned closer to Grace's ear. "Doctor is very worried he'll turn *septic*. Blood poisoning."

"But the damage . . . if he survives . . . will he . . . ?"

"Be able to have children?" The nurse shook her head doubtfully. "Who knows? Doctor says he's never seen such a terrible set of lacerations. And *he* served in the first war. Afraid he'd have to amputate, he was. But it hasn't come to that yet, and I'm sure I hope it never does. If it turns gangrenous, of course . . ."

"May I see him?"

The nurse wheeled abruptly and led her down the hallway of Churchill's villa to Ian's bedroom. It was next to the Prime Minister's, whose door was closed. Lord Moran had been dancing attendance on his Great Man's lungs now that the Tripartite Conference was over. It wasn't the first time Churchill had contracted pneumonia, but Moran was frank in saying it was the worst case he'd yet had. He was having difficulty breathing. Off his feed and off his sleep. It was uncertain whether Churchill could be moved in the next few days, and his return to Britain had been postponed. Even low-altitude flight would strain his lungs. Moran would not be answerable for the consequences. He had cabled Downing Street and Chequers and Whitehall with the news. Pamela was flying home the next morning, but Sarah was spending long hours in her father's room.

Ian's door was ajar.

The nurse grimaced at Grace and left her.

She tapped lightly on the panel.

"Come," he drawled.

Bored already, she thought, and peered into the room.

He was propped up on his elbows, face downward, leafing through a book. A sort of tray arrangement had been erected over his buttocks and the sheet was drawn up over this, hiding the damage that had so horrified the delegation when he'd been carried, unconscious, from the compound gate up to the British Embassy. It was Grace who had insisted he be brought in, ordering the military police to find a stretcher. She had seen him thrown from the lorry seconds before it exploded and was not about to let Ian be trampled by hysterical goats and Persians.

They had doubled-timed it up to the embassy that morning, past the open car carrying Churchill bravely toward a doom that had already escaped him. It was Sarah who had whipped around in her seat and shouted at Grace, "Isn't that . . . ?"

"Yes," Grace had cried. "Go on to the airstrip. We'll follow."

It was another day before she and Ian flew out of Iran in Lord Leathers's plane, Ian lying prone. The embassy doctor supplied Grace with several doses of morphia and told her on no account to disturb Ian's dressings until he was in the hands of medical personnel in Giza. He ought to have been placed in the British garrison's sick bay at the Old Citadel in Cairo—only Churchill wasn't having any.

"Fleming is a hero," he decreed, in the foghorn voice pneumonia had caused. "Chip off the old block. An Englishman to the core. Moran shall see to him."

And so he had been brought to the villa in Giza, where Churchill hoped they would both convalesce.

"Ian," she said.

He shot her his familiar quizzical look, one eyebrow raised, and slapped the covers of his book closed. "Gracie, by all that's holy. Let me have a look at you. I understand you saved my life."

"You saved your own," she said roundly. "I saw you straddling that lorry. How you did it, in your condition—"

"Nerves. Wonderful things, when one's about to die. Go into all sorts of gyrations one never anticipated."

She came toward his bedside slowly and looked about for a chair. There was one in the corner of the room, near the window framing the Great Pyramid. She drew it close to him and sat, feeling suddenly awkward and tongue-tied.

"How are you?"

"I won't say *Never better*. But better than yesterday. That's my motto for the next few weeks. I'm to be here awhile, apparently."

It was ludicrous talking to him like this, lying as much at ease as though he were on the shingle at Biarritz, attempting to brown his back. In reality he must be in constant pain, and the uncertainty about his prospects—

"I understand Lord Moran is pleased. You're healing."

His lips quirked. "The doctor views me as a valuable experiment. He's dosing me with a laboratory bug that's supposed to save lives when Overlord goes down. It's called penicillin, if you can manage the mouthful, and they're rushing production to have enough in hand by May. Doesn't look good for the jolly lads on the French beaches, does it, if they're already worried about torn flesh and infection? This war only gets better with each passing year."

"I hate it," she said. "I hate what it does to us all. Listen to you—nattering on like Bertie Wooster when you know—you must have heard—"

She came to a full stop. Ian's gaze didn't waver, but the humor had leached from his eyes. "That the bastard is dead?"

"Don't call him that."

"It's what he was."

"Yes." She dropped her chin and studied her hands. "I'm sorry."

There was a silence.

"I know I shall have to think about it," he said. "All of it. Why a fellow I loved from a child became a man I never knew."

"People grow apart, Ian."

"We'll say it was that," he agreed. "We'll say I refused to accept that we'd gone our separate ways in the years between Eton and Dunkirk. That I wanted to believe in him. Or what he represented."

"Which was?"

"Immortality. That because both of us were rotters, we were doomed to live forever."

"You're not a rotter, Ian."

He shrugged. "I'm no hero, either, Grace. I'm not sure they exist. Except in that most dangerous of places—their own minds."

"Well, I hope you've satisfied that itch of yours. To do more than a desk job, I mean." Her eyes skimmed hastily over his form. "I should think this result would cure you forever."

He glanced at her evilly. "I have itches in places, my dear girl, I wouldn't dream of mentioning."

"I have something for you." Grace drew a packet from her purse and placed it on the bed beside him. "A girl from the Soviet Embassy called at our legation, the day you were brought in. Nobody knew who she wanted at first, because she asked for *Bond*. But I remembered what that meant. She said she'd met you in the bazaar. You were delirious and the girl had a plane to catch, so she trusted me with this."

"Was she blond?"

Grace nodded. "Rather a stunner."

His fingers curled around the envelope, but his eyes were on her face. "What happened to Stalin, that day?"

"Nothing," she said. "Churchill drove through the gate first, you know."

"He would." Ian attempted a smile, but his expression was suddenly tragic. As though he were looking backward at hideous things Grace could not ask him about.

"Can I get you anything?" she said hurriedly. "Tea—or . . . or . . . some of your Laphroaig?"

"Is there any vodka in the place?"

She looked blank. "I've never been asked for that before. *Vodka.* How do you drink it?"

"In a martini. Shaken, not stirred."

"I'll hunt down a barman."

She kissed him lightly on the cheek and left.

When he was alone, Ian's fingers fumbled at the packet. It was too light to contain much. A few words of farewell, perhaps?

He tore open the envelope and drew out its contents.

A glorious length of saffron silk.

He held the softness to his face and breathed deep.

Do svidaniya, Siranoush.

ACKNOWLEDGMENTS

As someone who loves a good spy story, I've been reading deep in the history of World War Two for years. It is impossible to thread one's way through that wilderness of mirrors without bumping headlong into Ian Lancaster Fleming—arrogant, athletic, ridiculously compelling, with his dark blue eyes and broken nose. As the assistant to the director of British Naval Intelligence in wartime London, Fleming was up to his eyeballs in secret plots. His shadow falls across many of the most daring and ingenious deception operations of the war, particularly disinformation campaigns against the Axis. A great number of myths have grown up around him as well—from the outset, he was a character meant for fiction. In an effort to pin down his elusive figure, I tore through Andrew Lycett's biography, *Ian Fleming: The Man Behind James Bond* (Turner Publishing, 1995). I recognized a fellow traveler. Fleming spent so many hours making up stories because in some ways he found invented lives preferable to his own.

But Fleming's history left me with questions. He was a caustic and a callous individual who was capable of brilliant insights and profound loyalties. A man who desperately needed the affection and support of women, he was inveterately misogynistic. Uncomfortable in his own skin, he invented an icon of male suavity: 007, James Bond. Genteel, privileged, and sheltered by family wealth, Fleming was fascinated by violence and the underworld. A complex and fundamentally lonely man, he looked at least seventy when he drank himself to death; he was fifty-six.

I began to explore him as a character in his own spy story—one who'd lost his father too young and spent the rest of his life attempting to live up to his myth. In the 1943 Tehran conference, which Fleming planned (but did not actually attend—he came down with bronchitis and was left behind in Giza), I found the kernel of my plot.

A good deal of research later, I can recommend the following sources for those interested in the events and people of this novel: *The Irregulars: Roald Dahl and the British Spy Ring in Wartime Washington*, by Jennet Conant (Simon & Schuster, 2008); *You Only Live Once: Memories of Ian Fleming*, by Ivar Bryce (Foreign Intelligence Book Series, 1975); *Ian Fleming's Commandos: The Story of the Legendary 30 Assault Unit*, by Nicholas Rankin (Oxford, 2011); *Operation Mincemeat: How a Dead Man and a Bizarre Plan Fooled the Nazis and Assured an Allied Victory*, by Ben Macintyre (Crown, 2010); *Alliance: The Inside Story of How Roosevelt, Stalin and Churchill Won One War and Began Another*, by Jonathan Fenby (Simon & Schuster, 2006); *Churchill, Roosevelt, Stalin: The War They Waged and the Peace They Sought*, by Herbert Feis (Princeton, 1957); *Hitler's Plot to Kill the Big Three*, by Laslo Havas (Cowles, 1967); *Beria—My Father: Life Inside Stalin's Kremlin*, by Sergo Beria and Françoise Thom (Duckworth, 2001); *SMERSH: Stalin's Secret Weapon*, by Vadim Birstein (Biteback Publishing, 2012); *Citizens of London: The Americans Who Stood with Britain in Its Darkest, Finest Hour*, by Lynne Olson (Random House, 2010); *Reflected Glory: The Life of Pamela Churchill Harriman*, by Sally Bedell Smith (Simon & Schuster, 1996); and, last but not least, *Cairo in the War: 1939–1945*, by Artemis Cooper (Hamish Hamilton, 1989).

I am indebted to my editor at Riverhead Books, Jake Morrissey, for his sensitive and thorough treatment of this story in manuscript; to assistant editor Ali Cardia for her shepherding of my words through the book process; and to my agent, Raphael Sagalyn, who is always an inspired critic and collaborator. This is, of course, a work of fiction—and all errors in the facts underpinning it are my own.

—*Francine Mathews*
Denver, Colorado
2014